Blonde Rose
And the Men
Who Wandered
Through Her life

Blonde Rose
And the Men
Who Wandered
Through Her life

JEWELYA

authorHOUSE®

AuthorHouse™
1663 Liberty Drive
Bloomington, IN 47403
www.authorhouse.com
Phone: 1-800-839-8640

First published by AuthorHouse   02/09/2012

ISBN: 978-1-4685-5144-0 (sc)
ISBN: 978-1-4685-5143-3 (ebk)

Library of Congress Control Number: 2012902729

Printed in the United States of America

Any people depicted in stock imagery provided by Thinkstock are models, and such images are being used for illustrative purposes only.
Certain stock imagery © Thinkstock.

This book is printed on acid-free paper.

CONTENTS

BLONDE ROSE I

And the Men Who Wandered Through Her Life.
My First Twenty-Three Years
Written By:
Jewelya

This Book is dedicated to my children and others,
Who only thought they knew me.

And mostly to Red on the Head for being my friend,
sticking with me through thick and thin, when no one else would.
If not for her, I would probably not be alive to write this.

This is a book of fiction taken from actual events in my life. The names have been changed to protect the innocent, but mostly the **guilty.** I collected men as some would collect rare stamps, some men are like rare stamps to be held in our hearts, but others should be stuck to an envelope and sent to the ends of the earth with no return address.

CHAPTERS

Chapter One

Introduction

Blonde Rose
And The Men Who Wandered Through Her Life.
A Story of Abuse, Sex, Love, Betrayal, Secrets and
Survival, Survival, Survival

W e women have a way of surviving whatever is put in front of us. Some of us are hurt so desperately we think; you have hurt me so much I am going to show you and hurt myself even more. They turn to alcohol, pills, needles and the streets. Me, I turned to the thing that hurt me the most; the men who wandered through my life.

Some tiptoed through, some stumbled, some ran, some stomped. Some wandered through quietly, some wandered through noisily. A few made it necessary for me to find a way to survive, the others made it possible for me to survive and survive I did.

I have a sex drive, I guess like my mother's, it doesn't fail me, it is always there and I hope it never fails me. Being much different than my mother, I didn't let my sex drive control my life or the lives of those I love.

In the latter part of my life, I chose younger men, or they chose me as I have always looked and acted younger than my age. Men my age have not been able to keep up with me nor satisfy me.

As I got older, looking back over my life I asked myself, "How did you survive?" There was never a time in my life that my survival was at question. I had seven children; no one could love them as much as I did so survive was what I did. But, I wasn't sure how I had survived and as my children grew and left to have lives of their own I continued to survive; with the men who continued to wander through my life. So I decided to decipher my survival and what pushed me to survive and believe me there have been times I didn't want to survive.

When I found out Jonathon, the love of my life had died, I was devastated. I cried for two weeks and tried to drown my sorrow in bubble bath and beer, neither worked, he was still dead. I thought if I kept this up, I would be a shriveled up drunk. I have had sex with and loved many men, but only one Jonathon. He made me feel like no other man has ever made me feel, before or since. I was finally "In" love; I had loved, but never been "In" love. Most of the men in my life who stayed for a while had chosen me, then I loved. Even though I was not "In" love with those men, I loved them and was true to them, well almost. There was one time, the bus driver. Then I guess there were the times I was juggling several men at the same time, but I wasn't committed to any of them, just finding my way. Men do this all the time, why can't women?

Jonathon and I chose each other and fell in love the first night we were together. After I found out about Jonathon's death and my tears slowed, I started mentally walking through the times Jonathon and I had, had. Reliving those wonderful sexual, exciting and loving times. While I was bemoaning my loses, I started thinking about other loves and sexual encounters I had had during those years and concluded that I am glad the only thing I got from my mother was her sex drive, that was my survival. I decided to put it on paper and let all the women out there decide if they related to me.

Women are told if we have promiscuous sex we are whores and sluts. If a man does it they get a pat on the back with an at-a-boy good job.

I had a male friend say, "I went out with this girl who looked like a model and fucked like a porn star."

What the hell is that all about, how many porn stars have you been with? We don't have to be like a porn star to be able to fuck good. Women do not "fuck" as he put it; we either have sex or make love, depending on the man we are with. Not that we are "in love" at that time, but we are making love to a man we feel is worth our time. I wouldn't think a porn star would be all that good, she gets paid to do it, I do it because I love sex, and I love men.

Ladies we are very, very, special people. Without us, men could not get that at-a-boy pat on the back they give each other. We are really the ones in control, isn't it about time the at-a-boys knew that. They really do know that, they just won't admit it.

Remember high school? If you did put out you were a slut. If you didn't put out the boy still said you did and you were still a slut and to the boy you were more than that. We just couldn't win.

How many times have we heard, "She is a ho, she had sex with me the first night." Well wasn't it your first night also dude? Doesn't that make you a he, ho?

Now as I am getting older I have found it is the same way, that at-a-boy who asks you to go home to your house or his for sex is a stud, guess what you are. Why is it okay for him to ask, but not okay for us to go. If all of us said no, what would those boys do? Old lady palm and her five daughters!

From the things that have happened to me in my life associated with sex, I should hate sex, but I love sex every aspect of it. What goes on behind closed doors between two consenting adults is no one's business except those two adults. I know there are some prudes out there, but there are a lot more of you out there just like me. Most of the prudes just don't want to admit to loving sex, because men and the snobs in this world may look down their noses at them.

George Sand said: "There are no more thorough prudes than those who have some little secret to hide."

I have now lived long enough to not give a damn who is looking down their nose at me.

Like what is said of men; 95% of men masturbate, the other 5% lie about it, why lie about it we all know you do it, but then we ladies sometimes do it too.

I guess I feel that it was men who tried to break me; it should be men who glue me back together.

Ladies, enjoy your bodies and the fires men start in them. Remember, they couldn't start that fire if we didn't let them. That fire is not only in us but in them also, maybe more so, as men can not go for long without the feel of that woman under them. What would men do without that fire we women start in them. Think back on all the passion you have shared with whomever, relive them, enjoy them and enjoy the ones you will have in the future, with a passion.

Scarlet told me, "The day you die, when they go to burn your ass up you will sit up and say, "JUST ONE MORE TIME!!!!!"

Scarlet also said she didn't think I thought I could live without a man in my life. I may be able to exist without a man, but live without a man in my life? hummm, good question. I guess it all depends on what we define life as being. It is like reading the bible; ten people can read the bible and you will get ten different definitions. Same as with life, we all define it differently. But, "Life is like a butterfly, if you don't keep your eye on it, it will fly away taking all its beauty with it." jr

Who are these men that adorned my life? There were some who came in and stayed, some a long time, some not so long. Some I wanted to stay longer some stayed too long. Some were one-night stands; after Jonathon, I attribute my sanity to these one-night stands. I didn't want love I wanted lust, and someone to hold me tight in his arms and make me feel safe.

Some of these men I don't even remember their names. I knew them at the time, just wasn't important enough to remember. I went into most of these relationships, long or short, not expecting them to last, not wanting them to last. This is called lust, not love. Lust is everywhere you wander, love is not. I guess if that makes me a harlot, then a harlot I am, and a harlot I will remain.

I am not saying women should go out and sleep with every man she sees, what I am saying is that when we do we should not be treated any differently than the men we are sleeping with. Women are not like men, women have to be drawn to the men we sleep with, there has to be some kind of spark. With men, if she has a pulse, he is good to go.

I have been married five times; I married one of them twice, not a good idea. According to the second, third and forth (third & forth same man) I should stay with them as no one else would want me. They told me I was ugly and stupid and lucky to have them. They almost convinced me, they say if you are told something long enough you begin to believe it, even if it isn't true. Even my mother, or as I call her my birth person, giving birth does not a mother make, told me I wasn't good for much of anything and I should use my head for something beside a hat rack. Oh how she loved me. HA, HA, HA.

The real men in my life, the ones who really loved me, told me how much they loved me, how beautiful I was and I was the only woman they wanted.

Their comment; "Why would I go out looking for hamburger when I already have sirloin."

But, I'm getting ahead of myself. We should start at the beginning when I was very young, when all the craziness of my life began. I have had a very interesting, for want of a better word, life.

Chapter Two

My Beginning

I was born in a small city in Iowa. I was delivered by a mid-wife before the doctor arrived. When I was born it wasn't unusual for a baby to be born at home and delivered by a mid-wife. My mother suckled me, probably reluctantly as she had no choice.

My birth person never tried to hide how she felt about me. When I was an adult I asked her why she hated me so much.

Her reply, "If it wasn't for you, I wouldn't have had to spend the last thirty-eight years with that son-of-a-bitch."

She meant my father, at that time they had been married thirty-eight years.

My father was in the Army during WWII and when he came home on leave she got pregnant with me. I believe she was planning on leaving him as she only had my older sister and she didn't think she could make it with two of us. She could have left me with dad, but she couldn't do that as that would make her look bad and she couldn't have that. Appearances were everything to her. But, why would you leave your husband when you can do whatever you wanted and he will take care of you and give you everything you want. Cannot say she was stupid, she knew exactly what she was doing.

My dad was a very soft-spoken man that worshiped my mother. He looked at her through rose-colored glasses up until about a year before he died. When he took those rose-colored glasses off, then he looked at me in a different way also, he actually saw me.

He said to me, "We haven't been very good parents have we honey."

"Not so much you as her." I told him.

His comment, "No, more me as I could have stopped her and I didn't and I am so sorry for that."

My mother loved men, all but my dad and she didn't care who knew it. I think she loved him as much as she could, but to her standards he was boring. He knew what she was doing, but turned a blind-eye to it. I think she married my dad to get away from a sexually abusive step-father. Her mom died when she was ten leaving her to be raised by her step-father. I tried to talk to her about her childhood, and she would tell me it was none of my business, and all I needed to know about him is he was a bastard and a son-of-a-bitch and she hated him. I tried to ask her about her real father, she said the last she heard about him he was somewhere in California and she really didn't care where he was. She cared; she just didn't want me to know she cared about anything.

I attribute my survival when I was little to my grandmother, my dad's mom. We lived with her while dad was gone to WWII, and she protected me from my mother. The only time I remember my mother while at my grandmother's was one day I was in the kitchen with grandma and my mother started yelling at me to get out of the kitchen and leave your grandmother alone. I was hiding behind grandma peeking out from behind her. I had one arm around her leg with those heavy stockings they wore back then and holding her apron with the other.

Grandma had her arm around me, and said to my mother, "Jewelya is just fine out here with me, she is helping me."

My grandma took me everywhere she went; I think mom was glad to get rid of me. Grandma had a strawberry patch, grape vines along the driveway, a cherry tree, a peach tree, a pear tree, a rhubarb patch and several apple trees.

She would take my hand and say, "Come on Jewelya let's go pick some strawberries and rhubarb." We would pick the strawberries then the rhubarb. Grandma would bring a wet cloth and a little bowl of sugar. She cleaned the strawberries and rhubarb then we would dip them in sugar and eat them. She would laugh at me because of the faces I would make from the sour rhubarb.

My first remembrance of my mother was when dad came home from the war and my sister, Janie and I ran out to meet him. He picked us both up and carried us into grandma's house. When we moved away from grandma's and into a house of our own, I missed my grandmother so much. She would have dad bring me over so we could pick strawberries and rhubarb, and I would spend the night with her. She would set with me on the couch with her arm around me and read to me. I think this is where I got my love of reading and books.

My first encounter with a pervert was when I was about eight and my sister Janie was ten. He was our mother's cousin. He was in his late teens at the time, and he would ride his bike to our house. The first time he came to the house, we didn't know what he was like. He rode up into the yard and yelled at me to come see his new bike. When I got close enough he grabbed my arm and pulled me next to him. That is when I saw he had his penis laying lengthwise on the cross bar of his bike.

I struggled to pull away from him, but he yanked on my arm and put my hand on his penis, it was gross and I started screaming. My sister came running out of the house yelling at him, he let go of my arm and rode off on his bike laughing and my sister and me ran into the house. We tried to tell mom and dad what he did, but they wouldn't listen. Mom said we were lying because we didn't like him and wanted to get him into trouble. When we saw him coming we would run into the house and he would set outside with his penis on the cross bar of his bike and yell for us to come out. One day I was outside by myself when he drove up beside me and it was too late to run. He had me by the arm and already had his penis out. I started screaming for my sister and she came running out of the house with a meat cleaver in her hand. He released my arm and took off down the road as my sister was screaming at him that if he ever came back she would cut his thing off. Again, we tried to tell our parents, but of course mom didn't believe us and if she didn't dad didn't either. Even if he did believe us, he would not cross her. In later years the pervert ended up going to prison for molesting a young girl. We wondered if our parents ever thought how they could have saved other girls from him had they listened to us.

We also had a great uncle, I don't know if he was maternal or paternal, but he was always trying to feel our breast by putting his arm around our waist and feel us with his finger tips. Or he would put his hand on our leg and slowly try to run his hand up our leg to our crotch. Again, we tried to tell our parents, but to no avail. Our cousins, told their dad our dad's brother, that he was doing the same to them. Our uncle lived out of town and when he came in he stayed at our uncle's. The first night after the girls told their parents what he was doing, they watched what he did. He went into the girl's bedroom and was running his hand under the sheets to touch the girls and my uncle turned the light on and threw him out into the night, never to be heard from again. When my sister and I told them he did the same to us we were asked why we hadn't said anything. Our parents denied we had said anything about the uncle or the cousin.

It didn't take my sister long to realize how to get on our mother's good side, help her ostracize me. My birth-person was not physically abusive to me on a large scale, but she played some of the most abusive mind games with me, that I believe she is the cause of some of my strange behavior.

She was physically abusive to my sister. There were times dad would have to pull mom off my sister yelling at her, "What is wrong with you woman, what are you trying to do kill her?"

My sister moved to Colorado when she was seventeen with her husband. I begged her not to go.

She said, "I have to go, there is not a state big enough for our mother and me to be in, let alone a city."

Years later when we were adults my sister called me from Colorado to apologize to me for her part in the things my birth person had done to me. I told her it was okay because if the situation had been reversed, I may have done the same thing, it was called survival. The weekend my sister passed away Roy and I had gone to see her. My birth-person went with us because she had the new car and our truck was old. We were there when she had her final stroke. She had had several strokes before this one and survived, but this one she did not survive. She passed away at the age of fifty-four, much too young.

No matter where we were, we kept in contact, I went to see her and she me, and I still miss her desperately.

My younger sister, Callie, was born three days after I turned eight. My mother was very sick after Callie was born and had to go back into the hospital. I remember watching the ambulance taking her away, but this ambulance looked like a hurse.

I asked dad, "Is she coming back?"

"Yes." he said.

I'm not sure if that was the answer I wanted to hear.

When she came home from the hospital, it took her some time to get better. But, when she did she had new energy and was on the move. Dad tolerated me, he worshiped my sister, Callie, and he never allowed anything to happen to her. After my birth person attained her new energy, I became my mother's slave and my little sister's mother.

My mother ran with her men I did everything else. Dad built me a stool as I was too short to reach the cupboard or stove. I didn't know a thing about cooking, but I could read so I taught myself and became a great cook. I did everything for my dad except have sex with him. I don't think anyone had sex with him, I'm sure my mother didn't.

Chapter Three

"LOREN"
My First Love

When I went to high school I attained a little more freedom, I was still her slave, just a slave with a little more freedom. Not a lot of freedom, but more than I had had. I had dreamed about going to high school and learning everything I could. I was considered a nerd in high school and not very attractive. But, I didn't care how popular I was, I was there to learn and then go to college. I wanted to be in all the academic programs that were offered, but I couldn't because my birth-person would not allow it. Most of the programs offered were held after school and as I had to go straight home I could not join them. The one program I could belong to was the debate program. It was held during school hours in room three-hundred. This was a room sort-of on the third floor, but there wasn't a third floor at T. J. I think it was part of the attic of the school where they could store things out of the way. There was a room at the very top of the stairs where we could do our thing without bothering any of the other classes.

When I was in grade school, I loved going to the library. I'm sure if my birth-person would have known how much I loved the library she would have put a stop to that also. The librarians knew what I liked and when I came in they would stop me at the desk and give me books that had come in they thought I would like. I would set at one of the short round tables and read all day. I went every where in the world and never left the library.

When I was about twelve years old I met my nearest, dearest, friend Scarlet, I guess they called her that because of her red hair. She is still my nearest, dearest friend. My birth-person hated Scarlet. In years to come, Scarlet would save my life many times.

Scarlet introduced me to my first love, Loren. Loren was a friend of her boyfriend. Loren was a musician and would play the guitar and sing to me. We were both very young, he sixteen and I fourteen. He had a Chevrolet convertible and he would pick me up at school then drive out in the country where he would play his guitar and sing to me. We would hug and kiss, we called it petting back then, but sex was never a part of our love we just wanted to be together. My parents knew nothing about Loren, his family knew me. Dad worked nights which worked out great for mom; she could do as she pleased as dad never questioned her. I would sneak out to see Loren as often as I could. I knew when dad got home from work and mom made sure she got home just before he did so I knew I had to be home before she got home.

When Loren decided to enlist in the Navy, he asked me to marry him before he left. Then, when I graduated from high school and he was out of boot camp I would go to him. I was fifteen and he was seventeen and we were in love. We went to Atlantic, IA with Scarlet, her boyfriend, and another couple, Wayne and Dee, who wanted to get married also and Dee's brother. We were not sure what we were going to do when we got to Atlantic. Loren's parents had signed consent, but mine had no idea what was going on. I do not know how we fooled them at the Atlantic courthouse or maybe they saw how much we loved each other and decided to let us get married. On April 15, 1955, Loren and I were married. He will always be my first love, but not the love of my life, but I do believe if my birth person would have left us alone we would still be married and he would have been the love of my life.

I made excuses to my parents that I was spending the night with Scarlet and Scarlet was going to lie if they called her, but they wouldn't call. Loren's older brother had an apartment where we were going to spend the night. We were both virgins and we were excited and scared. We had petted in the past, but nothing more. Loren had the key to the apartment so we could let ourselves in. Once in, we just stood there looking at each other, like what do we do now. Loren took my hand and led me into the bedroom. I had on one of those popular box suits that Scarlet had bought me to get married in. Loren started unbuttoning my jacket, then pulled it down over my shoulders and laid it over a chair. My skirt was next, then I was standing there in my bra, slip and panties.

He asked, "Are you okay? Do you want to do this?"

"Yes," I replied, "I am scared, but I am now your wife and I want us to do this."

Neither of us knew what we were doing, but we forged ahead. The rest of my clothes fell to the floor and Loren just stood there looking at me.

"What's the matter?" I asked.

"I've never seen you, uh, a naked girl, I've only see women in magazines."

"Are you disappointed?" I asked.

"No, no, you look great." He said as his clothes quickly joined mine on the floor and he pulled me into his arms. This was the first time either of us had done this. We stood there holding our naked bodies tight against each other, and I could feel him grow against my stomach. We sat on the edge of the bed still holding each other tight. He slowly reached over and took one of my breasts in his hand. I have always been well endowed and I think he was surprised at their size without clothes on. He sucked in his breath, leaned over and brushed his tongue across my breast. He lay me down on the bed and lay down beside me. He was caressing my body as I was staring at him thinking how handsome he was and how much I loved him. He was trembling as he ran his hand across my body; I could feel him getting rigid against me.

My body was feeling things I had never felt before, I thought how is this going to feel, will this hurt? Loren would never hurt me; he loved me as much as I loved him. He rolled over and placed himself over me and pulled my knees apart to reveal my reddish-blonde fur ball. He was so absorbed in looking at my body he scraped my knee against the stucco wall and took the top layer of hide off my knee and it started bleeding. When I yelped in pain, his penis went limp in fear he had hurt me and pulled himself off me. We ran into the bathroom to get the bleeding to stop. When we finally got the bleeding stopped we looked at each other standing there in the bathroom, naked.

We started laughing, he looked at me and said, "I love you and we have the rest of our lives to make love. I just want to hold you in my arms and feel you next to me, till we are together again."

We walked back to the bedroom; lay down in the bed and curled up in each other's arms. We lay there holding each other talking about what our lives were going to be like when we were together again for good. Then we fell asleep thinking we had the rest of our lives together.

Our problem was we underestimated my birth person and what she would do to keep her slave.

The following morning Loren and Wayne were to leave for boot camp. We were all at the bus depot to see them off. Loren and I were clinging to each other praying the bus would never come. I was crying saying, "Please write to me and I will write to you everyday, until we are together again."

He said, "Listen to me; we both know how your mother is. No matter what happens don't let her come between us. If she finds out she will do anything to separate us."

"She won't find out, she can't find out, how could she find out?" I asked him.

He didn't say anything except, "I love you."

Loren and Wayne got on the bus and we watched the bus until it was out of sight. Loren was my first taste of passion, such as it was, and I wanted to go farther to find out why my birth-person loved men so much.

My birth-person didn't have to do too much to find out about our marriage, it was in the local newspaper. She was livid. When I came home from school she asked, "Is there something you want to tell me?"

My heart was in my stomach and it felt like my brain was going to explode, but all I said was, "No." I knew the tone in her voice meant nothing good.

She threw the newspaper at me and yelled at me, "You didn't think it would be in the newspaper did you. That shows how stupid the two of you are. What did the two of you plan on doing? Who in the hell is this boy? Where did you meet him, how did you meet him? I'll bet that Scarlet had a hand in this"

"I want to be with him and he wants to be with me. When he is done with boot camp, and I graduate then I will go wherever they send him. We love each other."

"The two of you don't know what love is. You really don't think I am going to let this happen do you? Have you slept with him?"

I said nothing.

Then she was shouting, "Have you slept with him? Answer me damn it!"

"We know more about how to love than you do, and yes I have slept with him." I shouted back at her. "You can't stop us, we want to be together." I wasn't lying to her we did sleep together, that is all we did was sleep, but I will never let her know that.

"You think I can't stop you? There will be a divorce I will see to that." The neighbors could probably hear her.

"We knew you would do this and we won't sign the papers. You don't care about me you just don't want to lose your slave."

Her face was so red with anger she was just stood there staring at, me then she turned to walk away from me, but stopped, turned back to face me and said, "There will be a divorce, I will see to that. You will find out he doesn't love you as much as you think he does."

I watched her back as she walked out of the room and I thought what is she going to do; I was so afraid of her I felt like I could throw up. I ran to my room and cried myself to sleep. When I woke up all I could think of was Loren and hoping I would get a letter soon, I missed him so. I wish he had never joined the Navy and was here with me.

I looked in the mailbox everyday when I got home from school, but no letters. My birth person would come home and mockingly ask, "Get a letter today?"

I came home from school one day and she was waiting for me. "Guess what I have here," she said as she was waving a piece of paper around in the air.

My heart sank, what had she done? Loren would never sign those papers, what had she done? But, in her hand were the divorce papers with his signature. I wanted to crawl into a hole and pull it in after me.

With that, ha, ha, ha look on her face she said, "I told you he didn't love you as much as you thought he did. Your court date is August 11th; I don't think she even remembered that was my sixteenth birthday.

We went to court on my sixteenth birthday to get a divorce from my first love. She didn't even acknowledge it was my birthday. I didn't care about that; I just couldn't understand why Loren had done this to us, had he stopped loving me?

The day of the divorce, I wanted to run as far as I could, but where would I run. She acted like it was just another day.

She said, "Someday you will thank me for doing this."

I stopped walking and mustered up the worst look I could and said, "I will **never** thank you for ruining my life."

From then on, I did not care what went on in my life. I went to school and continued being my birth-person's slave.

In 1978 I went back to school and graduated from Business College. There were three of us that hung out together. One of the girls was from Detroit and couldn't stay for graduation so the three of us went out to celebrate on our own. We went to a nice steakhouse for dinner, then we went to a bar where we could dance. While on the dance floor with the girls I thought I heard my name called. I looked around the floor, but could see no one that would have called my name. We started dancing again when I heard my name called again.

One of the girls with me asked, "Do you know that guy on the stage?"

I looked up to the stage and there was Loren playing in the band. I walked over to the stage my heart pounding.

He leaned over and asked, "Can I see you on break?" I just nodded. On break he jumped off the stage, took my hand and led me to a table.

We stared at each other for a few moments, then I opened my mouth and blurted out, "Why didn't you write to me? I waited every day for a letter from you."

He said, "You really don't know what your mother did do you? I did write to you, almost everyday, you didn't write back. They sent divorce papers three times and I refused to sign them, the forth time I had no choice. Your mother found out who my C.O. was and wrote to him telling him we were married. As I enlisted as a single man I was supposed to change that to married, I didn't know that. If I didn't sign the divorce papers I would be court marshaled and discharged from the Navy. Since you didn't write back I thought you had changed your mind about me and signed the papers."

"I waited and waited for your letters. She taunted me everyday about not getting a letter. She must have taken them; I knew she was up to something, she was not about to give up her slave. I never changed my mind about you; I missed you so and wished you would never have gone to the Navy. I never forgot the night we had together, that was all I had. I relived that night over and over again in my mind. I never stopped loving you, you were my first love, but I thought you had stopped loving me."

"I will never love anyone as I loved you; you were my first love also. I too, will never forget the night we spent together nor the other times we had, we just didn't have enough of them."

"Are you with someone now?" I asked.

"Yes," He said. "We have been together for some time now. We have a little girl. You are married aren't you?"

"Yes, I have seven children. I understand you have children from another marriage."

"Yah, I came home one day and found she didn't take our marriage as serious as I did."

"Sounds like your wife and my husband should be together. He runs all the time, as soon as my children are old enough to understand I am going to leave, someday soon I hope."

"If my mother would have left us alone we could have been so happy. You have no idea how evil she can be."

"Oh yes I think I have a good idea. I just don't know how a mother can treat her child the way she has you."

"I couldn't believe it when I saw you dancing out there; you have not changed a bit. You are the same as I remember you. I guess I'd better get back to work, you take care of yourself Jewelya." He said.

He kissed me on the cheek and headed back to the stage. My heart felt that familiar tug as I watched him walk away then jump back on the stage. He was still so handsome, and I was remembering when he sang for only me. "Strawberry Pink Apple Blossom White" was the song he sang the most for me.

Why I never said anything to my birth person about this, I don't know. Maybe I figured it wouldn't do any good. She would say she did it for my own good. She never did anything for my own good. Then maybe, just maybe, I didn't say anything because I was still afraid of her, I don't think I ever got over being afraid of her.

When my sons decided to delve into my past, to find out things about their mother that was none of their business they found out about Loren. I had not kept him secret I just didn't think he was any of their business, I still think that. In the process they dug up the divorce papers my birth-person had served on him. She depicted him as being a very violent man and that I was in fear of my life from him. When we went to court for the divorce she took all the papers so I had no idea what was in them. She didn't want me to know because she knew I would find out where Loren was and go to him as we had planned. But I thought he had stopped loving me and didn't want to be with me anymore. I was in shock, if she hadn't already died, I would have been on her like stink on shit, yeh right, I probably would have done what Jewelya does best, nothing. What made her hate me enough to do this to another human being, just to hurt me? This was about as far from the truth about Loren as anything could be. He was a very gentle man that could never hurt anyone.

When he read this it would have broken his heart if he hadn't known what my birth-person was capable of. Neither of us had stopped loving each other, these papers had been sent to him three times before he was forced to sign the forth.

When we met that night he never mentioned to me what was in those divorce papers, I'm sure it was because he knew I had nothing to do with it. I would never have said anything like that about him. He was my first love and I still think of him with love in my heart. No matter how long you live, you never forget or stop loving your first love.

Chapter Four

CARL I

D omestic violence has been around since the existence of mankind. Cavemen would pick the woman he wanted then pull her by her hair to his cave. Whether the pictures depicting cavemen pulling women around by their hair is really true or not, I don't know. I don't think it has ever been proven, but I think it is true as I have had a man pull me around by my hair more than once. Then, if the caveman wanted he would get himself another woman, and they would do as they are told or suffer the consequences. Not much has changed. Domestic violence is not getting better, it is getting worse.

Women have more options now than I had then, but the thing that still remains is fear, because some men never stop until one is dead and the dead one is usually the woman.

Many years ago when I was with my abuser, there were no shelters and if your family didn't help you, you were sunk and my parents moved me out of their house to live with him. But, as you can see, I survived, he didn't.

I believe that when a woman finally, out of desperation, kills her abuser there should be at least one person on the jury that has been abused, whether that person is a man or a woman as there are battered men. About five to ten percent of the abused are men.

MURDER

In 2005, 1,181 women were murdered by an intimate partner.[1] that's an average of three women every day. Of all the women murdered in the U.S., about one-third were killed by an intimate partner.[2]

DOMESTIC VIOLENCE (Intimate Partner Violence or Battering)

Domestic violence can be defined as a pattern of abusive behavior in any relationship that is used by one partner to gain or maintain power and control over an intimate partner.[3] According to the National Center for Injury Prevention and Control, women experience about 4.8 million intimate partner-related physical assaults and rapes every year.[4] Less than 20 percent of battered women sought medical treatment following an injury.[5]

SEXUAL VIOLENCE

According to the National Crime Victimization Survey, which includes crimes that were *not* reported to the police, 232,960 women in the U.S. were raped or sexually assaulted in 2006. That's more than 600 women every day.[6] other estimates, such as those generated by the FBI, are much lower because they rely on data from law enforcement agencies. A significant number of crimes are never even reported for reasons that include the victim's feeling that nothing can/will be done and the personal nature of the incident.[7]

IMPACT ON CHILDREN

According to the Family Violence Prevention Fund, "growing up in a violent home may be a terrifying and traumatic experience that can affect every aspect of a child's life, growth and development . . . . children who have been exposed to family violence suffer symptoms of post-traumatic stress disorder, such as bed-wetting or nightmares, and were at greater risk than their peers of having allergies, asthma, gastrointestinal problems, headaches and flu." In addition, women who experience physical abuse as children are at a greater risk of victimization as adults, and men have a far greater (more than double) likelihood of perpetrating abuse. [13]

LEGISLATION

In 1994, the National Organization for Women, the NOW Legal Defense and Education Fund (now called Legal Momentum), the Feminist

Majority and other organizations finally secured passage of the Violence Against Women Act, which provided a record-breaking $1.6 billion to address issues of violence against women.[15] However it took nearly an additional year to force the Newt Gingrich-led Congress to release the funding. An analysis estimated that in the first six years after VAWA was passed, nearly $14.8 billion was saved in net averted social costs.[16] VAWA was reauthorized in 2005, with nearly $4 billion in funding over five years.[17]

RESOURCES

[1] Bureau of Justice Statistics, *Intimate Homicide Victims by Gender*
[2] Bureau of Justice Statistics, *There has been a decline in homicide of intimates, especially male victims*
[3] Deptartment of Justice, *About Domestic Violence*
[4] Centers for Disease Control and Prevention (CDC), *Understanding Intimate Partner Violence* (PDF)
[5] National Coalition Against Domestic Violence (NCADV), *Domestic Violence Facts* (PDF)
[6] Bureau of Justice Statistics (table 2, page 15), *Criminal Victimization in the United States, 2006 Statistical Tables*
[7] US Census Bureau (page 12), *National Crime Victimization Survey* (PDF)
The Violence Against Women Act: Celebrating 10 Years of Prevention
[13] Family Violence Prevention Fund, *The Facts on Children and Domestic Violence*
[15] NOW, *The Violence Against Women Act: Celebrating 10 Years of Prevention*
[16] University of North Carolina, *Analyses of Violence Against Women Act suggest legislation saved U.S. $14.8 billion*
[17] NCADV, *Comparison of VAWA 1994, VAWA 2000 and VAWA 2005 Reauthorization Bill* (PDF)

(This was printed from http://www.now.org/issues/violence/stats.html)

I wanted to have children from the time I was very young, ten or eleven. I wanted to prove that not all mothers are the way my mother was. I truly believe that had Carl lived, my sons may not be the good men they are today. If Carl had not died when he did, it would not have been long before he killed me, as his violence escalated on a daily basis. Carl experienced, as a youngster, violence in his parent's home. There was violence between his parents and infidelity in the home, on both sides. He hated his father for his violence against his mother, but he was the same way with me, probably worse.

Carl was probably the most violent, angry man I ever met, but he still had his lucid moments. When he was growing up after his mom and dad split, he lived with his mother and sister in a second-floor apartment. He told me about the times he set outside on the roof waiting for his mother and sister to get done with their men before he could go in. He would cry and I would hold him in my arms until he would realize how vulnerable he had made himself and became angry with me for seeing this side of him, a side he never wanted anyone to see.

At fifteen a girl should not be looking for someone to love her, but I was. I didn't know that was what I was doing. A fifteen year old girl should already have someone to love her, her family. I didn't realize at the time, but I was a train wreck looking for a place to crash, and I crashed many times. But I was like the Phoenix, from the ashes I would rise to crash and burn again, and again and again, and I am still crashing and burning and rising.

When I met Carl I didn't realize how bad I wanted someone to love me. I wanted to be loved so bad even bad love seemed to be better than I had. Bad love is never good. Bad love is an oxy-moron and it didn't take long to find that out.

My school friends, Scarlet and Terry and, I used to walk between our houses. I lived at 35th & Ave. "B", Terry lived at 35th & Ave. "A" and Scarlet lived on 35th & 7th avenue.

On 35th & Broadway was a car lot with a little building in the corner of the lot. The three of us were walking past the lot when Carl walked out of the door of that little building. He was so handsome with beautiful brown eyes, wavy brown hair and when he spoke with that silver tongue there was nothing Scarlet and Terry could say or do to stop me.

I was mesmerized by this man. He seemed so understanding about how I was treated at home. He knew he couldn't pick me up at home so I would meet him at the car lot where he was one of the salesmen. He told me he was just out of the Navy and hadn't decided what he was going to do.

(Later, he told me he had been in the Navy only ten months. He had been in a mental institute the last three months of his ten months in the Navy. He was discharged with a medical discharge, stating he was mentally incapable of dealing with Navy life and he was to get psychiatric care when he arrived home, which of course he never did.)

The first couple of weeks sneaking out to meet him was so exciting I had butterflies in my stomach just thinking of him. I was having a wonderful time with this man. I was in love and nothing was taking him away from me.

One evening he called me to meet him at the car lot. When I got there two of his friends were with him for me to meet or should I say for me to be their meat. I didn't realize at the time what was happening.

One of his friends worked at the filling station across the street from the car lot.

Carl said, "We have to over go to the station, Conner is going to change the oil in my car for me. He has to do it after the station is closed, that way I get it free."

I said, "Okay" and we walked across the street.

When we got there Carl said, "Let's set in the back seat of the car while he's changing the oil." All we had done at this point was make out. I got in then Carl got in then one of the others got in.

As I was asking, "Why is he getting in?" the car started going in the air.

Carl was on one side, his friend on the other side. I reached over Carl for the door handle, the door swung open to air, the car was at the top of the hoist, I had no where to go. I was pushed down in the seat; I felt hands going inside my blouse under my bra.

I was crying, "No, please stop." As another pair of hands was pulling my panties down.

I was trying to scream, but Carl put his penis in my mouth and said, "If you bite me I will beat you half to death."

The other was forcing his penis inside me with such brutal force I thought I was being ripped apart.

I don't think any of them realized I was still a virgin that probably would have made them feel manlier. The penis in my mouth was choking me and flooding my mouth with such vile I started vomiting.

One of them hit me in the head and said, "Swallow bitch." I realized it was no use to struggle, so I just lay there praying for it to be over. I felt the car lurch as it was being lowered.

When we reached the floor Carl threw a shop rag at me and said "Clean yourself up." I was sobbing hysterically,

Carl grabbed me by the hair and yelled at me, "Shut up or I'll do more than pull your hair. And don't even think of saying anything about this to anyone. From what you have told me about your mother she wouldn't care anyway or wouldn't believe you."

And he was right, if I would have had a mother or a father that gave a damn, I could have gone to them or if I wouldn't have been fifteen and he almost twenty I wouldn't have been so stupid.

As soon as Carl let go of my hair, I was out of the car and running up the street.

I heard Carl yelling at me as I ran, "I'll be calling you honey."

I ran up the steps into the bathroom to take a bath as hot as I could stand it. I scrubbed and scrubbed and cried and cried. What do I do if he does call, I just won't go. I didn't feel I had any options except to try to stay away from Carl. That proved to be easier said than done. He didn't call for about a week, I thought he had forgotten about me. When he called, I answered the phone. When I heard his voice my heart dropped. I was reliving that night all over again, and was scared to death.

The first thing he said when I answered was, "Don't hang up; I need to talk to you. I'm at the car lot, I'll come by to pick you up."

"No" I said.

"If you don't come out, I'll park outside your house and honk until you come out."

Dad was home and he knew I was home, so if Carl did what he said, dad would know he was honking for me. I went down the stairs and out the door, just as Carl pulled up. I motioned for him to go around the corner so know one would see me with him. I was horrified to see one of his friends was with him, in the back seat. Carl reached over and opened the door. I hesitated, not wanting to get in.

The look on his face made my stomach turn. "Get in the damn car, now!" He yelled.

For the next few months this was my life and I could see no way out except that if he decided he didn't want me anymore.

He told me each time they were done with me, "If you ever tell anyone about me I will tell your mother and father and those two friends of yours what a tramp you are."

I was told for so long how useless and stupid I was, my self-esteem was so non-existent, it terrified me to think of him telling them what was happening.

I tried to bury myself in school and my books. My room was on the second floor, and I loved to read and set out on the roof outside my room listening to my 9-volt transistor radio. When you read a book you can go anywhere and never leave home, and I needed to go as far away in my mind as I could. I watched my birth person come out in her housecoat as a car pulled up in front of the house. She would get in the car and in a couple of hours come back and run back into the house. I don't think she ever knew I watched her come and go.

In late June early July, Carl and his friends picked me up and they took me to Conner's house. He said his parents were on vacation so he had the house to himself. I never knew where I was going to end up. This time I felt different inside. I felt anger, sickness, despair and a need to end this. Carl pulled his car in to the driveway, when the car stopped I opened the door as though to go into the house, but turned away as I approached the door and started to run.

Carl grabbed me by my hair and said "Where do you think you are going?"

"Home," I said.

"I don't think so," he said as he was pulling me by my hair back toward the house. I tried to pull away from him, but one of his buddies grabbed my arm and was dragging me into the house.

I was yelling at them, "You are not going to do this to me anymore. Tell anyone what you want to tell them, but no more, no more."

Carl pushed me in the back so hard I lost my balance and I ended up on my stomach in the front room. That's when I started crawling and they were grabbing me. I knew to survive, I had to escape and escape I did.

I was lying on my stomach, crawling trying to get away. I felt hands around my ankles and my wrists. I was flipped onto my back. One had my right leg another had my left. My hands were being stretched above my head by another. My legs were being pulled apart as I was trying to pull my knees together.

Someone yelled, "Pull her legs apart so we can see it."

The fear and hate I had for him and his friends was so much stronger than my fear of her, all I could think of was getting away from them. I started kicking and screaming, jerking my legs as hard as I could. I kicked one of them in the mouth and he let go. As soon as I felt my leg free, I started kicking at the other with my free foot still screaming as loud as I could.

Someone yelled, "Shut her up."

The one holding my hands let go of one hand and put his hand over my mouth. I bit down on some part of his hand until I tasted blood.

He was screaming, "The fucking bitch bit me."

I was crawling across the floor as fast as I could trying to get to my feet. Once on my feet I could see a door and headed for it still screaming as loud as I could "leave me alone, leave me alone."

I could hear them behind me. One of them was yelling, "Shut her up, someone will call the cops."

I made it out the door into the darkness, the sweet, sweet darkness where I couldn't be seen. When I hit the darkness, I knew I had to be quiet. The night was silent, too silent. I could hear my heart pounding in my ears, trying to run as quickly and quietly as I could so they wouldn't hear my footsteps. I weighted maybe ninety-five pounds and was barely five feet tall. I was going from tree to tree hiding behind each one hoping none of them would see me.

I could hear them behind me yelling, "Find her, we can't let her get away."

I flattened myself against the trees and stretched myself as tall as I could, how I thought that was going to help, I don't know. I was a young girl running for her life.

Conner's house is about two to three miles from my parent's house. I was running hard through yards, and hiding behind trees.

I don't know how long it took me to get home, it seemed like hours. Every once in a while, I would see Carl's car drive by as slowly as he thought possible without drawing attention to himself. I kept running from tree to tree and down alleys so as not to be on the main road when I felt something warm running down the inside of my legs, and realized I didn't have my panties on and I was peeing down my legs into my shoes and socks. I ran up the alley to my house, in the back door and up the steps to my room. My heart felt like it was going to explode in my chest.

I ran up the stairs to my room and closed the door behind me. I stood there with my back against the door until I felt my legs give out from under me. I slid down the door setting on my wet skirt and cried. I knew I was alone in the house, dad worked nights and mom ran anywhere she wanted. I hadn't turned on any lights in the house, as I didn't want Carl and his buddies to know I was home. I crawled over to my windows, as my windows came down almost to the floor; I could set on the floor on my wet skirt and still see out the window. Carl drove by a couple of times, making my heart start to pound again with fear, complete and total fear.

First, mom pulled in the drive, must be about time for dad to come home. She always managed to make it home just before him except for bowling night. Bowling night she had an excuse, like she needed an excuse. I guess she though having an excuse made her look better. Everyone knew what she was doing; they just didn't put it in her face.

I heard her scurrying around downstairs trying to get into bed and feign sleep before dad came in. When dad drove in I tried to move and realized my legs had fallen asleep from setting on them for so long. I pulled my legs out from under me and sat down on the floor on my bare butt, realizing again my patties were gone. My skirt was still wet, but at least it was warm wet.

I pulled my wet shoes and socks off thinking, it's a good thing I do the laundry. How would I explain my clothes smelling like pee? I went into the bathroom to wash my shoes out so they would be dry by morning. I got a dirty towel out of the clothes hamper, wrapped my wet socks and skirt in it and took it back to my room. I didn't know where my patties were and didn't care. I hoped one of Conner's parents would find them in the house and he would have to think fast and explain how they got there and who had left them there.

The next morning and many mornings after that when I left for school, I would slowly make it out the back door looking everywhere, scared to death they would be there waiting for me.

After that night Carl called the house a few of times, but when mom or dad answered he would hang-up. I guess they thought they were wrong numbers.

I tried not to answer the phone, but when I did and would hear his voice say, "Jewelya" I hung-up. I didn't know what I would do if he told anyone about what had happened, but he never did.

Now, I know he never would have, because that would have put him in jail. If he would have told my mother, she would have done nothing, but if it was made public knowledge she would have to save her face, and do something about it. He knew how afraid of my mother I was, that is what he used against me.

I would not walk past the car lot alone. This meant walking a few extra blocks, but I would have walked a few extra miles to stay away from them. I would make excuses to Scarlet and Terry to go another direction. One hot summer day we decide we wanted to go to Lake Manawa for a swim.

As we were walking past the filling station across from the car lot, Scarlet said, "Let's get your boyfriend to take us."

I said, "No, he isn't my boyfriend. I don't see him any more. Can't you get your dad to take us Scarlet?" I couldn't tell them what had happened inside that filling station.

My stomach was churning from fear remembering being in the backseat of a car up in the air on a hoist in that filling station.

Carl appeared out of that little building on the corner of the lot. My fear was so intense, I wanted to run as fast as I could. But, I knew I couldn't do that. Before I could object, one of the girls asked Carl to take us to the lake.

He said, "Sure, but I need to talk to Jewelya, I think she is mad at me."

I tried to protest, but he grabbed my hand and was leading me across the street. I didn't know what to do. I didn't want to go, but what could I do without Scarlet and Terry wondering what was going on.

Cochran, the pig, that owned the car lot, was setting in one of his cars. I think Cochran was his last name. I don't know what his first name was, puke I think, no that's what he was. He was old, bald and fat with a fat slobbery mouth and squinty eyes.

I asked Carl, "What do you want. I don't want to talk to you. We don't need you to take us to the lake."

He had hold of my arm and before I knew what was happening he had pushed me into the car. I was between Carl and the pig. Carl had his arm around me holding me down. We ended up by the Missouri river under the bridge. Carl opened the car door and I tried to kick him to get out.

Carl was holding me down, with his hand over my mouth. The pig was pulling on my jeans. I was kicking and trying to bite Carl's fingers. I felt my zipper in my jeans break. The pig got my jeans down far enough that I couldn't move my legs. I felt the pig's fat face coming down on my face, and his fat body coming down on me. I pulled my head up and spit in his face. He started cussing me and calling me vile names as I felt his sticky goo on my stomach. I kicked him in the face as he was getting off me.

He just kept cussing at me, and yelling at Carl, "I thought you said she was into this. She better not say anything to the cops or it is your ass."

I was laying there quietly crying. I could feel the tears running into my ears.

Carl still had his hand over my mouth. "I'll let go if you shut-up." he said. He let go of me, I sat up and took a swing at him hitting him on the side of his head. He hit me across the head so hard I flew backward on the seat landing against the pig. The pig started cussing me again and pushed me back into Carl.

Carl threw a rag at me and said, "Here, clean yourself up. When we pickup your girlfriends, keep your mouth shut. If you know what is good for you."

At this point in my life all I wanted to do was die, but I knew that wasn't too likely.

I don't know why Scarlet and Terry didn't see that something was wrong but, when we got back to the car lot, Carl said, "Jump in girls, I'll give you a ride."

The pig got out, waddled to his office, and we went to Lake Manawa as if nothing had happened.

I don't remember how we got home; I guess that doesn't matter now.

After that I would make excuses to Terry and Scarlet to not meet them, or meet them somewhere that I didn't have to walk past the car lot. Carl called a few times. I tried to never answer the phone. I think he hung up on mom and dad if they answered.

When I answered I would hear, "Jewelya" and I would hang up, then lay the phone on the cradle, but off the receiver so it would ring busy because I knew he would try to call back.

Late one summer evening, I was setting on the roof outside my bedroom window. Mom was off on one of her escapades and dad was at work. I would set on the roof for hours listening to my 9-volt transistor radio and read. When it was too cold to be outside I would set on my bed or on the floor beneath my windows and listen to my radio and read. I had an earplug for my radio so only I heard the radio.

One day as I was setting on the roof, through the music I could hear a horn honking and a motor racing. I looked up from my book to see Carl in his car by the curb. I took the earplug out and turned my radio down. He was motioning for me to come down. I kept shaking my head no.

My stomach was flopping so much I could feel it in my throat. My heart was pounding like the night I was running for my life. What do I do if he gets out of his car? His car started rolling backwards past the driveway then he pulled into the driveway. He opened the car door and started to get out.

Being in the driveway it made him closer to me, now I could hear what he was saying.

"Come down and talk to me," he said.

I couldn't say anything, just nodded my head.

Again, only louder he said, "Come down here I want to talk to you."

"No, I won't come down, go away." By now he was out of the car and coming toward the house. I jumped through the window and into my room thinking, "Were the doors locked? Would he dare come into the house?"

He yelled at me, "Keep your mouth shut, do you understand me?"

Then I heard a familiar voice say, "Can I help you young man?"

My neighbor was standing on her front porch with her big red chow dog on a heavy leash. This was probably the meanest dog I had ever seen. When she was gone the dog stayed in the basement. When my sister, Janie and I would walk up the driveway he would be at the basement window barking furiously, showing his teeth. We thought he would come through the window and eat us. If not for the metal bars across the window, he would have as the glass would not have stopped this dog. But, when he was with her he didn't move unless she told him to do so.

Carl looked over at the dog, got in the car and with one last glance pointed his finger and thumb at me and drove away. I stepped back out onto the roof.

My neighbor asked, "Are you alright Jewelya?"

"Yes," I replied.

"I got his license plate number before I came out if you want to call the police."

"No thanks, I'm fine. I don't think he will be back, Thank you so much for being here, I think you scared him half to death."

My knees were shaking so bad I slid down the outside of the house and set down on the roof. Thinking what would I have done if she would have called the police instead of coming out with her dog. How would I explain that to mother.

She knew how mom was so that may have been why she did what she did. Now being an older and wiser woman, her calling the police would have been the best thing for me.

A few months later I thought I had been saved, mom and dad had bought a new house on the other side of town. I guess I should say mom wanted a new house and mom always got what she wanted, always. Once we were moved I though I was free of Carl. I was going to graduate from high school next year then go to college. I wanted to teach English to third and fourth graders. At that age their little brains are like sponges and they want to know everything.

The best laid plans of mice and men and a teenage girl in the wrong place at the wrong time. My plans would soon be falling down around me. I knew I was pregnant, but I thought I had more time. I had no idea what I would do with more time, I just wanted more time. On January 14, 1956 in the wee hours of the morning I awoke in such pain. I must have been making noise because mom came in. She had no idea what was happening until she saw me. She called her quack doctor friend who was in the Civil Air Patrol with her and was as flaky as she was.

My son was born Wednesday, January 17th 1956 at 9 p.m. He was so tiny no one thought he would survive. I will never forget those three days.

I had no idea what was going to happen, but knowing my mother it could be anything and it would not take her long, and it would not be good.

Thursday morning, January 18th the day after my son was born, a nurse came into my room with papers she wanted me to sign to give my son away. She said, "I see you haven't named your son yet, it would be best not to name or see your baby as that makes it easier to let go."

I almost screamed at her, "Not name my baby or see him, just leave him here? I'm not signing those papers I will never sign papers to give my baby away."

"Your mother said you wanted to give him up for adoption. Isn't that what you want?"

"No I don't want to give him away. I never told her that."

"What will you do?" the nurse asked. "You are only sixteen and it doesn't sound like your parents are willing to help you. What about the father, will he help you?"

I snapped at her, "He doesn't have a father, only me."

"The decision is yours to make. Your parents can't make it for you, and they cannot just leave you here. You are a minor and they are responsible for you, they have to take you home with or without your baby. If you change your mind just push your button." she said as she left my room.

I lay there in bed crying, wondering what I was going to do. I was sixteen years old, with a baby and no one wanted us.

Later that evening there was a knock on my door. A man and woman walked into my room. I didn't recognize the woman, but I did the man. He was one of the men who would be with Carl when he came after me. The woman was his wife and I wondered what he had told his wife, that I was Carl's girlfriend and they should come to see me as he was Carl's friend.

I didn't know why he was there at the time, but I realized later he was probably trying to find out what I was going to do, as he knew there was a chance this baby was his.

I didn't care about him. All I knew was I didn't want my birth person to find out. I did a good job of that, she never did find out what really happened to me that summer. For many years, no one knew what happened to me that summer, not even Scarlet. If my birth-person had known, I'm sure she would not have cared. All she was concerned about was her image. No one knew, not even me, the lengths she would go too to protect that image and to get rid of me and my child.

The next day she came to see me. I had refused to tell her who the father was. She asked me, "Are you ready to tell me who?" I nodded my head.

"You didn't sign the papers?" Again I just nodded.

"Does the name Carl Harmon ring a bell?" I though I was going to throw up, I was so scared. I felt the blood drain from my face. Please God, let me die, that would solve all my problems, like before, that was not going to happen.

"He says he wasn't the only one, there were others. Is this true? Were there others?"

If at that point I had been older and not so afraid of her I should have said, yes, and told her why there were others.

Instead, I said the stupidest thing I had ever said, "Not that I remember."

She didn't even flinch, like she hadn't even heard what I had said. But I knew she had heard me, now she had her way out.

She raised herself out of the chair and said as she when out the door, "Now we know who is going to support this kid and it sure as hell won't be me."

I firmly said, "This kid's name is Big, please call him by his name."

As my son, was born almost three months early, he wasn't able to come home when I did.

I asked dad, "What do you think she will do when my baby comes home?"

"I don't think there is much she can do. Don't worry honey everything will work out. Famous last words of a fool, and my father was one of the biggest fools I knew, beside me. Oh everything worked out; just not the way I would have liked them to.

My wonderful grandmother worked in pediatrics at the hospital where Big was and she would go to see him every morning when she got to work. He got jaundice shortly after he was born and grandma said his head looked like an orange as he was so small. Every morning she went in to work she expected he would be gone as he was a very tiny, very sick baby. But my son is a fighter like his mom and he survived.

Not to long after that she came home from work with, "We have to talk. Now that we are in agreement as to whom the father is to this child, his name, not ours needs to be on the birth certificate. The only way for this to happen is for the two of you to get married."

I jumped to my feet and almost yelled at her, "No, I will never marry him. He is a terrible person. I'm afraid of him." I wanted to scream at her. You don't know what he has already done to me, but would you care if you knew, no never, you would find a way to blame me.

"Don't panic," she said. "You don't have to live with him. For him to be legally responsible for his child, the baby has to have his name. Marry him, send a letter to the department of records in Des Moines to get the boy's last name changed so he has his father's name, and then we will go from there. (It was as if she thought if she didn't call Big by his name he wasn't real to her.) Carl will pick you up tomorrow and I will meet you at the court house to sign the application for permission for you to marry him." I could see there was nothing I could say to change her mind.

Carl picked me up the next day. The sight of him made me cringe. I stood behind the door trying to hide from him.

I don't know who I was more afraid of, him or her. When I first saw him I thought he was the most handsome man I had ever seen and I was in love. Now, I was so repelled and afraid of him I was shaking.

"Hey," he said. "What the hell is wrong with you; open your mouth, talk. Let's go, get this over with."

On the way to the courthouse I asked Carl, "Why are you doing this? You don't want to marry me any more than I want to marry you. I would rather my son keep my last than to marry you."

"You don't think I'm doing this because I want to do you? Ask your mother; now I know why you are so afraid of her, she is just plain ass evil."

I thought to myself, "Takes one to know one."

Later that night I said to her, "I asked Carl today why he was so willing to do this. He said he wasn't doing it because he wanted to and to ask you why. I don't want to do this either, I like my son's name the way it is."

She was standing in the kitchen; I was standing in the doorway to the front room. She swung around to face me her face distorted with anger.

Her face was beet red as she was screaming at me, "That kid needs his father's name not ours'. He needs to be responsible for him, not me.

I will not have people talking about me behind my back about my kid having a kid out of wedlock."

"I will get a job. I will take care of Big; his name is Big not kid."

She was still screaming at me, "You can't take care of yourself you proved that by getting yourself pregnant. Let his father take care of him and to do that he has to have his name."

I was too young; I had no idea what she had in mind and too young to realize we didn't have to be married for my son to have Carl's name.

On Saturday, February 11, 1956 Carl and I were married by the Justice of the Peace just outside of town.

On the way home Carl said, "We will stay at mom's place tonight. She isn't going to be home tonight."

I felt panic welling in my throat. "No I am not staying with you, take me home."

"You are my wife now you will do whatever I want you to do. You got me into this mess I should get something out of it."

I screamed at him, "I got you into this mess? I think you made this mess not me, now take me home."

He was laughing at me as he pulled the car into his mom's drive. As soon as the car slowed down I opened the door and tried to jump out. He grabbed for me and got a handful of my hair. I thought he would pull my hair out by the roots, but I didn't care if I was bald I needed to get away from him. He let go of my hair to steer the car and I was out and running as fast as I could. I ran the seven or eight blocks home not slowing down till I was in the door.

Dad was setting in that ugly green chair of his. I ran up to him in tears begging him, "Please daddy, don't make me go with him again. I am so afraid of him."

"No. honey, we will figure something out." Again, famous last words of a fool, my father the fool, or was I the fool, my father would never go against my birth-person.

A week or so later I brought Big home, he was still so tiny. Boy did I underestimate my birth person; this was just the calm before the storm. My son was the wiser of the two of us, when she came in later that day she leaned over the bed as I was changing his diaper and he peed in her face.

The following Wednesday Big and I had gone with Scarlet. When she brought us home mom and Carl were in my room backing mine and my son's things.

"What are you doing?" I was yelling at them, "Put our things back."

"What does it look like we are doing." she said. "You have a husband now that is where you belong."

I ran out to the front room where dad was. "Daddy, you said I wouldn't have to go with him again."

My father turned that ugly green rocker around to stare out the front window and never said a word to me or anyone else. I ran back into what used to be my bedroom in tears begging my birth-person to not make me go with him.

Scarlet came running into my room yelling at my birth-person, "What are you doing, you can't send her with him he will end up killing her, he is crazy."

My birth person screamed at Scarlet as she pointed at the front door, "This is none of your business and get out of my house, now!"

Carl looked up from his packing and said, "You don't think either of us has a say-so in this do you?"

They carried our things to Carl's car. I was holding my son tight in my arms sobbing uncontrollably. I was sixteen with a tiny baby, being thrown to the lions. Scarlet stood in the middle of the road watching Carl drive me to what could only be described as hell.

Mine and my son's new home was about the size of my bedroom at what was once my home. I walked into our new home. To the left was a single bed with a baby bed at the end. A small rocker was setting between the beds. Behind the baby bed was a dresser and small closet. To the right was a stove, refrigerator, table and two chairs. Straight ahead was the bathroom we shared with whoever was in the middle apartment.

"Stop bawling," Carl yelled at me. "I'm going to tell you right now, I do as I please. Don't ever try to tell me what to do."

"I don't care what you do; stay away as much as you want." I was yelling at his back as he went out the door and I sat in the rocking chair with my son for hours.

Carl didn't come back till the following Friday night bringing a bimbo home with him and wanted me to sleep with them. His bimbo sat in the bed watching me get the first of the many beatings to come in the next six years nine months and eleven days.

He knew as well as I did how I got pregnant with Big so neither of us knew who the real father was. He said it couldn't be him as he was "shooting blanks." So every month I didn't get pregnant, I got a beating. I begged my mother to let us come home as I was afraid that one of these times, he would beat me to death.

Her comment, "You made your bed now you have to lye in it."

Carl came home from work one evening, sober. He had come home to tell me we were moving into the middle apartment for more room. We had one little room, now we had a little room and a pretty good sized kitchen, and still shared the same bathroom as before. I really didn't care about much anymore except my son. I just made do with what ever I had, but it was nicer having more room.

He hadn't brought one of his bimbos home for sometime, but nothing he did surprised me. In the wee hours of the morning I heard him come in the door, but he was not alone I heard a female voice. I quietly got out of bed and got into my rocking chair. I figured once they made their way to the bedroom I would move out to the kitchen and set at the table. The kitchen chairs were the only other chairs in the apartment. As they moved into the bedroom, I started to rise out of my chair to go to the kitchen.

Carl grabbed my arm and said, "No, you can stay, and be quiet we don't want to wake up the kid, if he starts screaming again you know then what will happen, you will have to kill me."

A week or so before tonight, Carl had come home earlier than usual and wanted sex. I told him no as Big was sick. He took Big from me and put him in his bed, and Big started screaming. Carl went to the kitchen, got the black pepper and put it on Big's fist and of course Big stuck it in his mouth, then he was really screaming. I grabbed him out of his bed and got a washcloth to get the pepper out of his mouth.

I was in Carl's face screaming at him, "You can do whatever you want too to me, but if you ever hurt my son again I will kill you!"

I thought, "I am now going to die," but he just walked away from me laughing.

Since the first time I refused to get into bed with him and his bimbo, he hadn't suggested it again, but now he was. I stood there frozen, when the female walked over to me. She was staring into my eyes. She was older than me, but I was only seventeen she would have to have been at least twenty-one to be in the bar. She was attractive with long brown hair, brown eyes I think, and what I could tell from her face she was slim built. She was not much taller than me, but she still had to look down at me, I wasn't quite five foot tall.

She put her hands on my breasts and said, "Not bad, good body. She looked at Carl and asked, "What do you want me to do?"

His reply, "Whatever you want to, I will watch. I told you, you would like her."

I could feel tears running down my cheeks.

Carl asked "What is wrong with you. She won't hurt you."

I begged, "Carl, please don't make me do this."

He just smiled and said, "Hey you never know you might like it."

The girl asked Carl, "Are you sure about this?"

"Yes," he said. "She does what ever I tell her to, she has no choice."

The girl looked at me, wiped my tears away and said, "Trust me, I would never hurt you."

She went to lift up my pajama top and I put my hands up to my chest. All Carl had to say was "Jewelya" and my arms came down.

She lifted my pajama top over my head then stood looking at my breasts. She gently took my breasts in her hands, I closed my eyes and tried to remember when Loren had done this, but the touch was much different.

She was fondling my breasts saying; "There is nothing more beautiful than young breasts."

I stood there rigid, not moving. I felt her pull the elastic on my pajama bottoms as she was pulling them down over my hips.

Carl took hold of the legs of my pajamas and pulled them down to my ankles as he said to her, "Get her underwear off."

She said back to him, "Do you want me to do this or do you want to?"

I'm standing there like a stone as they discussed who would get me first.

Carl let go of my bottoms while she took hold of my underwear pulling them down over my hips.

As she was pulling my underwear down, she stopped by my reddish-blonde ball of fur and said, "You really are blonde aren't you." As she lifted herself up from taking my pajamas over my feet her hand went between my legs.

While I was standing like a stone by the bed she started undressing and asked, "Do you want to help me?"

I said nothing and didn't move.

When she was completely undressed, she took my hand and led me to the bed. "Lye down," she said.

I knew there was no use objecting, just like with his buddies try to relax and let her do what she wanted to then it would be over. I sat on the edge of the bed and she sat down beside me. Carl was setting in my rocking chair staring at us going from body to body.

She took my shoulders and gently pushed me down on the bed. She bent down to take my breasts in her mouth one at a time. She reached down with one hand to get between my legs again. When I didn't open my legs Carl reached over and pulled them apart. She put her hand between my legs inserting her fingers inside me.

She quietly said to me, "Try to relax, I promise I won't hurt you I want to make you feel good and that will make me feel good."

Since the night Loren had held my breasts in his hands I had not known gentle sex. Carl and his buddies were not gentle. She was moving her fingers around inside me pushing them further inside me, then she took them out of me and put her fingers in her mouth sucking on them.

She had me laying on the outside of the bed so Carl could watch what she was doing to me. I think she enjoyed him watching us.

She pulled me close and said so Carl couldn't hear, "A man has no idea how to make a woman feel good only a woman knows what another woman wants."

She tried to kiss me, but I turned my head away, but she gently turned my head back toward her and put her lips on mine, this time I didn't resist. She parted my lips with her tongue searching for mine. I was so surprised to find that it wasn't as bad as I thought it would be. Not like kissing my Loren, but better than Carl. He didn't kiss me very often, but when he did it was disgusting. as there was no love on either side.

When I first met him he was so loving and kissed me with such passion, but he was in his conquering mode then.

While she was kissing me she put the palm of her hand between my thighs and inserted her fingers inside me again, this time I let her, I had no choice.

She was sucking on my breasts going from one to the other. She took her fingers out of me, raised her hand and put them in my mouth. I expected this to be disgusting, but it wasn't, so this is what I taste like. She continued her way down below my belly button then she pulled my legs apart so she could get between my legs.

She lowered her head down between my legs, and when she felt me tense up she said, "Remember what I said, I won't hurt you."

I relaxed and she lowered her head down between my thighs, first just licking all around my man in the boat (at that time I didn't know that was what it was called, I didn't even know I had one) and around the lips inside my fur ball then I felt her tongue go inside me. I was so afraid to show how much I was enjoying this. This was the first time I had experienced this, and it was by a woman and it felt good. She was right, only a woman really knows what a woman likes, but I so hope a man does this to me some day. If it feels this good by a woman how good would it feel by a man that loves you and you love him.

She was licking and sucking and moving her tongue in and out of me while her fingers were caressing my man in the boat ever so gently. I felt a gentle throbbing start slowly then grow inside me and spill out onto her fingers and tongue. I had never felt such a feeling before. She kept sucking on me until there was nothing left to suck.

She pulled herself up beside me, took my hand and put it between her legs and said, "Put your fingers inside me and feel me throb as my tongue felt you throb."

I put my fingers inside her as she said, "Move your fingers around, push them in as far as you can."

She was holding my hand pushing on it so my fingers went in farther then she was moving my hand up and down using the palm of my hand to caress her man in the boat. She was moving her hips up and down while holding my hand tight against her until I felt her start throbbing and my fingers were getting wetter. I heard her release a big moan as she held my hand there until the throbbing was done. Then she pulled my fingers out of her, raised them to her mouth and was licking them, then she moved them to my mouth. I clamped my lips together and turned my head. She was right she hadn't hurt me and I had almost forgotten Carl was watching us.

The next thing I knew Carl was beside us saying "My turn."

I was hoping he meant her, but he meant me. As he was watching us he had gotten a huge erection, I had never seen him this big. He was hovering over me; he grabbed the back of my knees, pulled my legs apart and lunged inside me.

I was wet from her tongue so he went in easily, but he went in so hard and so far. He pulled my butt up off the bed to get me closer to him and was going in and out of me so hard and so far it felt like he was going to my belly button and the pain was horrible.

I screamed at him, "You are hurting me."

Of course he paid no attention to me. He was pushing himself in and out of me so fast and so hard it didn't take him long to explode inside me. He rolled off me onto the bed. I was struggling to get out of bed.

I noticed the girl was dressed and setting in my rocking chair.

She said to me, "You and your body are too good to waste on him." Then she got up and went out the door.

Carl asked. "How'd you like that? Where did she go?"

"I don't know, she got dressed and left." I didn't tell him what she said.

"That was great watching you two. Nothing a man likes more than watching two women having sex together."

By now I was in the bathroom washing myself trying to get all of Carl off me, when I noticed how sensitive I was to my touch, I liked the feel of my own touch. I inserted my fingers inside myself and found I felt inside like the girl did. I removed my fingers from inside me and put them in my mouth, and found it was not as bad as I thought.

I realized that day, at seventeen, I really enjoyed the feel of that throbbing she had created inside me and I would be able to create that feeling myself. So from then on when Carl got done with me, I went into the bathroom and took a bath and used my fingers to create that feeling.

Big and my life went on a usual; wondering, is this the day I'm going to die? Carl was gone most of the time and I dreaded it when I heard him come in. He was angry with me for ruining his life; I guess he though mine was great.

Carl brought the girl home with him a few weeks later. This time I wasn't scared, as I knew she wouldn't hurt me, and she made me feel good. She undressed me and this time I helped her undress as she had asked me the first time. Carl was very quiet setting in the rocking chair watching us. We lay down on the bed facing each other, when she started kissing me I responded to her by letting her.

She was caressing my breasts and this time I reached for hers. They felt somewhat like mine, but smaller. I heard that same deep moan as I had heard from her before. Our hands went between each others legs as we spread our thighs to insert our fingers inside each other. Her fingers went deep inside me and I pushed mine further into her both of us moving them around inside each other.

She turned around to place herself above my face and mine in hers, I said, "I don't think I am ready for that yet."

She asked, "Is it okay if I do? I love the taste of you."

I didn't say anything just let her do what she wanted. She was between my legs and her lips and tongue were licking every part of me. Her tongue was moving around inside me, until I felt that throbbing slowly start from my belly button flowing out onto her tongue and into her mouth. I again heard that deep moan coming out of both of us.

I could hear Carl breathing hard so I knew it wouldn't be long before he came after me. He pulled her off me and had another huge erection that he lunged into me so hard and so far I screamed in pain.

She yelled at him, "Stop that, you are hurting her."

Of course Carl ignored her until he was done. Then he stood up and yelled at the girl, "It is none of your business what I do to my wife. She is mine not yours so this will be the last time you will be coming here."

She looked at me and said, "If you ever get tired of him, let me know. I will take care of you and your son."

I wanted to yell at her to please take me with her, but I knew Carl would never let that happen and all it would do was maybe get her hurt. So I said nothing.

I went to pick up my son as the yelling had woke him up.

As I passed Carl he grabbed my arm, "You were enjoying what she was doing to you weren't you? What are you now a lesbo?"

"What difference does it make? I do whatever I think you want me to do so I don't get beat on. Now if you want to beat on me do it before I pick Big up. He let go of my arm and I picked Big up and went into the kitchen to get his bottle. When I walked back from the kitchen I had to go past Carl, he grabbed my arm again. I pulled my arm away and sat down to feed my son. Carl reached over and slapped me across the face; at least it was a slap it is usually a punch.

I asked, "Did that make you feel good?"

"Yah," he said.

"Then why not hit the other cheek. Make yourself feel even better."
so he did.

"Did that make you feel better?" I asked.

"Yah. "he said, "Should I make myself feel even better?"

I rubbed my cheek and said, "No, I think you feel good enough."

From then on when he brought one of his bimbos home she was for him only. After the last time with the girl he thought if I was enjoying this, he didn't want it to happen anymore. Like my birth-person, if she likes it don't let her do it. Sometimes he would come home with a bimbo in the car and come in and tell me he had to take care of her then he would be in. I think he was finally realizing I didn't care what or who he did. He could not hurt me, physically yes, but unless he killed me, bruises heal.

When I finally got pregnant with Gene, Carl's attitude changed toward me. He became obsessed with me, and those friends of his were not allowed around me. The beatings never stopped, anything or nothing would set him off.

With another baby coming, we moved to the front apartment with two bedrooms. He came home from work one day, drunk as usual. I had fixed supper, but it wasn't what he wanted and said he was leaving to get something decent to eat.

As he walked past me I said, "You really don't have to come back you know."

The next thing I knew I was on the floor and he was kicking me. I got to my feet and was trying to run out the door when he grabbed my arm and threw me across the room, I landed on my stomach on the foot stool. I had to be in bed not moving trying not to abort my child.

Gene was born, July, 1958. Carl was not there nor did he take me to the hospital, Scarlet of course took me and stayed until Gene was born.

When Carl brought me home from the hospital he said, "You may want to change the sheets on the bed, I had company while you were gone."

Less than a year after Gene was born Wayne was born. When I got pregnant with my third son I was sick with the flu. Carl came home on his lunch time and wanted to have sex. I told him no as I was so sick and didn't want to have sex, so he went to the kitchen, got a knife and forced himself on me with the knife at my throat. This became one of his favorite things to do as he saw how afraid of knives I was. I prayed he would get the flu from me, no such luck.

One day there was a knock on the door. I opened the door to see Conner, one of Carl's "buddies" standing there.

"Carl isn't here." I said.

"I know," he said. "It is you I wanted to see."

"Why do you want to see me?" I asked.

"I just wanted to tell you how sorry I am for the part I played in what we did to you that summer."

I just said, "Fine, but you had better go, if Carl would see you here I would catch hell."

He said again, "I am sorry, I am so sorry."

Then he turned and walked off the porch and got into a police car. Then I noticed he had on a police uniform. Was he really sorry for what he had done or just afraid of what may happen if it came out about that summer? I don't think he would have that uniform on anymore, but I wasn't going to say anything. Not because he said "I'm sorry," but why bother. Somehow I would be the victim again. I had others that were very good at making me the victim; I didn't need to do it to myself.

As I watched him drive away I remembered a time in the backseat of Carl's car, Conner was the last one to have me, sloppy third's I guess you would call it.

As we were putting ourselves back together, Conner said to me, "I wish you felt about me like you do him." He nodded toward Carl as he spoke to me.

I said to him, as I got out of the car. "I do, I hate both of you."

My mother would take me to the hospital after Carl would beat on me then take me back to him again and again with, "You made your bed now you have to lye in it."

I finally stopped asking her and dad for help it was doing no good. When he beat on me, I took care of myself.

I tried to hide from him, but he would always find me. The boys and I had moved into an out-of-the-way house north of Broadway, where I didn't think he would find us, ha, ha, ha. The boys slept in the one bedroom and I slept on the couch. I woke up with Carl over me with a knife. I tried to get up, but all that did was make him push the knife harder down on my throat. When he was done and was moving off me, his pants down to his knees I pushed him and he fell which gave me time to run. I ran to the back of the house that made a circle back into the dinning room where the phone hung on the wall. I grabbed the phone receiver out the cradle on the wall and as Carl came through the door way I hit him on his forehead between his eyes with the phone receiver as hard as I could, and the blood flew.

When he saw his blood, he grabbed his head and was running out the door yelling, "I am going to kill you."

I thought to myself, "You are going to die."

My sister and her husband had moved back to Iowa from Las Vegas, as her husband had gotten into trouble with the mob and had to get out of town. They lived in a trailer court in Manawa where a small trailer was for rent. It was out of the way and we didn't think anyone would see us there. Again, the best laid plans of mice and men. The trailer court owner had added a small bedroom and bathroom on the side of the trailer. Wayne's crib was in the small bedroom and Big, Gene and I slept in the middle and only bedroom. The bed was pretty small and when the boys went to sleep I would go out to the couch to sleep. Things went pretty good for a month or so, and then I awoke in the middle of the night with a knife at my throat. Carl was staring into my face. We were almost nose to nose as I raised my knee into his groin. When he went down I went through the trailer out the back door. I don't think he realized there was a back door. I knew he wouldn't bother the boys he was there for me. I ran out the door in my baby doll pajamas screaming at the top of my lungs.

My sister's husband came out of their trailer with a shot gun in his hands. He yelled at Carl to stop chasing me. Carl kept coming after me so Rick shot his gun off into the air. Carl stopped dead in his tracks.

Rick said, "The next shot goes through you."

Carl turned and was running out of the court yelling at me that he would be back. I called the police, but because there was no knife to be found there was nothing they would do.

I guess Carl's sister had seen the boys playing outside and told him where we were.

I moved out of the trailer into another house, again he found me. He raped me again, with a knife at my throat. When he was done I pushed him off me and again I was running through the house and he took off. The neighbors had heard me screaming and called the police. This time there was a knife and the police picked him up. When they had him in custody, they called me to the police chief's office. They had brought Carl to the chief's office while they were trying to talk me into pressing charges against Carl for rape. Carl was a mess, he had two black eyes bruises on his face and he wasn't walking to well.

One of the officers asked," Harmon, what happened to you?"

Carl said, "I fell down a flight of stairs."

The officer said, "I wish I would have been the stairs."

Carl was glaring at me as the police were trying to talk me into pressing charges, they were begging me.

I said, "This has never been done before. Do you have any idea what he will do to me if this doesn't happen? Most people don't think a husband can rape a wife."

"If he goes to jail, he will be gone for five years or more. Lots of things change in five years."

"Not him," I said. "If I put him in prison, he will spend his time in there deciding how to kill me when he gets out."

Carl was glaring at me across the room, and I knew exactly what he was saying without him saying a word. When I left the police station they told me to call if I needed them, but I knew there was nothing they could do for me. I was on my own; it was up to me to survive. I wondered if his "buddy" that was the police officer was ever aware of all Carl had done to me.

If he was really sorry for the part he played in what they had done to me, he would have done something about it. We both knew why he was there to say I'm sorry, it was to save his ass not mine.

So, that day I finally resigned myself to the fact that I was on my own. Scarlet was the only person that would help me. I don't know how many times she saved my life. Back then if your family wouldn't help you, no one would and my family put me there. There were many nights I would stand over him in bed with a butcher knife wanting to run it through his heart, but I would hear the sounds of my sons in the other bedroom and wondered how I would explain to them their mother had killed their father.

There wasn't a day that went by I didn't ask myself, "Is this the day I'm going to die?"

The Dixie Chicks has a song, "Earl Has to Die," Scarlet and I had been saying for a long time before that, "Carl has to die."

After Gene was born I decided to go to work. After years of trying to hide from Carl, I realized that wouldn't work. I was tired of living in apartments and wanted a home for my boys. I went to work at a food factory where most of the work they did was for the government. They made canned products to send overseas where troops were stationed. I worked up to the time Wayne was born, and when he was two weeks old, I went back to work.

I got laid off there when their government contract ran out, then I went to work at a hair products company in Omaha where I made better money.

After about a year we bought a house or should I say I bought a house. His name was on it, but I paid for it. Not much change with Carl, but I had learned how to avoid some of the beatings. When he came home drunk, I would feel out his mood then go with my gut as to how to handle him. Never a dull moment, sometimes I was right and escaped a beating and some times I was wrong.

After my parents had moved me out of their house and into that little one room apartment with Carl I didn't think much about how the bills got paid, I just knew they did. I knew Carl spent his money as fast as he got it, so one day I asked him how the rent got paid and who bought the food at that time.

His comment was, "You don't think your parents paid for anything do you?"

That was when I realized his mom and step-father were paying our rent and buying the groceries. I guess a mom will do anything to keep her little boy out of jail, or maybe it was her guilty conscious getting the best of her, she had created this monster.

When the bank called to have us come in to sign the papers on the house his mom was not able to watch the boys.

I told Carl, "The boys can come with us they behave fine when I take them anywhere."

"I'm not taking these kids to the bank. Call your sister, have her watch them for an hour or so it won't hurt her."

So I called my younger sister, she was about twelve at the time and I didn't like the idea at all. She agreed and I went to pick her up. Mom and dad were not home from work yet and I told her she should be home before they were.

Carl and I went to the bank, got the papers signed and went home. Things were going okay till we got home and I tried to take my sister home, Carl wanted to take her. I gathered he wanted to take her home then go out, which was fine with me. When he didn't come home I was not concerned as he did this all the time, I loved him not coming home. Then the phone rang, it was my birth person screaming at me. I guess as Carl was taking my sister home he tried to get touchy feely with her and when he stopped at the stop sign she jumped out and ran home.

My birth-person was screaming at me, "This is your fault; you should have brought your sister home not him. You tell that husband of yours to keep his hands off my daughter."

I screamed back into the phone at her, "Why are you not calling the police, why are you screaming at me. I'm your daughter also and look what you let him do to me. I didn't bring him into this family, you did. And when he ends up killing me that will be your fault also."

And I hung up the phone. Nothing was ever again said about the incident amongst any of us. I didn't even tell Carl my birth-person had called. He probably didn't think he had done anything wrong.

There were times when Carl's anger could be funny, as long as it was not aimed at me. The first year we had the house Carl's mom had her tax man come to our house to do our taxes. Carl's birthday was April 15 same as tax day and he had procrastinated about doing the taxes, but of course because it was his birthday he had to have a few drinks before he came home. The tax man was already there, which of course Carl didn't like because that meant there was a man alone in the house with me. When the tax man finished figuring our taxes we owned $3.00 to Uncle Sam. Carl grabbed the tax man by the arm and was throwing him out the door calling him a dirty crook, among other things and this poor man was scared to death. He was trying his hardest to get out the door without Carl hurting him. The tax man was yelling at me to help him, but I figured he was a man he could help himself and I was not about to get beat on for a tax man.

As the tax man was being thrown out the door, Carl's mom and step dad were coming up the walk with a birthday gift for Carl, oh what timing. As Carl's mom had sent the tax man over it was her fault we owed the $3.00 to Uncle Sam so he was screaming at her to get the hell off his property that this was all her fault. She handed him his gift and was retreating as fast as she could as her gift went flying past her grazing her head, good thing it was a shirt so it was soft. As I was an innocent bystander watching this unfold it was taking all I had to control myself and not burst into laughter, rejoicing that his anger was not aimed at me. He was so angry he got into the car and sped off rocks flying behind him. I stood there watching everyone making a run for it and I was laughing so hard I was almost crying. What a sight, everyone running from this crazy man and none of him was aimed at me. I was an innocent bystander this time, he was gone and the boys and me would have the night to ourselves, there is a God.

I never knew what was coming next, I don't know if he thought them up as he went along or if he put thought into them. He came home one night, drunk of course and pulled me out of bed.

He quietly said, "Take your pajamas off cocksucker."

I had learned a long time ago not to argue with him so I took my pajamas off.

I was standing by the bed naked when he said, "Put them back on cocksucker."

So I put them back on. Then I was ordered to take them back off again, this went on for maybe an hour, on, off, on, off. While I was taking my P J.s on and off he got into bed. When I thought he was asleep I put my pajamas on and started to get into bed.

He said, "I didn't tell you, you could get dressed or get into bed did I, cocksucker? You can get in bed when I tell you, you can."

My pajamas came off again and I was standing naked by the bed. When I heard him snoring, I pulled my pillow down to the floor and pulled myself into the fetal position to cover as much of my body as I could with my shirt that was in the chair by the bed. I lay on the floor tears running onto my pillow, praying to God to please let this end.

There were times I created my own misery, but there were times I just couldn't help myself. Carl hated the smell of coffee and I have always loved coffee, but had to refrain from having it when he was home. One morning without a blink while he was showering for work, I went to the kitchen and made myself a pot of coffee. The fury came bounding out of the bathroom and of course because I had disobeyed him I was bounced around the kitchen a few times then the coffee pot went onto the floor then he flew out the door screaming what a bitch I was. My body ached, but I picked myself up cleaned up the coffee on the floor and made myself another pot of coffee with a smile on my face.

Another time I just couldn't help myself. As I worked nights I would make something for their supper Carl could heat up for him and the boys. One night I came home from work with him yelling at me what a lousy supper I had made, that dog food would have better. So the next day I left a can of dog food and a can opener on the table with a note saying, "Enjoy your supper, the boy's supper is in the fridge." Guess what I got when I got home. This could have been called; suicide by Carl.

We had been in our house about a year when Carl came home relatively early and sober. I always froze when I heard him come in. If I pretended to be asleep he would shake me and bounce the bed until I acknowledged him. If I said something when he came home then I was a nagging bitch staying awake to see when he came home. Like I really cared if he never came home.

This night he was not drunk, but calm. He lay down beside me saying he had to tell me something.

I just lay there and asked, "what?'

"I've met someone. I just came home to get some of my things. I have been seeing her for a while now. The boys know her they have been at her place."

He said he needed to be with her as one of her girls was in the hospital. I just lay there not saying anything. My heart was pounding one hundred miles an hour. I couldn't believe what I was hearing.

He asked, "Don't you have anything to say?"

"I expected this would happen someday. You have to do what you have to do to make yourself happy." I couldn't let him see how happy this news made me.

He said, "Mom will still watch the boys so you can work and I'll help with the boys too."

He got up, got some of his things and said, "I'll come back and get the rest of my things later."

I waited until he got out the door and heard his car go up the road to get up and dance around the bed a few times.

I stopped dancing around the bed, and put my hands together and looked up to the ceiling and said, "Thank you God and please God, make this last don't let him come back."

I didn't care if he took the boys to her house. My boys were everything to me and I knew Carl nor his mom would let anything happen to them.

He knew I meant it when I said, "Do anything to hurt my boys and I will kill you."

When Big started school it was a battle with him every day to get him to school. He knew that when he got out of school, mommy would not be there so he didn't want to go to school.

I would try to get him into the car and he would hang on to the car door handle for dear life saying, "Please mommy don't make me go, I want to stay with you."

One day I pried his fingers off the car door handle, picked him up and sat on the porch with him in my arms. He was crying so hard my heart was breaking and I could feel the tears in my eyes.

I told him, "You have to be mommy's big boy and watch out for your little brothers when you get home from school, because mommy has to work to make money for us. I wish I didn't have to leave you either, but I have to. You can help grandma by playing with your brothers. Gene and Wayne love you to play with them. Mommy needs you to help her out okay? Mommy loves you all very, very much and will be with you as soon as I am off work."

My beautiful son stopped crying and said, "You need me to help you mommy?"

"Yes I do, I won't worry as much about all of you if I know you are helping grandma with your brothers."

Big sucked in his breath, wiped away his tears and said, "Okay mommy, don't cry I will help you."

After that when it was time to leave, I would carry Wayne to the car and Big would get Gene by the hand and say, "Come on Gene, mommy has to go to work to get us money."

My boys went everywhere with me. I always had a car with two tires in the grave and the other two on a banana peel. I had one that had to have a piece of wood wedged in the solenoid, so I carried small pieces of wood in the glove box. One day the car stopped on Broadway in front of our local department store. I got a piece of wood out of the glove box as I told the boys to stay in the car while mommy fixed the car. This wasn't the first time this had happened so they knew what to do. I lifted the hood of the car, climbed under the hood and inserted my piece of wood into the solenoid. I closed the hood of the car and the boys and I were on our way.

The next night on the front page of the local newspaper, was a picture of me or should I say my legs sticking out from under the hood of my car. I am so short I had to lie on my stomach on the fender with only my legs showing, as the solenoid was on the back firewall of the car.

You could see my little boys' heads as they sat quietly in the back seat waiting for mommy to fix the car.

The caption read: "Mom fixes own car while kids set quietly in the back seat."

I left the hair company to go to work at a food plant in Omaha where I could make more money. I worked evenings as nights paid more per hour than days. I car pooled with a girl up the street, so each of us drove every other week. One night when we got off work, my car had been stolen. Why anyone would want my piece of junk I don't know they must have been hard up. We went back into the plant to call the police and to get a ride home. My friend's boss said he would drive us home (I think he was sweet on my friend) we stopped at a little café that set in front of Playland Park.

While we were drinking our coffee, I looked out the window and there was my car stopped at the stop sign just outside the café.

I yelled, "There is my car" as I ran out the door.

I ran up to the car and stuck my hand inside the window to pull the car door handle up. The outside handle was broke so you had to open it from the inside. I pulled the door open and as I was pulling the man out of my car my friend's boss was behind me pulling me away from the man. I had the man out of my car and on the ground when the police arrived.

The police asked me if I was crazy, doing what I did. "He could have had a gun or a knife, he could have killed you, is your car that important?"

I just said, "I'm sorry, I guess I didn't think, I just wanted my car back. I need my car to get to work to take care of my boys."

Then I realized what a stupid thing I had done. What would my boys do without me?

When I got home it was late and of course Carl didn't believe me, so I told him, "Call the police station, they will tell you."

He called; they told him what I had done. He told them to let the guy go, we had our car back and no harm was done. The police said they couldn't do that. I guess he was a transient and was going to Colorado and was practicing driving in Playland Park. He had taken a stolen car across a state line which was a federal offense.

Carl just told me how stupid I was and went to bed. The next day on the front page of the local news paper again, "Woman recovers own stolen car." Local woman has car stolen from Omaha parking lot, then later the same night recovers own car from the thief who stole it. The whole story was on the front page, I guess I must be a little crazy. Duh, I wonder why?

Chapter Five

"BOB"
The Man Who Showed Me
I Was Worth Loving

When I dropped the boys off at Carl's mom's house I wondered if she would say anything to me about Carl leaving. I didn't think she would mention it as I'm sure she knew about Carl's girlfriend all along. All she said was that she didn't want me to pay her anymore for watching the boys as she knew it was going to be rough for me.

I just said, "Thank you, but I really want to pay you something for watching the boys. Otherwise I would have to leave them with a stranger, and I don't want to do that."

When I went back to work it was just like any other day for me, work was work. I didn't mingle much at work, but I did have lunch with one girl once in a while, Doreen. I was on the floor where she worked when she was going to lunch and motioned for me to go with her. While we were at lunch I told her about Carl leaving. After her telling me how sorry she was for me, I told her not to be sorry for me it was the best thing that could happen to me he was a very abusive man, and I hoped he would be happy were he was and not come back, or that a bus might hit him to be sure he didn't come back.

She laughed and said, "Then if you are a free woman, why not come to this bar down the street some time with me and a couple of other girls."

I wasn't sure if I should go because no matter what Carl was doing, if he knew I was in a bar he would kill me. I finally decide to go, I couldn't live scared all my life and that is what I have been all my life, was scared.

The next time I saw her I told her, "I don't drink, but I would like to go just to know there is no one that can tell me I can't, that is as long as Carl doesn't find out."

This was when I realized how seductive I could be without knowing it. The first night I went to the bar with them I was like a kid with a new toy. I was out in a bar, a very nice bar. It was a long narrow tavern with the bar toward the back on the left side, and booths along the right wall to the front windows with tables in the front. We sat at one of the tables in the front. When the waitress came and took our order, I looked up toward the bar. There was a very handsome man standing at the bar looking our way. I looked back to talk to the girls, then looked back and he was still looking our way.

When the waitress came back with our drinks, she said, "These are compliments of Bob, the man standing at the bar."

We looked up toward the bar and he toasted his beer toward us. I wondered which of the girls he knew. Later, I needed to use the restroom which was at the back of the bar so I had to walk past Bob on the way. When I came out, he stepped out in front of me, I almost ran into him.

He said. "I haven't seen you in here before, are you with anyone?"

"I'm just with the girls from work." I answered.

He leaned down to whisper in my ear, "If I go get your drink for you, will you set at the bar with me?"

I started to say I didn't think I should, but he was already on his way after my drink. He sat my soda on the bar and pulled a bar stool out for me.

He took my hand to help me onto the stool, and then said. "You are so tiny I should have picked you up and set you on the stool."

I looked up to see he had beautiful sky-blue eyes, he told me later one of them was glass. He had wavy light brown hair, clean shaven, but I saw curly brown hairs spiraling out of his shirt.

He was well dressed with dress pants, dress shirt, jacket and shinny black shoes. And did I mention he was very handsome?

"I come in here quite a bit, but I've never seen you in here. I know the girls work at Campbell Soup, did you just start there."

"No, I have been there for some time now, but this is the first time I have come in here. I don't drink so bars aren't my thing. I'm not sure this is a very good idea setting up here with you." I answered.

The girls motioned they had to go so I started to get down off the stool. He stopped me and said, "Will you stay for a while, do you have to go? I can take you home."

"I have my car here," I said, "I don't like to go anywhere without my car. I guess it won't hurt to stay a little longer, I'll go tell the girls."

Before I could say anymore he was walking toward the girls to tell them I was staying for a while. I watched him walk back toward me and I was thinking to myself, "Self, what the hell are you doing, you don't even know this man."

He must have read my thoughts and said, "As you know my name is Bob and I am harmless, ask the bartender."

He nodded toward the bartender and the bartender nodded back. Like that meant something to me.

"My name is Jewelya, and I can't believe I am setting here with you. I'm new at this going out thing, what do I mean new to it I've never done the "going out thing." I answered back.

"Divorced?" he asked.

"Not yet, but soon I hope. How about you." I asked.

"Never been married, haven't found anyone I wanted to marry."

I was getting nervous about getting home to get the boys so I said, "I should go, I have to pick up my boys." I had told him earlier I had three boys with a sitter.

He lifted me off the barstool and as we were walking toward the door he took hold of my hand, and I didn't stop him.

Outside the door walking to the parking lot he still had my hand and he pulled me into his arms and looked into my eyes and said, "Can I?"

He lifted me up to him and was kissing me before I could say anything. Soft, gentle, arousing kisses that made my body shiver. The last soft and gentle kisses I had had were from a female. If he knew that what would he think of me, but he would never know that. My mind was saying stop him, but my body was screaming for more. I was remembering how my Loren had made me feel.

He stopped kissing me, but kept his arms around me holding me tight then asked, "Where have you been, blonde hair, green eyes, tiny little thing, where have you been? Can I see you again and when?"

"Are you asking me out on a date?" I asked.

"Yes I am. When you walked in the door, I ask the bartender who you were, he didn't know, so I had to know. I don't want you to leave now, but I know you have to."

Then I was back in his arms tasting those wonderful kisses and I wanted more of them.

We made a date for the following Saturday. Carl would have the boys for the weekend so I was free. I was praying Carl's love affair would last, but I was so afraid it wouldn't.

By Saturday I was a nervous wreck. I met Bob at the bar as I wanted to have my car at hand. Bob was waiting for me at the bar where we had sat the night we met. I had dressed up for the occasion and when he saw me come in, he started walking toward me.

He took both my hands and turned me around and said, "My god you are gorgeous, all this for me?"

I couldn't believe someone was telling me I was gorgeous. I had bought a black dress with a plunging neck line. It clung to me and flowed down my body to just above my knees. Underneath the dress was a black lace bra with matching panties, and black garter belt holding up black stocking with three-inch black heels. We had a drink there, Bob had a beer, me seven-up.

Bob took my hand and said, "Let's go someplace where I can show you off."

We went to where we could dance and when we danced Bob held me so close I could feel his heart beating. He had his face nestled in my hair telling me how good I smelled. I snuggled closer to him, thinking, please don't wake me up!

We had been there for about two hours when he asked me, "Can you stay with me? When do you have to be home? I will make you breakfast"

"Yes, I will stay with you and I have to be home tomorrow afternoon before he brings my boys home. I would love to have you make me breakfast. I have never had a man make me breakfast"

"I have an apartment down the hill from the bar, can we leave now? I want to be alone with you. I'll take you to your car and you follow me okay?"

He didn't wait for me to answer, he had my hand and we were going out the door.

When we were back at the bar he helped me into my car, kissed me and said, "Follow me, I will keep an eye on you."

I followed him down the hill and he turned into a parking lot by a large brick apartment house. He came to my car lifted me out of my car shut the door with his foot and carried me to his apartment. His apartment was on the first floor; he let me down long enough to unlock the door then picked me back up and carried me in kicking the door closed behind us. Inside his apartment I was thinking to myself, what am I going to do I have never been in this position before. What is he going to do? He must have seen the expression on my face.

"Jewelya, what's wrong, you look scared to death. I won't hurt you. We don't have to do anything, just sleep if you want; I just want to be with you, curl you up in my arms."

"No, no," I said. "I want to do this, but I have only been with one man in my life and he wasn't very good to me. Just being kissed by you makes me feel things I have never felt before. Just take it slow with me okay?"

"I will be so gentle with you, anytime you want me to stop, just say so and I will. When I saw you in the bar, the look you had in your eyes was not what I thought it was. You have no idea what those green eyes can do, do you? You could have any man you wanted, just by looking at him with those eyes. I was staring at you trying to get your attention, and when you finally looked at me I knew I wanted to be with you; I still want you so bad; but for different reasons. You are still a scared little girl, but I hope by tomorrow you will be a happy content woman."

He picked me back up and carried me into his bedroom.

His apartment was very tidy for a man, but I guess some men like clean homes. He carried me over to the bed and pulled the blankets back on the bed.

He looked into my eyes and said, "I could never be mean to you or hurt you there is already too much pain in there."

He stood me on the floor and bent down to give me one of those sweet wonderful kisses and I knew this was going to be a night I would always remember. His tongue was slowly looking for mine and mine for his. I had to stand on my tiptoes, even with heels to get my arms around his neck. (I have had many men since then tell me I am a good kisser and lover. I guess Bob was a good teacher of many things.)

He pulled my arms from around his neck and said, "Can I undress you or do you not want me to?"

"Yes, I want you to undress me." I remember how it felt when the girl undressed me and I want this to be so much better.

He reached around behind me to unzip my dress. I felt my dress come loose and he pulled it down over my shoulders.

"Just let it drop to the floor." I told him.

I could feel my dress flow down over my hips to the floor and another shiver went through my body as I stepped out of my dress and was left in my bra, panties, garter-belt, black stocking and heels.

I stepped toward him to start undressing him and he stopped me and stood staring at me and said. "You are so tiny."

He took my waist and pulled me to him. "I will be so careful with you."

I pulled him down to me and whispered in his ear, "Please make love to me, I won't break, and I know you will not hurt me."

I pulled his jacket off his shoulders and lay it on the bed. I unbuttoned his shirt then unbuckled his belt and unbuttoned his pants to pull his shirt off. I then saw his beautiful chest full of brown curly hair and I buried my face in his chest. I just now realized how much I loved a hairy man. Carl didn't have hair anywhere except his penis, his head and what he shaved off his face. Maybe that is why I love a hairy man.

He reached behind me again to unhook my bra and pulled it off my shoulders and let it fall to the floor.

He stopped and was staring at my breasts then said, "Can I hold them?" I nodded and he cupped each one in his hands, I heard him sigh then bend down to kiss each one on the nipple, I was in heaven. His mouth on my breasts was so much better than the girl's. He hooked his thumbs in each side of my panties and slowly pulled them down over my hips taking my heels off so I could step out of my panties.

As he stood up he stopped at my large ball of fur and put his face into it, then stood up and was holding me tight again.

He took a step back and said, "Every part of you smells good. What a sight you are. How can you have three boys and look like this? How much do you weigh, one hundred pounds?"

"I think I weigh a little over one hundred pounds, soak and wet. I guess it keeps me in shape chasing those boys around. I'm glad you like what you see and that you appreciate a woman's body." Only the girl had appreciated my body, Carl just used and abused it.

I unzipped his pants and let them fall to the floor then pulled his shorts down exposing him and all I could do was stare at him.

He took my hand and said, "Are you okay Jewelya?" Nothing would come out of my mouth so I just nodded then he picked me up and lay me down on his bed then placed himself between my legs. He unhooked my stockings and was rolling them down over my feet laying them beside us. I heard him sigh and realized he had stopped at my reddish-blonde fur ball. I tried to pull my legs together; how was he to know he was the first real man I had ever been with and I wasn't sure what to do.

"Tell me what to do, make love to me." I said. "Show me what it is like to really be made love to."

He pulled me close and asked, "What has been done to you? Now I know what those eyes were saying to me."

He lay down on the bed beside me and said," I am going to make such good love to you that you will never forget tonight. (As you can see I have never forgotten that night nor Bob. After all, he was the first man to really make love to me.) He pulled me close against him my breasts pressed into his hairy chest, and it felt so good to be held and feel safe. He started kissing me very gently his tongue again looking for my tongue he didn't have to look far I willingly surrendered it to him.

Every place he touched he set on fire. He kissed and nibbled gently on each breast until each nipple was rigid. He was kissing every part of me from my belly button to my reddish-blonde ball of fur down to the tips of my toes. As he made his way back up my body, he stopped with his head between my legs. He lifted my legs up at my knees and I could feel his tongue touching every part of me then his tongue darted inside me and I was moaning with such pleasure.

"Bob, please come up here with me."

He was beside me asking me, "Are you okay?"

"Yes, I am more than okay. I want you to show me how to do that to you."

He looked at me in surprise and asked, "You have never done this before?"

I said, "It is a long story, but no not really. I want you to teach me how to make you feel as good as you just made me feel."

"Okay," he said, "But I have never taught anyone how to do this before."

He lay back on the bed up on his elbows so he could see me and I was between his legs. He took my hand and placed it low on his penis and closed my fingers around it.

"Reach under my penis with your other hand and hold the rest of me in your hand and massage them."

I had never felt anything like this before. I was amazed with myself at what I was doing and how much I was enjoying doing it.

"Now, slowly place my penis in your mouth." I lowered my head and took his penis in my mouth and started to suck on him.

"Not that way," he said. "Pull him out of your mouth a little and use your tongue to circle around his head. Then move your head up and down clenching your lips tight against him. Not to tight, loose enough so you can move your lips up and down easily and run your tongue around him."

I could feel him growing in my mouth as he moved his hips up to me. I was getting so excited I could feel myself getting wet.

Then he said loudly, "Stop, stop."

I stopped and asked, "Did I do something wrong?"

"No, no you are great; I almost came in your mouth. I don't want the first time I make love to you to be that way. I want to be inside you so we can come together. I want you to know how that feels, you don't know how that feels do you."

He was quickly towering over me his penis standing straight out as he lowered himself down to me. He pulled my knees up and slowly entered me. This was the first time a man had ever gently entered me and wanted to make me feel good and feel good I did. He reached under me, took hold of my butt cheeks and lifted me up to him, then he wrapped my legs around him. He slowly pulled himself in and out of me. Each time I could feel him going deeper inside me.

He asked, "Are you okay? Am I hurting you? You are so tiny; I don't want to hurt you. You feel so damn good"

"You are not hurting me, please keep loving me don't stop until we drown each other. I want to feel you come inside me."

His rhythm was getting faster and I could feel that throbbing begin deep inside me. "Don't stop, please don't stop. Hold me tight and come with me."

The throbbing inside me was getting stronger and stronger and I felt his throbbing mix with mine and I was in heaven. I could hear his moaning along with mine as our fluids mixed together. He slowly relaxed on me then started to roll off me, but took me with him as my legs were still around him so he was still inside me. I felt him slide out of me as we rolled over to our sides still facing each other.

"How did I do? Did I make you feel good? Did I learn well? I didn't want it to end; I don't ever want it to stop. Am I rattling on?" I asked him.

"Yes, you are rattling on, you are so amazing and we will make love again, we have all night. You made me feel wonderful, you had me going as soon as he was in your mouth, but you had me going in the bar as soon as you looked at me with those eyes."

Again he said, "You have no idea what you can do to a man, the right man with those eyes. (I didn't know then what he meant, I know now.)

We lay there for a few minutes just holding each other. Then he said, "Shall we shower? I want to lather your whole body and wash every part of you, then rinse that beautiful body of yours then lick you dry."

"I would love to shower with you, and lather every part of you then rinse that beautiful body of yours then lick you dry. I have never been washed by a man before, I can't wait. You are showing me all kinds of things, and then can we do this again?"

He looked down at his lazy penis and said, "As long as he is willing, and I'm sure he will be I will do anything you want."

He stood up by the bed, lifted me off the bed, wrapped my legs around his waist and carried me into the bathroom. He reached into the shower to turn on the water not letting go of me. We stepped into the shower then he unwrapped my legs from around him and stood me on the shower floor. He handed me a bar of soap and he had one and we starting rubbing each other's bodies until we were full of lather. We were laughing at each other as soap bubbles were flying everywhere. He held my face in his hands, kissing my soapy lips. I had died and gone to heaven.

He was lathering between my legs as I was lathering his penis and he began to grow. He lifted me up and wrapped my legs around him again, this time his penis was standing straight out so when he put my legs around him his penis slid inside me. He was so hard, but he was so gentle and with the lather he went deep inside me. He had me leaning against the shower wall not moving, but pushing his penis deeper inside me.

He whispered in my ear, "Am I going in to far, can you come again?"

I didn't have to say anything as I could feel that wonderful throbbing start deep within me and I could feel him coming as he pushed himself deep inside me. I had my arms and legs wrapped tight around him until our throbbing stopped. He stepped under the shower still holding me. After a few minutes, I unwrapped my legs from around him and when my feet hit the shower floor I didn't know if they would hold me up. I leaned against him and put my arms around his waist, he put his arms around me and we stood there under the shower letting the water run over us. (All I could think of was, so this is what sex is supposed to be like, is this what my mother was looking for?)

When the lather was gone and we stepped out of the shower, Bob said as he looked down at his penis, "I think we need towels, I don't think he is up to anything else tonight."

I looked down at him and agreed with him. He got us two big fluffy towels and we dried each other off. His beautiful penis tried to move, but decided not to so I gave him a kiss. When he dried my fur ball she tried to move then decided not to, we were both exhausted.

He took my hand and led me into the bedroom; we lay down in his beautiful bed. Bob pulled the covers up over us, then pulled me into his arms and clinging to each other we fell asleep. With his arms around me nothing could hurt me, for tonight I was safe.

I woke up with the sun coming in the window, when I opened my eyes; Bob was up on his elbow staring at me.

"Good morning sleepy head. I have been watching you sleep. I noticed last night; you don't wear any makeup so you look as good this morning as you did last night. Hair is a little messy, but that was my fault, the shower. How did you sleep? I slept great with you in my arms."

He didn't give me a chance to answer as his mouth was on mine.

I pulled away and said, "No fair you brushed your teeth, I probably have morning breath."

"No," he said. "I haven't brushed my teeth, that would wash away the taste of you, and your breath is wonderful."

He started kissing me again, and all the desire we had felt last night came flooding back over us and we were tangled in each other's arms again.

I could feel his penis against my thigh growing as we kissed, "I need you so," he whispered in my ear.

"Make love to me Bob; make believe this is the first time we have ever made love."

When he was over me looking lovingly into my eyes, I opened my legs and took hold of his butt and pulled him down on me, as he entered me a shiver went from my head to my toes. I wrapped my legs around him and raised my hips up to meet him. With each movement he went deep inside me then I could feel that familiar throbbing inside me and our desire was mixing together.

When our desire had been satisfied again he said, "Can I ask you something?"

"Oh my, you sound so serious. Of course, ask away."

"What has been done to you? He asked. What I saw in those green eyes the other night was sadness and longing. They are so much brighter this morning. What has this world done to you?"

I looked up into his beautiful blue eyes and answered as best I could. "It is a long story, and someday when we know each other better we can talk about it. Just put it this way for now. You are the first person, male or female that has treated me good. Most of my life, for as long as I can remember, I have been abused in every way there is, until now. Now, no matter what happens in my life, my life will be brighter because of you."

He brushed the tears away that were running down the sides of my face into my hair and pulled me into his arms and held me tight and, for probably the first time in my life, I felt safe.(except for the brief time I had with Loren, like Loren I will forever hold this man close to my heart.)

He said, "I will do everything I can do to make you happy. I could never be mean to you or hurt you."

"Now can I ask you something? You are a handsome man. I can't believe you have not been taken. Isn't there anyone in your life?"

The next thing he said put a rock in my stomach. "There was a girl, I was dating on and off before I met you. She was nice and fun to go out with, but I didn't love her. I have never found a woman I thought I wanted to spend the rest of my life with, until now.

I broke the sadness we were sharing and said, "I thought you were going to make me breakfast. I feel so safe in your arms, but I have to be home before he brings my boys home."

"How about bacon and eggs and hash browns?" He asked.

"I am a great cook, I can help." He opened a drawer, pulled out one of his t-shirts and put it over my head. I don't want anything to happen to that body." Then he started laughing.

"What?' I asked.

"You are so little my shirt goes down almost to your knees. I thought I would be able to see that cute little butt while we cooked." He lifted the back of the shirt up and gave me a kiss on each cheek and there went those shivers again.

When I went to leave, he asked, "When can I see you again, soon?"

"I'll come by the bar Friday night after work. I will miss you. You were so sweet and loving to me. You made me feel beautiful."

"It wasn't me that made you feel beautiful, you are already beautiful. Will you be able to stay with me again?" He asked. "You know where I live. Come by anytime you want, if my car is here I am here, surprise me, please surprise me."

I drove away wishing I could stay with him forever. I thought of him every minute. Thinking in my head how could I see him again? Even if Carl was living with another woman, if he knew about Bob, there would be hell to pay.

By Tuesday, I couldn't stand it anymore. I made excuses to Carl's mom to leave for work early. I took Big to school, then crossed the bridge to go to Bob. When I pulled into the parking lot I saw Bob's car. I knocked on his door and in a few seconds he was at the door with a surprised look on his face. He stared for a few seconds then swooped me up in his arms kicking the door closed behind us and was swinging me around in his front room kissing me.

He stopped swinging me around and said, "My god am I glad to see you. I missed you so much."

He was pulling my clothes off as I was pulling his off. He abruptly stopped undressing me and asked, "Is this okay, can I make love to you?'

I said nothing just kept undressing him. He carried me into his bedroom and we fell down onto his bed. We were both so ready for each other and he was so hard, he was immediately between my legs. He pulled my legs up and wrapped them around him as he gently entered me, he felt so damn good. I felt my muscles inside me clench onto his penis. He unwrapped my legs from around him and rolled onto his back, and lifted me up by my waist so he wasn't so deep inside me.

He said, "Set up on your knees and slowly settle down on him. I don't want to hurt you and with you setting on him he will go in further."

I slowly lowered myself down on his penis and was amazed at how good this felt.

"When you feel comfortable with how far he is in set straight up. Go slowly and let your body adjust to him." he said.

When I was setting up straight with my knees beside him, he started slowly pushing my knees further away from his body and his penis was going deeper and deeper inside me. He took my hips and started moving them back and forth.

He kept asking me, "Are you okay, am I hurting you?"

"You are hurting me in such a wonderful way. It hurts and feels good at the same time, and I love it."

He stopped moving my hips and rolled me over so I was under him again. He wrapped my legs around him and was moving his penis in and out of me.

He was going in so deep I could feel myself start throbbing. "Come with me, I want to feel you come with me."

I felt his penis pulsing as he filled me again. We were both moaning so loud it is a wonder the neighbors didn't hear us, maybe they did. I was clinging to him so tight my arms and legs ached. We lay in each other's arms getting our breath.

He raised his head to look into my eyes and said, "Did you know your eyes are blue today, with a little green in there."

"They do that sometimes, but not to often. Must be because of who I am with. I hate to leave, but I have to go to work. I will see you Friday. That seems so far away."

"You know, you can surprise me any time I am here. I miss you every minute you are away."

I met him on Friday and sat as close to him as I could get. We sat in one of the booths along the wall where it was hard to see us. I wanted to feel him so bad, I unzipped his jeans and pulled his penis carefully out. We had been kissing and feeling each other everywhere we could so he was getting hard. I leaned down and put him in my mouth, I heard a loud sigh come out of Bob. I ran my tongue around the head of his penis and could taste his juices.

He whispered, "Oh baby lets go out to the car, you are making me crazy. He put some money on the table and we left.

In the parking lot he opened the back door of his car, I got in and he followed.

I unzipped his jeans again and had my mouth down on his penis, he pulled my head up and said, "I want to make love to you, as he pulled me down in the seat to get my jeans off one leg then he was over me and inside me.

He sat up pulling me with him; he was still inside me pushing his hips up to me and holding me down tight on him. That was all it took, he had his face buried in my neck holding me so tight we were flowing into each other.

He said, "Don't move baby, don't move just feel me come inside you, let me feel you. Oh my God you feel so good. I love you Jewelya, I am falling in love with you."

I was again in heaven and I didn't want it to ever stop. It didn't matter where we made love or how many times we made love, it was always like the first time.

We pulled our clothes on and sat for a few minutes in the back seat of his car not saying anything.

Then he turned and looked at me and said, "I meant what I said. It wasn't the sex talking; I am falling in love with you. All I think of is you and when I can see you again. I have never met anyone like you and I have never told any other woman what I just told you. I want you with me all the time."

"I do love you too; I know that in my heart. All I think of is you and being with you, my heart aches when I am not with you, but I have three boys Bob, remember?" They will always come first in my life, they are my life. I have to be sure of us before I bring them into this. They are dealing with that with their father. I never want their father back in my life again; he is a very violent man. If he knew about you I don't know what he would do, but it would not be anything good."

For the next month or so, we devoured each other every chance we got. Bob was a district manager and had to travel sometimes. When he would return from one of these trips, we would spend a whole day, more if possible making love and showering. He liked me walking around his apartment in his t-shirt and sneak peeks under it and it was easy to get off when he wanted me. He would pick me up in his arms and throw me onto his bed, pull the shirt over my head and stare at me then straddle me and rub lotion all over my body. He would be so hard, but we didn't make love till he was done rubbing my body.

He would tell me, "You have such a beautiful little body I can't get enough of it. You feel as good on the outside as you do one the inside." Then he would ravish my body and we would be in heaven again.

If we didn't have much time, we would meet in a park between his apartment and where I worked. If we went to his apartment, we had absolutely no control, we would have to make love and I would be late for work. That happened more than once so we decided that when we didn't have much time we would meet in the park, it was better than not seeing each other at all.

Then one morning Bob called telling me he had to see me. Something had come up he needed to talk to me about, to meet him in the park.

My heart sank he sounded so upset, what could have happened. Before he hung up he said, "I love you so much, no matter what I love you I will always love you."

Now I was really scared. When I got to the park he was setting on the bench where we usually met, with his head in his hands. I sat down beside him and saw the sadness in his eyes.

"Bob, what is wrong, what has happened?" I put my arms around him.

"I'm going to lose you. I don't know what to do. He was almost in tears.

"Just tell me, we will figure it out." I answered.

"Remember the girl I told you about, the one I dated before I met you? She stopped by the apartment last night to tell me something."

Before he could say anything more I sat up straight on the bench and said, "She is pregnant isn't she?" I could feel the tears welling up in my eyes, and my heart was breaking in two.

Bob sat up and said, "I don't know what to do. I know it is mine she didn't go out with any one else. If I describe her to you, you will probably know who I mean. She has a scar on her face and neck from boiling water when she was little. That bothers some guys, but not me. She was a nice person and fun to go out with."

"Do you love her?" I asked.

"No, I love you; I am in love with you. I know you have been hurt so much in your life and I promised you I wouldn't hurt you, now I am probably hurting you more than anyone has. She isn't a very strong person, and I don't think she can handle this on her own."

"I know Bob. That is one of the things I love about you, you are a very good man. If you did leave her on her own, we would not survive. In time, our guilt would sour our love for hurting someone else. This baby did not ask to be brought into this world. My boys are my life, I would die for them. This is why I didn't want to bring them into our relationship until we knew where it was going. They too have gone through too much in their young lives. Your baby is the same, he or she deserves two parents to give it the love and protection it needs."

"She knows about you. I guess news travels fast at the Campbell soup line. She also knows how I feel about you, but that I will do the right thing. I love you, I will always love you and I will always hope that someday we can be together."

I took his face in my hands, kissed him and said, "I also love you, part of my heart will always love you. After all, you are the man who showed me I was worth loving."

I got up from the bench and walked out of the park to my car, and didn't look back.

Chapter Six

MANNY I

My heart ached every minute for Bob, but my boys were my treasures and I was glad I had not brought them into Bob and my relationship. Every morning my boys would come into my room and crawl into bed with me. We would wrestle around in bed then spend what time we had together before I had to go to work. They would set with me on the couch and I would read to them. Gene would set on one side of me and Big on the other side of me and Wayne in my lap. I saw as little of Carl as possible.

When I went to work, I stayed to myself as much as possible. When J.F.K. was president and our country was being threatened by Cuba and Russia, we were all told to go to the lunch room that our president was making a statement about the seriousness of the situation. I sat down at one of the tables not paying much attention to anyone else. Someone sat down beside me, but I paid no attention to who it was.

"You are not very friendly are you?" a male voice said.

I said without looking around, "As friendly as I need to be." I was not looking for another man in my life. I felt the male beside me get up so I though he was gone. Instead, he was on the other side of the table where he was right in front of me.

He said, "Don't you ever talk to anyone?"

"Yes," I said, "If necessary." Then I saw who he was, he was one of the bosses on one of the floors where I got my samples. I had seen him several times, he would nod at me and I would nod back and keep going. He was a very good-looking man, but Bob was so fresh in my mind he didn't interest me.

"Do you ever go out?" He asked.

"Yes, sometimes, not too often." I answered.

"Some night after work when you have nothing else to do stop across the street at Frankie Payne's bar."

I said nothing, when the president was done we all went back to work.

A few days later I was on his floor getting samples from his line. I worked for quality control and went from floor to floor getting samples of food made on that floor to test in the lab. My lab coat sleeve got caught on a bolt and was pulling my arm into the machine. He was watching me as he usually did when I was on his floor, but this time because he was watching me he saved me from losing my hand in the machine. He stopped the machine and cut the sleeve off my jacket so I could get out of the machine. I was so scared I was sick to my stomach and every part of me was shaking. He was holding me up and yelled at his back up he was taking me to the lunchroom. He sat me down and went for a glass of water.

When he sat down beside me he asked, "Will you talk to me now?"

By now, the reality was setting in and I realized how close I had come to losing my hand, and the tears started to fall and I couldn't stop shaking. He put his arms around me and let me cry.

When the shaking and the tears stopped I said, "Thank you so much, I was scared to death. If you wouldn't have seen me there I would have lost my hand."

"I always know when you are on my floor. Come across the street tonight; let me buy you a drink"

"Maybe," I said. Later that night I decided to take him up on his offer, how could it hurt? Famous last words of a fool. (Manny would turn out to be my biggest nemesis)

He was very surprised to see me walk in the door. When he saw me at the door, he came to me and led me to a table where others from the plant were setting.

He said, "Next time you want to come over let me know, I'd rather you didn't walk over here alone. This is not the safest neighborhood." His name was Manny and he introduced me to every one at the table.

"How did you know my name?" I asked him.

"I have known your name for a long time. I have been trying to get your attention, but you paid no attention to me. It took almost losing your hand to talk to me."

He was very handsome and charismatic and not pushy. He was, I believe, Mexican with almost black hair and very dark brown eyes, mustache, but other wise clean shaven. Not too tall, but still quite a bit taller than me, but then almost everyone is taller than me.

He would make a point of talking to me when I was on his floor and kept asking me to join him at the bar. I got to where I stopped more than I wanted to, but I would tell him so he could walk me over or watch for me. Still looking for someone to love me I guess. I missed Bill so much and I was so lonely. When I went to the bar, Manny would always walk me to my car when we left.

One night while he was walking me to my car he asked. "Can we talk for a while?"

He took the keys and unlocked the door for me as he always did, and I slid over so he could get in.

"What do you want to talk about?" I asked.

"You are so quiet at work, you don't talk to anyone. Are you married?" he asked.

"I guess I don't have much to talk about. Yes I am married, but he doesn't live with us he lives with someone else. I have three boys they are my life."

"So your husband lives with someone else, you have three boys, you work, so you are pretty much on your own, right?"

"Yes, but don't feel sorry for me. When he told me he was leaving me for someone else, once he was gone I danced around the bed. He is a very abusive man and if I never see him again it will be too soon. My boys are what makes my life worth while."

He moved closer to me, took my face in his hands and gently kissed me. Not a long kiss, but a good kiss. He pulled me even closer to him put his arms around me and was kissing me again. He pulled me tight against him so my breasts were against him. It was a very gentle kiss to begin with, but I think the feel of my breasts made his kiss become more ardent and passionate. His lips were slightly open and I could feel his tongue on my lips. It wasn't the worst kiss I had ever had nor was it the best, he wasn't my Bob.

When I went to his floor the next night he asked, "Can I see you tonight, not at the bar just you and me?"

"I guess that would be okay, I can't stay long I have to pick up my boys." I answered.

"Wait for me at the guard's shack in front. I don't want you out there alone. It won't take me long to get my car."

The door where I come out is right in front of the guard's shack, so I pretty much there when I came out.

The guard stuck his head out of the shack and asked, "Are you Jewelya?"

"Yes, I am," I answered. "Why?"

"Manny asked me to have you wait in here, he doesn't want you out there alone." the guard said. I stepped inside and knew why they call it a shack, because it was a shack.

I hadn't been waiting long when I saw Manny coming up the street. I started to step out of the door and the guard said, "No wait for Manny to get you. By the way my name is Less, Manny and me are good friends. He has good taste in women. Nice to meet you Jewelya."

Manny came to the door, took my hand and led me to his car. He was very charming; as he opened the car door he took my hand as I got into his car.

When he got in the car he said, "Come closer."

I moved closer to him and felt safe with him as he put his arm around me. We went to a little bar down the hill.

We had one drink then he asked, "Can we go where I can hold you closer, where we can be alone?"

I answered, "If you mean motel or such, I don't have that much time. Remember I have to pick my boys up before long so you will have to take me to my car pretty soon."

When we got to my car he pulled me close to him just holding me tight. He said, "You feel so good."

He had his face in my hair and asked, "Do you smell this good all over? I want to take all your clothes off and see what smells so good. Will you go out with me on Friday or Saturday?" He asked. "I want to spend more time with you."

He was pushing all my buttons. Not pushing me, being polite making me feel safe. How easy it is to make a woman feel safe, with manipulation and I would find out he is the master.

We went out on Saturday. I don't remember what we did before we ended up at the motel. He did all the right things, he was not the lover Bob was, but he made me feel good.

He started undressing me as I was undressing him. He held me so close my breasts were pressed against his chest. He had no hair on his chest, but he felt good anyway. He held me at arms length to look at all of me. He didn't say anything about what he saw, but I could tell by the way he was breathing he liked what he saw.

I walked up to him and asked him, "Do I look as good as I smell?"

He moved me toward the bed and gently lay me down, then he lay down beside me holding me in his arms so close I could feel his breath on my ear as he whispered, "Yes, you do look as good as you smell, you are beautiful, I want to make love to you."

For the first time he was holding my breasts, then his body was over my body. He lowered himself down between my legs and was slowly sliding inside me, he stopped raised himself up so he could see my face, then continued sliding inside me. He was sliding himself slowly in and out of me as he was staring into my eyes. Then he lay down on me, pulled my knees up and wrapped my legs around him. He took my butt and pulled me up toward him and was going deeper inside me. I could feel him growing and throbbing inside me as I felt myself throbbing as we came together. He relaxed on me, ran his fingers through my hair behind my ears and pulled my face up to his and began kissing me again. I wrapped my arms around his neck and was kissing him back, running my tongue over his lips and just inside his mouth.

I could feel him start to grow inside me again. He rolled me over so I was on top and pulled my knees up and was pushing them out so he went in deeper. He took my waist and pushed me up so I was setting straight up. He held my waist staring at my naked body. He began pushing me back and forth and he was moving up to me. He pulled me down on top of him and rolled me back over with my legs around him and was moving faster and harder inside me. I clenched my muscles around his penis. We were both breathing so hard and moaning as we were coming again, it was awesome.

"You feel so good, just let me hold you, don't move yet." We lay there for a while, him still inside me just enjoying the feel of each other. We finally rolled apart laying on our sides facing each other.

"When ever I saw you on my floor, I always wondered what it would be like to hold you and make love to you. I knew loving you would be good, I just didn't know how good."

We got up and showered, washing each other and I was remembering not too long ago I had been doing this with Bob.

I said to myself, "Do not compare, you no longer have Bob."

We got back into bed and as I didn't have to get the boys until tomorrow I curled up in his arms and went to sleep. It felt so good sleeping in a loving man's arms again. If Manny could have stayed this way I would have been with him forever.

He woke me in the early hours kissing my back as I was still curled up in his arms. I rolled over to face him and he pulled me close. He took hold of my butt and pulled me closer, I could feel his penis rigid against me and I wanted him inside me. He rolled me over on my back, pushed himself slowly inside me then wrapped my legs around him again.

I whispered in his ear, "Push yourself hard inside me, let me feel you come deep inside me, and then I will come with you."

He was pushing against me hard as he was pulling me up to him. I could feel him filling me with his fluids as mine were mixing with his. We were both moaning again with such pleasure.

After that we would steel our times together as best we could as I was limited for time as I had to pick up the boys. On some weekends we could spend at a motel in each others arms. Sometimes our motel would be in the backseat of his car or mine. We would get so heated up we would fog up the windows. It is amazing what you can do in the backseat of a car when that is all you have, even a little car. Manny was limited in the type of sex we had, but I still enjoyed what we had. Was this one of the times I was mistaking lust for love, because I always wanted to be with him because he made me feel good and safe. I was never afraid when I was with him. He would protect me from everything and everyone else, but who would protect me from him.

They were having cutbacks at work and I was one of the newer ones, so I was laid off. About the same time I realized I was pregnant. After I was laid off I didn't see Manny as often and I was beginning to think something was wrong. And when I got one of these feelings I was usually

right. I called Lester the guard to tell him to have Manny call me I needed
to talk to him. I didn't hear from him. After a few times calling the guard
I called his floor. I told him I needed to talk to him. He told me to come
over on his lunch hour. I was not prepared for what was going to happen
even though I knew something was terribly wrong. When he came out he
didn't get in the car just stood outside my window.

"What do you need to talk to me about?" he asked.

"What is going on Manny? Why haven't you returned my calls? I am
pregnant, what is going on with you?"

He looked stunned, but calmer than I was. "I was going to call you.
I have been talking with my ex-wife in Wyoming and we have decided to
try our marriage again. I am leaving tomorrow."

"Tomorrow, what about me, I didn't want to go out with you in the first
place, but you wouldn't leave me alone until I did. I should have known
better. All you men are alike. You get what you want then off you go. Now
I'm having your child. If you were still involved with an ex-wife why didn't
you leave me the hell alone? You had no intentions of saying anything to
me; you were just going to leave weren't you? You are a bastard just like
the rest of the men in my life." I was yelling by now.

"I will help you, but Lorie is expecting me to leave tomorrow." He
took my hand and put some bills in it.

I screamed at him, "Fuck you, fuck Lorie and fuck your money."

I didn't even look to see what he had put in my hand; I just threw it
out the window at him and left.

I said to myself, "Self, how the hell did you do this to yourself again."
All men are the same, do I have stupid written on my forehead? YES
STUPID!!!"

All I could do was go home and do what I usually do, take care of
my boys, take care of me and now a new baby. This was my baby, no one
else's and I will take care of it. I guess the only person that can keep me
safe is me.

Chapter Seven

CARL II

N ow that I was laid off I could draw unemployment and spend more time with my boys. When the weather was good the boys and I spent a lot of time outside. We were outside one afternoon when a car pulled into the driveway. It was Carl; my heart took a nose dive. I did everything not to come in contact with him, and here he was. He came over on the grass and sat beside me.

I ask him, "What do you want?"

"I want to come home." he said.

I was hearing what I always knew I would hear and prayed I never would. I jumped up, gathering up the boys and headed for the house.

"No, you stay with your girlfriend; I don't want you to come back." I yelled at him.

"I don't want to be with her anymore, I want to come home."

I was screaming at him, "No, No!"

Before I could get into the house he was on me immediately, grabbing me by the hair shouting at me, "You don't have a choice, this is my home also. My things are in the car, get used to it."

Oh, my god what do I do now. He is going to kill me when he finds out about this baby.

I got the boys in the car and said, "I have to go to the store, be right back."

To Scarlet's I went. "What the hell am I going to do?" She already knew about the baby and whose it was. I never kept anything from her, except the nasty four.

She said, "You are probably going to die because Carl is going to kill you. You know he thinks he can do anything he wants, but you can't. I was afraid he would be back he was probably as bad to her as he was to you, it just took her a little time to throw him out. She knew he would run back to you. You will have to do something soon as it is going to be very obvious before long."

When I got home Carl was setting on the porch waiting for us. He said he was very sorry about yelling at me and pulling my hair. When I put the boys to bed I stayed in their bedroom. Carl came in and asked why I was in with the boys.

I said, "Wayne is cutting teeth and not feeling very well so I'm going to sleep with him tonight."

I was surprised he didn't argue with me, he just turned and went into the other bedroom. I was so afraid that nothing had changed about Carl that he would be as mean as ever. I knew there was no waiting for a good time, there would never be a good time to tell him about this baby. I was hoping he would change his mind and leave again, but no such luck.

As the next day was Sunday Carl didn't have to work, but I figured he would be going somewhere. After breakfast, the boys and I went outside and Carl followed.

He sat down on the grass beside me and said, "I really do love you, I don't want to be with anyone else"

I asked him, "If you love me so much why are you so mean to me? You hated your father for what he did to your mother and you do the same to me. You hated me when my mother forced you to marry me, that wasn't my fault, but I have been paying for it for years. I didn't want to marry you either. I don't even know how she found out about you, I refused to tell her anything about you or your buddies."

"I know, and I am really going to work on being better, I promise." He said.

I didn't believe him for a moment, but I figured this was as good a time as any so I jumped right in and said, "Then I have something I have to tell you. You will either accept it or kill me. I am pregnant."

Silence, he said nothing. The silence was deafening.

Finally he asked, "Who and where is he?"

I couldn't believe how calm he was. I thought, any minute I am going to die.

I answered, "Someone I was dating at work, but he is no longer there he moved to Wyoming, going back to his ex-wife."

Story of my life. (All of these men, who left me, came back. How the hell did I get that damn lucky?)

"Does he know about the baby?" Carl asked.

I lied and said, "No, he was already gone when I found out I was pregnant. I have no idea where he is in Wyoming and I don't give a damn. I will take care of my baby."

I thought I would go into shock when he said, "No, we will take care of our baby."

I don't care what he is saying now, I don't trust him, men like him don't change. And he may be saying how much he loves me, but I don't love him now, I have never loved him and I will never love him in the future.

I gathered the boys up to go into the house, it was getting late and it was time for their supper. After supper I got the boys ready for bed and again stayed in their room.

This time Carl came to the door and said, "Please sleep with me tonight."

I was afraid to say no, so as always I did as I was told. I learned my lesson with Carl a long time ago. I now had a baby inside me I had to worry about. He beat on me when I was carrying my boys, so with this being another man's baby, if I didn't do what I am told he will do the same. I took as much time as I could, then walked into our bedroom where Carl was lying in bed. I lay down beside him, my heart was pounding. He rolled toward me and put his arm around me.

He felt me tense and said, "Jewelya, I promise you I am not going to hurt you."

He lifted the top of my pajamas up and pulled the bottoms down past my belly.

He started rubbing my bare belly and said, "You are already getting a pouch. How far along are you?"

"About five months. My due date is around my birthday. As I am always early it will probably be sometime in July."

He started rubbing past my belly, I asked, "Do we have to?"

"I told you I won't hurt you." When I was pregnant with the boys he didn't care if he hurt them. If he wanted sex he just took it and was not gentle about it, so I was concerned for my baby. I can only remember a couple of times Carl had gentle sex with me.

He sat me up in bed and unbuttoned my pajama top, and dropped it on the floor. He lay me down and was working my pajama bottoms and panties down my legs and dropped them to the floor.

He said, "It has been a long time since I have seen you like this. I almost forgot what a great body you have."

He took my breasts in his hands and said, "They are bigger now because of the baby, right?"

"Yes, I said, "Please don't hurt me or my baby, I know it isn't yours, but it is mine so please be careful."

He started kissing me and rubbing my body down over my belly to between my legs I was just lying there wanting it to be over. He then did what he usually didn't do; he pulled my legs apart and had his head between my thighs. He lifted my knees up and was kissing my pussy. His tongue was darting inside me. I couldn't believe he was doing this.

He pulled himself up and over me, I pulled my legs together and he pulled them back. "I told you I won't hurt you."

I relaxed my legs so he could enter me and surprisingly he was being careful. I was actually enjoying this; he was really being gentle with me.

He was moving very carefully in and out of me, he was breathing harder and harder, and then I could feel him come inside me. He pulled himself up and reached on the table where he had placed a wet washcloth and began cleaning me, which also felt good. He lifted me up and lay down on his back.

He said, "I want you to straddle my face then lower yourself down on my face, I will hold you."

I spread my legs apart over him; he took my hips in his hands and pulled me down to his face.

He said, "I am going to do this until I feel you come, so relax and enjoy it. I will."

He started to lick me all around my pussy then I felt his tongue go inside me. He held on to my hips and was moving me back and forth as his tongue was darting in and out of me. I was holding on to the headboard to keep my balance. I couldn't believe how good this felt and I could feel that familiar throbbing deep inside me then a rush of fluid flowed out of me and he kept sucking on me until there was nothing left to suck out. He let go of my hips and took my waist and laid me gently on the bed.

He said, "See I told you I wouldn't hurt you or the baby. I can be gentle and still make us both happy." I didn't say anything.

He asked, "The father of this baby, did you love him?"

"No." I said, "Just lonely and he was very good to me until he left. I saw no reason to try to find him, I couldn't have meant as much to him as he said or he would still be here. Now, can we no longer speak of him again? What has happened to you, you have never been like this. Did your girlfriend teach you how to make love to a woman?"

I saw that look on his face and thought did I push him too far? "No, I just missed you, and we won't talk about her again either."

I didn't love Carl now, I have never loved him and I will never love him, but would tolerate him this way for my boys, but this was never going to happen, men like him don't change.

Carl was really trying to be different for a while. But, the drinking started getting worse, and when he came home drunk I stayed away from him. My baby was moving around and I could feel it growing daily. The boys would rub my belly and ask me hard questions that I answered as best as I could.

Tommy would touch my belly and say, "Baby mommy?"

I would answer him, "Yes honey, baby."

They loved coming into my bedroom in the morning crawling in bed with me to feel my belly, and they would start laughing when they felt the baby moving.

My daughter was born July, 1962. Carl was with me when my baby was born. He chose not to be there when his sons were born. I think somewhere in Carl he really wanted to be different, he just didn't know how. Carl was there to hold my daughter after she was born; he was in awe of her. I wondered where Manny was and if he ever thought about me or his baby.

I wasn't home from the hospital long when things started getting worse and worse, and my fear for my children and me grew daily.

He would come home from work drunk and want to pick Callie up out of her bed and swing her around. He would get furious when I would try to take her from him. He started disappearing for days at a time, which didn't bother me. I was hoping he was going back to his girlfriend, but she probably didn't want him back.

He came home one day really drunk and I didn't have dinner ready for him and he was furious. I tried to calm him down telling him I would fix him something that I didn't know when he would be home.

He threw me across the room and proceeded to take all the food out of the refrigerator and throw it all over the kitchen. He emptied the catsup, mustard and anything in bowls on the floor. He broke a dozen eggs into the silverware drawer. Any jars were smashed on the floor. The boys were crying scared to death and Callie was crying in her crib. I grabbed them to get them into their room to get them away from this monster.

He opened the door and yelled at me, "This will be cleaned up before you come to bed."

I got the boys and Callie settled down and went to the kitchen and just stood there and stared at his mess. I would be up all night. The floor was so slick I had a hard time standing up. I was trying to sweep it into a pile so I could pick most of it up with the dust pan, then scrub the floor. It was all I could do to keep from throwing up cleaning the eggs out of the silverware drawer.

Tears were streaming down my cheeks as I was thinking how the hell do I get out of this. I finished in the wee hours of the morning and I went into the boy's room and climbed into bed with my children.

I was just about asleep when the door came open and he was yelling at me "What the hell do you think you are doing, you belong in bed with me."

He grabbed me by the hair and was dragging me out of bed.

The boys and Callie woke up and started crying again. I said, "Okay, okay, let me get the kids settled down and I will come in."

He yelled back, "Don't take too long or I will be back."

I got Callie back in her bed and the boys settled down by telling them that when it was morning and daddy was gone they could come in and get in bed with mommy.

They kissed me and said, "Okay mommy." I loved my babies so much, what am I going to do?

I went into the bedroom where "he" was and lay down beside him. I tried to be very quiet, hoping he was passed out, no such luck.

He rolled over facing me and said, "It's about time. He started pulling on my pajamas.

"Please Carl, don't hurt me." I begged.

"You are my wife; you will do what I want you to do." was his response.

"What happened, you said you were going to be different?"

He yelled at me, "You are my wife and I will fuck you any time, you are not pregnant now and I want you to know it is me fucking you and not your boyfriend."

He was over my head pushing his penis into my mouth; I wanted to bite him but what would my boys do without me as he would kill me. I was trying to do what he wanted finally he took himself out of my mouth and pulled my knees up and out and lunged himself inside me. He was so brutal pounding at me so hard I wanted to scream in pain, but I put my hand over my mouth so my children wouldn't hear me. When it was over I went into the bathroom to clean up and because it hadn't been that long since Callie was born, I was bleeding again.

He came home one night, pulled the covers off me and said, "I want you to start sleeping naked so when I get home I don't have to mess with pajamas."

"No," I told him, "Please don't do this to me anymore, you are going to hurt me."

He said, "Hurt you, I want you to know this isn't your boyfriend fucking you," then he dragged me out of bed by my hair and started hitting me on both sides of my head. He threw me back on the bed so hard my head hit the headboard of the bed. I could feel blood running down my head where I had hit the headboard. He ripped my pajamas off me and had a huge erection; he must get a hard on when he beats me.

He was as brutal as he ripped into me, when he was done he threw me on the floor and said, "From now on when I get home and you are in bed, you best not have any clothes on."

I went into the bathroom to clean up and looked into the mirror. I had knots on my head. There was blood running down my cheek from the cut on my head I had bruises all over my face and one eye was almost swelled shut.

I sat down on the toilet and said, "Oh God what am I going to do, one day he is going to kill me."

I went into the kitchen and got a butcher knife and was standing over him wanting to run it through his heart, but I heard my babies in the other room and thought, "How would I ever tell them I had killed their father."

All I could think of was Bob and how much I missed him. From then on whenever Carl would do this to me I would close my eyes and put a picture of Bob in my mind.

The last time I received a beating from Carl was on a Saturday in late October sometime around Halloween. When he came home from work he was in a lousy mood, as usual. I tried to stay out of his way, but that usually didn't work. I would hope for him to pass out, sometimes he did sometimes he didn't. This time he didn't. The boys, Callie and me were setting on the couch watching T.V.

He grabbed me by the hair and dragged me off the couch screaming at me, "You been fucking your boyfriend?'

"I told you he went to Wyoming and he isn't my boyfriend. Why don't you go back to your girlfriend and beat on her or is that why she threw you out." I yelled.

This was the wrong thing to say as he was livid and started beating me. My oldest son, Big, jumped on his back. Carl threw him off and I yelled for Big to call Aunt Scarlet. Big was six so when I taught him our phone number, I also taught him Scarlet's.

He called Scarlet telling her, "My daddy is killing my mommy."

Before long Scarlet was coming through the door butcher knife in hand.

Carl was standing over me with a small wooden baseball bat, screaming at me. "I will kill you if you ever let another man touch you."

Scarlet yelled at Carl, "Move away from her or I will cut off your balls and stick them down your throat."

I was scrambling to my feet waiting for that baseball bat to hit me in the head, but it didn't. Scarlet was a crazy redhead, still is, I knew as well as Carl did that she would do it.

She said, "Grab some clothes for you and the kids, we are getting the hell out of here and you are never coming back."

As we were heading out the door I could hear Carl yelling at me, "Jewelya, you better not leave you know I will come after you."

I yelled back, "I am never coming back, never."

Scarlet and I both knew we were in big trouble. Carl would arrive every night at different times. Scarlet slept with her knife under her pillow. Carl would arrive; Scarlet would go after him with her knife. Each time we would call the police, but he would be gone each time before they got there. They told Scarlet if she used the knife to make sure Carl was at least on the porch before we called them.

After about a week, Carl disappeared. One evening the phone rang, it was his sister, screaming at me I had had her brother committed. I hung the phone up. It rang again, this time it was Carl's step-dad. He asked if I would talk to him.

I said, "Only if you are not going to yell at me."

Carl had committed himself to St. Bernard's mental hospital and told his family I had committed him. I told Carl's step-dad I had nothing to do with Carl being in the mental hospital, but that is where he needed to be as he was crazy.

Two days after their phone call, one of the psychiatrists that were treating Carl called wanting me to sign papers to commit Carl to St. Bernard's. I refused telling them what he had done and if I committed him, when he got out he would kill me.

"He may kill you if you don't. He is a very sick man and is a danger to himself and anyone else that gets in his way, especially you. If you don't want to commit him, stay away from him."

I knew it was only a matter of time before it started all over again.

The next day Scarlet's oldest son had to have surgery so that left me home alone. I heard a truck out front and when I looked out the door I saw Carl coming up the front walk. I gathered the kids up and headed for the bathroom. I put the kids in the tub shushing them putting my finger to my lips and closed the shower curtain. My two older boys were in school and I had spoken to the school officials about Carl and to never let him pick them up from school.

I could hear Carl stomping through the house searching for me. He went through the kitchen down the basement steps all the time shouting my name. When he came up the steps he stopped in the kitchen. I could tell he was staring at the bathroom door.

He was yelling at me, "Open the door or I will."

He started banging on the door. This was an old house so the dead bold on the door went into the doorframe it's self. The door swung out, not in so it made it almost impossible to pull it open.

This didn't stop Carl from giving it his best shot. He was cursing me and pulling on the door so hard I thought the knob would break off in his hand. Then I heard him stomping through the house and out the front door. The silence was deafening. I looked at the kids still in the tub amazed at how quite they had been.

The phone started ringing and ringing and ringing, then would stop then start again. The phone hung outside the bathroom door so

I quickly opened the door grabbed the phone and locked the door again.

Carl said. "Don't you think its time you and the kids came home?"

"I'm never coming home as long as you are there." I told him.

He asked, "I have the bug spray, a razor blade and my grandfather's shotgun here. Which one do you think I should use?"

"It's your life, use whichever one you want. You have been threatening to kill yourself for more than five years now?"

A wave of fear ran through me as he said, "Maybe I'll come back there with the shotgun. I bet this shotgun will open that damn door, then I can take all of you with me."

"If you want to die, that is up to you, but the kids and I have a lot of living to do."

I heard a gun shot and I heard Carl say, "Jewelya" then silence.

I was screaming his name into the phone. Back then the caller had to hang up or the phone did not disconnect.

Again, I instructed the kids in the tub to stay in the tub and be very quiet. I ran next door to use the phone. I first called 911 babbling into the phone incoherently. The voice on the phone was very calm while firmly telling me to calm down and explain what had happened. I slowed down my babbling and explained what had happened. In my mind I pictured Carl setting in the basement laughing at me. He had been threatening to kill himself for five or six years now and he hadn't yet and I didn't think he had this time. I told myself he is okay, he won't do this, and all the while I was hoping he really had this time. In the passed five or six years his way of getting me to return to him was by threatening to drink fly spray, cut his wrists with a razor blade, eat rat poison and now using the shot gun. Why should I think this time was any different? I could still hear him call my name, then the silence. To this day I still do not believe he planned on killing himself, he was trying to scare me and the gun went off, it was just his time to go.

After calling the police, I called Scarlet at the hospital. Her son was back from surgery and in his room so she was heading home. I got the kids out of the bathroom and set them on the couch and waited for what seemed like hours. I was pacing from the front door to the back door. Mine and Scarlet's babies watched me pace back and forth. I hoped none of them would remember any of this. I had been through so much with this man there was nothing he could do that would surprise me. About an hour after I had talked to Scarlet, a policeman opened the front door and walked in with Scarlet close behind. She looked like she had seen a ghost.

Scarlet had been at the hospital at the farthest northeast end of town. Carl and my house was at the farthest northwest end of town. Instead of Scarlet coming to her home, in her infinite wisdom, ha, ha she decided to go to my house instead, and she arrived there before the police. My house was a split-level home, if you chose to go through the garage, you could either go down two steps into the basement or up a few steps into the house. Scarlet chose to go through the garage, as the garage door was standing open. To the right were the two steps going into the basement.

Scarlet saw Carl lying on his side facing the wall. She walked over to him and nudged him with her foot. He rolled onto his back exposing a gapping hole in his stomach. She turned and ran screaming from the garage and ran into a very large policeman. To this day, we have no idea how Scarlet was able to get there before the police. We have a good idea why it took them so long.

Scarlet ran to me, put her arms around me and said, "He really did it this time. He is dead. I saw him, he shot himself, it is over it is really over."

I sat down on the couch where I had set all the kids. One of the police officers squatted down beside me, patted me on the shoulder and said, "I understand how you feel."

"No. I don't think you do." I said as tears rolled down my cheeks.

"Yes I do," He said "We have been here many times and we always wondered which one of you it would be. We always thought it would be you."

I looked into his eyes and saw that he really did know that my tears were of relief not grief.

November, 1962 my nightmare ended. Tonight, Scarlet and I would go to bed without the knife. I wondered how will I ever be able to tell my children about today, but for now, I knew I would never again have to ask myself, "Is this the day I'm going to die?"

The day of Carl's funeral was a very cold November day. Cold in many ways as Carl's family blamed me for his death, but I will deal with that later. Scarlet sat with me in the family room. As we watched everyone go by his casket, the last person was a woman in a black dress with a black hat and veil. She stopped by the casket, stared down at Carl then turned and walked back out not looking in either direction.

Scarlet asked, "Do you think that is her?"

I just shrugged and walked up to his casket alone; Scarlet said she had seen all of him she wanted to see. As I stood looking at my husband lying in his casket, I heard someone behind me. I turned around to see my parents standing there.

My mother said, "You have been through more in your twenty-three years than I have been in my forty-three years." My father just stood there as he usually did, in my mother's shadow.

I just looked at them for a few seconds then said, "And I do believe, I have the two of you to thank for that."

Scarlet was standing in the background at the end of the first pew. I walked passed my parents, took Scarlet's hand and the two of us walked up the aisle to the door. We opened the door to be greeted by the sun shining brightly.

Scarlet looked at me with a smile and said, "Jewelya, isn't this a beautiful day?"

I smiled back at her and said, "Yes, Scarlet this is a very beautiful day. Someday I will die, but it won't be today."

After going to the cemetery Scarlet and I had to listen to Carl's family tell me how I was going to live the rest of my life, taking care of Carl's boys.

When we left there she said, "I know you don't drink, but today you do. Carl is gone and you don't have to worry about someone killing you anymore. I am taking you to a quiet little bar where we can decide what you should drink."

We went to a little bar in downtown Omaha. We sat at the bar and Scarlet introduced me to the bartender (I don't remember his name, surprise). She told him to give her a Miller Lite and a shot of Jack Daniels.

She asked the bartender, "What do you think she should start out drinking? She has never drank so she should start out with something that won't kill her the first time around."

He said, "How about a Salty Dog, vodka and grapefruit juice in a salt rimmed glass."

"How about no salt." I said.

"Give her a shot of something too." Scarlet added.

"How about a shot of peppermint snapps?" The bartender asked, "That is a fairly mild drink."

We had had a couple of rounds when the bartender told us the two men at the table behind us wanted to buy us a drink.

I wasn't to sure about that, but Scarlet said, "Sure why not."

We turned and thanked them for the drink. We drank that one then they wanted to buy us another, we said okay. They came up to the bar, one beside Scarlet one beside me.

The one setting beside Scarlet said, "You girls seem to be having a good time all by yourselves."

Scarlet said, "Yes we are, we always have a good time all by ourselves, but today we are celebrating."

The one setting beside me asked, "What are you girls celebrating?"

Without looking up I answered, "We buried my husband this morning."

They looked at the bartender, the bartender nodded at them they looked at each other, and the one setting by me said, "Well you girls have a great day." then they turned and almost ran out of the bar."

The bartender said, "I think you two scared the hell out of those two."

Chapter Eight

Being Free

"Scarlet," I said. "We are only twenty-three years old and look how much we have been through. What do you think the next twenty-three or so years will bring us?"

She put her arm around me and said, "I have no idea what is in store for us, but I bet we do it together."

We raised our glasses and clinked them together toasting each other because we knew that what ever the next twenty-three or so years brought us, there would always be us.

Both of us were afraid to go to the house to get anything out. When we had to go to get clothes for me or the kids we would plan what we needed and where it was before we went into the house, then we would run like hell, get the things we needed and run like hell to get out. We knew Carl was dead, but there was still the fear Carl had put in us so deep we couldn't help still being afraid of him. The real estate company that sold me the house bought it back and they had everything packed up and moved to storage for me. As the interstate was going through there, they moved the house to thirty-fifth and avenue "G" so they probably got paid pretty well for the property. We didn't care what they did with it as long as we didn't have to go into it again. (I wonder if the people that live in that house now know what happened in that basement?)

While I was writing about this man who viciously wandered through my life, "The Burning Bed" with Farah Faucet came on T.V. This is about a woman who sustained so much abuse from this man she felt she had no choice but to do what she did for her and her children.

I never get tired of watching the movie, Deloris Claiborne, about another woman who got her abusive husband drunk during an eclipse. Then made him angry enough to come after her. She led him up to the hill where she had found a very deep well that had been boarded over. She jumped over the opening as she knew it was there, he wasn't so lucky. The boards were very old and very rotten. She stood at the edge of the well as he hung onto the rotten beam across the opening as he begged her to help him, then he fell in never to be seen again. Every one thought he had just left the island they lived on. This man had beaten Deloris for many years and know one would listen to her. Then she found out he was sexually abusing their daughter, it is one thing to beat on me, but hurt my child and I will kill you.

It has been forty-eight years since Carl died, and all of those terrible memories come rushing back when I see or hear of a woman being abused. There is so much fear that you become sick to your stomach. It doesn't matter who the women are, their stories are mirrors of each other. These men are the same and we women are the same, we are sisters in fear. All those years and it seems like it was yesterday.

But, we have only the future to look forward to. Looking back into the past is not the problem; dwelling in the past is and only dims the future, as long as we learn from the past our futures will be brighter. Tomorrow is your future yesterday.

We do not know what tomorrow will bring, but we are ready for it, "Aren't we Scarlet. Scarlet, hey Scarlet, we are ready for it, aren't we?"

Come walk with me into my next twenty or so years, see what I will do next and meet the men who continue to wander through my life.

BLONDE ROSE II

And The Men Who Continue To Wander Through My Life
My Second Twenty or So Years
Written By:
Jewelya

This Second Blonde Rose is Dedicated to:
All the Passionate Women Out There
Who Have Found Their Own Way To Survive

CHAPTERS

Chapter One

Learning How To Live

It took me some time to realize I didn't have to hide anymore or be afraid of every sound around me or a knock on the door. My boys and my daughter were everything in my life. Now, I didn't have to worry about dying and leaving my children. I kept them close to me, having them sleep with me so I could reach out and touch them. Will I always feel this afraid?

The one thing I have learned over the years is: There is always something to be afraid of, the difference is: learning how to deal with it.

(I loved my mother so much; I would have died for her as I would my children. All I wanted her to do was love me back, but I finally realized that was not going to happen. I also felt that if I loved my children unconditionally they would love me back the same way, and the more children I had the more love I would be getting back, well that ain't necessarily so. I would find out in the future that, just because you give love does not mean you are going to get it back.)

Scarlet, me and our total of seven children moved into a larger house. Her house had one bedroom and she used the dining room as a bedroom, you don't put seven children into a one bedroom house.

My boys seemed to be adjusting pretty well without their father, but they never saw that much of him anyway and most of the time he was drunk and violent. I had them in counseling for quite some time to make sure they were adjusting, but how do you know what it will be when they are grown.

Carl's family did everything to make my life miserable. Phone calls at all times of the day and night. One evening I was making supper, fried chicken, the kids loved fried chicken. A car horn started honking in front of the house.

Scarlet asked, "Are you expecting anyone? I'm not."

I looked out the window and there was Carl's dad and sister. I told Scarlet, "Watch the chicken."

I went out to the car; Carl's sister opened the door and told me to sit down. They were telling me they knew I had had Carl killed and they were going to prove it and take my kids away from me. Not Callie, as she wasn't Carl's and they didn't want her.

I started to get out of the car and Carl's sister grabbed my arm and said, "I know you say my brother beat on you, we don't believe you. It takes a lot to make a person hit another."

I looked at her hand on my arm and said, "Right now if you do not take your hands off me it will not take much more for me beat the hell out of you just like your brother did to me." She let me go and I ran into the house.

Scarlet had the chicken out of the pan and the kids were at the table, and the chicken was raw in the middle.

I looked at her with my look and she said, "Hey, you should know better than to leave the cooking to me." (And Scarlet still does not cook, her husband does. His comment, "I ain't lettin' her in my kitchen.)

We both started laughing then the kids were laughing and I turned the stove back on and finished cooking the chicken.

I finally had to get a lawyer to send Carl's family a letter telling them if they didn't leave me alone he would take them to court for harassment. They finally left me alone.

Scarlet worked and I took care of the kids and the house. I was a good cook and she was a terrible cook, so she wasn't allowed to cook. I started drawing Social Security and Veterans as Carl had been in the Navy. We did pretty good, we never had any money left over, but the bills were paid and we always had food and we had each other. We slept good, without a knife under the pillow.

Scarlet was an excellent pool player. One of the T.V. stations had pool a tournament on Monday night and Scarlet was on almost every Monday. Men would get so pissed at her as she beat them all. As long as you were winning, you were playing pool on Monday night.

She was getting ready to go one Monday night and she asked," Why not go with me. We can get a sitter you will have fun."

Have you heard of Murphy's Law? Well, Scarlet and I lived by it. I went with her and stood in the background behind a door.

She was right; I did have a good time but, the next day oh my God. Our phone started ringing and boy was I getting my ass chewed. I guess the door I was standing behind was right in line with the camera and I was on television that Monday night almost as much as Scarlet. Carl's family was livid, screaming at me that I had no business doing anything except raising Carl's boys, and if I didn't take better care of them they would take them away from me, and again, not Callie.

My birth-person showed up at our door and said I should show more respect for the dead, and to be more discreet. I guess she meant discreet, as she had always been.

"I will show as much respect for the dead as he showed me while he was alive. I am tired of being afraid of everything around me. The best thing that ever happened to me and my children was him killing himself." I told her.

"Don't you talk like that. You should never be glad when someone dies the way he did." She was almost yelling at me.

"I'm not glad he died the way he did, but the only way I was going to get away from him was for one of us to die. There was no one that could or would stop him and there was no one that cared what he did to me. So one of us dying was the only option. Someday I will have to explain that to my children, I hope they understand. Until then, I will do as I please. When my daughter grows up if a man raises a hand to her I will kill him. I will never allow a man to do to my child what you allowed Carl to do to me." I was now yelling at my birth person.

She said nothing, just looked at me in surprise and I turned and walked out of the room, and she left without saying anything else.

Chapter Two

Bob II

A few days before Christmas the phone rang, it was Bob. I will never forget the sound of his voice.

It was like music in my ears to hear him say, "Jewelya, this is Bob."

"How did you know how to reach me?" I asked.

He remembered me talking about Scarlet and called information.

"I heard what happened. Are you alright? How are you doing?"

"I'm fine; this was something a long time in the making. It was bound to happen sooner or later. We all thought it would be me, that he would kill me. He tried, but I survived, he didn't."

"Now, I think I have an idea of some of what has happened to you. Can I see you; I want to see you so much?"

"You are still married are you not?" I asked.

"Yes, but just this one time. I need to see you, hold you; I miss you and love you so much, please."

I wanted to see him again and have him hold me one more time. "I have missed you also and think of you every day. Where and when? I asked him.

"Tomorrow, I will call you early morning to tell you where."

I didn't sleep most of the night thinking of the next day.

He called early the next morning and asked, "Do you know where the motel is at on fortieth and Douglas?"

"Yes I do."

"Room 104, I am already here, can you come right away? We can spend the day together."

"I am ready; I was waiting for you to call." Scarlet was home for the day so I could spend it with Bob and not worry about the kids.

She said, "Go, have fun, it has been a long time since you have had any fun. Don't worry about the kids. Good-bye, get out of here."

I knocked on room 104 and the door swung open and there was the most beautiful man in the world. He wrapped his arms around me and was kissing me as he was pulling me into the room. I was crying, tears running down my cheeks.

He said in my ear "I have missed you so, you are still beautiful, your blonde hair and green eyes. What the hell has been happening to you?"

"I had a baby girl last July. What did your wife have?"

"A girl also." He answered.

"I wish I could have had your baby, not her. Then I wouldn't have been there I would be with you and you would be mine, I would be your wife not her."

By now I was sobbing. "At least this time when you leave me I don't have to go back to him. Every time he would take me I would put a picture of you in my mind and that made it easier. I want you to make love to me all day. I don't want to talk about anything else, just make love to me. Take my clothes off and kiss me all over don't miss a spot, it has to last me along time"

He was wiping away my tears and kissing me at the same time. His kisses were so sweet and gentle; it was like it was yesterday.

He started undressing me, and when he pulled my sweatshirt over my head he saw I didn't have a bra on. When he pulled my jeans down, I didn't have panties on either.

"You had a baby in July? You now have four children and your body is the same as it was, beautiful."

I was pulling his shirt off, unbuttoning his jeans and pulling them down along with his shorts. I was on my knees with my arms around him pulling his penis into my mouth as far as I could without him chocking me, he tasted so good.

He lifted me off my knees and lay me on the bed. Just the touch of my mouth on his penis had made him stand straight out. He was over me pulling my knees up and out as he lowered himself down onto me. I could feel him gently enter me then slowly push himself deep into me.

"I want to be as far inside you as I can get, tell me if he hurts you." He was so deep inside me our pubic hair was mixing together and I could feel the rest of him lying against me.

"I don't care if it hurts because it is you making me hurt, and I love you so much."

He would pull himself out then push himself all the way inside me again and hold him there then pull himself out. I could hear myself moaning along with him.

It felt so good I could feel him start to pulse inside me and that familiar throbbing was starting at my belly button.

When he was deep inside me I said, "Stop and just hold yourself deep inside me as far as you can so you can feel me come and I can feel you come." I had my legs wrapped around him and he was holding my butt pulling me tight against him, we could feel the friction from our pubic hair crushed together, then we were both moaning with such pleasure. We were both coming so hard it was like an explosion deep inside me. We lay there clinging to each other not wanting it to stop. Bob lay there on top of me still holding my butt and with my legs wrapped around him.

"I don't want him to come out, you feel so damn good. I wish you would have had been the one to have my baby. Then I wouldn't be in a motel with you, we would be in our home and we could make love anytime we wanted to."

"Bob, my love, we can't think of what could have been, only what we have today. Let's shower, remember how our showers used to go? We still have a few hours, let's not waste them."

He raised himself up and I felt him slid out of me and I let out such a sigh he started laughing.

I asked, "What are you laughing at."

"You are the most exciting woman I have ever met. No one will ever make me feel the way you do. Sex with you is always a new experience. I love you, no matter what, I will always love you. You are the love of my life and I will carry you with me always."

He leaned down and took my breasts in his mouth one at a time and those shivers went up and down my body as they always did when I was with him.

"We should shower, I don't think we are done with each other yet."

He stood by the bed and picked me up. "You are still so tiny. How tall are you? Four foot something?"

"I am five foot I'll have you know. I guess chasing kids around all day keeps me thin."

"You are not thin, you are perfect." He carried me into the bathroom as he always did, but this time when he left me I would probably never see him again, but I'm not going to think of that right now.

We lathered each other washing ever part of our bodies. This shower was too small to do very much in so he carried me out to the bed both of us still wet. We were hanging on to each other not wanting to let go.

"Set down on the edge of the bed." I said.

He did as I had asked; I got on my knees and wedged myself between his legs pushing them apart. I took him into my mouth slowly moving my lips up and down rolling my tongue around his penis, as he had taught me. I was holding his penis in my mouth with one hand and with the other I reached under his penis and took the rest of him in my hand massaging them, rolling them around in my hand, these jewels are amazing. I felt him growing in my mouth, he was moaning deep in his throat. I was making him feel so good he had lain back in the bed. He took hold of my hair and pulled my mouth from his penis.

"What are you doing?" I asked.

"I want you up here with me so I can taste you too."

He pulled me onto the bed with him placing me over him then turned me around so my fur ball was over his face with my knees beside his head. He pulled me down and pushed my knees out so his face was buried in my fur ball. I took his penis back in my mouth and reached under him and took his jewels in my hand, excited by the feel of them. His mouth had engulfed my pussy and was licking my man in the boat as his fingers were deep inside me. He took his fingers out of my pussy and started running his tongue all over her then his tongue was darting in and out.

He raised me up so he could say, "If we keep this up I won't be able to stop him, do you want me to do that? I want you to come all over my face. I want to taste everything on you."

"No, I don't want you to stop him; I want to taste everything on you too." My lips went back around his penis and his face was again buried in my pussy. He pushed my legs out away from his head so I was as close to his face as he could get me without smothering him. He tasted so good; I wanted him to fill my mouth. He had his arms wrapped around my butt holding me close. I could feel him start to throb and I pushed my head down on him so I could feel and taste all of him. I felt the throbbing start deep in my belly and came rolling down to my pussy. I could feel my wetness run out into his mouth I could hear him moaning as he was sucking everything out of me. His fluid was filling my mouth and it was wonderful, I kept swallowing to enjoy all of him. When my throbbing stopped he was still clinging to me and when his penis started to get limp I was licking everything I could from him. (This was nothing like when those pigs were forcing me to do this) When you love someone as much as I loved Bob, it is awesome.)

I collapsed on Bob I was so spent. I rolled off him and turned around to face him. We were both panting, trying to get our breath. He leaned over and kissed me and I could taste me on his lips. I remembered the girl and her fingers in my mouth, this was so much better, this was Bob and me.

"Now I know how I taste, I am on your lips, but you taste so much better, that was wonderful." I said. "Oh God how I wish we had a lifetime."

"That is the first time you have done that isn't it." He said.

"Yes it is and you taught me. How did I do?"

"You were perfect; your mouth on him is like nothing I have ever had. When I was coming and you kept him in your mouth every part of my body was feeling you."

"Well," I asked. "How many women have you done that with?"

"Like that, you are the only one; you will always be the only one. When I felt you coming I wanted all of you in my mouth so I could taste the sweetness of you. I didn't want it to stop. You taste better than beer and I really like the taste of beer. I want you to always remember me, no one will ever do that to you as good as I did."

I took his face in my hands and was kissing his eyes, his nose, his cheeks, his lips I held his head between my breasts and said, "They will miss you, what will they do without you, no one will ever make them feel as good as you have, never!"

We lay there clinging to each other. We didn't have to shower we had licked each other clean.

The day was going so fast, and we had no way of stopping it. We lay on the bed watching the sun trying to go down.

He rose up and lowered his lips down on mine. "I want to kiss you and kiss you and kiss you. I may never be able to kiss you again. I want to make love to you one more time, I want to be inside you one more time, I want to have my fingers inside you one more time, and I want to suck on your breasts one more time."

He was kissing me everywhere, and his hands were exploring my body as if they had never been there before and my body was again on fire. I took hold of his penis massaging him up and down, and I could feel him growing in my hand, what a feeling it was to know I could do this to a man. He was over me and I spread my legs and welcomed him inside me by lifting my hips up to him.

I whispered in his ear, "This time do it hard, I want to remember how big he is, how hard he can get. I want to remember how you feel inside me forever. This will be the last time I will have you."

He took hold of my butt and pulled me up toward him to get further inside me, then he pushed hard on me as he pulled me up to him. My arms were wrapped tightly around him. He wrapped my legs around him and pulled me closer to him. He was gently moving in and out of me. I felt him go so deep inside me, then both of us started to come, it was so intense we were both moaning so loud they could probably hear us in the next room. I had never felt him come this hard nor had I ever come this hard. It just kept coming and coming, I never wanted it to stop.

I was crying and telling him, "Please don't stop, stay inside me and love me I never want it to stop." If it only worked that way.

We both collapsed onto the bed panting. I rolled over into his arms and started crying and sobbing. "It is going to be so hard leaving you, but we had today and no one can take our memories away from us."

(As you can see I still have mine and I'm sure he still has his also. I have found that through out my life, men don't tend to get over me. Candice Bergman said on an episode of Boston Legal, "I am phenomenal in bed and men don't tend to get over me.")

I knew he had to leave soon, he had a wife, and I no longer had a husband, thank God. I got up, went into the bathroom to clean myself off somewhat. I took a warm washcloth back to wash him off, he smelled like me, a woman would notice, and then I put him in my mouth one more time and gave him one more kiss before he left me. He shuttered as I ran my tongue around his penis.

He grabbed me and pulled me close to him through his tears he said, "What am I going to do without you. I will never be able to turn your green eyes blue again. I will miss you so much."

We finished dressing, put our coats on and walked out to the parking lot. He walked me to my car, put his arms around me one more time and said, "I am not going to say goodbye, I will never stop hoping someday we will be together."

His kiss on my lips was wet with both our tears. We clung to each other not wanting to let go.

I got into my car started it and said, "I love you Bob, as I said before, part of my heart will always be yours. Try to be happy, I will do the same. Until we meet again and someday we may, if not on this earth, another."

I drove away like the last time and didn't look back. I cried all the way home.

Bob was a good man. I knew he was a good husband and excellent father. I had never seen him with his daughter, but I didn't have to I knew him. I just wish it was me he was with, not just in love with. I had his love, she had him.

I drove out of the parking lot where I had just left Bob standing. I was not going to look back to see if he was still standing there, I'm sure he was. This was as hard on him as it was me. The tears were streaming down my cheeks as I was heading home where of course, Scarlet was waiting.

When I walked in the door, she put her arms around me and let me cry on her shoulder. Then she said, "Go take a shower and brush your teeth, you smell like sex. We are going out. I'm going to show you a few things. Put on a sexy dress."

"How are we going out, we don't have any money? I think I have thirty-five cents on me."

Her answer, "That is thirty-five cents more than I have. That is one of the things I am going to show you. A woman, if she knows what she is doing, does not need money. Most women do not know that we, women not men, rule this world, we just let them think they do, use what you have woman."

Scarlet was and still is a red-head, with the fire of a red-head, and we were both built the same, great. She was about four inches taller than me, but we could wear each others clothes, and she was already in a sexy dress.

I took my shower, brushed my teeth, put on my sexy black dress, the one I had worn on my first date with Bob.

When I came out, she just said, "That will work." And out the door, we went.

That night I learned more about what Bob had said, "You have no idea what you do to a man just by looking at him with those green eyes."

Every bar Scarlet and I walked into, we turned heads. Scarlet was the redhead with a great body and I was the blonde, learning I had a great body, as Bob called it, a gorgeous body. We danced, we drank, and we had a great time and came home with $2.35. We had men buy drinks then come and want to set with us?

Scarlet would say, "You can set, but your drink only buys you conversation nothing more."

Most of them asked for our phone number, but none got it I was not ready for a man yet. I think men just liked setting with good-looking women. When we left, they wanted us to come back, soon.

I had a great time, but missed Bob so much. I said, "Self don't go there, he is gone."

Chapter Three

Another Man Returns
I Shouldn't Have Let This One Return
MANNY II

The days went by and the nights went by and all I could think of was Bob. I would go out occasionally with Scarlet, but she had met Perry one night when she was playing pool so I didn't want to be the third wheel. I was asked out all the time when I went with her, but I refused all of them. She didn't like leaving me alone as she knew how much I missed Bob.

One afternoon I was rocking my daughter, Callie, when the phone rang and a familiar male voice said, "Jewelya, what are you doing."

I said," I am rocking your daughter," It was Manny, I felt a shiver go down my back, there was that old fear of losing control of my life, again.

He asked, "Can I come see you and my daughter? I know you are really angry with me, but I would really like to see you."

(Why do these men who leave me keep coming back only to hurt me again? Because I let them!)

"She is your daughter, I'm sure you would like to see her." I didn't even ask him if he knew where we were, he just said he would be right over. When I heard the knock on the door, my knees were shaking as I walked across the room. I still had Callie in my arms when I opened the door.

There he stood, as handsome as ever. He took Callie from me and said, "She is beautiful."

"Of course, she looks just like me." I said.

We both laughed as Callie looked just like her father. Her eyes were so brown they were almost black and she had dark, dark brown curly hair and beautiful brown skin. He is Mexican and I am blonde, hard to hide that.

He reached over to touch my cheek and I pulled back. "I know you are angry, but I not only wanted to see Callie I wanted to see you. I missed you so much and made a big mistake by going back to Laura. It wasn't any better the second time than it was the first time. Please let me make it up to you, let me take you out show you how much I missed you and love you."

"Oh, now you love me. You left me carrying your baby. You were going to protect me from this vicious man I was with. Instead you left me to deal with him alone. By the way, he loved your daughter as his, we were lucky he didn't kill us all."

He walked over to me with Callie still in his arms, put his arm around me, kissed me on the cheek, and said, "Let me try, I love you and I think you still love me. You are not with anyone, not because you can't, but because you don't want to."

Boy did I fall for that one, "again."

That night, Manny was in my bed. We went out for a while with Scarlet and Perry. Scarlet gave me daggers eyes all night long, she knew what he was up to, but no one could tell me anything, its that stupid sign on my forehead. Manny kept holding my hand, rubbing my back, patting my butt and saying, "I want to get closer to you; I want to hold you and make love to you again."

By the time we got back to the house all I could think of was being in his arms, I'm not sure if it was so much his arms as it was being held by a man that would not physically hurt me and I had always felt safe with Manny.

We were undressing each other as we went into the bedroom. He was kissing me with such passionate kisses, as he lay me down on the bed I could feel him growing against me.

He was rubbing my body everywhere, then he was over me looking into my eyes saying, "I love you, I want you, do you want me as bad as I want you?"

I didn't get a chance to answer as his lips came down on mine running his tongue just inside my mouth and I met him with my tongue as he was lowering himself down on me. As he entered me, I wrapped my legs around him to get closer to him and felt him going deeper inside me. He was slowly moving himself in and out of me while he was still kissing me. He stopped kissing me and pulled me closer to him as I could feel him coming so I clenched my muscles around his penis as I was also coming. Manny had his head buried in my neck and his arms were holding me close against him. We both relaxed our hold on each other, but he was still holding me tight in his arms.

"I never forgot how you felt; I love you so much I will never leave you again. I want you to marry me, will you marry me?"

All I could think was, oh shit! I wiggled my way out of his arms and jumped out of bed and ran into the bathroom. I cleaned myself up and just set there on the toilet thinking, "Oh my God, Now what do I do?"

When I returned to the bedroom, Manny was setting up in bed. "Well?" he asked.

I answered him, "I don't want to get married right now, I think it is too soon. We can talk about it later." I crawled back into bed with him and said, "Hold me Manny, for tonight just hold me."

I needed to feel safe, and in his arms I felt safe. Even with Carl gone I was still so afraid, will I always be afraid?

My birth-person stopped by the next morning. Of course, she had to stop by when a man was there. I introduced them and before I knew it, Manny was telling her he wanted to marry me. She didn't know this man from Adam and to her it was a good idea. She knew what Carl was and still thought it was a good idea to give me to him. I guess this was another way to give me to someone else. Here we are again, back to trying to say no to my birth-person, it wouldn't happen this time either. Especially when Manny told her he was Callie's father, she decided Callie should have her father in her life, like Big had to have his father in his life, crap, so I had no choice but to marry Manny. I was just an innocent bystander, again.

I said, "I would like to wait at least a year, before we get married. It would just look better. Carl has only been gone six months; don't you think that is a little soon?"

Manny said, "I may not be around in a year."

My birth person said, "You have a man that is willing to marry you. Look at you, as she pointed at a mirror on the wall, and you have four children. You should jump at the chance to marry this man."

I just stood there in the middle of my front room with these two people deciding my life for me and I let them. I know what I should have done, I just didn't do it. So we, or they, decided we would marry July, 1963.

Early one morning my phone rang and my heart almost stopped, it was Bob. I will never forget his voice. I stood up by the bed as he said, "Jewelya?"

"Yes this is Jewelya, Bob?"

"I can't believe I am talking to you." He said. "Don't say anything, I have to tell you something and ask you something. My wife died two months ago from a brain aneurysm. I have been offered a job in Miami, FL, and I want you and the kids to go with my daughter and me. I didn't want this to happen like you didn't want your husband to die to get away from him, but it has happened and I love you so much, I have never stopped loving you, please go with us."

I was in shock, why is this happening now?

I quietly said, "Bob, I have never stopped loving you either and never will, but I can't uproot my kids. Why do things like this keep happening to us? A year ago I would have followed you to the ends of the earth."

I could hear his voice crack as he asked. "Are you with your daughter's father? Is he there with you?"

"Yes," I answered.

"I am so sorry about how much I hurt you. When I watched you leave the motel, I knew you would not be alone long. You were not meant to be alone. Just remember I will never love again as I loved you, be happy Jewelya."

"I will try, I have to do what I think is best for my children, you know that. I will never love the way I loved you and you be happy too. Remember, as I will, those wonderful times we had together, you showed me that I was worth loving."

Before he hung up he said, "Those memories will always be with me. I will never forget what we had. I am not going to say goodbye as I will always hope to someday see you again."

And he was gone again, this time in my heart I knew I would never see my love again.

As Alfred Lord Tennyson wrote, "'Tis better to have loved and lost than to never have loved at all."

I slowly sat down on the edge of the bed. Manny asked, "Are you okay?"

What could I say, I just told the man I love goodbye. I did what Jewelya does best, pretend everything is okay. Again, my life had been ruled by what someone else wanted.

Manny and I were married, July 07, 1963. I should never have married him, his cheating started before we were married. I just didn't want to admit it. For the third time I had lost Bob. I think at that time, I felt the only thing I had left, was to have the children I had always wanted, and Manny could give them to me.

I had always wanted three things in life, to be an English teacher to second and third graders, when their little brains are like sponges and absorb everything they are taught, a writer and a mother. It didn't look like I was going to be a teacher, but a mother I could do. Scarlet always said the reason I stayed with Manny was because he gave me my children, I guess maybe she was right.

Our first son was born May, 1964, our second son was born July, 1966 and our last child, a daughter was born January, 1968. This is when I really realized what I was to Manny, the same as I was to my mother, his slave. My last daughter and I both almost died as she was so early, my doctor had to wake him up to get his permission to save my daughter's and my life, then he left the hospital.

Later that day when I woke up my doctor was in the chair beside my bed, not my husband and my doctor asked me, "Do you plan on having anymore kids? If you do you are on your own, I don't think I can do anymore of these, you know we almost lost both of you in there."

As he was walking out the door he turned and said, "By the way, when are you going to get rid of that worthless husband of yours? He has given you all the kids you need and he gives you nothing else."

I made the newspaper again. I loved to bowl and the only time I could bowl was in the mornings as Manny didn't allow me out after dark or to do anything unless the kids were with me. The bowling alley had a day care there so I could take the kids with me. I bowled on Thursday morning and it was 3 a.m. Friday when I went to the hospital to have Deniece.

In the Friday evening Newspaper my name was in there for having high game and high series for bowling Thursday morning, and having a baby on Friday morning. How's that for multi-tasking? The Newspaper loves me, I am newsworthy.

The next few years I devoted to my children while Manny did as he pleased. My children were my life. What ever my kids were involved in so was I. I was the den mother, brownie leader, and what ever else they needed me to be. I knew my boys' paper route as well as they did. In the winter on Sunday mornings I would take the boys to get their newspaper bundles, then I would make hot chocolate for us to drink while we rolled the newspapers and placed them into the plastic sleeves. We would pile the newspapers into the station wagon and be off to deliver them.

There was baseball, softball, football, and wrestling. My house was the house where all the kids in the neighborhood wanted to be.

We built snowmen and snow forts for snowball fights. One year we decide to save snowballs for summer for a snowball fight. Manny found them in the freezer and asked why they were there. I told him we wanted them for summer.

He said, "How stupid are you, they will be ice balls by summer."

They were, but he didn't have to call me stupid, and we still had fun with them.

We had food fights in the kitchen, which I started. Then we would all pitch in to clean it up laughing so hard we were crying. Each child had their own birthday party. Christmas at our house was magic. At Halloween, we made most of the costumes and I went trick or treating with them until they were old enough they didn't want me to go, but I would set on the porch waiting for them to come home to see what they got, I got most of the Snickers. I taught them how to play penny-anti-poker and on Friday nights the kitchen was full of kids having a great time.

One Christmas my boys got ten speed bikes. As soon as it was warm enough, they were out riding them.

I was outside watching them one afternoon when one of them said, "Mom, why don't you ride one of our bikes, its fun you will love it."

I have never been well balanced and have been called clumsy by the best of them, mother, Carl, Manny, so I tried to decline, but my boys would have none of it.

"We will teach you how." they promised.

Well they tried to teach me, but I failed to learn very well and instead of pulling the back brake I pulled the front brake and went flying over the handle bars. The boys came running over to me to be sure I wasn't hurt. When they found I was okay we were all setting on someone's front yard laughing so hard. But, I never tried that again, my bike with the regular brakes on it was fine.

I told my boys, "They don't call your mom grace for nothing."

When Manny left for work in the afternoon, it was never clear when he would come home, that would be when ever he wanted. He would have to step around boys as they would be all over the front room. We would pop popcorn, make cool-aid and watch movies till the wee hours and the boys would fall asleep on the floor. Manny would be pissed they were all there, but I just ignored him. Some of the boys that came to my house for refuge told me years later if it hadn't been for them being able to come to our home, their lives would not have turned out as well as they had.

Until one day, everything came undone. I had borrowed money from the bank to remodel my kitchen. As I had my own income, I was able to do it without him. He told me not to, but I ignored him. When he came home, I told him they were starting on my kitchen in the morning. He was furious that I had done what he had told me not to. He wanted the money for a motorcycle, and when I refused to give him the money, he doubled up his fist and hit me as hard as he could between my eyes and I went down. I guess he didn't hit me as hard as he could as he had been a golden gloves boxer and if he would have hit me as hard as he could he probably would had killed me. My sister Callie, who my daughter was named after, would come to stay with me from time to time and she was there that day. She came running into the kitchen and jumped on his back with her arms around his head and legs around his waist, trying to beat on his head with her fists.

When they both saw I was bleeding, Callie let go of him and came running to me. Manny got some ice out of the freezer and was trying to help me.

I screamed at him, "Get the hell away from me. I told you I would deal with your girlfriends, but don't ever hit me, remember?"

I had told him before; I would take almost anything from him except him hitting me. I spent six years nine months and eleven days being beat on and once they start they don't stop. The next morning I filed for divorce, he didn't think I would go through with it so he ignored the notices.

When the final papers came in, I gave him a copy and said, "Now it is my turn to dance." Manny's mom was always telling him, "You may be dancing now, but someday she will be dancing and you will not like it." so he knew what I meant.

Manny's mom and I were very close and she hated the things he did. She told him he was like his papa, but he ignored her. His dad was a womanizer also, one night Manny's dad was with one of his girlfriend's and he tried to outrun a train because he was drunk, guess who won. His girlfriend died in the wreck and he was in a coma for nine months, Manny's mom took care of him, but said his punta (whore) got what she deserved.

Manny didn't come back to the house, I don't know when he came after his things. I was alone again, except, of course, for Scarlet and my children.

I started going with Scarlet when she shot pool. The bar she shot pool for needed a substitute so when someone couldn't make it they had a sub for her. As I always went with Scarlet, they always had a sub when needed. Scarlet had been working with me teaching me how to shoot and I was becoming very good. It wasn't long before I was a regular member of the team and I loved shooting pool, still do.

The bar Scarlet took me to was to become our home away from home. Scarlet had known the woman who owned the bar for a long time. Her name was Nicky, she had taken it over when her dad retired. I have been to many bars since then, but none compare to Alderman's. In this place I would, in the future, meet many men and women that I would call friend and some of the men I would call lovers, after all my life was about collecting men.

Chapter Four

Another Bob

One afternoon my sister came by and wanted to know if I wanted to meet someone.

"Who," I asked her.

"A friend of Ron's. He saw you once when he and Ron dropped me off, you were pregnant with Deniece and he thought you were beautiful. He wants to go out with you. Ron and I will go too so if you don't like him we can bring you home. He looks like Paul McCartney. I'm sure you will like him, how about this Friday?"

"Make it Saturday; Manny is coming after the kids Friday night.

When Manny came to pick up the kids he would try to have a conversation with me, but I would ignore him. I don't think I trusted myself around him; he had this way of pulling you into his web. I think that is called manipulation.

Saturday evening I heard a car in the driveway, I didn't look out just I waited for the knock on the door. I opened it to a man who really did look like Paul McCartney.

He said, "My name is Bob, your's is Jewelya right?

I just stared for a minute I couldn't speak, Bob, another Bob.

I wanted to ask, "Can I call you Paul?" Don't compare Jewelya; you no longer have that Bob he is in Florida probably happily married, because you sent him away.

I found my tongue and said, "Yes I am."

He bent down to look into my face, as he was quite a bit taller than I was. "You are still pretty, even if you are not pregnant."

"I understand you like pregnant women." I said.

"No, not all of them, just you. When I saw you standing in the doorway, you were beautiful and I wanted to see you again, I didn't think that would ever happen, but here we are."

He took my hand and led me to the car. Callie and Ron were in the car waiting. This was the beginning of quite a love affair.

Bob and I were good together, must be the name. The first night we made love, we were with Callie and Ron and ended up in a motel together all four of us, same room, and two queen size beds. I thought to myself, how is this going to work, same as if we were alone I guess, just quieter. My sister and I told each other everything, this time we wouldn't have to because we were together.

Bob pulled everything off the top of the bed except the sheet to cover with. He pulled the sheet back and lay me down under it, and then he crawled in beside me.

He pulled the sheet up over our heads and said, "I don't mind being in the same room with them, but I don't want Ron to see you."

He wrapped his arms around me and pulled me close and started kissing me. He was a great kisser, mouth slightly open with his tongue searching for mine.

"Can I undress you?" He asked.

I whispered in his ear, "I would love for you to undress me."

He pulled my shirt over my head and put it beside me, then he reached behind me to unhook my bra. My jeans were next I could hear his breathing get heaver. All that was left were my panties; he was rubbing my body everywhere.

He asked, "If I wrap the sheet around you can we go in the bathroom?"

"Why?" I asked. He still had his clothes on so he stood up by the bed pulled the sheet up around me so no one could see me and carried me into the bathroom.

Bob turned the light on then started unwinding me from inside the sheet. Finally, I was standing in front of him in just my panties.

"You have a perfect body. How do you do it with seven kids? How tall are you five feet? He put his hands around my waist lifted me off the floor and asked me, "Do you even weight one hundred pounds?"

"Yes, I am five foot and weigh about one hundred and ten pounds. I guess chasing seven kids around keeps me fit."

He sat down on the toilet then pulled me close and buried his face between my breasts. He sat me down on his lap with my legs around him, holding me tight.

He took hold of my hair and pulled my face back so I was looking into his eyes. "You have beautiful green eyes, eyes that go right through a man. (I was told that by another Bob. Do not compare Jewelya)

"Are we going to stay in here all night?" I asked.

"I just had to see you in the light." He said. He got up, wrapped the sheet around me again, then picked me up and carried me back out to our bed. Back under the sheets, I unbuttoned his shirt and lay it beside me with mine. I scooted under the sheet to his pants, unbuckled his belt, unbuttoned and unzipped his jeans then pulled the jeans and his briefs down to his knees, then he scooted himself out of them the rest of the way. We were both under the sheets, he found my breasts and started caressing them, then they were in his mouth. I reached down and took hold of his penis to find he was already hard.

I asked him, "Are you glad to see me?"

"You have no idea how long I have wanted to see you." His mouth was again on mine we were so close I realized he had hair on his chest. I pressed my breasts against him as close as I could. He was sliding further under the covers pulling my panties down as he went. He stopped when he got to my fur-ball spreading my legs apart so he could get between my legs. His lips were softly kissing my pussy I could feel her getting wet I was squirming around so I was under him and his penis was above my head. I pulled him down so I could put my lips around him, it had been so long since I had had this kind of sex, and shivers were going up and down my body. I could hear him moaning quietly. I wanted to scream with passion, but we were not alone.

He stopped me and said, "Turn around I want to make love to you. I want to be inside you. I have been waiting for this for so long." His penis was good size, so he had to enter me slowly; as my pussy got wetter he slid into me I heard a sound coming from me.

Then my brain over road my pussy and I said, "You can't come inside me, I don't want to get pregnant. I'm not on the pill yet."

I don't have any rubbers, and I want to feel you come. I will hold it as long as I can so you can have your's then I will pull him out and into the sheet." He pulled me so close against him my breasts were buried in his hairy chest. He wrapped my legs around him and took hold of my butt to pull me closer to him.

I was trying so hard to be quiet, but that was so hard for me to do. "You don't have to move to much just stay all the way inside me and hold me tight."

It didn't take long, I could feel that throbbing inside me, and I surrounded his penis with my fluids. He pulled himself out and I wrapped my hands around his penis and felt him start to throb. He pulled the sheet around my hand and his penis while he was throbbing into the sheet.

All of a sudden, Ron yelled, "Keep it down over there you two the neighbors will hear you."

We started laughing, all four of us. We were so involved in what we were doing we didn't realize we were being so loud.

He pulled the bottom sheet off the corners of the mattress, wrapped it around me, and carried me into the shower. In the shower, he was rubbing soap on me and I him.

He said, "The next time we will be alone. I don't want to come in the sheets; I want to come in you."

"I can figure pretty close when I can get pregnant, but I have been planning on getting some birth control, but had no reason to before now. We were standing under the water letting it run over our bodies.

He reached for me and I went into his arms, he felt so damn good. "I want you so bad again, but I can wait till we can do it right."

He called the following week to see if I could go with him on Friday, and could I stay the night with him. Yes, yes, yes. I was so excited; it had been so long since I had had someone make love to me like this. It had been almost seven years since my Bob and it was as if it was yesterday. I could lie in bed at night, close my eyes and feel his touch and I had learned a long time ago how good I could make myself feel.

Bob picked me up Friday after Manny picked up the kids. I always tried not to have a conversation with Manny. He was always trying to talk about something. I would talk to him about the kids, but that was all.

Bob asked me if I liked the Spaghetti Works. Who doesn't, I asked him. We sat in a back booth so we could be alone. He pulled me close, put his arm around my waist and slowly moved his hand up to hold my breast. Bob had them bring us a bottle of wine, very good wine.

When we had finished the bottle of wine, he asked, "Are you hungry? Do you want something to eat?"

I said, "Only you." He was up and out of the booth taking my hand. He put some money on the table and we left. He had already reserved a room for us and had the key. We were undressing each other as we went in the door, clothes fell where they may. When we were naked, he lifted me up in his arms, he had his arms wrapped around my waist and I wrapped my legs around him.

"Will it be okay tonight? Can I make love to you without stopping?"

He sat on the bed with me still wrapped around him, I could feel him grow. I just nodded and he unwrapped my legs and lifted me up enough so his penis was standing up between my legs. He slowly let me down and I slid down over him. I tried to settle down further, but he had grown so I wasn't able to set completely down.

He said, "Just relax and let him go in on his own, you will adjust to him." I sat there and I felt myself slowly go down further on him. When I was completely down on him I wrapped my legs around his waist and my arms around his neck. He was holding me so tight and he was so far inside me I could feel that familiar throbbing start deep inside me. I could feel his penis start pulsing, he was filling me with his fluid, and we were both moaning. I could feel our wetness run out of me onto him, it felt so good. I let my arms relax from around his neck and he relaxed his grip around my waist.

He took hold of my hair and pulled my head back so he could look into my eyes. "You are amazing, you felt so good, how could a man ever let you go?"

Bob stood up and again carried me into the bathroom and into the shower. "When I lift you off me goo will go all over us. In the shower, he lifted me off him and goo ran out of me and down my legs.

He said, "See what I mean"

He got the soap and washcloth and started washing me. I just stood there enjoying the feel of him washing me everywhere. When he was done, I started washing him, and his penis started growing again.

"Look what you do to me all you have to do is touch me. In the restaurant when you looked at me with those green eyes all I wanted to do was grab you and hold you. I was afraid you didn't want to go so soon."

We didn't even dry ourselves off we ran back into the bedroom and was in each other's arms.

I straddled him and sat on his stomach and said, "Just relax; I am going to make love to you."

I started with his lips kissing him; he had both his hands on my breasts holding them as if they were precious stones. My tongue went down his chest to his nipples and ran my tongue around each of them; I could feel them get rigid as I sucked on them. Then my tongue went down to his belly button then down to his penis and it was waiting for me. I took him into my mouth and heard him moaning. I had my lips loosely around him so I could move up and down and run my tongue all around his penis. I lifted his penis, found his jewels, and had them in my mouth one at a time. I went back to his penis still holding his jewels in my hand.

He said, "You will make me come do you want to do that?"

"Yes," I said.

"Then turn around so I can taste you." He said. Keeping him in my mouth and hands, I turned around so my fur-ball was in his face. He took my hips and pulled me down to his lips. His tongue was running all around my man in the boat then his tongue was going deep inside me as he was pulling my pussy tight against his face. I could feel him growing as big as he was before. He was getting so big I had to pull my head up to keep from choking. He started coming I closed my lips around him so I could taste all of him. I could feel my pussy throbbing as his tongue was deep inside me. When our throbbing stopped, I turned around and curled up in his arms. We were both breathing so hard we were like panting dogs.

He wrapped his arms around me and pulled me so close, then lifted me up on top of him and put his legs around me and was kissing my face, my eyes my hair and said, "I have never been made love to quite like that before. What do I taste like?"

I said, "Salty-sour Mayonnaise. What do I taste like?"

He said, "Sweet, sweet pussy." We fell asleep in each other's arms and again, I felt safe.

Bob had a thing of wanting to have sex everywhere, I have found that most men are this way. He called one night he had worked late and wanted to see me. The kids were home so I couldn't leave, but there was an alley behind my house. He said to watch for him and run out he wanted to hold me and don't wear any undies. I put on a long shirt and took off my undies. When he pulled up, I ran out to the alley and got in his truck. He moved to the middle of the seat then lifted my shirt above my breasts. He was sucking on my breasts as I unzipped his pants and took hold of his penis and found he was already growing. He took hold of my waist and lifted me on to his lap. I was on my knees straddling him; he slowly lowered me down on him. I wrapped my arms around his neck and settled down on him. He slid down in the seat so my pussy could adjust to him and I was all the way down. I was moving back and forth on him as he was moving his hips up and down. We were both moaning and he buried his face in my neck holding me tight against him.

I said, "Stop moving just feel me throbbing against you hold me down tight on him so I can feel him throb inside me. Do you feel me; can you feel me coming on you?"

We were both coming so hard, he was holding me down on his penis, and it was the greatest.

When he could talk, he said, "I was afraid I was going to hurt you."

"When you get that far inside me it does hurt, but such a good hurt. Any woman worth her salt enjoys a little pain. The end result is worth it, don't you think?"

He was kissing me with such soft lips, then looked into my eyes and said. "Every time we make love I don't think it can get any better, then it does. I just think of you and he gets hard, that can be embarrassing, but I can't stop thinking about you."

A few days later my sister called me and asked, "What are you doing to Bob. Ron said he has never seen him like this. He thinks Bob is falling hard for you. How do you feel about him?"

"I love being with him, sex is great, but he isn't divorced from his wife yet, so I am being careful. I am the one who always gets hurt."

We would go to the motel and look for Ron's car, when we found it we would honk until Ron or Callie let us know where they were. They did the same thing, but we didn't get as wild with our sex when we were with them, but we were not bashful anymore either.

One night we decided we wanted to be alone and knew they would be looking for us. So Bob gave me the key to the room and dropped me at the door then parked on the other side of the lot. It was one of the nights we had as long as we wanted so we wanted to be alone. We undressed each other and sat like Indians in the middle of the bed looking at each other's nakedness. I loved his body and he loved mine. He was holding my breasts in his hands then moved closer and put them in his mouth one at a time.

When he released my breasts, his hand went down to my fur-ball. "Your hair is soft on both ends and blonde on both ends. All that woman in such a tiny body."

He pulled me closer and pulled my legs over the top of his. His fingers found my pussy behind all my hair and when he touched me, shivers went up and down my body. He was moving his fingers around inside me, I pulled his fingers out of me, then put them in my mouth, and licked them, he made a strange sound and I put his fingers back inside me. I pulled his fingers out of me and replaced them with my fingers. I put them as deep inside of me as I could, with my other hand I wrapped my fingers around his penis. I could feel how wet I was getting from what he had been doing with his fingers. He was staring at what I was doing with my fingers inside me. I then pulled my fingers out of me and put them in his mouth.

He took hold of my hand, licking each finger, and said, "You have such a sweet tasting pussy."

While he had my fingers in his mouth, he moved his hand back down between my thighs and my body was on fire.

He pulled me close, lay me down and asked. "Can I make you come this way?"

"Yes, I want you to feel me come on your fingers. I lifted my hips up and he had his fingers as deep inside me as he could as I was holding his hand against my pussy moving his hand up and down. I could feel me start throbbing from my belly button down; he was holding his hand close to my pussy as his fingers were deep inside me.

He was saying, "Oh baby, I can feel you coming on my fingers, your pussy is throbbing so hard."

I could feel my wetness flowing out onto his fingers and hand. I pulled my knees together to hold that feeling inside me as long as I could. When the throbbing stopped I relaxed my knees, but he left his fingers inside me.

"That felt so good." I looked at him and said, "Can I do that to you? Use my hand to make you come? I have never done that before, but you can show me can't you?"

"If you really want me to show you, I would love you to do that." he said.

He took my hand and placed it around his penis. "Hold him, but not to tight and move your hand up and down. Start slowly, when he starts getting bigger do it faster, I'll tell you when. With your other hand hold my jewels and roll them around."

I took hold of him and started moving my hand up and down, he felt so good in my hand.

I had those shivers go up and down my body. I was watching him grow in my hand. I was getting so excited.

He was saying, "Start going faster. I could feel him pulsating in my hand and a stream of fluid was slowly oozing out of his penis.

Bob dropped back on the bed saying, "Faster, don't stop. His fluid was streaming into the air and came down on his stomach and my leg. I hung on to his penis until he was limp in my hand. Bob was spread eagle on the bed not moving.

I asked, "Are you okay?"

He just said, "Am I okay, I am better than okay."

He pulled me down on him rolling our bodies around in his come, it was awesome. He picked me up and carried me into the bathroom and into the shower. That night we spent nine hours making love and showering. We always got a room with two beds, so when we showered we didn't even dry off, just went from bed to bed. I had found another lover. How long would he stay?

When he would call me and one of the kids would answer, he would tell them he was Charlie Brown. (This was the first of a very few men I gave my phone number to.) We went to the same motel so much he said they should send him a Christmas card. This Bob was my mad man, the adventurer, the thrill seeker, the risk taker. He called one night to say he had found a new motel.

"Where is this "new" motel? I asked.

"It is the Express Way Motel in the south end of town. I'll pick you up in a few minutes, Okay?"

The kids were with their dad, so when Bob pulled into the drive I was waiting for him. All I knew was he was going to make mad passionate love to me, he always did.

We pulled into a big parking lot of eighteen-wheelers. "What is this," I asked him. "This is not a motel."

"Yes it is." he said. My dad owns these trucks so take your pick which one do you want."

I took his hand and led him to the first one. "Now, how do I get in?"

He jumped up on the step pulled the door open jumped back down picked me up and set me on the step.

He went past me into the truck then grabbed my waist and lifted me into the truck. He pulled the curtain back to see a very clean bunk.

"Enter my lady," he said then jumped in after me.

I was setting at the end of the bed when he said, "I want to watch you undress. Slowly, okay?'

My hair was long and I had a pin holding it up. I slowly took the pin out of my hair and it fell to my shoulders. I started unbuttoning my blouse to expose my bare breasts. I had decided not to wear a bra, as I knew we were not going anywhere.

He said, "You don't have a bra on, I couldn't tell." When the blouse was gone, he was holding my breasts so gently. I had worn a pair of slacks with an elastic band and no panties. So when the slacks were gone, I was setting like an Indian in the bed of an eighteen-wheeler, naked.

Bob was staring at my naked body smiling and said, "No fair, you cheated."

"I didn't cheat, just saved time and lunged for him. My arms went around his neck as he was reaching for his pants I was laying on top of him and said, "Now I want to watch."

I rolled off him as his shirt was coming off over his head. He got on his knees to undo his pants. When his pants fell to his knees, he was already getting hard. I laid him down and pulled his pants off him. My first stop was to take a lick on his penis then up to his lips for those great kisses. He rolled me onto my back then lay gently down on me.

He had his fingers in my hair pulling my head up to his face kissing me as he was saying, "I love you."

I whispered, "Please make love to me, slowly make love to me."

He pulled my knees apart and slowly lowered himself into me. We were both moaning, as he was moving himself slowly in and out of me.

I said, "Don't come to soon, I want it to last."

He slowed his pace somewhat. We were enjoying each other so much. I had my legs around him slowly moving up and down against his body. Our bodies would touch then pull away from each other, causing such a pleasure inside me.

But with his "Jewelya, are you ready I can't hold it to much longer your pussy is sucking it out of me, come with me."

He pushed down on me and me up on him, I tighten my legs around him to stop our movement then we were coming at the same time, both of us throbbing.

"Push in harder," I said, "Hold him there let me feel you deep inside me." It was as if his heart was beating inside me. "Do you feel me, do you feel me come?"

"Oh baby, yes can I feel you, He was groaning loudly as he held me tight and came so far inside me. We collapsed when the throbbing was done, but he stayed inside me.

He raised enough to look at me and said, "One of these days you are going to kill me, but what a way to go. I have never known a woman who enjoys sex as much as you do, and I am so glad you enjoy it with me. You are as crazy as me, you don't care where we do it as long as we do it."

We lay there with our arms and legs wrapped around each other, and again I felt so safe, at this moment I was not afraid of anything.

One night he said, "Where do you want to go? You decide."

"To the 103 Club in Omaha. It is just north of 40th & Dodge."

"That was quick, you been there before?" He asked.

"Yes I have, a long time ago." When we got to the bar, Bob opened the door for me like my Bob used to. I looked all around the bar; it looked the same as it had back then. I looked at the bar where Bob had stood that first night. I wasn't sure this was a good idea. Bob interrupted my thoughts, "Good memories or bad ones?"

"I guess a little of both." I answered.

"Who did you come here with? If you don't mind me asking." he asked.

"No, I don't mind you asking. Believe it or not Bob, his name was Bob. That is why I had a hard time talking the night you introduced yourself to me. I thought this apropos, maybe not. They were mostly good memories, just not enough of them. We don't have to stay if you don't want too."

"No, it is nice here set where you want I'll get us a drink." Bob sat down beside me and put his arm around me. I had a short skirt on and he had his hand on my bare leg, which sent a thrill through me.

He asked, "Are you cold? I felt you shiver."

"No," I said, "It is your hand on my leg." He pulled his hand back.

"No," I said, "Put your hand back I love your touch. That is what caused the shiver."

He put his hand back on my leg, but further up the inside of my thigh. I shivered again. He said, "It is good to know I can do to you what you do to me."

"Bob, my love, your touch sets me afire. I have to pee be right back."

When I returned, Bob got up to let me scoot back into the booth. I took his hand and put it back on my leg, but placed it further up under my skirt. I spread my legs so he could feel I had removed my panties.

He looked at me and said, "You are so bad. I love it." He was setting so close to me with his arm around me and his other hand under my skirt. His fingers were finding their way up my thigh. I spread my legs further apart so his fingers could enter me, I was on fire again. I reached over his leg to feel his crotch and he shivered.

I put my leg over his leg so his fingers could go deeper inside me. I was moaning low.

He asked, "Can you do this without making a lot of noise?"

"Yes, don't stop." I lay my head on his shoulder and raised my hips so his fingers could go deeper inside me.

He whispered in my ear, "I can feel you coming on my fingers, what a rush, you are something else. You just made another good memory with this Bob. But, we need to go soon I need you so bad." The waitress asked if we needed anything else.

Bob answered, "No thank you." He paid the bill and we went to his truck in the parking lot.

Bob helped me get in the passenger side of the truck and I said, "Get in beside me." When he was in, I unzipped his pants and pulled his already growing penis out. I pulled up my skirt, put my leg over his legs, and sat down on his penis. He slid right in as I was wet from his fingers. This time he was moaning and I could feel his fluids fill me it felt so good.

He had his arms wrapped around me and said, "You are nuts, you know that don't you."

"Yes," I said, "And you love it." I didn't want to move, when he was inside me was when I felt the best. He lifted me off him and we both sighed at the same time.

We started laughing and Bob said, "We need to get to the motel, are you as gooey as me?"

"Yes, probably more," I answered.

This Bob was my wild one and he was up to doing anything.

He called one night when he knew the kids were down for the night. "I want to take you somewhere, can I pick you up? We won't be gone long."

I woke Big my oldest, to tell him I would be gone for just a little while. Bob picked me up in the alley in his truck. At that time they were putting in the interstate which was a mile or so behind my house. Bob headed south down 35th street, at the end of the street he drove around the barricades.

Now he was on the partially finished interstate, he stopped his truck turned it off looked at me and said, "Come here woman."

He was pulling my pajama bottoms off while he was kissing me, and I knew what he was doing.

I pulled my face away from him and said, "You want us to be the first ones to have sex on the interstate don't you?"

I jumped into his arms and helped him get my pajamas and panties off. He lay me down in the seat and was quickly making love to me. Things like this excited us so much it didn't take us long to finish.

When we were done, he had his arms around me saying," I am so glad I found you, you are as crazy me."

He drove me back to the alley kissed me goodbye and I ran back into the house, checked on the kids and cleaned up.

When the phone rang late in the evening, I knew it would be Bob. He called one evening wanting to know if I could meet him in the alley.

I told him, "If you want to go back to the interstate it won't do much good it is that time of the month."

He said, "That's ok I just want to see you."

He picked me up in the alley and headed to the interstate.

When he stopped the truck he scooted over to me and put his hand between my thighs, "No padding," he said.

"I don't use pads, you know that." He was tugging on my pajama bottoms again and I let him, if he didn't mind I didn't either.

He pulled me onto his lap and as usual, when we were being bad he was hard. He carefully slid into me and pulled me close and pushed up against me while I pushed myself down on him holding him tight against me.

Again it didn't take long to finish. I sat up in his lap took his face in my hands and kissed him, he was smiling and his eyes were sparkling like a bad boy and said, "It felt like someone was in there with me. I've never done that before, I wanted to know what it felt like."

"Well?" I asked.

"Great as usual, but that thing will still come out won't it? I didn't push it in too far did I?" He asked.

I laughed, "No, that can't happen, it can only go in so far."

Another time he called to ask I could go for a ride with him and look at the stars. He picked me up in the alley and was not in his truck, but was driving a very nice car, Toronado, I believe it was.

"Nice car." I said. When did you get this?"

"Just picked it up today. Come on," He said as he took my hand and was pulling me out of the car. He reached in the back seat and pulled out a blanket then spread it out over the hood of the car. He stepped up on the bumper and pulled me up with him. We lie back on the blanket and lay there staring up at the stars. He pulled me close and put his arms around me.

"Do you think we can make love up here?" He asked.

"Yah, we probably can, but we may fall off, I'm game if you are, but I get on top." I answered.

I pulled my jeans down and unzipped his jeans; he was already hard because we were doing something daring. I straddled him and we made love on the hood of his new car. We didn't fall off as it was a pretty big car with a big hood. When we were done we slid down off the car and Bob had this big grin on his face, the one he got when he had done something bad.

"What?" I asked

"You are going to kill me." He said. "You are going to be so mad at me."

"What are you talking about, why will I be so mad at you what have you done?"

"This is my x-wife's new car not mine. You would never have done this if I told you that before, would you?"

I was livid, I lunged at him and he took off running around the car. I was screaming at him, "I am going to kill you when I catch you, you are such an asshole."

He stopped running and I ran into him and he folded his arms around me so I couldn't hit him as I had my fists swinging at him.

"I'm sorry, I'm sorry." He was saying. "But don't you think this is funny. Thinking about the next time she drives this car she will be looking out over the hood where we made such great love?"

"Give me a little time; right now I don't think it is so funny. Now I have to ride home in your ex's car. You are such an asshole and I am so angry with you right now."

We rode to the alley in silence. When I got out of the car he was out also and had his arms around me again, kissing me all over my face how could I stay mad at him for long.

The next day thinking of where we had made love the night before, I smiled to myself.

Bob's wife was my sister's friend as Bob and Ron were close friends. Even though Bob and his wife were getting a divorce, when she found out about us she started asking Callie questions about me. I guess Bob had not been a very faithful husband, so at first she thought I was just another one of his bimbos. Our relationship had to cool, because she no longer wanted a divorce. Bob was not rich, he is now, but he was comfortable and his family was rich; therefore he was afraid she would try to take it.

I just told him, "You can't snuggle up to a pile of money at night and get from it what you get from me. Don't expect me to set and wait for you to decide you want me again."

When Bob came into my life, I wondered how long I would have him, now I know.

I decided to go to work for some extra money; I was tired of the kids and me doing without. Manny paid his child support minus the health insurance he made me pay for as I didn't ask for it in the divorce. Later I found out he didn't have to pay for the insurance, it was one of his benefits. Other than the child support, he did nothing for our children. I applied for a cocktail waitress job at a large hotel and bar in Omaha. The manager wanted me as a bartender in the hotel restaurant, which was an upscale restaurant. I loved that job; I met so many business men with money. But, most of them were very nice men, happy at home. I still got hit on, but none of them turned me on. The bar in the restaurant only had five stools so no one stayed too long. One evening as I was mixing a drink,

I heard someone pull a stool out and looked up to see Bob standing there. I was frozen in time, my mouth was open, but nothing was coming out.

"Can I see you after work?" He asked. "I miss you so."

"I'll meet you outside in the parking lot, I get off at ten." I answered.

My heart was pounding so, what am I going to do?

He was parked beside my car when I got off work. I climbed into his truck and sat down. He was beside me in a flash, kissing me and I was kissing him back, his lips felt so good. His hands were going under my blouse finding my breasts.

I stopped him and said, "What are you doing. We can't do this."

That night I decided to do what I said I would never do, sneak around to see a man. I couldn't resist him, (what a lousy excuse, I wanted sex from him he made me feel good, and I felt safe when I was in his arms, maybe that is what he wanted from me, sex was what we had in common.) He followed me home and I met him in the alley. We were all over each other.

He said, "You can't do without me anymore that I can do without you. We can make it through this. I love you, I think you love me."

"I do, I do, just make love to me." My body was on fire, I wanted him to pull my clothes off and violate me. And he did, we were like two animals pulling at each other's clothes.

All I wanted was him inside me and to feel that throbbing we both loved so much.

He had his head between my breasts holding them together against his cheeks. When we were naked I pulled him down on me and wrapped my legs around him, we were breathing so hard and I was begging him to hold me make love to me. I had my arms and legs wrapped around him his hands were under me pulling me close to him and I felt him quickly go inside me as far as he could.

Then he was pulling himself in and out of me with such force it didn't take us long to feel that wonderful throbbing we lived for. The only thing more important to me than that feeling, were my kids. I would give up that feeling for them only, but I had gotten good at hiding my secrets. I had a great teacher, Scarlet.

Scarlet and I still saw each other every week to shoot pool, but usually had a date afterward. I met Bob one night after shooting pool at a little bar not to far from my house. I suggested it for that reason and there was a little motel across the street from the bar. It was winter and had snowed a lot so I didn't want to be far from home. When we pulled into the motel, there setting in the parking lot was Scarlet's big boat of a station wagon. I wrote in the snow on her car; Red on the Head, I was the only one who called her that so she would know who it was. When we came out a few hours later in big letters was written on my car, BITCH and that was what she always called me when I got the best of her. We still laugh about that one along with others, many others.

Bob was my wild one, but also my sensitive one. We went out lots of times to have fun, but more often than that we were together to have sex.

One night after we had sex in his truck, I said, "Sometimes I think all you want from me is sex."

He sat straight up under the steering wheel and said "How can you say that, you know I love being with you. But, if that's what you think, let's see who can go longer. I am not going to have sex with you for a month."

All I said was, "Yah, right." Famous last words of a fool. We would go to the Spaghetti Works, have a bottle of wine have something to eat, then he would take me home. He would kiss me, hold me, feel my breasts, but no sex. We would just go for a ride roll around in the truck suck face and all that good stuff, then he would take me home.

One evening we went for a ride and ended up parked across the road from our favorite motel. I begged him to please make love to me.

"Okay," He said. "On one condition. You go in and get the room, pay for it, then admit I can go longer than you."

"Okay, okay whatever you want." He drove into the motel, I ran in got the room, jumped back into the truck and gave him the key.

When we were inside the room I was pulling my clothes off, he was standing there laughing. "What, I said.

"I didn't think you were ever going to give in. I don't think I could go have gone another day without you."

"If I didn't want you so bad, I would be so mad at you." I told him. "Now take off your clothes."

"No, you do it." he said. I was pulling his shirt over his head and unbuttoning his pants at the same time. I pushed him back on the bed pulling his shoes and socks off then pulling his pants and briefs off. He was laying there on the bed with his penis sticking almost straight out. I was between his legs with him in my mouth sucking so hard on him. He pulled me up on him turned me over and made such wonderful love to me.

When it was over he was holding me hard against him and whispered in my ear, "Let's not ever do that again. I can't go without making love to you."

We still couldn't see each other as often as we would like and me being who I am was not to be left alone to long. The "Bobs" who had wandered into my world had made sex a necessary part of my life.

(At the beginning of this I said I needed to figure me out. I think I am beginning to see a pattern here. I lived for so long in fear of everything and everyone around me. I had been programmed from the time I was old enough to understand, that I did as I was told, no was not in my vocabulary. The only kind of sex I had was violent and hurting, except for the girl. When my first Bob came into my life he gave me something I had never had before, the feeling of being loved, loving in return and feeling safe. I felt safe when I was in his arms, while he was making love to me. I felt he would protect me from anything or anyone. When he was gone the fear was back. Then Manny entered the picture and I felt safe when I was in his arms, while he was making love to me. Manny would have protected me from anything or anyone, but who would protect me from him? Then my wild Bob came into my life, he had the right name, my Bobs had made sex something I never want to do without.)

Chapter Five

How Did I Manage This

I was at work on a not so busy night so I was doing some cleaning. Out of the corner of my eye I saw a uniform set down at my bar. I turned to see a flyboy setting there.

"Can I help you; are you meeting someone for supper?" I asked him.

"You can help me, but no, I'm not meeting or having supper with anyone. I stopped in the bar next door and all that is in there are yuppies. I asked if there was another bar close, and the bartender said to go next door, Jewelya will take care of you. You must be Jewelya."

This is one, I remember the uniform and he was handsome, blonde, blue eyes, very polite, but don't remember his name as we never had sex, we danced. We may have had sex if it would have lasted longer.

As the night was pretty slow in the restaurant, we were able to talk and the conversation turned to dancing.

He asked, "Do you dance?"

"I love to dance, what kind of dancing." I asked.

I was so surprised at his response, he liked ballroom dancing and so do I. We sat there most of the night talking, then he asked if I would go dancing with him some night.

I said, "Sure, what night I have to make plans for my kids."

He asked, "How about Saturday night. There is a dance at the Livestock Exchange Building. I can pick you up or meet you there."

"I would rather meet you there so I can have my car with me." I answered.

He said, "I don't blame you, if I were a good looking blonde that's what I would do."

"You are a good looking blonde also, so I'll meet you there about seven p.m. okay?"

I decided this was a dress-up night. I had a red dress that fit me good, showed a little, hid a little, garter, stockings and high heels. Things to drive a man crazy and I loved to drive a man crazy.

He was waiting for me at the door, and I am sure glad I dressed up, because he did. He was gorgeous. Nice slacks, black shinny shoes, dress shirt and sport jacket.

He took my hand and turned me around and said, "You look fantastic."

When we got to the top floor the band was about to start playing. We went by the bar and got our drinks and he led me to a table just as the band was starting to play. He took my hand and led me to the floor then, I was in his arms and we were dancing to a slow song.

He said, "I was hoping the first song would be a slow song so I could hold you against me."

But, he was a perfect gentleman. We danced all night to almost every song.

When we sat out a couple of songs to get our wind back he asked me," How many children do you have?'

"Seven," I said.

"What? A woman doesn't look like you and have seven children." My standby comment was they keep me young chasing after them. Maybe that was so, but I don't know what other women look like that has had seven kids. I didn't do much of anything to keep thin, so maybe it was chasing them round.

He walked me to my car after the dance and asked, "Can I kiss you?"

I lifted my head up to him; he had to lean down to find my lips. He lifted me off the ground and held me up with his arms around my waist. He said you are such a tiny little thing, then his lips were on mine, but I didn't have that shiver with this kiss as I usually did. He did, as I could feel his passion grow against me.

We went dancing the following week at Peony Park. He was a marvelous dancer; I wish I felt differently when he kissed me. He was such a gentleman he would never be aggressive with me. Maybe that was it; he was too much a gentleman. If he would have tried harder I would have let him, I still would have enjoyed sex with him. What the hell is wrong with me, do I always have to have a bad boy?

He said, "When I asked if you could dance I didn't expect to get what I did, you are an excellent dancer. You follow my every move, I could dance with you and hold you every night, but there is someone else isn't there."

"He is not in the picture anymore." I said.

"He may not be in the picture anymore, but he is still with you. I know I have been there. You need time to let go. I would love to make love to you, but I won't push you, I love being with you."

Why couldn't I feel about this man the way I feel about my Bob. We woman are nuts. The ones we should keep we throw away, the ones we should throw away we keep. Love cannot live without that fire.

There was a very popular dance hall in Council Bluffs that was having a ball room band we were going to. I always dressed up when we went dancing, I think he liked showing me off and I liked him showing me off. I started looking in the mirror more often and realized what these men were saying just might be so. As we were leaving the dance floor, he was holding my hand. I had made up my mind if he didn't make a move tonight, I was I needed to be held.

When we sat down he asked, "Do you know that man standing over there?"

"Where," I asked

"Over there at the edge of the dance floor. He has been watching us, you I think. You never notice when men are watching you do you? That's one of the things I love about you, a beautiful woman who doesn't know she is beautiful."

I looked where he said and there stood Bob. My heart was in my stomach. He was just standing there staring at me.

I said, "I'll be right back."

Bob never took his eyes off me as I walked across the dance floor toward him.

"You are a great dancer; I've been watching you and your partner. Do you want to stay here with him or go with me, I love you please go with me."

When it came to Bob, I was not in control; not going with him was not an option. I walked back across the dance floor to the table, then looked back at Bob, he was still standing there.

My dance partner stood up and said, "That is him isn't it."

"Yes," I said, "And I am so sorry, I never wanted to hurt you."

"I know," he said, "I could tell by the look on your face he is the one. Be happy, Jewelya, I don't think you have had too much happiness in your life. Go, you have to do what you have to do."

I grabbed my purse and jacket from the chair and turned to go, Bob was still standing at the edge of the dance floor. I walked up to him; he took my hand and walked me out the door.

We went to his truck he unlocked the door took me by the waist to lift me in; instead he turned me around in his arms and said, "When I saw you out there in his arms I didn't know what to do. I almost left, but I couldn't I had to let you know I was here and let you do what you had to."

Then he was kissing me all over my face. "I want to be with you please stay with me, I miss you so much. I watched you walk toward me and watched you walk away from me, along with every other man in this place, and every one of us undressed you as you floated across the floor."

"Won't your wife get mad if you are out all night?" When I saw the look on his face I said, "I'm sorry I know you are doing the best you can and yes I will stay with you. I need you to hold me so bad."

We were undressing each other as we made our way into the room. By the time we got to the bed all we wanted was sex, pure sex. He picked me up threw me down on the bed and as my body was bouncing on the bed he was over me. I put my arms around his neck and pulled him down on me, I opened my legs willingly so he could see what was waiting for him, he was inside me moving in and out of me like a mad man and I was loving every moment.

He said in my ear, "I missed you so much."

"Me too." I said, but I thought to myself I may have left the best man behind, again.

Bob knew me well, he knew if he left me alone to long I would be on the prowl.

Manny had the kids most weekends and I was not one to stay home alone. I loved to dance and there was a bar not to far from home, the same place I had gone with my dance partner. I didn't usually like to go to bars alone, but I needed a partner to dance with, and there were plenty there. I knew a lot of the people in this bar, so I didn't mind going by myself.

One night when leaving the bar I heard someone say, "Blondie."

I looked around and saw no one. As I opened my car door, I heard again, "Blondie."

Now I was getting concerned, then a man in a uniform walked out of the shadows. He was tall, but with the lighting I couldn't see him very good. He walked to where the light was, and motioned for me to come over. He was in a fireman's uniform so I didn't figure he was a danger. I walked under the light to see a very handsome man, light brown hair, clean shaven man. Strike one; I like hair, but what the hell. He walked toward me and I stopped.

He said, "Don't be afraid of me. I have been watching you come and go from here for some time now and you always leave alone, I always wondered why you are always alone? So I decided to ask you tonight, why are you always alone?"

I stood there staring at him, then asked him, "Why have you been watching me?"

He said, "You are not supposed to answer a question with a question and I haven't really been watching you, but I set out here a lot when I'm at work and I would see you leaving here, then I started watching for you?" I could not see as much as I wanted to so I decided to talk to you."

"Well," I said, "Are you happy now?"

He said, "I will be as soon as you say you will go out with me. Do you have time to have coffee with me? We always have coffee on in the firehouse."

"I don't have much time; I have kids at home with a sitter." Which was a lie, they were with Manny.

We went into the fire house to the kitchen, he got out two cups and asked, "How do you like your's?"

We sat and drank our coffee and talked. His name was Bill, not a fireman an EMT, divorced with two children.

"How about you," he asked. "You mentioned children?

"I have seven children." I always start out about the kids; if they are going to run they run then.

"You have seven children? How could you have seven children? You don't look like you are old enough to have seven children."

My favorite line, "Running after seven children keeps me young I guess. I really have to go now. Thank you for the coffee and conversation."

As I got up to leave he took my hand and said, "I want to see you again, not just watch you in the parking lot. Will you go out with me, Friday night?"

"It would have to be later in the evening; the kids' dad picks them up about seven. I can meet you here about seven-thirty or so."

When I got up to leave he took my hand and said, "I will walk you to your car, there may be someone else watching you."

He walked me to my car opened the door said good night and watched me drive away.

Bill hadn't said where we were going on our date, so I just put on some jeans and a blouse. He was waiting out side when I got there. I parked and he led me to his car.

He was the perfect gentleman, there's that gentleman thing again. We went to a bar at the other end of town where they had dancing also.

He said, "I don't want to go where everyone knows you, I don't want to share you tonight."

While we were dancing he looked at my eyes and said, "Green eyes, the sexiest eyes there are."

"Really?" I asked.

He laughed and said, "I really don't know about any other green eyes, just your's. You are telling me something with your eyes, but I'm not sure what it is yet."

He kissed me lightly while we were dancing and held me tight against him. He smelled so good, not like cologne, like man.

He drove me back to my car, but before I could get out of his car he moved over in the seat beside me, "Can I kiss you, really kiss you. Nothing else, I won't push you for anything else just a kiss?"

I turned my head up to him so he could kiss me and what a kiss. This was not just a kiss, his lips were lightly on mine at first then he parted his lips slightly and parted my lips with his tongue. He pulled me close and my breasts were against his chest, and I could feel that shiver go down my back. He was caressing my tongue with his tongue then the kiss got more ardent for him and me.

He pulled away from my lips and said, "We have to stop this, kissing you makes me want you so bad, and I told you I wouldn't push you but, when can I see you again? I work two days on two days off, I'm yours when ever you want."

I wanted to crawl into his back seat, but he was being such a gentleman I should act like a lady, I guess.

I looked at him and said, "When is your next day off and I will make arrangements for the kids."

"I am off this Wednesday and Thursday. Can you do that?"

"I can get a sitter, but I can't stay late because of school. The earliest I can get here would be six after their supper, or we have to wait till a Friday you are off."

He said, "I'll be here Wednesday waiting."

When I got there on Wednesday, he was waiting. I parked and got in his car, he asked, "Where to?"

My response was, "Where you can hold me, kiss me like you did the other night and make love to me."

He just sat there staring at me, then said, "Really?"

"Yes really," I said, "That is what I want to do."

We went to the north end of town to a little motel I had forgotten was there. He went in to register, jumped back into the car, pulled me close and was kissing me, then we went into the room. We lay down on the bed as he was kissing me like he did before and I was melting. I was kissing him back as I was undressing him.

He took my hand to stop me and said, "I want this to last, I have been watching you and wanting you for so long I want to enjoy every part of you."

He sat me up in bed facing him, and pulled my shirt over my head. He unzipped my jeans then lay me down to pull them over my hips. He stood by the side of the bed then took my hand and pulled me up to stand facing him. I was standing there in my bra and panties.

"You are beautiful, I just want to look at you, your body is just like I imagined it." He moved toward me, I reached for his pants to unbutton and unzip them; he let them fall to the floor.

He had a great body, not real muscular, but very good shape, no hair on the face, but hair on the chest not a lot, but enough for me.

"You are beautiful also." I said. "I want to see the rest of you."

He said, "Me first, there is more of you to see, and I want to see every inch."

My goose bumps were coming back. He put his arms around me to unhook my bra, (guys are really good at this) and let it drop to the floor.

He stared at me, "They didn't even move, they are beautiful. Can I hold them?" He asked.

"How do they stay up like that, you have good sized breasts." I moved closer to him and took his hands and put them around my breasts. He was holding them so gently. I moved his hands down to my panties, he put his hands inside each side of my panties and pulled them down to my ankles and I stepped out of them. As he was standing back up he stopped at my fur ball took hold of my butt and buried his face in it.

He stepped back from me took my hands and said again, "You are beautiful, you really are a blonde."

I was staring at his penis as he was staring at me. "You are beautiful too and I want him." Then we fell onto the bed holding each other. He had his head between my breasts, kissing them sucking on them then he was kissing me with those great kisses.

"Make love to me.' I whispered "Hold me tight and make love to me. I want him inside me"

He was over me looking into my face as he lowered himself down to me. I wrapped my legs around him and lifted my hips toward him as I felt him go inside me. He was holding himself up so he could see my face as he was loving me. He was going in and out of me slowly; I reached up and pulled him down on my breasts and told him to hold me tight, really make love to me. I felt him grow bigger inside me as I clenched my muscles around his penis, his movement got faster and harder and I could feel that throbbing inside me coming from my belly button. We were both moaning as we came together. He was holding me tighter and tighter, I wrapped my legs around him tighter to hold him inside me. When he felt my legs relax around him, he relaxed his hold on me also.

I said, "Don't let go, just hold me a little longer." He rolled over, but didn't let go of me. His arms were holding me tight. I felt safe again.

We lay there in each others arms for some time, then he said, "What has happened to you in your life. You are a beautiful woman, very in control, but underneath you are a scared little girl."

Oh Bill, I thought, if you only knew. What happened to me with Carl no one knows but Carl and me and he isn't telling anyone.

"Shower with me, okay?" I asked.

He picked me up in his arms and carried me to the bathroom. In the shower he said "I want to bathe your whole body, okay?"

I handed him the soap and said, "Don't miss a spot."

When we were done he carried me back to the bed. It felt so good to be in a man's arms again.

"Do we have time? Can I make love to you again? I still want you so bad. I just look at you and I want you."

He lay me down on the bed and I reached down and wrapped my fingers around his penis and felt him growing in my hand. I heard a big sigh come out of him. His hand went between my legs his fingers finding his way through my fur ball to inside me.

He put his lips next to my ear and said, "Can I see what she taste's like?"

"You don't have to ask, do what you want to as long as it doesn't hurt me."

He looked startled and said, "Hurt you, I could never hurt you. If I do anything that hurts you tell me and I will stop." He took me in his arms and was holding me tight again.

He was kissing me then his lips were going down my body till he was at my fur ball. He spread my legs apart and put his lips and tongue on my pussy and my hips were moving up to him.

He lifted my hips up further so his tongue could find everything, his tongue was inside me and I was moaning, he lifted his head and said to me, "I want you to come this way, can you?"

"Yes, Yes, don't stop." I said. He was running his tongue in and out of me, around my man in the boat. His hands were around my pussy caressing it. I took hold of his hair rubbing his head as I felt that throbbing inside me and my fluids came flowing out into his mouth. When the throbbing stopped he was beside me, "Can I make love to you?"

"I told you, you don't have to ask," as I rolled him onto his back, and put myself over him and saw how ready he was.

I lowered myself down over him; he took hold of my waist. "I don't want him to hurt you he has grown a lot."

He said what both my Bobs had said, lower yourself slowly and you will adjust to his size. He was big so I let him hold on to me till I felt him slide further inside me and I settled down on him moving my legs out so I could feel all of him. I started moving back and forth on him our pubic hair rubbing against each other. He still had his hands around my waist. He was moving his hips up and down while he was pulling me back and forth. I could feel his penis start to pulse and he pushed him inside me as far as he could. I was setting up straight on him arching my back holding him tight with my pussy muscles.

I told him, "Come hard, I want to feel you come deep inside me." He stopped moving me and pushed up on me holding me down on him and I could feel his penis throbbing and pulsating inside me. He reached up to hold on to my breasts; I leaned down so he could take them into his mouth. I didn't want to get up, he felt so good.

He pulled me down to his lips and kissed me one of those great kisses and said, "You are amazing, but I knew you would be. I wish you were happier."

In the following months Bill did his best to make me happier.

When I got home Big said Charlie Brown had called earlier. I loved being with Bob, but I wasn't going to wait around for him. I had found another lover who made me feel safe.

There was a little bar up the street a couple miles where Scarlet and I liked to shoot pool. Another friend of mine liked to go there also. I decided one night to go down to see if she was there as Manny had the kids. When I got there she was there with her boyfriend and his brother, Joey. I had seen Joey in there before and every time he would ask me out and I refused. He was tall, not as muscular as Bill, but built good, black hair, brown eyes, and my favorite; a mustache and full beard that went down into his shirt which meant hairy chest, but younger than me by about eight years. To night my friend had a straw waving it in the air and she asked, "What would it take to get you to go out with Joey, he is driving us nuts."

She asked me. "If his tongue is as long as this straw will you go out with him?"

"Sure." I said. Not thinking his tongue would be that long. He stuck his tongue out as far as he could and it was as long as the straw.

Joey was right beside me saying, "Okay, when are we going out, I can go right now."

"No, not tonight. I can't stay long. I have to get home. I'll come back on Friday, think of something to do." I told him.

Joey said, "You won't back out will you, stand me up?"

"No." I said, "I wouldn't do that. I'll be here."

He called during the week to ask me if I could go away for the weekend. He wanted me to go to the rodeo with him, but we wouldn't leave until Saturday morning.

"Good," I said. "I can spend Friday night with my boys."

We still liked to have the penny-anti poker parties on Friday night so that worked out great. I loved playing card with my boys. Manny would have the kids for the weekend and my boys were old enough to be alone. So I told him okay as I loved the rodeo.

When I got to the bar Saturday morning Joey was waiting. He asked, "Can we take your car it is newer than mine."

"I would rather take mine anyway." I had a new car; I don't blame him for wanting to take mine. When we got there he had a motel reserved for us, a man that plans, wow and a young one at that. I thought, what am I going to do with him, or what is he going to do with me. The rodeo was great, I love watching the cowboys, and everything that goes with it. He held my hand everywhere we went or would put his arm around me. When the day was over, we made our way back to the motel.

Inside our room he asked me," What do we do now?"

I asked him, "What do you want to do?"

He had a big smile on his face showing very nice white teeth, and said, "You have to know what I want to do."

I took his hand and lead him to the bed and pulled him down with me. "Just hold me for a little bit, Okay?"

He pulled me close and wrapped his arms around me. "I can't believe I am laying here with you. I have wanted to be with you for so long and you kept saying no."

He took my face in his hands and placed his lips on mine so gently. His lips were so soft and his mustache and beard were caressing my face and lips and I shivered.

"Are you cold, do you want a blanket?" he asked.

"I'm not cold, it was your kiss." I answered.

He had me lying on my back; he was over me looking into my eyes and said, "Whenever you came into the bar, I made sure to get your attention. You would talk to me, but you never really saw me your eyes were going right through me and you kept saying no. You have such sexy eyes that talk to a man, do you know that?"

"You know I have been told that before, but I don't know I'm doing it." I answered

"But I'm looking into them now and that look isn't in there anymore. You look so content now."

I thought to myself, because now I feel safe.

"Are we going to stay like this or can I undress you and make love to you." He asked. "If all you wanted me to do is hold you all night, I would do that, but I really want to make love to every inch of you" he said.

"I want you to do anything you want, just hold me tight and make me feel good."

He was kissing me as he was unbuttoning my shirt as I was unbuttoning his. He pulled my shirt off then unzipped my jeans taking them off. I unbuttoned his jeans and unzipped them then pulled them down and he kicked them off the end of the bed. I was in my panties and bra, he was in his shorts. I rolled over so he could unhook my bra, then he pulled my panties down. He leaned down and kissed each cheek of my butt, then turned me over and sat up on the bed staring at my naked body.

"I have waited so long to see you like this."

"Was it worth the wait?" I asked

He said nothing, just started to kiss me again, this time he parted my lips with his tongue and was inside my mouth looking for my tongue.

I said, "I love your kisses, but I want that tongue somewhere else." He took his lips off mine and was running it down my body past my breasts to my fur ball. He pulled my knees up and spread my legs apart and was running his tongue through the hair around my pussy, it felt so good I started moaning with pleasure. I felt his tongue find its way inside me as his fingers were massaging my man in the boat. I was twisting and pushing myself up to him as his tongue was going in and out.

I pulled him up to me telling him, "Make love to me, I want you inside me."

As he found his way inside me he took hold of my hips and pulled me toward him so he could go in further. He lowered himself down on me and wrapped my legs around him. "Am I hurting you?' he asked.

"No, I said. "Make love to me." He was going faster in and out of me and I could feel me starting to come.

He said, "I can't hold it are you ready, come with me baby, come with me, and I did, my pussy was throbbing against his throbbing penis and we were clinging tightly to each other. We finally relaxed, but just lay still clinging to each other, exhausted.

Joey said, "I have died and gone to heaven. You are everything I thought you would be and more."

He pulled the covers down from under us then pulled them over us. He moved closer to me wrapped his arms around me and said, "I want to feel your naked body against me as long as I can." And we fell asleep in each others arms, and I was safe again.

I woke up as the sun was coming up. Joey was behind me rubbing my butt; I could feel he was hard, morning hard on.

"Do you have to pee?" I asked.

"Already have." He said. "I was watching you sleep."

"I have to!" So I jumped up and headed for the bathroom, peed, cleaned a little. and crawled back under the covers with him. I started to crawl back into his arms again when he turned my back to him.

I said, "No you can't do that. That would hurt too much."

"I'm not going to do that," He said. "Just relax, I would never hurt you." So I turned my back to him again.

He said. "Let me make love to you the way I want, you will love it."

He lifted my leg up and was directing his penis toward my pussy as his fingers were going all around where his penis was going in.

He put my leg up over his then reached around me and had his fingers massaging my man in the boat and I though, oh my god what is he doing. He took my hand and put it down on my pussy where his hand was.

"We are going to come together; I can feel with my fingers when you are ready. Can you feel your pussy with your fingers? Do you like it this way; does it feel as good to you as it does to me.? You will feel it when you are starting to come, so leave your fingers with mine and we can feel each other come."

My fingers could feel him and me coming. He pushed his penis inside me as far as he could and was filing me so full it was running out onto our fingers. His fingers were over mine and he was rubbing me with my fingers, it was awesome.

I rolled over to face him and said, "I'm glad I changed my mine about you." and rolled back into his arms. This was the first time I had thought about Bob.

(It is amazing to me how much men are alike and how different they are from each other. They all do the same thing, but in different ways. It is just that some are much better at it than others.)

Now I was juggling Bob, Bill and Joey. I guess I thought that wasn't enough so I had to add another one to the mix or should I say, Scarlet added another man to the mix.

Scarlet called and was shooting pool in North Omaha at the local bar. She said. "The bartender is good looking, he looks like Elvis and will probably give you drinks, wear a pair of shorts and halter."

"In North Omaha, are you nuts?" I asked her.

"Well, forget the halter where a tight shirt, show off those boobs. I'll meet you there."

I don't remember his name, but he was good looking. I did know his name and I can see his face and we did have sex several times, well quite a lot of times. But I don't remember his name. That was a long time ago, I remember the sex and that's what I was looking for.

He was so good looking, with almost black hair, dark brown eyes, Italian dark skin, and a beautiful almost black mustache with long Elvis sideburns. When he smiled his eyes sparkled and showed very white teeth. He had sharp features like Elvis. I wore the short shorts, not a halter top, but a not to tight shirt.

Scarlet's car was in the parking lot so I walked in the door of the bar. In a bar when the door opens everyone looks, but when a good looking blonde, in short shorts and a not to tight shirt over her good sized boobs walks in they really look. The bartender was at the far end of the bar when I walked in and he did look like Elvis.

When the whistles started he looked up and saw me, Scarlet told him I was coming over so he was heading toward the door telling the boys I was there for him.

He took my hand and said, "I have a stool waiting for you at the end of the bar. Scarlet was right, she said you were good to look at, all of you."

"The shorts and the tight top were her idea."

"Good idea." he said. He was nice and did give me drinks; I think the shorts did it.

When Scarlet was done shooting pool she had one drink with us then said she was leaving to meet Murray, one of her toys. Scarlet loved men as much as I did.

She asked him, "Will you make sure she gets to her car and gone?" He nodded to her and she gave me a hug with a, "call me tomorrow."

When the bar closed he locked the door to clean things up and put the money away.

He walked me to my car then said. "Can I set with you a minute?"

We got in my car; I thought what is he going to do. He was looking at me strangely.

I asked him. "Why are you looking at me like that?"

"I can't imagine a man letting you go. You are divorced aren't you?"

"Yes I am, but he didn't leave me I threw him out because he had to many girlfriends."

"That is what I mean, why would he need a girlfriend having you?"

"They are usually younger than him, so maybe he wanted younger women. He wanted them and me. I really don't want to talk about him anymore. What about you? Scarlet said you were divorced or on the way."

"Yes, I guess I wasn't a very good husband either. I'm staying with my mom and dad until it is final or I can get an apartment. When can you come back and when can we go out?"

Then he said one for the books, "Can I kiss you to see if you want to see me again. I understand women are into kissing."

I laughed and said, "That is a new one. Why not, you might be right, I don't know about other women, but this woman is into kissing. The way a man kisses tells us a lot about the man."

He pulled me out from under the steering wheel held me against him, but not to tight. His lips found mine and was slowly kissing me barely toughing my lips. He was running his tongue along my lips, then his tongue was inside my mouth and he pushed his lips down harder on mine. He put his hands behind my ears then ran his fingers through my hair and pulled my head back to look into my eyes then pulled my lips up to his. He let go of my hair then his arms were around me and my breasts were against his chest. It was a gentle, demanding kiss. He dropped one arm down to my butt and was gently rubbing me and pulled me over on his lap. I was setting sideways on his lap when he freed my lips. My heart was pounding so hard I thought he could hear it.

He had his fingers in my hair again and he turned my head up to look into my eyes and asked, "Did I pass, was that a good kiss?"

I said, "Yes, do it again."

He turned me around and said to me, "Kiss me back more, I don't bite."

I put my legs on either side of him, put my arms around his neck and returned his kiss.

This time he was holding me tight against him. His put his tongue inside my mouth and found my tongue as I was searching for his he was moving his head from side to side as I was. My tongue moved his and was licking his lips with my tongue. I felt his hands move up to my breasts, my hands went between his legs to feel he was getting hard. I unzipped his pants to expose his beautiful penis. My shorts were stretchy so I moved them aside so he could enter me. He was sliding slowly inside me as I was lowering my body down on him. He wrapped his arms around me pulling me tight against him. He buried his face in my neck and I could feel his hot breath and a sound of pleasure was coming from him. He pulled me down tight against him as he was moving me back and forth on him. I could feel him start coming as I was. We kept moving back and forth until there was that wave of throbbing going through both of us.

When we relaxed, he took my face in his hands and said, "That was one hell of a kiss, we have to do that again soon."

I agreed by just nodding my head.

When I went to the bar, he liked me to wear my short shorts and my shirt tight over my boobs, so when the guys would whistle when I came in they knew I was there for him. The bartender and I made plans to spend the whole weekend together, from Friday night after the bar closed until Sunday. I hadn't heard from Bob, but Bill called and I told him I was going with Scarlet over the weekend. He had to work that weekend, but asked me to stop by the firehouse so he could see me before I left.

So on Wednesday evening I stopped by to see him. We set outside for a while with a couple of other firemen. After a while they went in saying they would let us have some time together alone. As soon as they left Bill had me in his arms.

He said, "I didn't think they would ever go in. Come downstairs with me everyone is in bed."

He led me down the steps into the kitchen where we had drank coffee. He straddled the bench and motioned me to set down. He pulled me over to him and put my legs around him. He pulled me on his lap kissing me all over my face. You don't know what you do to me. I was moving around in his lap and felt him growing.

He asked "Can we do it here?"

"I don't know, do you think anyone will come down?' I put his hands under my shirt so he could feel my breasts as I hadn't worn a bra or panties. I unzipped his pants and pulled his penis out. I had my short shorts on so I moved them aside, then I slid down over him as he took my face in his hands and was kissing me harder than he usually did, but it felt so good.

He was all the way in me, I told him. "Don't move just hold yourself tight inside me till we come. I tighten my muscles around his penis then relaxed them then clenched them again.

He asked. "What are you doing, how are you doing that?"

"Don't talk just hold me tight, he took hold of my hips and pulled me closer pushing himself deep inside me. We both could feel each other come as I sat tightly on him. We relaxed when we stopped coming, but we hung on to each other loving the feel of each other.

"When I stand up we are going to be wet. I hope you have another pair of pants." I said.

He reached on the table for some napkins and handed them to me, we were both soaked. "I can smell our sex, it is great." he said smiling at me.

Bill was a good man and I would end up breaking his heart. Again, I probably left the best man behind.

On Friday night I went to see my bartender, we were going to spend the weekend together. When the bar closed he asked me if I was hungry,

"No, I want to be in a bed with you." I answered.

All we had had so far was the backseat or front seat of a car. He had already gotten our motel. We had teased each other in the bar with kisses and touches so we were ready to make love.

Just inside the door he took me in his arms and said, "Lets take it slow, we can sleep late if we want. We have the room for two nights, and you are mine."

He pulled the pin out of my hair and my hair fell to my shoulders. He took my head in his hands and pulled my lips up to his for one of his great kisses, this was when I realized how tall he was, taller than any other man I had been with. What I also realized, it all levels out when you lay down.

While he was kissing me he unbuttoned my blouse then unzipped my pants, while I was doing the same to him.

When he had my bra and panties off he said, "Let me look at you, I have never seen you in the light with all your clothes off."

I heard him suck his breath in and say, "I need you so bad."

He lay me down on the bed and I opened my arms and legs for him to lay down on me so he knew how much I wanted him.

He had dark brown hair on his chest and I pushed my breasts against him. "Just make love to me, I need you too."

He lay down on me and slowly slid inside me and wrapped my legs around him. "I want it to last." He said, "Go slow the first time."

"Just make me feel good, make me feel good." I said.

He was slowly going in and out of me, it felt so good. I wanted it to last too.

He was whispering in my ear, "I will make you feel so good; I promise I will make you feel so good."

He rolled me over so I was on top of him setting me up moving me slowly back and forth.

He stopped moving me and said, "Stay still, don't move I don't want us to come yet you feel too good for it to be over."

I was still for a few moments when he turned me back over and wrapped my legs around him again and started going in and out.

I couldn't take it any longer and said. "You have to go faster I can't hold it any longer I want to feel you come, I need to come."

He started moving faster and going deeper as I was raising my hips up and down to him. I had my arms and legs wrapped around him; he had his head buried in my neck holding me tight as we both came. We were throbbing so hard we were locked together. When we finally relaxed our hold on each other, he looked up in my eyes and the first thing he said was, "Damn, you sure smell good."

"That's all you have to say?" I asked, "I smell good?"

"Well, amongst other things, Yah, you sure smell good."

He was laughing now, "You are one of a kind. I want to wash you all over, make you smell even better, okay?'

I said nothing, just sat up in bed and said, "You have to carry me, if I'm not too heavy for you."

He had me in his arms kissing all over my face, lifted me off the bed and carried me into the bathroom. Instead of turning the shower on he plugged the tub and started the water running into the tub. We had both brought a small bag with our clothes and essentials in them. He had a little bottle with bubble bath in it and was making a bubble bath for us. "Do you like bubble baths?" he asked.

"I love bubble baths, I answered. "How did you know?"

"You just looked like a bubble bath girl." He said.

He lifted me up stood me in the tub and held me while I sat down then he got in behind me. He took hold of my breasts and pulled me close against his hairy chest. Bubbles were every where.

"This is not working," he said, "I want to see you," he took hold of me and turned me around.

As soon as I was facing him, he pulled me close. He moved us to the center of the tub so I could put my legs over him. I reached between us and pulled his penis up so it was standing up between us its head sticking out of the water. I was running my fingers over and around the head of his penis. I watched him grow and grow. With my other hand I wrapped my fingers around his penis and slowly started working my hand up and down as my fingers were tracing the head of his penis. I heard him moaning and when I looked at him he had his eyes closed.

He opened his eyes and said, "Do you have any idea how you are making me feel, every part of me wants you."

I let go of his penis and pushed it down so it was straight between us and put my arms around him. He took hold of my waist and pulled me close while his penis was sliding into me. He was going inside me so far because of the bubble bath and he felt so damn good. He pulled me tight against him and I wrapped my legs around him as tight as I could. He had his arms wrapped around my waist with his head buried in my neck. I was kissing his neck his cheeks his ear, running my hands through his hair.

He whispered in my ear, "Come with me, are you ready?"

I pushed on him harder and he put his hands on my butt and pulled me as close as he could. I could feel us coming so hard; it seemed to go on and on and was awesome.

When our desire had been completely spent I said, "I have never had sex in a bubble bath before."

"Me neither, was it as good for you as it was for me. You felt so good. Just your touch gets me hard."

"I love it when you respond to me like you do. I can't be satisfied if you aren't." I said.

"You don't have to worry about that, You always satisfy me. Shall we shower the bubble bath off us?"

We let go of each other and when I pulled myself away from him I felt his penis slide out of me and I groaned. After our shower we dried each other off then went back to our bed I curled up in his arms, and in his arms, I felt safe again.

We must have worn each other out; we did sleep late and woke up at about the same time. I was still curled up in his arms with my back to him.

I rolled over to face him and said, "Good morning, what a wonderful sleep. I slept so good in your arms, how about you."

He opened his eyes, and kissed me on the nose, "Good morning to you beautiful. I slept great also, with you in my arms."

He pulled me close, and I felt him hard against my stomach already. I scooted down under the covers and took him in my mouth. I rolled him onto his back and placed myself between his legs. I reached under his penis and was caressing his jewels while I was going up and down on his penis in my mouth.

He took hold of my head and pulled me up to face him. "Let me make love to you, how I want to make love to you, you just lie there and let me love you"

He rolled me over and was kissing me everywhere. From my forehead, my lips, my neck when he got to my breasts he spent more time holding them kissing them sucking on them, then he was at my belly button running his tongue around and inside it. From there he went to my fur ball, he pushed my hair back and ran his tongue from my man in the boat to inside my pussy. Then he turned me over and was kissing both cheeks of my butt. He pulled me up on my knees and pulled my butt cheeks apart and was running his tongue through my butt crack. I could feel the shivers and goose bumps running all over my body.

Suddenly he stopped and turned me over and was between my legs with his penis so hard and said, "I want to do more, but I can't I need to love you, I can't wait."

He pulled my knees up and out and was inside me so fast and buried himself deep inside me. He had his hands under me pulling by butt up to him as he was going in and out of me then I could feel him start to pulse and fill me with those wonderful juices.

He rolled me over on top of him and said, "I am so sorry, I hope I didn't hurt you, but woman you make me like a mad man, I can't get enough of you. You didn't come did you? I am sorry, but he just couldn't wait any longer. I will make it up to you."

I looked down at him and said, "I know you will make it up to me and you smell so damn good."

We were both laughing, and agreed it was time to shower, go get something to eat and do something besides making love.

"Then we can come back here and you can make it up to me, you owe me one." I said.

We went to a little restaurant not far from the motel, then we went to the mall just to walk around and hold hands. We decided to go to his bar for a drink and shoot a couple of games of pool. After we were done playing pool we sat in a back booth drinking our drinks. He had his arm around me pulling me close, kissing my ear and cheek. I turned my face up to him for one of his great kisses.

We had to be careful in there as everyone was watching us. I had my hand lying between his legs; he whispered in my ear, "Do you know what you are doing?"

"Of course I do, I said, "I want you in my arms, I want to go."

He slid out of the booth, I slid out behind him, he took my hand and told everyone goodbye that we had an appointment.

When we got out to the car I was in his arms and he was hugging me and lifted me up with my legs around his waist so he was looking into my eyes and said, I can't believe I met someone that enjoys sex as much as I do. All men enjoy sex like I do, most women don't."

"I'm not most women, now will you stop talking and get in the car so we can go, you owe me one remember?"

He let me down and opened the door on the driver's side for me to get in then he was in beside me. I sat close to him so our legs were touching and I put my hand between his legs.

We were undressing each other as soon as we got in the door. He picked me up and lay me in the bed then lay beside me.

He pulled my naked body next to his naked body and said, "I want to finish making love to you my way, okay? I promise you I won't hurt you. You will love everything I do."

I told him, "It is okay to do what you want as long as you don't hurt me."

"I could never hurt any part of this great body." He had set up and his eyes were going up and down my naked body. He was kissing every part of me again from my forehead down to my belly button. He pulled my legs apart and was between my legs so his tongue could trail down to my fur ball. He pulled the lips of my pussy apart and ran his tongue around it put his tongue inside me. I was moaning with pleasure as he turned me over and pulled me up on my knees and pulled the cheeks of my butt apart and was running his tongue up and down from my pussy past my taint and to my anus. I could feel my pussy getting so wet. He put his fingers inside me and was rubbing my wetness on my anus. He took a tube out of his bag and was rubbing a gel on himself and me. I tried to move away from him.

He held on to my butt and said, "Jewelya, I promise I won't hurt you, if it hurts tell me. It may hurt a little at first, but then it will feel like nothing you have ever felt before."

He pulled my butt cheeks apart again and I could feel his penis trying to enter my anus. He said, "Lay down on your chest so you are closer to me, let me have your hand."

He took my hand and put my fingers inside my pussy. "Now move them around, think about how that feels."

I did what he wanted, then I felt the head of his penis go inside my anus, I tried to pull away by instinct, but he was still holding my butt close to him.

He whispered, "Relax baby, just relax. Once he is in you will love it. If it hurts tell me." He pushed my fingers back inside me and was slowly pushing his penis inside me. I relaxed and thought about what my fingers were doing.

Then I felt his penis go so far into me I felt his body against my butt. "Does that hurt baby, he is all the way in just relax and like him being in your pussy, you will adjust to him."

I was amazed, it hurt, but not like I thought it would.

Then he started to slowly pull himself out, then slowly was going back inside me. "Is that okay? Can I start going faster? I don't want to go to fast or I will come too soon and I want to wait for you. Talk to me baby, do you want me to stop or can I keep going?"

"No, I don't want you to stop. It doesn't hurt like I thought it would, but how do you make me come this way." I asked

"I don't, you do, but what I am doing will make you so hot, your fingers will make you come." I could hear in his voice shiver with pleasure.

He was slowly moving himself in and out of my anus while my fingers were as deep in my pussy as I could get them. He put his arm around me and put his hand on top of mine and his fingers were in my pussy moving around inside me with my fingers.

"Move your fingers around with mine and you will be able to feel my penis, can you feel him?"

"Oh my, I can feel you back there, that's amazing." I said.

He was right, his penis in my anus was making me so hot, our fingers were in as deep as we could go moving them together.

We were both breathing so hard. "Oh Gary, I am going to come, come with me, I want to know how this feels. Move faster, it doesn't hurt at all, help me come. His hand was on mine and my juices were flowing out on both of us.

Then I heard him moaning and saying. "Baby, baby I am going to fill you, he pushed himself in me as far as he could and held my butt tight against him. I could feel his penis pulsing inside me and he was filling me. My arms gave out my knees gave out and I went down on my belly with him on top of me still inside me. He slowly pulled himself out of me and we both groaned. Then he rolled me over on my back reached between my legs and was massaging my pussy.

He licked his fingers and said, "Can you come again, with my fingers? Let's try."

His hand went back down to my pussy rubbing her all over, his fingers went inside and he was moving them around inside me. He put his arm around me and pulled me on my side putting my leg over his so he could get his fingers further inside me.

I could feel the throbbing start and so could he. "Let it go, baby. Come all over my hand I want to feel you, you come so hard."

He was moving his hand faster and faster as he felt me coming. I put my hand over his to hold it still against me. I tighten myself against him and was moaning and groaning with such pleasure. When I relaxed my hold on his hand and his fingers came out of me we were both soaked with our come. His penis was lying against my thigh wet and sticky.

He pulled me over on top of him and said, "You have never done that before so I need to tell you something. I came a lot inside you, just like I do in your pussy. You know how it comes out of your pussy? It has to come out of your rear also, but louder. Go in the bathroom and set on the toilet. It will start coming out of you and you will see what I mean."

I went in and sat on the toilet and I could feel the come start to run out of me, but then air was coming out too and it sounded like I was farting. I could hear Gary laughing hysterically. I must have set there ten or more minutes till I thought I was done.

I cleaned myself then went back to the bedroom and said, "I have now had my first fucking enema."

I jumped on the bed bouncing him up and I farted again, we were both laughing so hard.

He pulled me down on him and said, "You are something else woman. See I told you I wouldn't hurt you, how did you like that? You have the greatest ass woman, to look at, to feel and to make love to."

"You are something else also my love, and yes I did enjoy that, I was surprised. It isn't something I would want to do everyday, but when the mood strikes or if we get bored with plain sex."

"There is no such thing as plain sex with you; everything we do is an adventure. There is nothing about you that is plain. Shall we shower? I'll wash you again."

That got me moving, I love to have a man wash me. (as you see while reliving my adventure with the bartender I remembered his name, Gary. Isn't it amazing what revisiting great sex can do for the memory?)

After our shower, we were exhausted. I asked him, "Are you as exhausted as I am?"

"Yes I am, all I want to do is wrap my arms around you and sleep, but if you wake up in the night feel free to wake me up."

We were really exhausted; we didn't wake up till the sun was coming through the window. I was curled up in Gary's arms and I could feel his penis against my butt. I scooted my butt closer to him.

He asked, "Do you want more of that?"

I quickly rolled over facing him and said, "No I do not want a fucking enema this morning, but I could use some of him," as I reached down and wrapped my fingers around his already growing penis.

He laughed and said, "I think we can arrange that. I just lay by you and he is hard."

"Kiss me, I said, "Morning breath and all, kiss me one of those great kisses."

He wrapped his arms around me my breasts pressed against his hairy chest and was licking my lips with his tongue then his tongue was in my mouth searching for mine. His kisses were soft and gentle then they became more passionate and he was kissing me harder and I could feel my pussy getting wet and his penis was so hard. He rolled over on top of me and took hold of my butt to pull me closer to him. My legs parted to let him in and I could feel him go so far inside me, he felt so damn good.

I pulled him down on me and wrapped my legs around him. "Push him inside me as far as he will go, don't move just hold me as tight against you as you can."

I could feel that familiar throbbing begin, "Hold me Gary, hold me tight," we were both moaning loudly as we both came.

When the throbbing was done and we relaxed, Gary said, "See what I mean, there is no such thing as plain sex with you, every time is like the first."

Another thing about my wild Bob, I think he could smell me. I didn't want to work nights anymore and I was offered a job at a bar in Council Bluffs working days. The Food and Beverage man at the hotel drove me crazy. He was in town almost every week and liked well-built blondes, problem was he was married and most of the time she came with him. He didn't care; he wanted me whether she was there or not. I kept refusing him telling him I didn't do married men, and not to mention he did nothing for me.

When he said, "Well your job may depend on it,"

I reached behind me to untie the apron that was over my scanty uniform. We were in his office and I saw from the big smile on his face he was expecting something much different than what I gave him. I took my apron off threw it in his face and walked out, what a rush that was.

I went to work at the bar in C.B. the following Monday. It wasn't a little bar, but not a big one either, but bigger than the bar I was used to so I was much busier. I had regulars that came in there also. There was a man that came in everyday around 10a.m. He was probably around sixty or so.

He sat at the end of the bar where I had a stool inside the bar I sat in when it wasn't busy. The second or third time he came in he said to me, "What are you doing working in a place like this?"

"Why, what do you mean? I like working here. What would you suggest?" I asked.

His response, "You are a gorgeous blonde, built great, great smile and you are setting on a goldmine!"

"What did you say? What are you talking about?" I asked.

"You heard me, you could make a fortune, you are setting on a goldmine."

After that, every time he came in he would have two of the same drink, stay for about an hour or so and when he left he would shake his head at me and say, "What a waste woman, settin' on a goldmine, yer settin' on a goldmine."

(If I would have taken his advice, I would probably be rich by now)

Late one afternoon when it was starting to get busy, guys getting off work, I wasn't paying much attention to the doors opening and closing as I would if it wasn't busy.

I heard a familiar voice say, "Can I get a beer here when you have a minute?"

It was Bob, my heart was about to pound itself out of my chest. I sat his beer in front of him and held out my hand.

"You're not going to buy me a beer?" he asked.

"I don't buy men drinks, they buy me drinks!" I snapped.

"Are we testy today?" he asked.

"No, just busy!" I snapped again.

"When do you get off?" he asked.

"Not till six, that's probably too late for you to be out!" I snapped again.

"Ouch," He said, "We are testy aren't we?" He drank his beer and left.

My heart sank as I watched him walk out the door. I didn't have time to think about him as it was getting really busy. It was a little after six when I went out the back door to go to my car and beside my car sat

Bob's truck. I stopped beside my car and just looked at him. He was out of his truck and by my side in a flash. He picked me up threw me over his shoulder, carried me to his truck, opened the door and almost threw me inside and jumped in beside me.

"What are you doing?" I asked him.

He said nothing just grabbed me pulled me onto his lap and started kissing me. I wrapped my arms around his neck and was kissing him back as tears were streaming down my cheeks. I didn't know until now how much I had missed him.

He pulled my head back and said, "Stay with me, I miss you so much please stay with me."

"I can't stay all night; my kids are home with a friend of mine that is staying with us for a while. I can call and tell her I will be home later."

I ran into the bar and called home, to tell her Bob was here. She was the one who introduced me to Joey so she knew about Bob."

When I got back to the truck Bob said, "Follow me to the Express Way motel."

We ran to the first truck parked on the lot. I was a pro at getting into these trucks now. Bob jumped up on the step then just pulled me in, a good thing I don't weigh much. In the bed of the truck we sat looking at each other, tears still running down my cheeks.

He asked me, "Why are you crying?"

"I hate myself for missing you so much, and I don't know why I am crying. What I do know is you are going to make such good love to me. First, I want you to slowly undress me and touch every part of my body, don't miss a thing."

I was setting Indian style on the bed. He moved closer to me and said, "I want to kiss you first, I need to taste your kisses, you have such great kisses."

Before I could say anything he was in front of me with my face in his hands kissing me with such love.

He pulled his face back looked into my eyes and said, "Jewelya, I love you, I don't know anything else, I don't know what to do except that I love you."

Then he was kissing me again. It had only been a little over a couple of weeks since we had seen each other but it seemed like months. We never went any longer than that, but it seemed like so much longer. As he was kissing me his hands were going through my hair. His pulled my shirt over my head, then he lay me down to pull my jeans and panties off. He sat me up and pulled me closer to him watching my reddish blonde fur ball as it got closer to him.

He reached behind me to unhook my bra and let my breasts fall free. He pulled his shirt off then was on his knees unzipping his jeans to pull them off. He pulled me close and put his legs around me, his penis lying against my belly, I could feel my pussy getting wet.

He took my face in his hands again and said, "I will make such good love to you." He pulled me around and lay down on me, pulled my knees up and my legs apart, then he slowly entered me, saying over and over, "Feel me, feel me, I want you to feel me inside you." Then he rolled over and sat me up on him.

"Oh, Bob I can feel you, I want to feel you so deep, I want to feel you come in me so deep. Don't move let me set here and come, hold me down tight on you."

He pushed my knees away from his body then took my waist holding me down on him as I was setting straight up on him arching my back to get him in as far as I could. We were throbbing so hard he was filling me so full of his fluids and mine mixed with his was running out into our pubic hair and down between his legs. We were both making such noises from our passion. I fell down on him, exhausted, I was once again in my Bob's arms.

Lying in his arms I asked him, "How do you find me?"

All he said was, "I always know where you are."

He pulled a towel out of a little alcove and was wiping me off. I took the towel out of his hand and was wiping him off and he started to grow.

He said, "See, I told you how much I miss you."

He then reached for me and I was in his arms and he was kissing me everywhere again. He lay me down, then was over me and looked into my eyes and again said, "I love you. You never say you love me, why?"

"I'm afraid to, I'm afraid to love, because when I love, I always lose." I answered.

I was remembering my other Bob. And I was beginning to feel this Bob would never be mine either, but for tonight I was in his arms and I felt safe.

It was getting to where when ever Manny would pick up the kids he was trying to get friendlier; I didn't want to be friendlier. He thought we should talk about the kids and with Christmas coming up we needed to talk. One Friday after he had picked up the kids and his we need to talk, I was finally alone, a Friday night alone.

The phone rang, it was Joey wanting me to come down to the bar, so I went, really not wanting to. When I got there he met me at the door and he had a drink waiting for me. When my drink was gone I told him I wasn't into the bar thing tonight and I was going home.

He had such a sad look on his face I said, "Come with me."

"What?" he said. "Are you serious, you want me to come home with you, to your house you never let anyone come to your house, do you?"

"No, but there is a first time for everything. I want to be home, but I don't want to be alone."

He left his drink on the bar and was by my side as I walked out the door. One of my rules, I never brought any man home with me, whether my kids were home or not. This was their home not mine, I bought it for them to grow up in. But this was different, Manny was making me crazy with his, let's talk crap. He was using my kids to get to me.

Joey walked in behind me and said, "This is a great pad, can I look around?"

I walked him through the house; the last thing I showed him was my bedroom.

"Let's watch a little T.V." I said.

We went into the front room and sat on the couch. He was beside me as soon as I sat down. He put his arms around me, pulled me close and asked, "Why did you let me come home with you."

"I guess I didn't want to go anywhere and I didn't want to be alone, is that good enough?"

"Yes, yes, it doesn't matter why, just that I am here with you. Can I make love to you in your bed?"

I took his hand and led him into the bedroom and pulled him down with me and said, "Then make love to me. In the morning I will make you breakfast, and you can make love to me again."

I pulled the covers back on the bed and started undressing him and me. I took off my shirt, then his, I unzipped his jeans, then mine, I pulled his jeans and shorts down and off over his feet, then mine. I still had my bra on.

I took his hands and put them around me to unhook my bra, when my breasts were free he sucked in his breath and said, "I want to suck on them and everything else on you."

I put my arms around his waist and pulled him down on my bed. "Don't talk about it do it." I said

Joey was such a lover that night, he took my breasts into his mouth and gently made my nipples rigid, then put his mouth on my pussy till it was so wet.

I pulled him up to me and said, "I want you to make love to me all night, lay on top of me and make love to me, slowly make love to me. Don't come too soon, I want you inside me all night."

He was on top of me then pulled my knees up and my legs apart and was inside me. He lay on me with his face in my neck kissing my neck. I could feel his penis inside me growing and I was so happy.

He started moving in and out of me slowly. "Don't come," I said. "I just want you to slowly move in and out of me, that feels so good I don't want to come too soon."

"If I do come, I can start again and I can start you again too." He said.

He was being so gentle and slow, then I felt that throbbing inside me as he was slowly pulling himself in and out of me. I wrapped my legs around him and he pulled my butt up to him, I couldn't stop and neither could he. Then all I wanted him to do was hold me, I had such a need of being held, and he held me close, and I felt safe again.

(When I started this book, I said I wanted to figure me out, and that I should hate sex because of the things that has happened to me. As you can see, it is quite the opposite. It is kind-a like the hair of the dog. When you have a really bad hangover, you drink what ever you had the night before, voila' hangover all gone. Is that what I am doing? Getting rid of a sex hangover? Even sometimes I want the sex to hurt, does that stem from the violence and pain I had experienced during sex when I was very young? Someone once said, "Any woman worth her salt enjoys a little pain." Must have been a man that said that, is it the same with men? Any man worth his salt enjoys a little pain? Duh, not even. If men had the babies, the population would stop growing because after the first baby, he would have no more.)

When Manny brought the kids home on Sunday he was giving me shit about my working at a bar. I told him it was none of his business. He kept at me about how much he missed me and how the kids needed both of us. "Self," I said, "Don't let him do this."

The following Friday Scarlet was shooting pool at the bar where Gary (my bartender) tended bar, so I thought I might as well go watch her. When I drove in the parking lot I saw Scarlet's car. I thought I really don't want to go with Gary tonight so I would tell her when I got in there to say she wanted me to go somewhere with her. When I got out of my car I thought I saw a familiar truck. I thought, that is crazy, Bob knows nothing about this place and he is the only one that would look for me. I started to walk toward the bar and that familiar truck pulled up beside me, Bob. He jumped out of his truck, wrapped his arms around my waist and lifted me into his truck.

"What are you doing?" I asked him. "How do you always find me?"

"I told you I always know where you are."

"If you always need to know where I am, then why don't you always want to be with me?"

"I always want to be with you, but you know why I can't."

"I know what you tell me, but if you really wanted to be with me all the time, you would be. Someday, you are going to lose me, then I hope that money keeps you company."

He pulled me close and said, "I do love you, please go with me. Stay with me tonight, I will hold you close all night."

How could I say no, he was my Bob, my wild Bob? He excited me, he set me on fire, and what woman wouldn't want a man that took the time to look for her, and always know where she was. Is that love or lust? Right now I don't know and I don't care, all I know is I wanted him as much as he wanted me.

We went to our favorite motel; the one he said should send him a Christmas card. The motel where he not only made me pay for the room, but go in and get the room because I told him all he wanted me for was sex. The motel where we made love and showered for nine hours. The motel where we would hide from Callie and Ron so we could be alone. We made such love to each other; it was like the first time we made love. There wasn't a part of each other's bodies we missed. Neither of us knew this would be the last time we would make love.

Chapter Six

MANNY II
What Was I Thinking?

It was getting close to Christmas and Manny kept pressuring me to go with him to talk about what we would do for Christmas for the kids. He kept asking me to go have a drink with him to talk about Christmas. I finally gave in and said I would go. "Oh crap, Jewelya what have you done? You know Manny is the master manipulator."

When Manny picked me up I told him this was not a date we were just going to talk about Christmas for the kids. Of course the kids were excited that mom and dad were going out. They had no idea what our marriage had been like, great for him lousy for me. I always felt that that was something between Manny and me and had nothing to do with our children. He took me to the same little bar he had taken me to when we first met. He played the song on the jukebox he always played, Ray Price's, Lay your Head Upon My Pillow; he was working it Jewelya, look out.

After we left the bar we went for a ride and also ended up parked at one of the places we went when we first met. He slid over in the seat by me and put his arm around me.

I pulled away from him, but he held on to me saying, "Jewelya, I love you I miss you and the kids. You know they want me to come home. It would be so much better, I will change it will only be you. And I would never hit you again; I have learned what is important to me.

He took my head and pulled me into a kiss. He was unbuttoning my shirt telling me he wanted to make love to me. He pulled my jeans and panties down then unhooked my bra. One thing Manny was never big on was my breasts, but tonight he was. He was actually holding them and running his tongue across them. He pulled me down in the seat and was over me telling me how he had missed making love to me. By the time the night was over he had me right back in that web. STUPID!!! is still written across my forehead.

(I have a hard time writing about this part of my life as I know now it was a very big mistake for me. I always thought it was good for the kids, but by not letting them know what their father was like, in time he was able to manipulate them also. Manny did so many things to me in the twenty-odd years we were together I could fill a book with them, but he is not worth my time. We did have some good times together, but not nearly enough good times to forget the bad times.)

He had been back a little over a week, it was New Year's Eve and we were to go out and it was getting later and later. When the phone rang and there was a strange voice on the other end telling me if I was waiting for Manny to come home it might be a while as he was at the bar across the street from his work, where he had taken me, dancing with his girlfriend. The first time in my life I checked on a man, they aren't worth your time ladies, but this time I wanted him to know I had seen him not just someone calling.

I drove over to the bar; he and his girlfriend were dancing. Others in the bar saw me and knew why I was there and just watched me walk across the floor. I walked up behind Manny and tapped him on the shoulder and as he turned his head around I punched him in the nose as she ran for cover then I walked out. He ran after me grabbed my coat sleeve and I wiggled out of my coat and went home. He came right home saying he had just gone to tell her he would not be seeing her anymore.

That was just the beginning of his girlfriends, nothing had changed. There goes my life, again.

One day something happened I knew would before long, when I answered the phone I heard that familiar voice, Bob, Charlie Brown. He wanted to see me and I had to tell him I could no longer see him.

He pleaded with me not to do it. "What will I do without you?"

I told him, "Bob I really didn't have you, you didn't really have me. I had you when it was convenient for you. I know you love me, but not enough to make me your life. I love you too, but I have to do what I think is right for my children. If I could have you in my bed everyday, not once in a while I would never have taken Manny back."

"I can work on that," He said. "In time we can be together all the time."

"How long have you been telling me that Bob? You will always be my love; a part of me will always be yours." I could feel the tears rolling down my cheeks.

He told me he would respect my decision even if he thought it was the wrong one.

He said, "I love you" then hung up.

Bob called me one more time. When I answered and heard his voice my heart was about to explode.

He said, "I know I told you I respected your wishes, but I had to call one more time, I want you to hear something; he put the phone down by the jukebox and played "The Way We Were" by Barbara Streisand the song we always played when we were out together. When the song ended, he hung the phone up and I cried and cried and cried. I have now said goodbye to my two Bobs, my sweet Bob that showed me I was worth loving and my wild Bob who made my life so exciting and I still miss them. Sometimes at night I close my eyes and I can still feel them.

Once in a while Manny would have me meet him at the bar with his friends from work. I had already told Joey I had taken Manny back he also though it was a bad idea, but respected my wishes. Manny knew about Joey, but didn't know this was the bar we went to. One night when we went into the bar and Joey was there. When we walked past Joey, Joey said hi to both of us, I responded of course Manny didn't. We had no more than sat down and Manny took my arm and said we were leaving. As we left we also walked past Joey and he again said good night, I responded, again Manny didn't. When we were out the door I heard the door open behind us. When we looked back Joey was behind us.

He addressed Manny and said, "Manny, if you have a problem with me, then you come to me, not Jewelya. You leave her alone or I will come to you, you don't deserve her."

Manny never said a word till we were home, then he told me to tell my boyfriend to stay away from us.

I told him, "You had a great opportunity to tell him yourself, but you didn't. That's what you get for thinking no other man would want me, you were so wrong, but you already knew that didn't you."

Joey called a few days later to see how I was and if Manny had said anything to me about our encounter at the bar. I lied and said he didn't mention it. I don't think he believed me, but Joey would not question me. I was very lucky with the men I had had my affairs with; they were all very loving and gentle with me, and would do nothing to hurt me.

Joey said, "I was in heaven when you decided to go out with me. Then you let me make love to you in your bed, if you ever need me you know where I am."

"I know Joey, I enjoyed every minute I had with you also, and you will always be with me. (as you can see, he is.)

I tried to fight for my marriage two more times; I mean literally fight for it. I knew Manny was still seeing his old girlfriend. At home I said nothing, as I said this had nothing to do with my children. I had made a commitment to my children when I let Manny come back, I would stick to it as long as I could.

We went to another bar that was owned by an old friend of my dad's, Joe. Joe's also had food and when Manny and I were divorced he would call me at night and tell me he had chicken or what ever left if I wanted to stop and I could have it for the kids, or he would drop it off at the house.

Joe wanted to be my sugar daddy; he always told me if I ever wanted to live the way I should live just to let him know, so I was pretty special to Joe. He knew what Manny did and one night asked me how long I was going to let this girl come into the bar and try to intimidate me. She doesn't intimidate me, but there isn't much I can do about it.

He said, "Kick her ass."

"In here?" I asked.

"Yes, "he said, "I want to see it."

Joe's had two levels; Manny and I were on the second level. When the group came in from Manny's work they set just below us with about three tables together. She would set at the end of the tables where she could see both of us and make eyes at Manny and stare at me. Before anyone realized what I was doing, except Joe as he was expecting it, I had climbed over the railing and was walking down the middle of the tables, drinks and bodies going everywhere. When she saw me heading her way she was going out the door. I grabbed a handful of hair to stop her then threw her down on the curb and was beating her ass rubbing her face into the curb. I felt hands pull me off her, when I turned around it was Manny, so I punched him in the nose, yelling at him that I wasn't doing it to fight for him, but to let her know that every time she came where I was I was going to whip her ass. Joe gave me thumbs up, and then I went home.

The other time was at another bar and I ran her and her girlfriend out and they jumped in their car. I was pounding on the window telling her if I saw her anywhere I was going to whip her ass and her friend's also. I told them both to get out I would kick both of their asses now. I had caused quite a stir in the bar and they had followed me out and were calling me tiger. Manny yelled at me that I had embarrassed him.

"Embarrass you, you asshole." I yelled at him, "How do you think I feel having your girlfriend follow us around. We went to one of your friend's house and she shows up there. I am done, she can have you I don't want you anymore. I will do what I have to do for my children, but as your mom tells you some day it will be my turn to dance again and this time my next dance won't end."

Sex between Manny and I had never been riveting to me, it was to him. When we got back together and he had made a short try at my breasts, but when I suggested doing other things he was livid.

He asked, "What the hell were you doing with those men you were with."

"Having a great time." I snapped.

"Well, if you were having so much fun why did you have me come back."

"If you remember right it wasn't my idea for you to come back, and if you wouldn't have come back, I would still be having fun and feel free to leave again anytime you get the notion."

My older boys were getting at the age where they would be moving out soon, but we still had our penny anti-poker parties on Friday nights. One Friday night my oldest said, "Mom, I want to tell you something."

"Yah honey, what?" I said.

"Well now that I have a fulltime job and eighteen I am going to see about getting my own apartment." The whole table went silent for a few seconds then the game continued. After that hand I said, "Deal me out this hand I have to use the restroom." I went into the bathroom, sat down on the toilet and was silently crying. My little boy was telling me he was moving out. The same little boy that I had to pry his fingers off the car door handle because he didn't want to go to school because when he got home his mommy would not be there.

There was a soft knock on the door and Big said, "Mom, are you okay? It will be a while before I move, please come out."

I wiped my eyes and threw some cold water on my face and opened the door.

Big hugged me and said, "It will be a while mom, I haven't even started looking yet."

My baby didn't move out until he was almost twenty-one and it was because he got married.

Gene, my second son, at seventeen decided he wanted to enlist in the Navy. His counselor at school said he was bored with school and thought it would be good for him. Gene was a very intelligent boy, but didn't always make the right choices and the Navy was one of his bad choices as he hated it. He went AWOL twice, and was almost thrown into the brig, but his mom talked the very large MP's into letting her get him to turn himself in to Fort Omaha.

I may have done the right thing for them but not for me. That's what moms do.

In 1978 I went back to school, which Manny was totally against, but I had my own income so I got a student loan on my own. I went to school days and Manny worked nights so I barely saw him.

When I graduated from business college I got a very good paying job and opened my own checking account. He was furious as he had always controlled me and my money, not anymore. Each check I had a bond taken out to save for my escape.

Manny continued doing as he pleased which pleased me, then I didn't have to deal with him. I never argued with him about anything, because I didn't care. When he left I hoped he wouldn't come back, but he had it made here why would he not come back. When Manny felt his empire crumbling he decided to work days because that was what I had wanted for years.

I told him, "Don't do it for me, I don't care anymore. I'd rather you stay on nights."

All the years I was with Manny I was never his wife I was his possession, he thought he owned me, no one is owned by another person.

Manny never did hit me again as he promised, but there is all kinds of abuse. As he thought he owned me I couldn't have any friends. He had all but outlawed me seeing Scarlet. One night he came home from the bar furious. Scarlet had come into Joe's bar, and if I knew Joe so did Scarlet and she knew how Joe felt about me. Manny was in there setting with some girl, which he said later was just a girl from work, sure she was. Scarlet plopped herself on his lap and asked the girl, do you know Jewelya?

The girl asked, "Who's Jewelya?"

"Jewelya, his wife you dumb ass." Scarlet said and went up to the bar to talk to Joe.

Manny told me to tell my red-headed girlfriend to stay the hell away from him.

I told him, "Tell her yourself or are you to chicken shit, like you were with Joey?"

When I went to work, Manny went on days and he felt his hold on me slipping away, he did what Carl did, he became obsessed with me and wanted to know every move I made. He always wanted to know where I was before, but it was different now, but I didn't care what he wanted, I was going to do as I pleased. I wasn't to go out for lunch; I was to brown bag it. If I had to go to the store or whatever after work I was to call him to get his permission. If I didn't, he would be waiting for me at the back door. He didn't even want me to see my sister, Callie, said she was a bad influence.

Scarlet and I started meeting once a week for lunch, sometimes we didn't make it back from lunch. I would get home after he did and he would be livid.

Scarlet and I loved to screw with people. One day after our liquid lunch, we left the restaurant with Scarlet following me. At the stop light on tenth street in the Old Market Scarlet ran into the back of my car. I jumped out of my car running back to her car cursing at her, shaking my fist at her telling her I was going to kick her ass for running into my car.

She flew out of her car running toward me shaking her fist at me, when we met we wrapped our arms around each other, hugged and kissed on the lips then jumped back in our cars and drove off. I think everyone was disappointed as they thought they were going to see a cat fight. We still laugh about that one.

I am not going to spend much more time on this part of my life, but this is where the bus driver comes in. When I was in a relationship with someone, it didn't matter what they did, I didn't mess around. We still went over to Janelle and Kyle's, the guard at Manny's work. They had a friend that came to their house sometimes. I guess he had dated their niece at some point; hence the bus driver. He started coming over more and more and would set with Joan and me instead of the guys. Again, Manny tells me he doesn't like the bus driver spending so much time with the girls and not out in the kitchen with the guys.

I told him, "If you don't want him around me tell him not me." Ha, ha, like that was ever going to happen.

I asked him, "What are you concerned about? You always said no other man would want me. We both know better than that, you have always known better than that. It just took me a long time to know that."

Then the bus driver asked me out. Janelle was always trying to talk me into going out with him. I told him I was married and didn't do that.

I was going to school part time on Saturday morning from 8a.m. till noon. A friend of mine wanted me to meet her across from her work after school. She was already there when I got there. When I sat down at the bar beside her, someone came up and set beside me, it was Donny, the bus driver.

"What are you doing here?" I asked him.

"The bus terminal is down the street. I just came in from a trip and I remembered you were going to be here so thought I'd join you. Is that okay." He asked.

He was good looking, blonde, blue eyes, medium build. Clean shaven except for a very thick well kept mustache, and goatee.

I said, "I don't care if Dee doesn't and you're buying not being."

Dee shrugged and said, "Don't matter to me. I'll have a beer."

We sat there for several hours talking and laughing at every thing we said.

Donny asked me, "Why won't you go out with me?"

Dee asked, "Yah, Jewelya why don't you go out with him?"

"Have you both forgotten I am married?" I asked.

"Manny is married too, but that doesn't stop him. Leo is married that doesn't stop him and I am married to Leo and that doesn't stop me, I am meeting Jay before long. I finally got tired of waiting for Leo to come home. Now I don't care." She slurred.

"I will have my day someday." I said. Well, I tried to do the right thing.

Donny asked, "Do you dance?"

"I love to dance, but I have to get home." I answered.

"Go dancing with me, I bet you are a good dancer, aren't you?"

"Yes, as a matter of fact I am a very good dancer. I can dance to anything you can." I answered.

I was about to do the same thing Manny had been doing to me. In my mind I was making all kinds of excuses, but it was still wrong. My head was saying don't do this the rest of me saying, go. We went dancing and he was a good dancer and so was I.

During a slow dance Donny said, "You really are a good dancer."

He pulled me closer took my chin and pulled my face up to his, then he was kissing me. His mustache felt so good on my lips. I hadn't realized how much I had missed this feel of a man. It had been maybe six years since my lovers and my body was aching. Manny was my husband, but definitely not my lover.

He pulled my head back and said, "Will you follow me home? It isn't like we've never met. You aren't happy with Manny, he isn't good to you. How he could have all those girlfriends when he has you at home makes no sense."

With his body against me I could feel him, and my body was on fire. I was no longer in control, my body and desires were. I didn't say anything just nodded my head. He took hold of my hand and led me out the door. Outside the door he took me in his arms, lifted me up to him and was kissing me, what a kiss.

Someone drove by and yelled, "Get a room."

Donny took me to my car and I followed him home. He lived with his dad, but he had his own door so he came and went without anyone noticing. When we were in his room he just stood looking at me. It had been so long since I had been in this position I wasn't sure what to do.

He broke the silence with, "What can I do? I want to do a lot."

"You do what ever you want to, if I don't like it I will stop you." I had already made the decision to do this, why stop now. My mind was telling me to stop, but my body was now in control.

"Can I undress you?" he asked.

"Like I said, you do what you want, don't ask. I will stop you if I don't like it."

He walked over to me and was slowly unbuttoning my blouse he pulled it off then was removing my jeans and panties. He reached behind me to unhook my bra and released my breasts.

He took a step back and was staring at me, then said, "Does Manny look at all of this very often?"

"No, he doesn't pay much attention to anything except getting on top and getting his rocks off then it is over. I often wonder if he is like that with his girlfriends. He has never really paid much attention to my body."

"To have a body like this around all the time and pay no attention to it is crazy. I would never leave you alone; my hands would be all over you as often as I could."

"Well, this body is here for you take advantage of while you have the chance."

He lay me down on his bed and stood in front of me while he undressed. He had blonde hair on his chest, lots of it. Then he took his jeans and shorts off and stood naked in front of me his penis wasn't huge, but it was getting there. He lay down beside me and pulled me into his arms and started kissing me and asked, "Can I kiss you all over?"

My body and I were remembering what we hadn't had in a long, long time and I said back to him, "I don't want you to miss anything."

He put his head between my breasts and was kissing them back and forth then his tongue was trailing down to my belly button and kept going. I spread my legs apart to let him know to keep going, by now I was squirming my hips around and I was so wet. He put his mouth over my pussy rolling his tongue everywhere then I felt his tongue go inside, now I was moaning and holding his head running my fingers through his hair. I could feel that old familiar feeling that I hadn't felt in so long. I held onto his head and was moaning, "Don't stop, please don't stop, do you feel that?" I lifted my hips up to him as far as I could and he was holding my butt up to him.

When that old feeling slowed he was over me, "Can I still make love to you. I felt you come. Can you do it again?"

I pulled him down to me and whispered to him, "Make love to me I want to feel you come inside me I will come again when I feel you. Don't come to soon I want to feel you inside me."

He lowered himself down on me I wrapped my legs around him as he slid inside me. "Go as far as you can. I will tell you if it hurts." He was slowly pulling himself in and out of me. Damn did he feel good.

"Can I go faster? Are you ready can you come with me?"

"Go faster and harder and I will come with you, just don't stop. He was moving faster and going deeper inside me with each push. I could feel his penis start that wonderful pulsing like his heart was beating inside me. We were both moaning and groaning as our fluids mixed and was running out of me.

When our throbbing stopped he relaxed on top of me still holding me and kissing me "I knew making love to you would be great, but that was more than great. I would never be able to get enough of you if you were mine."

"It has been a long time since I have been made love to like that. Manny is not a great lover, but he is my husband and I really need to get home, I am in deep shit."

"When can I see you again? You can't do this to me and not see me again. I want more of you."

"I'm sorry," I said, "I should never have let this happened. This is what Manny does, not me and it won't happen again while I am married to him."

Of course, when I got home I was in deep shit, but I did my best to ignore him. I sat on the picnic table in the back yard while he was yelling at me telling me what a terrible wife and mother I was. I said nothing back as I agreed with him, at that point I was a terrible wife and mother. He didn't know what I had really done that night, but I did. Why do I have a guilty conscience and he doesn't?

(Going back to the first part of my book, just because a man thinks it is okay to do it; it is not okay for a man or a woman to do it. Adultery is wrong for him and/or her.)

Donny would call me or go to Kyle and Janelle's when Manny and I were there. Manny would yell at me later when Donny came to their house. I would tell him, if you are worried about him tell him not me. I can't help it if men are attracted to me, you always said no other man, but you would want me, remember?

At one time I believed that myself, but I now know it is quite the opposite.

Chapter Seven

Free Again

I finally had had all I could stand when it was my birthday and Manny asked me what I wanted to do for my birthday.

"Why are you asking me? We will do exactly what you want to do not me." I responded

The Saturday after my birthday, which was my sister's birthday, we went to Joe's for a drink, then we went to a popular fish restaurant in South Omaha. When we left the restaurant Manny said one of his friends he worked with was having a party and had invited us. When we went into the basement of their house I was again a ten year old girl. My birth-person had told me on my tenth birthday I was having a birthday party with the girl down the street whose birthday was the same as mine. When we arrived at her house everything there was for her, no one even knew it was my birthday, I ran home in tears. I should have know better, my birth person had never really acknowledged my birthday, why should she now, just wishful thinking on my part. I was again ten years old at someone else's birthday party and know one there knew it was my birthday. So again I ran home, or should I say drove home in tears and left Manny there to fend for himself. When he came home he was furious with me and told me I had embarrassed him in front of his friends and I needed to start behaving like a wife. THAT WAS THAT!!!

I grabbed my purse and my keys and said, "I am leaving and I am not coming back except to get my things and my kids"

"You are not going to take the car."

"Then I will take the truck."

"You are not taking the truck either."

"Then I am fucking walking as I can no longer take this from you." And I walked out.

The next day I came for my kids and some things for us.

As I was leaving Manny told me, "You will pay for this, someday you will pay for this, women don't leave me I leave them." Manny wanted to blame Donny for my leaving, but as I told him the only man that caused me to leave Manny was Manny.

Manny was like my mother, I loved him probably more than any man I was ever with, but he couldn't give that love back. It was like he was also looking for something that didn't exist. He wanted to control me not love me. After we had sex he would turn over and go to sleep he never held me after the loving. Most of the time he didn't even kiss me just fuck me then go to sleep. I felt like he should slip a fifty dollar bill under my pillow. In all the years we were together sex was great for him, but lousy for me. That wonderful feeling I had become accustomed to with my lovers, was non existent for me with Manny.

He has spent the last thirty plus years getting even, even though he has been remarried for twenty-seven years, he has finally made me pay for the mistakes he made. He has manipulated my children the way he did me. I did not leave Manny for Donny, but that one night with Donny was like the time I had with my first Bob, I am worth a lot more than what Manny was giving me, not just in bed, but in life.

When my last son, James was born I knew he was different and that he would need more attention from me than the others.

When James and I talked about him being gay he had said, "I know mom, you have always wanted me to have a wife and children and living in a house with a white picket fence around it."

"No James, what I want for you is what ever you want for you. The white picket fence, that was what I wanted for me."

James also told me, "Mom, I don't think you have ever gotten over what dad did to you." I told him he was wrong that I was over what his dad had done to me the day I walked out, but maybe, just maybe James was right.

I thought at one time I wanted to spend the rest of my life with Manny, because he had given me the thing I wanted most, my children. I wanted that white picket fence with a daddy that came home to be with his family.

The only thing I got from Manny was my children and I thank him for that. His other women were more important to him than his family. I stayed as long as I could.

Again, I am on my own, but I believe I have always been on my own, except for Scarlet, of course. I have now had three husbands and I took care of two of them instead of them taking care of me. My birth-person did not give the first one a chance to be my husband; with him maybe I would have had that white picket fence, with the daddy that came home to his family.

I have now had another taste of being held by a loving and sexy man and feeling safe in his arms. I had felt physically safe when I was with Manny in our first marriage until he showed me different, but in our second marriage I never felt physically nor emotionally safe with him. Looking back, I do believe Manny was more abusive to me than Carl, black and blue heals, emotional black and blue does not. The emotional black and blue I received from my birth person and Manny has never made it to the back side of my brain as the physical abuse I received from Carl has. The pain of the beating from Carl has left me, the pain of the mental abuse from them all is still there I have to fight it everyday.

Where do I go from here? Anywhere and everywhere I can and I doubt if I go it alone. Scarlet, here we go again.

Again, come with me, follow me through the next twenty or so years of my life, it only gets better, anyway I think it just gets better, I guess it depends on what you would consider better, you judge for yourself.

How many of you women out there are reading this and saying to yourself, "This is me, this is about me. Maybe not word for word, but this is me." We women are masters at keeping secrets, about ourselves. This is how we maintain our sanity.

Since I started writing this book I look at women I see just walking down the street or in a mall or putting gas in their car, and ask, "What are the secrets you are keeping about yourselves that makes is easier to for you to survive?"

BLONDE ROSE III

And The Men Who Continue To Wander Through My Life

Free Again

Written By

Jewelya

Blonde Rose III is dedicated to me.
Knowing how I survive, but still not knowing why I survive.

CHAPTERS

Chapter One

Free Again

A fter finally walking out on Manny, again, and vowing not to do that again, I moved with three of my children into a duplex as Manny wouldn't move out. He says he was no longer cheating, but two weeks after I moved out he moved his young girlfriend into my house where our oldest son stayed with his dad. It took me a year to get a divorce as he was trying to make me pay. My attorney wanted my children in court as they could testify that I was always home with them not running around, I refused, this is between Manny and me, not my children.

I started discreetly seeing Donny, but as he was a bus driver he was out of town a lot. My older boys were on their own now and the others were gone a lot with their friends and with Manny. I worked two jobs to keep the kids and me going as Manny refused to pay me any child support even though he had been ordered to by the courts.

I was a supervisor at a saving and loan during the day and worked in the watch department of an upscale department store across the street. I had been taking care of myself and my children for a very long time, and this was no different.

Chapter Two

Alderman's Bar

I started shooting pool again with Scarlet and picked up where I left off, I guess it is like riding a bicycle, once you know how, you never forget.

One night she said, "I think you are getting good enough to shoot pool on our league. We are just starting up again so I want you to come with me tonight to the bar I shoot pool for. By the way, there isn't going to be any more Manny is there?"

"Good God no. I have had as much of him as I can stand."

I had never suggested Manny go to Alderman's with me as he would think he was to good for it. The real reason was it was my bar, my friends and there was no way he was going to associate with my friends. He wanted me under his thumb, to do what I was told, he would lose that hold eventually if he went with me, but they would not have liked Manny because they would have seen right through him

Scarlet said, "Your know this bar, we have been coming here for a long time. You haven't been here for some time, too wrapped up in Manny and doing everything he said to do. Don't ever do that again."

I knew what bar she was talking about when we turned on to Leavenworth. It had been a long time since I had been here, but this is one bar that once you are here you never forget it.

This bar, most of it's patrons called; "Our Cheers."

When I walked back into this bar, I knew this was where I would always come back to, this was always going to be my bar, Alderman's Bar.

When I first divorced Manny in the early seventies, Scarlet and I had come in here a few times, but I had so much living to do I didn't make it in as much as Scarlet.

Now, I need to dig deep into my memory bank as we had been coming here since we were seventeen or eighteen years old, but my memory bank is very vivid as you have probably noticed by now. You are thinking how did you do that, drinking age was twenty-one. You are right, but back then if you didn't drink, they didn't pay much attention to you and Scarlet nor I drank.

We went in with our idiot husbands and were ordered to set in a corner booth, anyway I was ordered Scarlet would not be ordered by anyone, but she always sat with me and we drank our sodas.

There were many bars on Leavenworth at that time, more so than now and when you went to one of these bars the name was not usually mentioned just we are going to the avenue. That meant you were going to one of the bars on Leavenworth, and you would make up your mind which one when you got there as it was usually more than one bar you would go to in one night. This would have been in the middle to late fifties, early sixties.

When Alderman's first came into being in 1937, it was little more than a chicken coupe with a pop-bellied stove in the back room for heat, a dirt floor and they sold beer in buckets. It's name has always been Alderman's Bar. There hangs a poster in the bar that reads; "Selling Liquid Stupid Since 1937."

Back then, Alderman's had sat on the front of the lot along Leavenworth. Eventually it was moved to the back of the lot, made larger and a cement floor poured.

I don't remember how Alderman's looked back then, Scarlet does as she and Mr. Alderman's daughter had been friends since they were teenagers.

Now, the bar sets facing south with a door on each end with beer posters and windows along about two-thirds of the south wall and Elvis pictures and posters of his concerts and records at the end of the windows to the end of the west wall. The long bar sets along the north wall with my favorite thing on the west end of the bar; two pool tables and a dart board, not my favorite thing, in the southwest corner. There is a popcorn popper at the west end of the bar always full of popcorn and there is always a smiling face behind the bar.

Behind the bar along with the sign, "Selling Liquid Stupid Since 1937," are numerous signs and posters that always bring smiles and sometimes loud laughter.

Where Alderman's is located is not considered the best neighborhood, but I feel as safe in Alderman's as I do in a bar in the best area, maybe safer as those inside this bar cares more about me.

Scarlet and I didn't go to the bar with our idiot husbands to often, but when we did there was always a fight. Most nights when we were not with them they got into a fight. Carl was different than most wife beater, most wife beaters are afraid of other men that is usually why they beat their wives or girlfriends. Not Carl, I don't think he was afraid of the devil himself, he is probably arguing right now with the devil as to who is in charge. No matter who or how big the guy was, if Carl wanted to punch him he punched him.

The night that sticks out in my mind did not happen at Alderman's, but across the street from Alderman's. Our idiots were playing pool and Scarlet and me were setting in our booth talking when all hell broke loose. Carl broke a pool stick on someone and they in return came back with a pool stick and broke it over Carl's shoulder, the war was on, but to our surprise Carl went out the door shouting he was going to get his grandfather's shotgun and come back and kill everyone in the bar. Of course all of us thought he was just blowing off smoke, but when we got outside he was in the car driving down Leavenworth. We didn't live to far from the bar so we figured he would be right back after us when he realized how stupid he was being. But, what we failed to remember was, Carl did not think anything he did was stupid. We saw the car coming back up Leavenworth and stop in the middle of the street. He got out of the car with the shotgun, the same shotgun a few years later he would use to blow a large hole in his stomach while I was on the phone with him and my name, Jewelya, was the last thing he ever said.

He was waving the shotgun in the air shouting as loud as he could that he was going to kill everyone in the bar. All the patrons in the bar hit the floor except for one old drunk setting at the end of the bar, he was oblivious of what was going on around him. I ran over to Carl trying to get the gun away from him but he just knocked me down. I was setting in the middle of Leavenworth with my arms wrapped around Carl's leg screaming at him to put the gun down, but that was not going to happen.

Cars coming down Leavenworth would see Carl and they would disappear down into the seat. Cars coming up behind Carl would make a u-turn and head the other way.

Scarlet's husband Glenn came up behind Carl and grabbed him with one arm around the neck and grabbed the gun with the other hand. Glenn was much bigger than Carl so there was no contest to who would win this one, but Carl was fighting him. Glenn was yelling at Scarlet to get in and drive and for me go get in front with Scarlet as he threw Carl into the back seat.

"Get off Leavenworth, go down to the Old Market and drive through slowly, don't go home yet." Glenn told Scarlet. We could hear the police sirens heading toward the bar. Carl was screaming and cursing all of us at the top of his lungs.

Glenn screamed back, "We could have left your ass there, but then they would have come after us, now shut the fuck up before I knock you out." Carl shut up.

Through all of this, the drunk on the bar stool never moved.

We drove around the Old Market a time or two then ventured toward home. For weeks, every time the phone would ring or there was a knock on the door or a strange car drove by, my heart would skip a beat. On the other hand, Carl could have cared less, I don't think anything bothered him, except me.

We found out later the reason he didn't shoot the gun was he was so drunk he couldn't get the safety off. He remembered it all, the only thing he was sorry for was he couldn't get the safety off so he could shoot all those sons-a-bitches in the bar. Carl very seldom had blackouts, he remembered everything he did and was never sorry for anything, except for sometimes when he beat me. He would say he was sorry and would never do it again, but there were other times he said I got what I asked for and there was always another beating and another I'm sorry, a vicious cycle of beatings and I'm sorry that finally ended November, 1962 with that same shotgun, this time he got the safety off.

Mr. Alderman owned the bar at that time and when he decided to retire his daughter, Nickie, took it over. She had spent so much time there she moved right in as the new owner of "Our Cheers."

At Christmas there was Santa and his elves with a stocking for each child, I have a picture of me setting on Santa's lap, for Halloween she had a bus that took the kids to haunted houses and a treat for each child. Once a year at football season she chartered a bus to take everyone that wanted to go to a Husker football game with tubs of ice stuffed with beer in the isles. There was always something going on at Alderman's.

Again, I was returning to Alderman's. In this bar I would find several of my lovers, I guess maybe they found me. Most of the time I didn't knowingly go in to find a lover it just happened, other times, that is exactly what I was doing and usually I got what I wanted. Some were good lovers some not so good, but that was okay they were only stepping stones to get me from one place I didn't want to be to another place I didn't want to be either, they just made the trip more fun.

We walked into Alderman's and it seemed like only yesterday I was here when in actuality it had been almost seven years. We sat at the bar and she introduced me to the bartender, Lee. I stuck my hand out and Lee shook my hand.

"Jewelya" Lee said. "So you are Jewelya, we have heard a lot about you its good to finally meet you. I hope to see a lot more of you." As his eyes were going up and down my body

Scarlet said, "Don't be surprised at anything Lee says or does. Give us a couple of glasses of beer Lee."

We sat there drinking our beers and talking so I wasn't paying much attention to what Lee was doing as he was walking back and forth behind the bar. I picked up my glass to take a drink when I heard a clink then Scarlet and Lee were laughing hysterically.

"What?" I asked.

Scarlet said, "Look in your glass." As she was waving her finger in the direction of my glass.

I looked in my glass and screamed as I saw an eyeball in the bottom of my glass. I almost threw my glass down as Scarlet and Lee were still laughing hysterically.

"What the hell is in my glass, is that a real eyeball."

"Well, yes and no, it is real but it isn't real, look at Lee." Scarlet said.

When I looked at Lee he had one eye the other was just a socket, it was his glass eye.

"Funny, real funny you assholes. Are you having fun. Is this really your eye?"

Lee picked up my glass and dumped beer and eye into his hand, then put the eye under the water and stuck it back into his socket. I thought I was going to barf.

Scarlet was laughing so hard she was crying. "Lee does that to everyone that comes in here, that is how we know if you are a true Alderman patron. You didn't throw it at him or leave, but I didn't think you would."

Lee and I would become great friends and lovers every once in a while. Lee was one man I could do both with, be a good friend and an occasional lover.

Scarlet and me shared a lot of things, but never our men. Except maybe Lee, Scarlet says no, Lee says yes. I believe Lee, sorry Scarlet, but I think she had the same relationship with Lee as I had, great friend and occasional lover. Lee would have our backs anytime we needed him, but he would also have our fronts and everything else on our bodies when we were in need also.

Scarlet rode a lavender 1200 Harley Davidson Dresser motorcycle that we rode all over. That Harley sat in the parking lot of Alderman's many times while we shot pool drank beer and smoked Anthony & Cleopatra cigars. The men loved us, even when we beat them at pool, and some of the women hated us. Scarlet and I were in Alderman's one night when one of the women who was a regular at the bar became angry with Scarlet for what ever reason and took her gum out of her mouth and dropped it in our pitcher of beer.

Scarlet calmly reached in the pitcher of beer pulled the wad of gum out and as she stuck the wad of gum securely in the girl's hair she said, "Here, I think you dropped this."

The girl ran out of the bar, the bartender brought us another pitcher of beer and we continued doing what we were doing. All was made up later, no one ever stayed mad for long at Alderman's.

There were relationships found and relationships lost. There were one-night stands for many, but some of those one-night stands turned into relationships that lasted many years. My thought on those lasting relationship found in Alderman's was; they continued coming into Alderman's together where they had the same friends who loved each of them equally.

Scarlet met her second husband, Perry, in Alderman's, I can't say it was one of those lasting relationships, but they brought two beautiful redheaded daughters into this world. Scarlet and Perry were redheads so what else would their daughters be, but redheads.

Scarlet and Perry's marriage didn't last long, but the friendship did. They were friends until his death. As I said before, when you were a patron of Alderman's you had family and when you had children they were also a part of that family.

Perry had always said that when he died he didn't want any fanfare, just his children and friends together to have a last beer to send him off. Perry died in December, 1991, a freezing December, but we didn't care we all went to his funeral and the gravesite then to Alderman's. Nickie set a pitcher of beer and glasses on each table and we all toasted Perry and said our final goodbyes.

That is what I want when I kick the bucket is to have my children and friends at Alderman's to have a last beer to send me off, **BUT I WILL BE BACK!**

After decades, Nickie decided to retire, much to the dismay of her patrons as she was like the matriarch of our family.

Nickie sold the bar to the present owner, Mark, who is doing a great job of keeping "our" bar the same as it has been for decades. Of course he has brought "Our Cheers" into the modern age, with Karaoke on Friday and Saturday nights, but has still kept it Alderman's.

There are new people that have made the bar their Cheers, but there are still many that have come into Alderman's for years as I have. Even when you leave for a while, there is always someone who remembers you and everyone welcomes you back with open arms.

I did some traveling this summer through some of the middle and southern states with the purpose of finding a small bar U.S.A. that would compare with Alderman's, didn't happen. I guess you could say I was bias, but I am also very open-minded.

I found one bar, in New Strawn, KS, Buddies Bar & Grill that came close, but no horseshoe.

I have frequented many bars/taverns in the C.B. and Omaha area and always come back to Alderman's.

Chapter Three

Damon

I started shooting pool with Scarlet again and realized how much I missed it and I was very good at it. Even after being off the charts for so long the men were still there. One night while shooting pool at our home bar I noticed a very handsome man setting at the bar watching every move I made. He sent over drinks for the team so I thought I should say thanks. I was almost forty, but looked maybe thirty and was still built very well. As I approached the bar his smile got bigger showing beautiful white teeth. He was setting on a bar stool so I wasn't sure how tall he was, but he was very handsome with dark brown thick hair, clean shaven, and very dark brown sparkling eyes. He was dressed in blue jeans and a Henley shirt showing curly hairs through the buttons, yes this will work I thought to myself.

"Thank you for the drinks you sent over for the girls."

"You are very welcome," He said.

I said, "My name is Jewelya" as I extended my hand out to him.

He took my hand and said, "My name is Damon. I guess my mom wanted to name me Damien, but my dad nixed that, it reminded him of the movie, The Omen, and that movie scared the hell out of him so she shortened it to Damon."

"I love the name Damien and not because of the movie and I doubt your mother wanted to named you after that movie, did she?"

"No, I don't think she really did but I like to tease her about it. I'm glad you like my name. You are a good shot; maybe we could play together sometime."

"Do you mean shoot pool together or play together?"

"I would really like to do both, what do you say Jewelya. Do you have anything planned right now?"

"How about we get acquainted shooting pool tonight and go from there?"

"Then can I take you home with me, I don't live far from here?"

I told Scarlet I was staying awhile and she just winked at me and said, "Have fun."

Damon was much taller than me, but almost everyone is taller than me he was probably six foot or more. He was muscular, but not to muscular just built very well, I definitely wanted to jump his bones. Every time he walked past me he made sure he touched me, not sexually just running his fingers across my back or down my arm or just take hold of my hand in passing. This man knew how to make a woman want him.

When the bar closed he asked me to go home with him, but I turned him down as my kids were home, but we made plans for the next night to meet here then go from there. He walked me to my car then lifted me up and set me on the fender, with his arms around me he pulled me close to him staring into my eyes and said, "Green eyes, beautiful green eyes that see into a man's soul. I could see those green eyes clear across the room, you talk with those eyes of your's, did you know that?"

"I have been told that a time or two," then he was kissing me, a soft wonderful kiss that set me on fire. His lips were slightly open and his tongue barely touching the inside of my mouth. He stopped kissing me, but was still holding me close and staring into my eyes.

He leaned against the fender of my car, wrapped my legs around him and whispered in my ear, "Kiss me back," as his lips returned to mine. I had not been kissed like this in a very long time, Donny was a good kisser, but Damon was Damon.

His ran his fingers through my hair and pulled my face close to his placing his lips on mine and turning me into a flaming torch.

He stopped kissing me, but our noses were still touching and his fingers were still in my hair as he said, "I want to make love to you so bad and I think you do too, but I also want to get to know the woman who is behind those beautiful green eyes."

We made plans for the following Friday as the kids would not be home. I didn't tell Damon I had the whole weekend till I saw how things went between us.

I met him at the same bar on Friday evening. He was watching the door when I arrived and he came across the floor to meet me. He took my hand and led me to a table in the corner where he had drinks for us. As soon as we were setting he pulled me and my chair next to him with his arm around me. He took hold of my chin to pull my face up to his for one of those great kisses of his.

"Is there anything special you would like to do tonight?" He asked me.

"I do have something special in mind. A couple of games of pool, a couple of drinks, good company, then I want you to take me home with you and make mad passionate love to me, then in the morning make me breakfast, did you have something else in mind?"

The look on his face was classic, "I think we should jump over the pool and the drinks, then take the good company to my house and go right to the mad passionate love making, what do you think?"

I didn't say anything just took his hand and led him out the door to my car then said, "I will follow you."

Damon had his own business and home. His home was a modest home, very well kept. We walked up the steps into an enclosed porch, as he unlocked the door he lifted me into his arms and wrapped my legs around his waist and kicked the door shut. He carried me across the front room into the bedroom standing beside the bed he asked, "Can I undress you?"

I unwrapped my legs from around him stood on the floor and said, "Please do."

He was like a little boy with a new toy. The shirt went first, then the jeans then he stood there just staring at me.

"What?" I asked

"You are so tiny, I knew you were little, but I didn't realize how tiny until now."

I turned around so he could unhook my bra then I cupped his hands around my breasts. I turned around so he could see what was in his hands. He ran his hands down my sides and pulled my panties down to my ankles. I stepped out of my panties as he picked me up and laid me on the bed.

As he was staring down at my nakedness I said, "You can't make mad passionate love to me standing there."

"You have a gorgeous body, seven children? All of them came out of that body?"

"Yes," I said as I stood up on the bed pulling his shirt off and saw that beautiful hairy chest. I buried my face in the hair on his chest and found his nipples and was running my tongue around them and nibbling on them. Damon removed his jeans and shorts then lifted me onto the bed. He was lying beside me running his hands all over my body as I was his. I wrapped my fingers around his large penis as his hand found his way between my thighs.

He rolled me onto my back and was again staring into my eyes, "Kiss me Damon, please kiss me and make love to me, I love your kisses, make love to me."

His lips were again on mine and I was on fire, he pulled my legs apart and was caressing my pussy with his fingers then he lowered himself down to me and I felt him slowly enter me. He was so gentle and so loving I was remembering my first Bob. He wrapped my legs around him and pulled my butt up to him as he was slowly going in and out of me. I could feel that wonderful throbbing start at my belly button. "Come with me Damon, I want to feel you come with me."

He pushed himself against me as my legs clung to him and our arms were wrapped tight around each other. We were coming so hard together it felt like our hearts were beating inside me.

"Hold me tight Jewelya, don't let go you feel so damn good."

When the throbbing slowed and we relaxed we still clung together not wanting it to stop.

Damon raised himself up enough to look into my eyes and said, "You are amazing I could feel you coming, I have never felt a woman come like that before. Can we do that again?"

"Can we take a shower first?" I asked.

"If we can do it together, I want to wash your beautiful body." The magic words, I loved having a man wash my body.

When he picked me up to go into the bathroom both our goo ran down my leg, but I didn't care I was going to take a shower with this beautiful man, it has been so long.

We lathered each other then he leaned me against the shower wall and lifted me up and wrapped my legs around him with the lather he was able to slide easily inside me. He had his hands under my butt holding me and kissing me as we made love.

"Open your eyes baby let me see your eyes."

I opened my eyes to see his brown eyes staring into mine. "Push him in as far as you can and hold him inside me and you will feel me come again."

"Hold me tight baby, don't close your eyes I want to see them while I make love to you."

When I felt him start to throb I could feel my throbbing start and we were coming together again.

When the throbbing stopped he said, "Your eyes are so beautiful. They are now blue with a little green in them; did you know they change color like that?"

"I have been told that before, but it doesn't happen to often. I think we need to shower again don't you?"

He slowly pulled away from me and I felt him slide out of me and we both groaned at the same time as my feet hit the floor.

I wrapped my arms around him to steady myself he laughed and said, "Did I make you as weak in the knees as you did me?"

After we showered again and dried each other off he carried me back into the bedroom. He pulled me into his arms and asked, "Is it okay if I hold you in my arms? I want to feel your body next to mine."

"Please, hold me tight don't let go of me." I went to sleep curled up in his arms and felt safe again.

We spent the weekend cooking for each other and making love. It seemed like the years I had spent being Manny's slave were far in the past and not worth thinking about. I was again being held by a man that appreciated being with a woman.

Damon and I had great times together. We did a lot of things together, pool, bowling, movies and just enjoying each other. I let him take me home one night after he had come to watch us shoot pool, as I had ridden with Scarlet, and he wanted to come in and make love to me in my bed. I refused, telling him I don't take men into my children's home even when they are not home. He seemed a little put out, but accepted it.

After a few months being in the duplex I had moved us into, my lawyer decided I should move back into my house. So I informed Manny that I was moving back and his girlfriend would have to move out. I didn't want to do this and wished I hadn't agreed to it as it just made things worse for my kids and me. It worked great for Manny as that gave him more time to make me miserable. His goal in life was to make me miserable, still is.

Once we had moved back into the house and I was finally divorced from Manny, I didn't tell Damon where our house was. I always insisted on meeting him somewhere even though he was always asking me where my house was. One night I was lying in bed reading when my phone rang, it was Damon.

"I want to see you can you come out?" He asked.

"I am in bed reading it is too late to get dressed to go out tonight. I can meet you tomorrow."

"You don't have to get dressed just come outside?"

"Where are you?" I asked.

"Parked across the street from your house. Please come out and see me."

"How did you find out where I lived? You know how I feel about involving my kids in my life outside of my home, and I am not coming out." I hung up and that was the last I saw of Damon. He would call, but I refused to talk to him and he finally stopped calling. I missed him terribly, but my children are more important to me than anything I was getting from him.

Chapter Four

New York via Chicago

W hen I graduated from business school I was offered a job with an insurance company as secretary to the vice president. It was a great job and it evolved into purchasing agent for the company. I had the greatest boss in the world and when he was offered a job in another city in Nebraska I decided it was time for me to move on and I was offered a position with a savings and loan in Omaha. As a purchasing agent I bought office supplies from several office supply companies, one of these companies was located in New York City. One day I received a call from the president of the company wanting to meet with me to offer me a job to run his distribution center in New York City.

Of course the first thing I did was call Scarlet. "You need to go to Chicago with me!"

"What the hell are you talking about? Go to Chicago for what?"

"I am supposed to meet with a Danny White about a job in New York City!"

"The Danny White?" Scarlet asked.

"When he called me to talk to me about the job and he said his name was Danny White, I said the same thing, "The Danny White?"

His response was "Yes, the Danny White of the Dallas Cowboys."

"No! I don't think so I know football and I know who Danny White is and that is not you. Danny White is the quarterback for the Dallas Cowboys. A good quarterback, but a crybaby. So what is it that you really want Mr. White?"

"Well I thought it was worth a try, how was I to know you'd know your football. What I really want is to talk to you about a job. I have been working with you for some time and you are great at your job. I am going to be in Chicago and I would like to meet with you. If you can get there I will pay your expenses, you can pick me up at the O'Hara airport; the company has a standing reservation at the Sheridan O'Hara. You can go to the Hotel and they will give you the key to the room. I will tell them when and where I will be coming in. What do you say Jewelya?"

"Can I bring my friend with me? I don't like to travel alone."

"Sure, you can, I don't blame you for being careful. I will leave your name with the hotel and will see you Friday when I get in. I will show you girls Chicago."

I relayed all this to Scarlet and she said, "When do you want to leave? We can leave Thursday morning and be there that evening."

Scarlet was at my house early Thursday. As Callie was old enough to stay with Deniece and James I didn't have to worry about them. I had just bought a new compact 1978 Chevrolet so we didn't have to worry about having a car that would get us there and back.

We got to Chicago before the sun went down and checked into the hotel. He was right the room was ready for us and the hotel was at our service. It wasn't just a room it was a suite with a kitchenette, wine cooler and room service. Danny's plane got in at 4pm and Scarlet and I were there to pick him up.

I told him we would be waiting for him as he came in, when he saw a good looking blonde and redhead that would be us, how could you miss us.

We had no idea what he looked like, but when we saw this man waving at us and walking toward us we knew who he was.

"You were right," he said. "How could I miss the two of you?"

Danny White was a good looking man, not a quarterback Danny White, but good looking anyway. A little overweight, but not too bad, light brown hair and eyes, clean shaven. Much younger than we expected for being the owner of his own company, later he told us he was thirty-two.

He was right, he showed us Chicago. First we went to dinner at a classy restaurant where we discussed the job he was offering me. It was an awesome offer, pay that I could never make in Omaha with a security apartment in downtown New York City where he lived, or a house outside of New York City where I could commute everyday and he would pay for the commute. Then he asked if we like to dance.

My response was, "I love to dance to anything."

We went to several night clubs and danced all night. He was a good dancer and could dance to almost anything. It was about four a.m. when we got back to the hotel. We didn't have to drive as he had a car, with a driver, waiting for him at the airport and we parked my car in the airport parking lot.

The suite was a two bedroom and when we got back to the hotel we talked for a while about the job he was offering me. We decided it was time to get some sleep as he had to go back to New York in the morning.

Danny said, "You can sleep in either room you want too you know."

"Yes, I know, but if I decide to take you up on your offer it might not be a good idea to sleep with the boss."

"Yah, I guess you are right. That's why I want you to work for me; you're smart and good looking. If you change your mind, you know where I am."

Scarlet and I went into the other bedroom which had a king size bed with a red velvet bedspread. When we turned back the spread we found red silk sheets. I had never been in such a place.

Scarlet saw the look on my face and said, "You know if you go to work for this guy your house will look like this. This could be the chance of a lifetime."

"I know, but what about the kids New York City is not the best place in the world to raise kids."

"You heard what he said; you could live outside of New York and commute."

"Shit Scarlet, this city would scare me to death, how would James and Deniece deal with it?"

"James fine, Deniece I'm not sure she is more like you it would scare her also. Let's go to sleep we can talk about it tomorrow."

I could not go to sleep, but Scarlet was asleep as soon as her head hit that silk pillow. I lay there for what seemed like hours then I slipped out from under those silk sheets and tip toed into the other bedroom and slid under another set of red silk sheets.

Danny rolled over to me and said, "I guess this means you are not going to move to New York." He pulled me into his arms and we made love.

The next morning on the way to the airport Danny told us to enjoy Chicago and we could have whatever we wanted at the hotel. Boy, did we take him up on that. We drank and danced at the lounge in the hotel until it closed. We were staggering up the hall to our room and couldn't get our key to work because we were trying to open the wrong door, as the people in the other rooms were good enough to tell us. We were making so much noise, just the two of us the other visitors were coming out into the hall. I guess it is Chicago so what we were doing was no surprise, and one of the men showed us to our door. We both had to pee so badly and it had taken us so long to find our room, by the time we got to our door it was two late. We were both laughing so hard, at what we still don't know just one of those laughing times that the pee was running down our jeans and into our shoes.

That night room service fed us, then the next morning we hit the restaurant for breakfast. Danny was right, they knew who we were and we could order anything we wanted.

As we were leaving the hotel Scarlet said, "Look around you, you dumb blonde this could be your's all the time."

I knew she was right, but still I had to do what I thought was right for my children, again.

Chapter Five

My Highway Patrolman

O ur trip home was very eventful; we went to Chinatown and other places I don't recall. On the way out of town we ended up heading for Gary, Indiana. How the hell we did that is also still a mystery amongst other things, but damn did we have a good time. We did what most stupid people did in the late seventies and early eighties, got us something to drink for the road. Scarlet, Miller light and me vodka and a six pack of grapefruit juice, bag of ice and a Styrofoam cooler. We had the radio blasting to drown out our singing as we raced across I-80 headed for home. We stopped for a sandwich to go at a truck stop. As we walked back to the car I saw a sack in the parking lot, so of course I picked it up. There was some kind of sandwich in a baggie and a banana which I hate so why I kept it I have no idea. I threw the sandwich in the trash and placed the banana on the console between the seats and we were on the road again.

The speedometer on the car went to eighty mph and Scarlet had it buried when she shoved her beer at me and said, "Hide this as there were red lights going around and around behind us. There was no place to put it so I just held onto it, what the hell I wasn't driving.

Scarlet rolled down her window and the patrolman asked, "Are you drinking?"

Her reply, "No, she is," and pointed at me.

He wrote her a ticket for speeding then walked around the car to me, I rolled my window down and the patrolman asked, "What is that in your hand?"

Caught with the evidence in my hand so I had no choice but to confess so I said, "A can of beer, no, an empty beer can."

He looked into the car and asked, "What is that laying between the seats?"

I looked at the banana and said, "It is a banana, what does it look like?"

Then he wrote me a ticket for public intoxication. "How can this be public intoxication, we were not in public we are in my car."

"Just sign the ticket and you can be on your way."

Scarlet said, "Will you just sign the damn ticket!"

"Okay, okay."

We drove off as Scarlet was telling me how fucking crazy I was, then there was a bang and the car was bumping down the highway, we had a flat tire. Scarlet pulled off the highway, popped the hatchback to get the spare out to find we had one of those damn doughnuts for a spare. Again the red light going around and around as another patrolman pulled in behind us.

The patrolman got out of his car and we saw it was not another one, but the same one who had given us the tickets. "Not you two again, here let me change that for you so you two can get out of my county."

When the tire was changed I said to him, "I think I love you."

He said jokingly, "I love you too."

"Well," I said as I was waving the ticket around in the air he had given me, "If you really loved me you would take this ticket back."

He looked at Scarlet, pointed at me and said, "Get this woman out of here before you both go to jail. I don't want to see either of you again, no speeding no drinking just go home."

I started to open my mouth again as Scarlet put her hand over my mouth and said, "Get in the damn car and shut up."

I pulled her hand off my mouth and said, "Okay, okay." I knew Donny was waiting for me and I didn't want to go to jail.

As it turns out I guess that patrolman really did love me. Big went to court with me and we waited for my name to be called. When it wasn't, Big went to investigate and found the patrolman had not turned the ticket in and didn't appear either so I was off the hook, so I was loved.

When I called Scarlet and told her she said, "You bitch, I still have a speeding ticket to pay."

"Well you were speeding not me, but I will pay for half of it, because I am loved by the patrolman."

"You are a crazy fucking blonde bitch, you know that don't you."

"Of course I am, but you love me too, because you are a crazy fucking red head and we belong together what can I say; men love me everywhere I go."

Danny White didn't stop trying to get me to go to work for him even though I did sleep with him. He said that would just be a plus for him, but had I gone to work for him I would never have slept with him again.

James and Deniece knew about Scarlet and my trip to Chicago and knew why, so they were anxious to find out what I decided.

James was so upset with me, "A chance for us to live in New York City, are you nuts mom? Think about it, it would be great living there. If we didn't like it we could come back." James would have fit right in; he would have loved New York City.

Deniece would go any where I went, but I knew she was happy we were not going to New York, as Scarlet said, Deniece was like me New York City would scare her to death.

When the Holidays came around that year Danny sent Deniece, James and me Christmas gifts. One of my gifts was wanting to know if I would like to spend New Year's Eve in New York City with him. I was ecstatic, going to New York City for New Year's Eve and watch the ball drop. He made all the arrangements for me to fly out of Omaha to Chicago then to New York, but the best laid plans of mice and men. I could get out of Omaha to Chicago, but Chicago was snowed in for God only knew for how long, so me going to watch the ball drop on new Year's Eve, in New York City didn't happen, that seems to be the story of my life.

Chapter Six

Iowa State Fair-Des Moines

Being back in my own house was great, after all I had bought this house before Manny and I had gotten married the first time, and this was the only house my children knew, they were either born while in this house or since they were very young so this was the only house they knew.

Scarlet call and said the motorcycle club was going to Des Moines for the Iowa State Fair did I want to go? Did I want to go, hell yes I was free again and can do what ever I want to do.

The following Saturday Scarlet picked me up on the lavender Harley, she says lavender I say pink, but whatever, then we went to the club house to meet the rest of the gang. When we grouped to head out one of the girls suggested I ride with one of the new members of the club, it was okay with me. He wasn't handsome, but attractive and built good so I climbed on the back of his Harley and we were off. As we drove down I-80 toward Des Moines it started to cloud up. We pulled off the highway to get our rain gear out of the saddle bags.

We hadn't been on the road too long and it began to rain, but motorcyclists are tough a little rain will not stop them, and some liquid stupid in the blood helps too.

When we arrived in Des Moines the fair was in full force and alive with activity. As we were all soaked to the bone we didn't bother to go to the motel we had reserved to change.

Scarlet said, "I don't know about you, but I have to pee so bad." We were walking around the fair looking for a bathroom that wasn't full of women trying to get out of the rain, we just wanted to pee, but we couldn't get through those crazy women. Next step, the men's restroom men are not as afraid of getting wet as women. Well that would have worked, but we were told we could use the men's restroom, but they got to watch. Oh I don't think so.

Scarlet and I were standing in a puddle of muddy water on the grounds of Iowa State Fair and I am sure we are not the first to do this and will not be the last.

Scarlet said, "I don't know about you, but I can no longer hold this." So in a muddy puddle of water at the Iowa State Fair Scarlet and I left our mark as the pee was running down our legs we were laughing hysterically. Everyone passing by thought we were nuts as they didn't know what we were doing. We did this same thing in the hall of the Sheraton Hotel outside our room, remember?

We all met at the entrance of the fairgrounds as planned at the end of the day. One of the girls rode a Harley Low Rider and as she was trying to make the turn to go out of the fairgrounds, she went over on her side. Her husband went running to her and got her up an on her way. Later we found out she had forgotten to unlock the wheel and it would not have turned no matter what, again that liquid stupid doing what it does best, make you stupid. I climbed on the back of the bike with the guy I came with, guess what, I forgot his name, can you believe that? I wrapped my arms around him and snuggled up close, but he was as cold as I was. By the time we got to the motel we were all about froze even though we had been filling up on liquid stupid all day. So why stop now, so we partied for hours on the balcony going from room to room.

Scarlet had reserved the room for us, but the guy hadn't as he was the spur of the moment goer so he would stay with us, but that was okay as there were two beds.

In our room we started stripping except for the guy.

Scarlet said, "What, are you shy or just like freezing."

"I didn't know if I should," Oh my God another nice guy. So he shed down to his skivvies and he looked blue he was so cold.

I said, "I don't know about you guys, but I am freezing I am taking a hot bath." and headed for the bathroom and said to nameless, "Come on a hot bath will warm you up."

I grabbed on of the little shampoos they have in motels and as I filled the tub with very warm water I dumped the shampoo in the water as the tub was filling then I shed my panties and bra and stepped into the water. He just stood there looking at me.

"Get in, I don't bite, too hard." I said. "You don't talk to much do you?"

"When I have something to say you will hear me," he said.

He stepped out of his skivvies and into the tub of bubbles, the shampoo did a great job. I was at one end of the tub he at the other end. Again he was just staring at me.

"Is that all you are going to do is stare at me? I'm sure you have see a naked woman in a bath full of bubbles before."

"Well, no not exactly." He said.

"What do you mean, not exactly."

"Not one that looks like you do. I didn't expect this under those clothes. You really are a blonde, I didn't expect that either."

"Is that all you are going to do is look?" I asked

He smiled and pulled me into his arms pulling my legs around him. With all the bubbles I couldn't see he was as ready as I was, but I could feel. He started kissing me then the bubbles flew. I can't say it was the worst sex I have had, but it was not the best either, better than Manny. We dried off with our towels and went out to go to bed.

Scarlet was already in bed and sat up and said, "You two have to sleep with me, I sold the other bed to a couple that didn't have a room and it is to cold and rainy to sleep outside in a tent as they had planned so crawl in."

She pulled the cover back and I crawled into bed in the middle and he was on the other side.

As he pulled me close to him Scarlet said, "Hey you two, no hanky panky, go to sleep." and we did we were all exhausted.

The ride home the next day was beautiful, no rain and the sun shinning down on us, it was a great ride home.

Later I found out my second son was very angry at me for going on this trip.

He said, "My mom has no business being on the back of some guy's motorcycle traveling around the country. She needs to be home."

It was his aunt he had said this to and she called me to tell me how upset he was.

She told him, "She spent a lot of years raising you kids and did a great job, now it is her turn, leave her alone let her enjoy her life now, even if it is on the back of a motorcycle more power to her."

He didn't pay much attention to her, he always thought I should stay home and make cookies for my grandchildren, like that is going to happen.

The next motorcycle club meeting I went to with Scarlet, they asked me, "What did you do to the guy you rode to Des Moines with?"

"I didn't do anything to him why?" I answered.

"We haven't seen him since then, we think you scared the hell out of him."

"Well, he did say he hadn't met anyone like me. Maybe I did scare the hell out of him. I didn't mean to."

Chapter Seven

Another Bob

At the same time I left Manny my sister and her husband split up. Her husband ran with other women also, must be in the jeans, not genes, but jeans and what is behind the zipper.

She had applied for a cocktail waitress job at a bar by the T.V. channel buildings. I would go see her sometimes when she was working; a lot of the people who worked at the T.V. stations came in there, thus the name Antenna Lounge.

I got acquainted with some of them so I was comfortable going in there even if my sister wasn't working. But then I am comfortable going in anywhere I choose to go whether I know anyone in there or not.

This job did not last long for my sister as one evening her estranged husband came into the bar, picked her up and carried her out of the bar, end of job.

(What I have found is there is an over abundance of men everywhere. As I have gotten older, that has not changed. I am an avid book collector; I am also an avid man collector.)

I was setting at the bar with someone from one of the stations and someone sat down beside me.

I didn't pay much attention until he said, "Can I buy you a drink."

When I turned to answer him I saw this very good-looking middle-aged man. He was slim build with very well-trimmed semi-gray beard and mustache with sky blue eyes you could fall into. He had a beautiful grey Stetson on his head that he promptly removed and lay on the bar. He had very thick brown hair with the same graying that was in his beard and mustache. I agreed that he could buy me that drink. Then he told me his name was Bob, I thought oh no not another one. He was in Omaha for the horse races as his son was a jockey and only seventeen so his dad traveled with him. He was from just outside Denver and was a child psychologist and the head of a psychology clinic. He had quit his job there to travel with his son. He invited me to go to the track with him the next day to met his son and watch the races. I liked the house races so I agreed to meet him there after I got off work.

He said, "I'm meeting my son for supper so I will see you tomorrow at the races, okay?"

I nodded my head and he slide off the stool and I saw why his son was a jockey. He was slim built and was probably around five-foot six or seven. To go with the Stetson he was wearing cowboy boots, jeans, a western shirt and leather vest, I would say very high-end clothes.

I met him at the track the next day and met his son who was a picture of his dad with out the beard and mustache. He was very good rider and won most of the races he rode in. I couldn't stay to long as I had to leave for the kids to be home and I bowled that night.

When I left he asked if he could join me at the bowling ally that night. I told him I wasn't sure if he could find his way as he was from Colorado and hadn't been here very long.

His comment, "I will find it, see you tonight."

I was so sure he would never find the bowling alley, I wasn't watching for him.

My bowling partner, Jennie, said, "Is that your friend up there? If you don't want him I'll take him."

When I looked behind me there he was Stetson hat and all.

When we finished bowling we moved to the table where he was setting. He was so handsome and like my other Bob, he took the time to find me.

"Can I take you home? I would like to spend some time with you."

"I have my car here."

Jennie spoke up and said, "I can take your car home with me and bring it back to you tomorrow when you call me, go with him have some fun."

That was all she had to say and I agreed to go with my new Bob. We didn't do much but go to the lounge and talk. We talked about everything. He was divorced, but they were still friends and she would only let her son be a jockey if his dad went with him, great mom I thought. When he took me home in his very big red truck he pulled me next to him and put my hand on his leg. Of course, that sent shivers through me. We made plans for a date the following weekend. Before we got to the house he pulled over to the curb and pulled me into his arms and that very soft beard and lips on my mouth was creating a fire all over me.

He pulled away from the curb and into my driveway, gave me a quick kiss on the cheek and said, "If you can make it to the track before the weekend, you know where to find me." I ran into the house feeling that old familiar feeling again.

James was asleep in my bed so I went to the basement to sleep in one of the beds the older boys had had.

This would come back to bite me in the butt when we went to court for the divorce. As my car was not at home and I was not in my bed Manny assumed I did not come home all night. This was something I had never done when my kids were home, not come home all night. But with all the other shit Manny had come up with, it was a he said she said and because I would not let my kids come to court to tell the judge I was at home, it didn't go to well for me, but what does.

I met Bob at the race track for twilight racing, and then we went to the Antenna.

He said, "I hope you don't mind but I made plans for us. If you don't agree we can change them."

"I'm sure I will agree, what do you have in mind?"

"I made reservations for Saturday night at the Sheridan Hotel restaurant and a room for the night and longer if you want. Is that okay? Please say it is okay."

"Okay!"

"Well that was easier that I thought it would be." He said

"I love a man with a plan."

I was getting pretty good at this juggling men thing. I was still seeing Donny, but as I said before he was a bus driver so he was gone a lot and I was not to be left alone to long.

I met Bob at the race track Saturday then when the races were over we went to the motel for our rendezvous. We had a wonderful dinner in the dining room of the motel then some dancing in the lounge. While we were dancing Bob was kissing my cheek and neck, I loved dancing with him as he was not very tall so I was comfortable in his arms. He whispered in my ear, "Whenever you are ready to go to our room just say so. I am ready when ever you are."

I lifted my head off his shoulder and said, "I am ready whenever you are."

We stopped dancing, he took my hand and we went to the elevator to go to our room.

It was a beautiful room with a king size bed and a bottle of champagne in a bucket of ice. He handed me a gifted wrapped package and said, "Here, I bought something for you."

When I opened it there was a beautiful see thru negligee inside. "Will you go in the bathroom and put it on, I want to see you in it?"

When I came out of the bathroom, he just stared at me. This was the first time he had seen me without clothes and he seemed surprised. "What?" I asked

"You are beautiful."

I walked across the room to where he was setting on the bed. He wrapped his arms around my waist and pulled me next to him then he pulled me down on the bed with him.

He pulled the ribbon that was holding my gown closed. He began kissing my lips then his lips were going down my body kissing everything and building that fire inside me as he went. He was undressing himself as he was caressing my body.

His body was over mine as he looked into my eyes and said, "You feel and taste as good as I thought you would. I am going to make such wonderful love to you."

He wasn't a very big man in stature, but he sure was very well endowed. He had to be careful at first as he was so large. Once my body had adjusted to him and he was inside me he wrapped my legs around him and was slowly moving in and out of me holding my body close to him. I could feel that wonderful throbbing start inside me as his penis was beginning to pulse along with me and we clung tightly to each other until we were exhausted.

He pulled himself off me and said, "Wait right here I will be right back." He came out of the bathroom with a warm washcloth in his hand and began washing me off. When he was done washing me he slipped my negligee back on me and said, "You are so sexy in this. Seeing your body behind your gown makes you even sexier."

He popped the top on the champagne and poured each of us a glass. We sat in the middle of the bed drinking champagne and taking each other in. Me in my see-thru gown and he in his nakedness. He had a beautiful body full of dark brown curly hair. A small but muscular body. When he kissed me his soft beard caressed me wherever he kissed.

We talked about everything from his kids to my kids, briefly our marriages and things we had done and things we wished we had done and things we wished we hadn't done. Then we were silent just staring at each other then he pulled me to him and wrapped my legs around him and I felt his penis finding its way inside me and he was again making such wonderful love to me. We made love all night, only stopping long enough to have a glass of champagne. At one point we had to call room service for another bottle of champagne. We ran out of champagne before we were done with each other. As the sun was starting to come up I curled up in his arms and we went to sleep. I woke up with his soft beard kissing my back and I rolled over into his arms and we made love again.

"Can I call the lobby and tell them we will need the room tonight?"

"Yes, please do." I answered.

We had breakfast in the hotel restaurant then went to the race track to see his son race. We had supper with his son then headed back to the hotel undressing each other as we went into the room. That night he told me he loved me and never wanted to be without me.

We spent as much time together as we could. He would be leaving as soon as the racing season was over. One weekend we went to Sioux City for the dog races on Saturday evening then to the horse races on Sunday afternoon. We spent the night in a very nice motel after we made love Bob said, "I need to ask you something."

"You sound serious, is there something wrong?" I asked.

"No, nothing is wrong; I have had such a wonderful time being with you I don't want it to end."

"Well, you will be leaving soon so it will have to end before long."

"Jewelya, I love you I told you I never want to be without you. I want you to come with me."

I felt my mouth drop open and just sat staring at him in shock.

When the shock somewhat wore off I said, "I can't go with you, what about my kids. I would never leave them here with their dad, and they can't go with me they are still in school. You know how much my kids mean to me I could never leave them. They are my life I brought them into this world so it is my job to take care of them"

I saw the disappointment on his face as he said, "I knew that is what you would say, but I had to ask just in case I know you could never leave your kids. Just as I could never let my son go on without me. Can we spend as much time together as we possibly can before I have to leave?"

"Of course we can, I will miss you terribly. Maybe we will see each other next year."

"You will never be alone that long; a woman like you should never be alone. I would never expect you to wait for me to come back."

The day he had to leave I was at home when the phone rang. It was Bob, "Will you come see me one more time? I am here on the interstate behind your house, please."

All I said was, "I am on the way."

He was standing outside that big red truck with the trailer attached to the back. The trailer we had made love in so many times. I jumped out of my car and ran to him. He wrapped his arms around me and was kissing me and wiping my tears away.

"Jewelya, I love you so much and I am going to miss you so much. I will always remember the times we had together. I understand how you feel about your children, that is why I am with my son. We are parents, that's what we do."

He let go of me and I watched as he walked to his truck as he pulled himself into the cab he turned and blew me a kiss then he drove off. I stood there on the side of the interstate sobbing.

The next racing season I looked in the newspaper everyday to see how his son was doing and he did very well. I had thought of going to the track and looking him up, but I didn't want to open that wound again and of course Bob was right I wasn't alone for long.

The following year I was watching breaking news on television and it was about a popular jockey coming in for the races and a pickup had crossed the center line and ran into the jockey's car head on, it was Bob's son. He died at the scene, his father watching knowing there was nothing he could do to save his son. Bob was behind him in his big red truck with the trailer attached. I struggled with the idea of going to see him, but decided it was no place for me to be. His mother was coming in from Colorado to take their son home to be buried. My heart ached for both of them. I always wondered how they were doing as this was their only child, maybe this would bring them back together, I hoped it would.

Chapter Eight

Washington D.C.

Scarlet called wanting to know if I wanted to go to Washington D.C. with her. She was a teacher and they were having conferences there for a week and she could get me plane tickets at her cost from the school she taught at. I had a job at one of the larger savings & loans in Omaha, making pretty decent money, but I hadn't been there long so I wasn't sure I could go. I had set up a new ordering system for them they had been trying to get for years. They were so happy with it they let me have three days with pay. I would have to come back before Scarlet, but that was okay.

Donny, my bus driver, was thrilled I was now able to go with him when he was on a trip. He had called and said he had taken a charter to Washington D.C. and to meet him at the Quality Inn to spend Saturday night with him. Scarlet had classes for school so she would be busy and would pick me up on Sunday.

We left early Saturday morning and I didn't have to be back to work till Thursday. My oldest daughter was almost eighteen she would be there with the kids. When we got to D.C. we rented a car and promptly got lost in the worst part of town, it was like North Omaha on a bigger scale.

How we found the hotel we figure was purely accidental. Donny was waiting for us in the bar. Scarlet had to leave as she had to go back to the hotel. She left us setting at the bar. I wouldn't go out with him while I was still with Manny, so now he was making up for lost time, and we made love as often as we could. I again felt safe lying in the arms of a loving man.

When Manny and I had sex he never held me in is arms, he very seldom even kissed me more than a peck then he turned over and went to sleep, so we didn't have sex to often. I could come up with some great excuses. I loved sex, but not with him. Anyway, he had enough girlfriends he didn't need me for sex, I had loved Manny so much at one time and now all I was, was his slave.

As soon as she was gone Donny turned toward me on his stool and asked, "What do you want to do first? I want to make love to you; I want to hold you in my arms. Can we go to my room, then I will take you dancing? They have a great disco band here in the hotel." Donny and I loved disco and we were good at it.

He knew me well; before I could say anything he took my hand and was leading me to his room. My heart was pounding so hard, I wanted him as much as he wanted me. Inside the door I was in his arms we were kissing each other everywhere and pulling clothes off each other.

He said, "Stop, stop. I want this to go slow don't rush it I want to undress you and see all of you it has been to long since I have seen your body." He pulled me close to him and started kissing me those wonderful kisses with his tongue searching for mine and his soft mustache tickling my nose. He unzipped my dress and let it fall to the floor. He lay me down on the bed staring at me in my panties and bra. His shirt and pants fell to the floor as I watched him pull his shorts off and his penis sprang out at me.

"Donny, please lay down beside me, touch me, kiss me, hold me. He was over me pulling my panties down over my hips. He was pulling my legs apart and putting his head between my legs. He placed his mouth over my pussy engulfing all of it. I lifted my hips up to him, I could hear myself moaning. He was beside me rolled me over to unhook my bra and was running his tongue down my back to my butt then lifted me up on my knees spreading my legs and my butt cheeks as his tongue went down my butt crack then to my pussy. "Donny come up here you are going to make me come and I want you inside me to do that."

He turned me over pulled my bra off and lay down on me. He was sucking on my breasts then while he was kissing my lips he lifted my knees up and was between my legs pushing his penis inside me. As he was sliding in I was moaning with pleasure and pushing myself up to him.

"Jewelya I missed you so much, you have such a sweet pussy. I wanted to suck on it till you came, but it has been to long I need to be in you."

He took hold of my butt and was going in and out of me; I could feel his hot breath on my neck as we were coming together. We were both coming so hard the throbbing was like our hearts beating inside me. I still had my legs wrapped around him as he rose up to look at me, "My god how I missed you."

"Can we do this again when we get back?" I asked

"We are going to make such good love when we get back. I want so much more of you."

We showered together, washing each other. We thought of making love one more time before we went dancing, but decided to save it for later as we had all night.

We stopped at the restaurant in the hotel for something to eat then we went to the bar. He was right; the band was a good disco band. We loved to dance to disco music and people liked to watch us because we were good together. What ever he did I followed.

Donny had to leave in the morning with the bus so he didn't drink at all so I didn't either. Our last dance was a slow dance and he was holding me so close I could feel his heart beating. My head was on his chest and it felt so good to have his arms around me again.

When we got back to the room Donny held me at arms length and said, "Where do I start, what do I do first."

I was laughing at him and said, "There isn't that much of me. Do what ever you want; I know I will enjoy everything you do."

I was undressing myself while he watched. When I got my bra off I started massaging my breasts and rolling my nipples with my fingers and thumbs until they were rigid. Then I pulled my panties down over my hips and placed my hand between my legs. Donny stepped closer to me as I spread my legs to get my finger inside me. He took my fingers out and put them in his mouth and placed his fingers inside me. I was removing his clothes, when I unbuttoned his pants and removed them he was already hard. He picked me up, lay me on the bed then was beside me. He started kissing my lips and holding me so tight then his tongue was going down my body again to my belly button, then he turned me over pulled me on my knees and was running his tongue down my back, spread my butt cheeks apart and ran his tongue through my crack and on to my pussy. He lay under me and pulled my pussy down on his face and was sucking on every part of her. His hands were caressing all around where his lips and tongue were and I could feel that throbbing start deep inside me, he raised me up and said, "Come baby, come, I can feel you, I want to taste your sweet pussy." He pulled my pussy back down on his face and was sucking that throbbing out of me. I was moving my hips back and forth on his face as I could feel me fill his mouth. He pulled himself up under me, took hold of my hips and pushed me down on his penis. I sat up so he would go farther inside me. I reached around behind me to hold his jewels as he was massaging my breasts. I moved my knees away from his body to feel his penis go deep inside me. We were both moaning with pleasure as I was moving back and forth. He pulled me off him and turned me on my stomach and pulled me on my knees and was pulling my butt cheeks apart again as he was placing his penis inside my butt. He took my pussy juice and rubbed it on me and him and was slowly pushing himself inside my anus. "I won't hurt you baby, let me love you, you will love it if you just let me."

If it hurts too much I will stop." He kept pushing and I could feel him going inside me. "Lie down on your chest and reach down and put your fingers in your pussy, move them around. You feel so good, I don't want to hurt you, but this feels so good. Are you okay can I go faster can I come in you?" I could feel his body against mine so his penis was all the way in my anus. I didn't say anything and he was pulling himself out then pushed himself back in.

"You feel good Donny; you can go faster I want to feel you come there. I can feel you with my fingers." He was holding my hips pulling himself in and out of my anus, then I felt him explode inside me. He pushed himself against my butt as he was holding my hips tight against him and I could feel him pulsing and filling me and he was making such moaning noises of pleasure. He slowly pulled himself out of me and fell onto the bed. I didn't want to bust his bubble and tell him he was not the first to do this.

I started laughing, He said, "What?"

I said as I pointed at his penis, "Look, I think we killed him."

He looked down and said, "Yes I think we have."

As he pulled me into arms. We were both soaked and sticky with our come and his come was noisily coming out of me. Now we were both laughing at my noises.

I said, "You gave me a fucking enema and I loved it. I wouldn't want to do it every time, but once in a while is okay."

"You really did you like that? Really? I thought you would be mad at me. I would have stopped if you had asked."

"I know you would have, you have taught me so much about making love and being made love to I know you would never hurt me. Now I think we really need a shower."

It felt so good to be lying in his arms knowing his arms would be around me all night. We fell asleep curled in each other's arms, and again I felt safe.

Scarlet picked me up the next morning; Donny was already gone with his bus.

When he left me in the hotel café to wait for Scarlet he asked, "Will you let me know when you get home? I'll worry about you till you get home."

He had good reason to worry, as Scarlet and I can be pretty crazy when we are out together.

Scarlet's conferences were at the Sheridan Hotel so she had a room there and we got all our meals as they had buffets all day long and there were parties all over the place.

She didn't have much to do on Sunday so we decided to walk around. Across the street from the hotel was a row of sidewalk cafes we decided to check out. We decided on one to have some coffee and what ever they had. Most of these sidewalk cafes were owned by foreigners. A waiter took our order, but another brought it to us.

Scarlet asked, "What happened to the other waiter."

"I wanted to serve you two ladies myself." He said.

He had an accent, don't know where, but was sexy. He was very good looking no he was handsome, very handsome.

Very dark brown hair and mustache, brown eyes medium build. "I am the owner of this little café; may I set with you ladies a little bit? You two are not the usual we see around here. You are not from around here are you?" He asked.

He sat down next to me and said, "You have beautiful green eyes, I had to see them up close. We do not see green eyes where I am from."

"We are here with the convention at the hotel, we are from Nebraska." Scarlet answered.

We all sat and talked for a while, then when we went to pay, he wouldn't take our money he said it was his treat.

As Scarlet and I got up to leave he put his hand on top of mine and asked, "Will you come back tomorrow? I would like to show you around. There are many interesting things to see."

As Scarlet had meetings all the next day I told him I would be over around lunch.

As Scarlet and I walked away from the café she said, "See I told you, use what God gave you, for you."

I was beginning to see what she was talking about, but I had no idea what I was doing it just seemed to happen.

He was at the same table were we had sat the day before. "I am having my cook make us a special lunch, is that alright?" He asked.

"Of course," I said. I love trying different foods."

I don't remember what we had, some type of salad, but I remember him. I would have liked to have gotten to know him better. We spent the day walking around as he was explaining what we were seeing. We stopped at a very large fountain and sat down. He was staring at me very silently, but intently as if looking for something.

"You have been looking at me all day the way you are looking at me now, what is it?" I asked.

"I wish you weren't leaving in a few days, I would like to get to know you better. You look with your eyes, but see with your heart. There is so much behind those green eyes I would like to know. He leaned over and kissed me, a short sweet kiss. I would love to hold you in my arms, make love to you, but you are not mine. I would only make love to you if I could keep you with me."

He walked me to the hotel, put his arms around me, pulled me close and kissed me with so much passion then looked into my eyes and said, "Try to be happy, come back to me if you ever want to stay." Then he turned and walked back to his café.

It was now Monday and an insurance convention had come to the hotel for the week. There were parties everywhere and Scarlet and I tried to make it to as many as possible. Later in the evening we went to the bar in the hotel. We sat at the bar, her with her Miller and JD and me with my vodka and grapefruit juice.

Someone sat down next to me, but I didn't pay much attention until he said, "Would you like to dance?"

I turned and saw a very good looking man with light brown hair, mustache and very well trimmed beard.

"I would love to dance," I answered.

While we were dancing, I noticed Scarlet was dancing also. We spent the whole evening in there dancing and drinking. He was a very good dancer, not as good a Donny, but still good.

As we were dancing a slow dance he pulled me close and asked, "Will you go to my room and spend the night with me?"

This was one of those men I can't remember his name. He was an insurance man from Indiana. He was married, one of the things I usually don't do, but I'm sure I wasn't the first nor the last. I guess this is what I told myself to sooth my conscience, it worked.

When we got to his room he had me in his arms kissing me. "I have wanted to do this all night. Can I undress you?" he asked.

I nodded and he was unbuttoning my blouse and unzipping my slacks. His arms went around me to unhook my bra. He was holding my breasts still inside my bra. I pulled my bra straps off my shoulders and let it drop to the floor.

He stepped back and was staring at my naked body. "Can I touch you, everywhere?" he asked.

"First, can I undress you? You know what I look like under my clothes, what do you look like under your clothes?"

He smiled as I stepped toward him pulling his jacket off then his shirt. I unzipped his slacks and pulled them off him along with his briefs.

I could hear him breathing harder as I brushed my hand across his penis. He picked me up and carried me to the bed and lay me down. He was over me kissing me everywhere. He pulled my legs apart and was kissing my pussy. Then his tongue was going inside me as I was pushing my hips up to his lips.

I took his head in my hands and pulled him up to me, "Make love to me." I said.

He was kissing me as he pulled my legs apart and lowered himself down to me. As he entered me, we were both moaning with pleasure. I wrapped my legs around him as he grabbed my butt and slowly was going in and out. As his pace got faster I could feel that feeling deep inside me. He lunged himself deep inside me and held himself tight against me as we were both exploding. We rolled over onto our sides, still holding on to each other.

He looked at me and said, "That was all I expected it to be and more. Will you shower with me; I want to wash your beautiful body."

We untangled ourselves then he picked me up and carried me into the bathroom. I said, "You know, I can walk."

"I know you can walk, but I love having you in my arms, and you are such a little thing it is easy to carry you."

After we showered he carried me back to the bed. He pulled me into his arms and asked, "Will you spend the night with me? I would love to have you in my arms all night."

I didn't answer him just snuggled up next to him and pulled his arms around me.

He woke me early kissing my back and I could feel his soft beard tickling my back. I rolled over to face him and we were making love again.

"Will I see you again before you leave?" He asked.

"I don't know what Scarlet has planned. I am leaving tomorrow as I have to be back to work Thursday."

"Shower with me again before I have to go, then you can go back to sleep if you want."

Before he left he gave me a business card and said, "Call me anytime. I will be watching for you tonight hoping you will come and see me again."

I knew when I left his room I wouldn't be back. He was a very good lover, but he was also married and one night was enough.

I had already soothed my conscience once by saying, "If it hadn't been me it would have been someone else." I don't think I could convince my conscience again.

I spent the day following Scarlet around the hotel going from room to room, this was a partying convention, but from what I understand all of them are.

Scarlet took me to the airport the next morning and I was on my way home. When I got to the airport I called Donny and asked him to pick me up.

All he said was "On my way."

All the way home on the plane I was thinking of Donny and being in his arms once more. But, I also knew Donny was not the one, if I loved him I wouldn't and couldn't have sex with someone else.

(Maybe I am that harlot I spoke of at the beginning of this book, oh well.)

Chapter Nine

Roy

Donny and I saw each other as often as possible when he was in town. I didn't stray too far from Donny as he kept me relatively content as far as sex was concerned. He knew me like my wild Bob did, don't leave me set too long. He always said that when he was on the road he didn't screw around, but I had my doubts. I never asked if he did or didn't, and I thought it was strange he wanted to make sure I believed he didn't. I guess I didn't care as if I ran into someone I wanted to have sex with I would. And I was always running into someone, I just didn't want to have sex with most of them.

Scarlet and I still played pool a couple of times a week so that kept me pretty busy also. Men still hit on me, but none I really wanted to go with. After Manny and I were divorced even a couple of his cousins tried to get me to go out. They hit on me before we were divorced, but they didn't try to hide it now. Men are such pigs.

I met Donny at the bus terminal when he came in and we had planned a couple of days together. We dropped my car at his place as he said he had to pick up a friend, as he said his best friend, at a bar and grill in south Omaha and take him home. As we walked into the bar I heard a familiar voice, a loud familiar voice. Donny had me by the hand leading me to the booth where the loud voice was coming from. I slide into the booth and Donny slide in beside me. Across the table was this drunk good-looking blonde. Beautiful sky-blue eyes, fair skinned with a red/blonde goatee and thick mustache. I recognized him but I don't think he remembered me. Donny introduced me to his friend of many years as Roy.

Roy sat staring at me and told Donny, "How in the hell did you get such a good-looking blonde to go out with you?"

"Jewelya and I have been dating for a while now. I have been trying to keep her away from you." Donny said.

I could tell he had no idea who I was and didn't remember meeting me, which was fine with me.

Several years earlier a friend of mine and I had gone Christmas shopping in south Omaha. We stopped at this bar and grill to have something to eat. I had never been there as this was when I was still married to Manny. I didn't drink at that time same reason, I was married to Manny. My friend said they had very good food and no one would know me there to tell Manny I had been in a bar even if it was a bar and grill. We ordered our food and I went to the jukebox to play some music.

As I was selecting my songs someone came up beside me and said, "Can I play one of the songs for you?"

"I guess." I said

He pushed the song he wanted and when it started playing I was furious. He had played short people; I am barely five foot tall. This is an obnoxious song. When I turned toward him he was hurrying across the floor to his booth. I followed him and told him I thought he was an obnoxious asshole. Then I went back to finish playing my music. He came back to apologize to me saying it was only a joke. I told him he was a joke and went back to my booth.

The waitress brought us our food with two more drinks which she said was from the two men in the back booth.

Then the two men in the back booth were standing by our booth, the blonde apologizing again and the other was in a police uniform and wasn't saying much.

I asked the police officer, "Are you taking him to jail? That is where he belongs."

"No, we are just friends; can we set with you girls and have a drink?"

I could tell my friend wanted them to set so I agreed. The police officer set by me and the blonde by my friend. My friend is a very large woman and I was thinking he must like big women. We ended up going to the blonde's apartment which was just a few block from the bar. My friend and the blonde went into the bedroom and the policeman and I sat in the front room talking. He told me he was married, but his wife was divorcing him. I told him I was also married, but had a husband that ran around, but as long as I was married I didn't run around.

He said, "Maybe someday when we are both not married we will run into each other again."

He was very good-looking and the uniform was a plus, but I guess I wasn't looking around yet because the thought of cheating wasn't there, I still loved my husband and I think he still loved his wife.

My friend and the asshole were not in the bedroom to long and we left as soon as she came out. I didn't ask and she didn't offer any information as to what went on in that bedroom.

Now, this obnoxious asshole was setting across from me in a booth in the same bar and grill as I had first come in contact with him and he didn't even remember me or playing that obnoxious song, Short People, for me and I was not going to refresh his memory.

As Donny was anxious to get me home he slid out of the booth taking my hand and pulled me out. Once in the car I slid as close to Donny as I could get as Roy was trying to get closer to me.

He leaned over as close as he could get and whispered into my ear, "I want to eat your crotch."

I didn't say a word just ignored him. He knew I had heard him, I'm surprised Donny didn't hear him and I never told Donny either. After all this was supposed to be his friend, I found out later they were not as good friends as I had thought they were.

Donny was working more or so he told me, I was beginning to not believe him so I started paying more attention to the men I met. One of these men was Manny's cousin. He had been asking me out for some time and was the bartender where I went quite a bit so finally one night I decided to go with him after the bar closed, why not.

Marcus was a good-looking Mexican, but like his cousin and most other Mexicans he was being divorced by his wife for the same reason I was divorcing Manny. I heard through the grapevine Manny had said if it wasn't for me going out with his cousin he would take me back. Excuse me, who the hell said I wanted you back.

I went out with Marcus on and off for about three months, then I started seeing him less and less, he was just a bigger version of Manny. He was much better in bed; he knew what to do with a woman's body. I really think the reason I went out with Marcus was to piss off Manny, and it worked. When I knew Manny knew about Marcus then he was of no use to me, I guess women can be pigs also. Sorry Marcus.

I was still working two jobs to keep the bills paid and food in the house. Manny refused to pay child support even when he was ordered to. He finally started paying when the judge told him he either paid or go to jail; he started paying but didn't like it.

I worked at the savings and loan during the day and at the retail store across the street selling high-end watches. The watch counter was setting in the front window. When it wasn't busy I had a stool I sat on and would stare out the window wishing I was anywhere else in the world. One evening I was staring out the window watching it snow when I a man walk up to the window beside the bus sign. When he looked in the window I saw who it was it was the blonde Short People man. He recognized me from when I was with Donny. As he came in the door I was thinking ugh, but I would be polite. He was not drunk so his attitude was different and very polite.

"Jewelya, Donny's girl, right?"

"Yes I am Jewelya, but not sure about if I am Donny's girl part. I don't think I'm anyone's girl except me, I belong to only me. What are you doing here?"

"I'm catching a bus to go home. When do you get off work?"

"I get off at nine, if you want to wait till I get off you can walk me to my car and I will take you home."

When I got off work he walked me to my car which I had to park about four blocks away. He cleaned the snow off my car as I got it started. It was nice to have someone walk me to my car as I usually had to walk alone in a not so good a neighborhood.

I let the car warm up for a few minutes then drove off. Roy said; "I live on south 10th street."

"I know where you live." I answered. "You don't remember me do you?"

"Yes, I do you were with Donny the other night when he picked me up."

"No, we met before that you just don't remember. I will take you home and you will see what I mean, then I will explain it to you." I drove him to his apartment house and pulled up in front.

"You live in the apartment on the south side last apartment."

I started describing his apartment to him when he stopped me and asked, "How do you know where I live, did Donny tell you?"

"No, the last thing Donny would want is for me to know where you live. What's that about I thought you two were best friends? Do you remember when two girls came into the same restaurant where Donny and I picked you up? One was rather large; the other was short, blonde, curly-headed and very well-built, with big boobs. When she went up to play some music, you came up and used her money to play short people while looking at her chest."

"Stop, I remember. That was about five years ago, that was you how could I forget you."

"Because you were not looking at my face, you were looking at my boobs. Look at my boobs then you may remember me!"

He started apologizing for that night and I interrupted him saying, "It is okay, you are not the first man that recognizes me by my boobs and that was a long time ago. Do you remember the rest of the night at your apartment and what you were doing while I was in the front room with your policeman friend? Would you like me to refresh your memory?"

"No. no I would just like to make it up to you, I remember that night very well. I would like to forget it."

That was the beginning of what was going to be a very different kind of, what I call living that lasted thirteen years.

Roy started stopping by each night I worked. I didn't mind as that way I didn't have to walk by myself to my car. One evening he asked me if I would like to stop to have a beer. There were two bars by his house, one across the street one around the corner, Scarlet and I had been to each of them shooting pool. When we walked into the one across the street all the guys started whistling and asking Roy how he had gotten so lucky. We sat at the bar and he ordered drinks for us.

"I see they have a pool table, want to shot a game or two?" I asked

"And the little blonde shoots pool also. How many other surprises do you have for me?" He asked.

"In due time," I said, "In due time, one surprise at a time."

"You shoot a pretty good stick Jewelya. Who taught you how you seem to know what you are doing."

"My friend, Scarlet, she is a very good shot, she shoots competitively and wins a lot. But I have to go my kids are waiting for me. I don't usually stop anywhere when I get off work."

"Will you go out with me again, when we can spend more time together? I would like to get to know you better. You are the only woman I know that can shoot pool almost as good as me."

"I can shoot as good as you, I think our games are even. But don't feel bad I usually beat most men I shoot pool with."

Christmas was coming up again and the store I worked at always had, The Grinch Who Stole Christmas on the ninth floor. There was a tenth floor, but it was the penthouse for the owner of the store. Roy had a young daughter he spent a lot of time with. He suggested he and his daughter and my James and Deniece and I go together to see The Grinch Who Stole Christmas. We had a great time and after the show we went to my house to roast hot dogs and marshmallows in my fireplace. When I took the two of them home, Roy kissed me goodnight and asked if we could do something on the weekend. As his daughter was running up the sidewalk to his apartment he whispered in my ear, I still want to eat your crotch. I gave him my phone number and said to call me. He had already been at my house and met my kids so I didn't think giving my number was breaking any of my rules as he already agreed having a man in the house when you still had children at home is a no, no.

Donny would call once in a while and I would tell him I was seeing someone and not to call anymore, but he didn't listen. Roy finally went to see Donny himself to tell him to stop calling me and he did.

Roy and I finally had our first date about a month after he and his daughter had come to my house. The kids were with Manny so I had all weekend, but I still was not comfortable having Roy at my house so we went to his apartment, which he understand and admired me for it. We went to the bar around the corner, which was walking distance from Roy's apartment.

He was still very surprised that I shot pool as good as I did he thought the first night was a fluke, but he said, "I can teach you more," and he did. After a while I was able to beat him and he was an excellent shooter.

He drank beer and I had my vodka and grapefruit juice. When I walked around the pool table he made sure to be by me so he could touch me, not sexually but lovingly, he was a complete gentleman. When we left the bar we were both feeling pretty good and he was holding my hand. When we got into his apartment we stood staring at each other, so I asked, "Are we going to stand here looking at each other or what?"

He smiled from ear to ear and asked, "Can I finally eat your crotch?"

He led me into his bedroom as we were undressing each other. Once he had all my clothes off he lay me down on his bed looking down at me.

"What?" I asked

"I have been waiting for so long to see you this way, now I don't know where to start."

"Start at the top and work your way down, make sure you stop in the middle. Or you can start in the middle and go in any direction you want."

He didn't say anything else just lay down beside me and took my advise and started at the top and worked his way down. Roy was a very good kisser. His mustache and goatee were very soft and it felt very good everywhere he kissed.

But, he had one thing to learn about me and my children, it doesn't matter where I am or who I am with my children always come first. One weekend when I was with Roy we had slept in the front room as he didn't have a television in the bedroom and we wanted to watch football. It was about one or two in the morning when the phone rang. Roy answered it then handed it to me, it was my third son he didn't live at home but my children always knew where to find me. After I talked with him I handed the phone back to Roy and apologized for the late call and lay back down to go to sleep.

Roy said, "Does that happen very often?"

"Does what happen very often? My kids calling me? They call me any time they need me." I answered.

"Well I have a hard time sleeping and when I get woke up I have a hard time getting back to sleep, can you do something about the late calls when we are here?"

I said, "I sure can." as I got out of bed.

"Thanks, why are you getting up?" He asked.

As I was getting dressed I answered him. "My children always come first no matter where I am or who I am with, if I am someplace where they can't call me then I don't need to be there, so I'm taking care of that problem for you." And I left before he had a chance to say anything else as I was furious.

He called a couple of times, but I wouldn't answer his calls. The following Monday he was at the store where I worked wanting to know what was wrong.

I was still furious at his behavior. "I told you my children are the most important things in my life and when they want to talk to me they will talk to me. I don't need you, but I do need them so leave me the hell alone. Even Donny understood that and it never bothered him."

"I am so sorry, I have never met a woman like you and that was very thoughtless of me as I do know how you feel about your kids and I admire you for it and that will never happen again. They can call my place anytime they want to. I don't want this to come between us as I really like you and want to see more of you."

"I like you also, but you have to understand how I feel about my children. How would you feel if your daughter needed you and she couldn't reach you because of me."

"I thought about that and the way I behaved was very bad, please accept my apology and know that will never happen again, now can I walk you to your car? I really miss you."

And it never did happen again.

Roy and I were married February, 1980.

The first few years were a little rocky or should I say a lot rocky. He thought I belonged to only him and James, my son, thought I belonged to only him so I was caught in the middle.

We moved to Oklahoma when the factory he worked for closed. I worked at a Wal-Mart in Checotah and he worked for a mattress company in Muskogee.

Roy started drinking a lot and not coming home and he and James were not getting along so one day he came home and I was packing a U-Haul trailer to go home.

I had already sent the kids home on a bus to their sister and as I climbed into the truck with Beethoven, my dog, I said to Roy as I drove out, "I am not leaving because I don't love you, but because I do and my James comes first. He is a child you are an adult, act like one." And I left Checotah to come home to, you guessed it, Scarlet.

(The ironic part of Roy and my marriage, in time my children would become closer to him than their own father, especially James. They became like father and son, Roy could not have loved James any more if he was his own. James would go to Roy when he needed to talk because he got from Roy what he didn't get from his biological father, love, compassion and understanding. My James was gay and his biological father never accepted that, Roy embraced James with everything in his heart. Roy ask me once if he would ever be as important to me as my children, Roy finally understood what I meant when I said, "No, never." As they were now his also.)

A few months later he called and had woke up in a dumpster just before they were going to empty it. He wanted to come see me he couldn't stand being without me, so I agreed as I missed him also.

Roy stayed for two weeks and had to go back to his job and I decided I would follow in a few months. James and Deneice were now in high school and wanted to stay with their sister to finish school. I reluctantly agreed and returned to Oklahoma and Roy. I had visited Roy on several occasions to be sure this is what we both wanted.

We found a small trailer in Checotah with the help of the only cabbie in Checotah, Lucas and his wife Lena. The four of us became great friends and would go driving around the country roads of Checotah drinking our beer and singing country music to the radio.

One night Lucas said, "I'm going to take you to see something that probably neither of you has seen. But, you have to promise not to tell anyone about this place."

"What place," I asked, "We have no idea where we are at."

Lucas drove a few more miles then turned the cab into a heavily wooded area where just passed the trees was a very large barn with a dozen or more cars parked around it. Lucas parked the cab and we all got out and walked to the barn. Lucas was right, inside the barn was something I had never seen before, a cock fight. There were men and women jumping up and down screaming and yelling at the cock they had bet on to kill the other one. I just stood there with my mouth open.

Roy took my hand and said, "You have never seen this before have you? They had them in North Omaha when I was growing up. Dad and my brothers went to them but I wouldn't go with them as I didn't like seeing the chickens killing each other."

Lucas said, "These are not chickens, they are roosters."

"Well, if roosters are not chickens may I ask what species they are?" I demanded.

I stood there for a few more seconds watching this craziness then I turned toward the barn door and said, "I will wait for you guys in the cab."

Roy grabbed my hand saying, "Wait for me Blondie!" Roy had always called me Blondie or I was his Blonde Kitty, almost from the first day we met, he was the only one who did.

Roy would be the one who taught me how strong I had always been. I thought I was weak and useless. He made me realize it was not my fault I was raped, that it was not my fault I didn't know who Big's father was. He was the first person I told about that summer of 1955, because I blamed myself as most rape victims do. Rape victims feel they should have done more to keep it from happening and we live with that rape all our lives we just find a way to survive, as I did. I thought Roy would be the last man I would need for my survival.

He also made me realize it wasn't my fault my mother didn't love me. None of us can make someone else love us, either they do or they don't. Roy loved me more than any man has before or since, a love like his is very rare. He loved me much more than he did himself, he would have died for me. He was not a well educated man and could not read very well, but he was one of the smartest men I have ever known.

We had so many journeys together as we loved each other's company more than any one else.

One night we were out shooting pool when a man came up to Roy and asked. "Do you two shoot pool like this all the time?"

"Of course." Roy answered. "Why?"

"You know where the bar is just coming into Muskogee from Checotah?" he asked

"Go there some night make some money. Tell the bartender you want to get into the game in the back. He glanced at me then said don't tell them she shoots or they won't let her in. Sign her up pay the entry fee then when they call her name, give them bogus names they never know, they can't say no once she has paid. I've never see a woman shoot the way she does. I'll be there tomorrow night, come by, make some money. Fifty dollar entry fee, winner take all."

We were there the next night. Roy signed us both up and we waited for our turns. When it was my turn, of course the man I was to shoot with did not want to shoot with a woman and wanted his money back. He was told by the owner to shoot or forfeit.

He said. "Fine, this won't take long."

My response was, "No it won't." And I ran the table on him. He was so mad he threw his stick on the table and left. At the end of the night, I took all the money home.

Roy and I loved to fish and we caught some of the biggest big and small mouth bass I had ever seen. There was a small private lake not to far from Roy's moms house that would let us fish there. We had a carpet we would take with us so we could make love while our poles were in the water. This was a very secluded lake so we were not worried about anyone around seeing us. One Friday we were out fishing at this lake listening to the football game between the Huskers and Sooners, we loved the Sooners. We were in the sun making love while where the football game was being played, Lincoln, NE, it was snowing and freezing cold. While we were making love Roy noticed his bobber going up and down. When he jumped up and was headed for his pole he yelled at me, "Jewelya, grab the net, get the net this is a big one. Both of us were, of course naked, we were making love. We were running along the shore Roy was just ahead of me trying to grab his pole before this big fish pulled his pole under and I was running behind him with the net. We both heard this noise above us at the same time, we looked up and there was a small plane just above us tilting his wings to let us know he saw what we were doing. We kept on going as we didn't want to lose the fish and the plane kept going. Roy caught the fishing pole and I got the net around it, this fish was huge Once we got the fish pulled in and was back on our carpet we remembered the plane and started laughing and though about the sight that pilot had seen. That had to have been a sight to see, a naked man with a naked woman running behind him with a fish net.

About every three months we would make the trip home to see the kids, I couldn't go any longer than that without seeing my kids. Fourth of July, 1984 my second son and his wife came to visit us for the holiday. We had a wonderful time and while they were there Roy wanted to take our son to his favorite fishing spots as our son loved to fish also.

The day after our kids left my world came crashing down. Roy became very sick and in a lot of pain. I took him to the E.R. there in Muskogee and he was having a heart attack. They were working on him furiously trying to save his life. I slid down the wall just outside of the room he was in and sat and cried. I was praying to God to not take this man from me, he was the best thing that had ever happened to me. Once he was stable they flew him by helicopter to Tulsa to undergo angioplasty to clean out his clogged artery and it worked.

His doctor said, "You are one lucky son-of-a-bitch, when I started this I didn't think it would work, but it did, someone is on your side."

Roy just said, "My wife."

He couldn't work anymore at the mattress company so we decided to move back home where our kids were.

We found an apartment right away and I found a job to keep us going till Roy could go back to work. When he was well enough he started working part-time for a cleaning company and became friends with the owner. The owner wanted us to be supervisors in some of his buildings so we decided to do that as it would be work that would be physically easier on him. We loved working together and we continued to go fishing and shooting pool. The tournaments we found were not near as lucrative as those we found in Oklahoma, but we loved the game. We did everything together and loved each other's company more than anyone else's.

Then on September 10, 1990 my world came crashing down around me again, Roy's heart gave out and nothing would help him this time, but a heart transplant and that was almost impossible as we could not get insurance on him because of the heart attack he had had before, without money we were sunk. I took our plight to the media, Roy was on television and in the newspapers trying to get him help. Finally a heart doctor contacted us wanting to help and the state of Iowa said they would also help and get him on the list for a new heart.

When the heart doctor saw him he said, "I wish I would have seen him a year ago. I'm afraid he doesn't have enough strength in his heart to keep him going. He only had seventeen percent of his heart and he has lost almost seventeen percent more since in the hospital.

Saturday, June 27, 1992 I had to call the emergency unit for him. As they were taking him out he stopped them saying, "I have to talk to my wife before you take me."

I told him, "We can talk later you need to go with them now, I will follow and we can talk in the hospital."

"No we need to talk now. I am not coming home this time."

"Yes you are coming home this time, you always come home with me you will this time too." I answered.

He proceeded to tell me. "The next time you decide to get married, marry for money not for love. Look what love has gotten you, marry the next time for money. It is as easy to love someone with money as one with out."

I put the oxygen mask back on his face and told the E.M.T. s to take him to the hospital. I saw him once more, when I could talk to him, before he went into a coma that he never came out of.

I stayed at the hospital 24/7 with him, as in Muskogee I sat on the floor of his room praying to God not to take him from me knowing that he was, it was only a question of when. Early Thursday morning July 2, 1992 I was in the waiting room getting some coffee when the nurses came after me that Roy's pressure was dropping fast and he probably wouldn't last much longer. I dropped the coffee down and ran down the hall to his room where my life in the form of a man was slipping away from me. I watched the machines that were keeping him alive slow down then stop and watched that straight line going across the screen, taking its trip around and around until one of the nurses unplugged it. The nurses called the kids and Roy's family and they started filing in for there last goodbyes.

One of my sons followed me home, but had wanted me to go home with him. I told him no I would be okay, but could he do something for me before he left.

"Sure mom, anything what do you need."

"Just go to the convenient store and get me a six-pack of Coors Light."

This must be where the bubble bath and beer came from when I am upset. Roy and I always had bubble baths together and when he got to weak to get in the tub with me he would set on the toilet and play our favorite cassettes and keep me supplied with beer. That is what I did that night, bubble bath and beer and I have been doing the bubble bath and beer since. When I got out of the tub wrapped in a towel as I always did I heard that kissing sound Roy always made when I got out of the tub. His ashes were setting on top of my wardrobe and that is where the kissing sound came from. I do believe Roy was with me that night and many other nights I bubble bathed alone. I have showered with many men, but bubble bathed only with Roy. I got thirteen years with Roy, we had wanted a lifetime, I guess we did get his lifetime. I still get angry with him for leaving me here so alone.

BLONDE ROSE IV

And the Men Who Continue to Wander Through My Life

This last book is dedicated to all my friends that I have met along the way and all the men who helped me survive.

CHAPTERS

Chapter One

MY BOOK OF JONATHAN RAY

Jonathan was the love of my life. He came and went in the blink of an eye. My shortest love affair, but by far the most of everything a woman could ask for and I was the same to him. In the short amount of time we had together we devoured each other, not just with lust, but love, compassion and everything else we could find.

I lost him the first time to a tragedy in Oklahoma, 1994, then to his death on my birthday August 11, 2007, while he was in prison. Most of those years we wrote to each other and we knew there was a good chance we would never see each other again. But, we both agreed that no one could take away the memories we had made together. We wrote often about those memories and kept them alive. I have never forgotten them and I know he had not forgotten them either.

When my husband, Roy died I was so tired as I had been his long-time caregiver. I loved Roy, but was not as in-love with him as he was with me. We were very happy together because he loved me so much and I was very content with him.

I needed a break and my children agreed with me. I decided to go on a trip to see some of my friends, Scarlet in Illinois, Laura in Texas and Lena in Oklahoma. I went first to Scarlet's then Laura's then to Lena's in Oklahoma to meet Jonathan and to never be the same again.

Lena and her husband picked me up in Muskogee at the bus terminal. Of course she had my Coors Light waiting for me and we sat at the kitchen table catching up on things.

She asked, "Do you want to go to Checotah tomorrow? I told them I had a friend coming in from Iowa and they want to meet you. They are having a bonfire party."

The next afternoon we left for Checotah, our first stop Lena's son and family then to the country. I drove as Lena had already started drinking and I hadn't.

She said, "We have to go to the house first to pick up my nephew, Jonathan, so he can show us the way."

She had me pull into a drive and up to a house where a young man was setting on the porch waiting for us. He stuck his head in Lena's window and gave her a kiss on the cheek. Little did I know this night was the beginning of a part of my life that would be with me forever and a love that would not diminish even by a small flicker.

Jonathan jumped into the back seat and Lena introduced us. I backed out of the drive and was told to go west on the road we had come in on. After a few minutes Jonathan directed me on to a narrow road through the trees.

He stuck his head between Lena and me asked, "Jewelya, why are you so angry?'

"I'm not angry, just tired." I answered.

Jonathan came back with, "You look angry, why are you so tired?"

Lena answered, "She was her husband's caregiver for a long time before he died."

Jonathan said, "I'm sorry to hear that, maybe I can help you get over being so angry."

I guess I must have snapped at him when I said back, "I am not angry!"

He said, "See, I told you, you were angry."

Maybe I was angry, but how did he think he could help and how rude he was.

We could see a large bonfire just beyond the trees. It was huge and awesome. Lena introduced me to everyone and someone handed me a beer. So many years ago and there is not one thing I have forgotten about that night and the following months. First, I was in heaven then I was walking through hell with no exit.

I was setting on the tailgate of someone's truck talking to everyone and watching the flames from the bonfire flickering into the star filled

Oklahoma sky. Then I noticed Jonathan on the other side of the fire staring at me, the flames flickering in his eyes. I looked back into the fire and watched the sparks from the fire sailing into the night air. When I looked back he was gone and my heart dropped down to my stomach.

I thought, "What is wrong with you Jewelya, he is too young."

Then, there he was setting so close to me our hips were touching. I looked into his eyes; he had his face so close to mine our noses were almost touching. Jonathan was small in stature, about four or five inches taller than me, but we probably weighed about the same. He had dark brown hair almost down to his shoulders. He had medium size dark brown eyes darker than his hair. I could still see the flames from the fire dancing in his eyes. I thought how strange for such a small framed man to have such a large full beard and mustache. When he smiled, he showed straight white teeth except the one in front was gold. He wore jeans, a t-shirt and a denim shirt over that and tennis shoes. He was staring into my eyes and I thought, "He is so handsome."

He leaned down to me and whispered in my ear, "I want to kiss you, can I kiss you?' There was no answer coming out of my mouth as his mouth was on mine. I could feel the softness of his beard and mustache on my face and I never wanted this kiss to end. I was frozen in time. It was a short kiss, but a kiss as I had never before nor since experienced. There were parts of my body that came to life I didn't know still existed.

He pulled my face close to his and asked, "Can I kiss you again?" All I could do was nod and his lips were again on mine. This time his arms went around me and pulled me closer to him. This kiss was longer, but so gentle, soft and caressing. His lips were slightly open with his tongue barely inside my mouth just touching my tongue. He released my lips, but kept his arms around me which was fine, I didn't want him to let go of me.

He took my hand and said, "let's walk, okay?'

I said nothing, just slid off the tailgate and followed him. I would have followed him anywhere. If he were here today, I would still follow him anywhere.

We walked down the hill hand in hand in silence. When we reached Lena's car Jonathan broke the silence, as he brushed the hair away from my face and he said," You are beautiful with the moon shinning on your face and in your eyes. I've never seen green eyes like yours before."

I could feel the blood rushing to my face. If he could see my face he would see I was blushing. I wanted to say something, but nothing was coming out. I have now had more men tell me I was beautiful than told me I wasn't. Maybe I am or they are all nuts.

Jonathan opened the back door of Lena's car and motioned for me to get in.

As he sat down beside me he said, "If we stay out there we will be eaten up by the mosquitoes. We sat for a few minutes just staring at each other, trying to see every detail of each other. Then we were in each others arms holding each other as though we would never hold each other again.

We released each other and I said to him, "What is happening here Jonathan? We just met and I can't keep my hands off you. I have never felt what I am feeling now."

"Me neither, when I first saw you it was like I already knew you and that I needed to know more about you."

Then we were undressing each other. He was unbuttoning my blouse as I was pulling his shirt over his head. We removed each other's jeans without a word spoken and still staring into each other's eyes. He was beautiful and every part of my body was screaming for him to touch me, so, he did, as I have never been touched before, nor since.

At first only his fingertips brushed across my skin. He moved closer and asked, "Can I take this off?" as he touched my bra. All I could do was nod my head. I felt my bra fall from my shoulders and to the seat of the car as my breasts were released from their prison.

He gazed at my breasts and said quietly, "I knew all of you would be beautiful."

He gently cupped my breasts in his hands as I heard him sigh. I watched his eyes wander around my body as if he had never seen a woman's naked body before. His touch lit up every sense in my body. His hands slid down to my waist caressing every part of me on the way.

He took hold of my waist and lifted me off the seat and pulled me over him. I straddled his beautiful frame, as my eyes stared at every part of him. He slowly sat me in his lap and I felt him slid inside me and my whole being welcomed him. His hands were again on my breasts fondling them as we stared into each other's eyes. I could feel him grow larger inside me and I pushed my body down on him. Jonathan released my breasts and pulled me so close my breasts were crushed against his chest. I wrapped my arms around his neck and he moved forward so I could wrap my legs around his small frame. We were kissing each other with such passion I felt the only way I could get close enough to him was to crawl inside him and I wished I could do that.

I could feel him welling up inside me, he stopped kissing me and buried his head in my neck whispering, "Oh Jewelya, hold me tight let me feel you come. You feel so good." I felt our hearts beating together as our bodies were throbbing together.

When the throbbing was over and our bodies relaxed I whispered in his ear, "Don't stop, please don't let it stop I still want you to make love to me."

He held me back and looked into my flushed face. "I will make love to you as long as you want me to."

He kissed my lips then was kissing my breasts and my body was so on fire again. He started moving his hips back and forth then slowly up and down, I was moving my body up and down against him and I could feel him growing inside me. He kept moving slowly back and forth then I could feel our rivers coming together to make an ocean.

"Hold me tight, don't move, hold me down tight on you I want to feel every part of you inside me."

I don't know where we had gone but we had gone there together, and I didn't want to come back. We were clinging together not wanting to let go. We were both sweating and the windows were fogged over.

His hand brushed my wet blonde curls away from my face and cupped my face in his hands and said, "You are so beautiful, I don't want to let you go and I have never felt so happy."

All I could whisper was, "Me too."

I was still straddling him so we were still somewhat attached. He took his t-shirt and started wiping the sweat from my body.

As he was wiping the sweat from my breasts I told him, "Careful your touch does things to my body I won't want you to move."

He took hold of my waist again and lifted me off him onto the seat beside him.

He pointed to his lap and said, "I know, I don't want you to move either, but I think he needs to rest. He cleaned the rest of me then himself and for a small framed man, he was well endowed.

We talked about everything and nothing. He asked me if I was going to move back to Oklahoma. I told him I had to go back to Iowa; my kids were expecting me back. One of my bigger mistakes. I had found my soul mate, the love of my life and because I still lived my life for my children, I would lose him too soon.

We had had every window in Lena's car fogged over, but they had cleared.

Jonathan pulled me over to him and said, "We need to fix the windows."

He started at my forehead kissing me, my eyes, ears, nose, cheeks, lips, chin. His tongue and lips made a trail down my neck to between my breasts. As his tongue found my nipples he lingered long enough for his tongue to encircle each nipple. His teeth would gently nibble each one of my breasts then as to make up for the nibbles he would kiss each one and gently suck on them. Then he would roll them gently with his finger and thumb till they were firm and erect and very happy I might add. He was awesome.

He then moved down to my belly button, as he couldn't go any further as I was setting up he pulled me down on the seat then started his journey again. He was taking his time kissing every part of my body and I was again ablaze with passion. His kisses followed that line of baby fine hair I have running down from my belly button to the large mound of reddish-blonde hair surrounding the lips his tongue and lips were searching for. His tongue never did venture inside those lips, but his kisses were everywhere. His tongue and lips wandered through that mound of hair as his fingers found there way inside me and I was on my way to the place we had been before. He left his fingers inside me moving them slowly. His lips started retracing the path he had taken down.

When he was beside me again he whispered in my ear, "Let's take it slow, I want to make love to you all night." He removed his fingers from inside me and was moving his body over mine. I felt his penis slide across my hips as he moved my thighs further apart so he could enter where his fingers had just been. He lowered himself down between my thighs and slowly and gently pushed himself inside me as far as he could go. I could hear myself moaning.

He pulled himself back a little and said, "You feel so good I never want to stop."

I didn't answer just pushed myself up to him. He wrapped my legs around him and said, "Don't move tighten your legs around me. I just want to feel me inside you. If we move it will be over and I don't want it to be over."

My muscles clenched around Jonathan's penis, he pushed himself hard against me, and he grabbed my butt and pulled me up to him we held on to each other so close we were like one. Then with a large sigh from both of us I felt his river flowing inside me and mine began to flow into his making an ocean and again we had gone to that place we never wanted to come back from. We lay there for a moment or two with my arms still tight around his neck and he still holding my butt.

Jonathan let go of my butt and I relaxed my hold on his neck. He rose up to look at me and sweat dripped off his nose onto my eyebrow,

He smiled and said, "Sorry about that." He used his hand to brush away his sweat from my eyes.

I just said, "That's okay, we are both covered with sweat, sweet wonderful sweat. I have never been made love to like this in my life." (I think it is safe to say I have been made love to like this before, the difference was, I was in love with Jonathan which made the love making a whole new experience.)

He just smiled showing his gold tooth through his beard and said, "Me neither."

We lay there enjoying the feel of each other's sweaty bodies. Jonathan raised himself up so we could see our faces. I could see the sweat glisten in his beard.

He started to pull himself out of me and I tightened my grip on him as my legs were still around him. "No, please don't move if you come out of me it will be over and I don't want it to be over."

"No," he said, "We will never be over."

He sat up and pulled me up. He had draped his shirt over the back of the seat. Our bodies were wet with sweat and we had fixed the windows with fog. We wiped the sweat from each other's bodies, again. I never want to leave here.

We sat for awhile again talking about everything and nothing. We stopped talking and sat staring at each other.

Then Jonathan broke the silence with, "You don't look angry anymore, I told you I could help."

We both were laughing. It had been a long time since I had laughed this way and it felt so good.

Jonathan said, "You have a beautiful smile, you need to do it more. Show those white, white teeth. When you smile, you smile with your whole face, even your eyes light up."

My mind was racing, is this lust or love. How can lust without love make me feel this way? Is he that good, or is there something more?

"I haven't had too much to smile about for awhile. Your smile is infectious. When you smile that wonderful smile I can't help but smile also and yes you did get me over being angry. I think I have been angry for a long time, I don't want to be angry anymore, I want to feel like this forever."

It felt so good to be held in a man's loving arms again. Roy had not been able to do much of anything for some time, which I understood. His heart was too weak and I know this bothered him more than it did me.

Jonathan's voice broke into my wandering mind, "Jewelya, where did you go?"

"Just thinking back," I said, "But I am here with you now."

As Jonathan was pulling me into his arms again he ran his fingers into my hair behind my ears then clenched his fingers into fists entwining my hair in his fingers. He was kissing and nibbling at my ears then my neck then his mouth was on mine. He pushed my head back onto the seat, his lips parted so his tongue could search for my tongue. I had goose bumps everywhere on my body. With his fingers in my hair he could move my head and mouth where he wanted. He was kissing me so ardently our teeth would clink against each other's.

He took his mouth from mine to ask, "Am I being to rough, is it okay?"

"Oh no," I said. "Don't stop, do what you want."

His mouth came back down on my with such ardent kisses my goose bumps had goose bumps. We were going to that place again. He pulled his fingers from my hair and engulfed my breasts with his hands and was kneading them as if they were balls of dough. He was staring at me as if deciding what to do next. Then his mouth was on mine again with those wonderful kisses and his beard and mustache against my face.

He pulled my knees apart and was lowering himself toward me. I could feel him start to enter me and held my knees up pulling me close to him.

He was making such love to me I had to brace myself, one foot on the back of the seat the other on the back window.

I couldn't contain my passion any longer, I said loudly, "Jonathan, come now with me."

One more lunge and I could feel our rivers meeting and turning into that ocean. This time our passion was so great I could feel our ocean flowing out onto Lena's car seat. We were at that place again where neither of us wanted to come back from. Jonathan's body collapsed on top of me. We were both sweating, but we didn't care we just clung onto each other wishing the night would never end.

After our breathing had calmed down and we could move again, Jonathan raised himself up to look into my face and said, "You are the most amazing woman I have ever known."

My legs were still wrapped around him and I never wanted to let go.

He looked out the window and said, "There is either someone out there with a flashlight or the sun is coming up."

"Oh my God, where did the night go? I have to find Lena."

"Don't worry," he said. "The family has made sure Aunt Lena is tucked in somewhere."

He pulled my face to his and started kissing all over my face and said, "I don't want you to leave, I have been waiting for you all my life. The last place I thought I would find you was in Oklahoma, but here you are. I guess they are right, it doesn't matter where you are, but who you are with. I could live in the middle of a cow pasture if you were with me."

There is no doubt in my mind, Jonathan and I fell "in love" with each other that night.

We fumbled around for our clothes, how some of them got in the front seat is still a mystery. We walked back to where the bonfire had been. I didn't see Lena so Jonathan and I started walking around calling for her.

Lena came stumbling out of the trailer. "There you two are, I was wondering where you were, looks like Jonathan took good care of you."

"Morning Aunt Lena." Jonathan said. "I'm going to cut through the trees to the house; you two have a great day."

I just stood there watching him walk away. He got to the edge of the trees then turned around and waved. All I could do was stand there and hold my hand up, close to tears; will I ever see him again?

I couldn't move, my heart was in my stomach and I jumped when Lena said, "Are you ready for coffee girl? Let's go to Checotah."

While walking to the car I had a thought, we should have left a window down a little. We had made love in there for hours it probably smelled like sex.

Lena said, "You drive, you are better at it than I am."

She didn't say anything; maybe she was just being nice. I drove out through the trees remembering Jonathan asking me why I was so angry and he could help me get over being angry, he did and now he is gone.

Lena and I were setting in the restaurant drinking our coffee and Lena asked, "Did you have a good time? Where did you sleep? I was so drunk I don't remember going to sleep."

"I don't think you went to sleep I think you passed out. I slept in the backseat of your car."

She looked at me over the top of her coffee cup and asked, "Alone?"

"No, Jonathan was with me." I answered.

"I knew it," she said. "I know that look and both of you had it. And when we got in the car, I know that smell also."

"Are you mad at me Lena?" I asked.

"Of course not. Jonathan needs someone like you. That family of his is crazy. And God knows you sure do need someone."

"That is your family too isn't it Lena?"

"No that is Sam's family, but Jonathan is adopted and he is a good kid, but his mom is nuts. She manipulates him; he needs someone to get him away from her. She doesn't let him get to far away from her.

"Why doesn't he just leave? I asked. "He is a big boy."

"He has left before, but somehow she always manages to get him to come back. He went to California one time, even got married and had a little girl, but the next thing we know Jonathan is back here with his mother and no one knows why."

"Well it doesn't matter; I said "I probably won't see him again anyway."

"Don't be too sure of that. I saw the way he looked at you and I know that look. We have to get back to my son's, they are making breakfast."

When we got to Checotah, the smell of bacon and sausage came through the door as we walked in.

Lena's son, said, "Come on in ladies, set down we were about to have biscuits and gravy Oklahoma style just for you, Jewelya."

"Thank you," I said, "It has been a long time since I had biscuits and gravy Oklahoma style." They say the way to shut a mouth up is to fill it with food and that is what we were doing.

About half way through breakfast there was a knock on the back door. Someone yelled, "Come on in."

I looked at the door as it opened and through the door came this beautiful, handsome bearded man and my heart was soaring.

Lena said, "Jonathan Ray, have ya had breakfast? Grab a plate, pull up a chair."

"Thanks," Jonathan said, "I already ate. I came to steal her from you, okay?" As he pointed at me.

Everyone looked at me as Lena said, "Go with him, go ahead have fun."

I got out of my chair and told everyone thanks, Jonathan took my hand and we were going down the steps. At the bottom of the steps Jonathan stopped, pulled me into his arms and we were kissing each other so hard, I had my arms around his neck he had his around my waist holding me so close I could feel our hearts beating.

He stopped kissing me and took my face in his hands, looked into my eyes and said, "Jewelya, I love you, I love you so much. I couldn't stay away. I knew you were here and couldn't stand you being here and me not being with you. Is it okay I'm here?"

"Is it okay? Oh my God it is more than okay. I love you too and all I can think of is you. I have missed you every minute since you walked away from me and disappeared into the trees. I can't believe you are here. Lena said you would come after me."

He pulled away from me pointing at something. I looked in the direction he was pointing and there sat a motorcycle.

He asked, "Do you like bikes, I hope so that is all I have."

"I love bikes," I said.

"Then, come my lady your chariot awaits." He took my hand and led me to my chariot.

Once he was on I stepped on the bar and swung my leg over the bike and snuggled up behind him. He took my hands and pulled my arms around him.

"Push your body against me as close as you can, I want to feel you against me."

I told him, "Not a problem, if I could crawl inside you then I would be close enough."

We went through the main street; there was only one main street in Checotah. We drove out of town and into the country. All I could hear was the humming of his bike and the feel of my knight. He pulled his bike to the side of the road; he slid off the bike put the kick stand down then slid back on facing me.

He sat just looking into my eyes, then pushing a blonde curl away from my face and said, "You are fascinating, do you know that? I look into those green eyes and see so much love."

He leaned forward to kiss me and my lips met his. He put his arms around me and pulled me as close as he could get me. This was one of his long gentle sweet kisses that I never wanted to end. His soft mustache and beard was caressing my face as he kissed me.

He stopped kissing me and said, "I want to take you somewhere. A place I go when I want to be alone. I want you to go there with me."

"I would go anywhere with you," I told him.

He turned himself around on his bike and we were off again. We road for a while with me tucked tightly against him. We turned off the road onto a narrow path, when the path ended we stopped "We have to walk from here. It is just beyond the trees. He slid off the bike and took my hand to help me off. He pulled a blanket out of one of the packs on the bike. We walked hand in hand to the trees; beyond the trees was a field that looked like a green, green field of clover.

"This is beautiful. How did you find this?" I asked.

"I was riding around wanting to be alone, I saw the path and at the end of the path I found this. Isn't this great? I wanted to be here with you so when you are gone, I can come here and know you were here with me."

We walked a short way into the field and he spread the blanket on the clover. He sat down on the blanket and beckoned me down with him. This was the softest ground I had ever been on. We were setting face to face. He scooted closer to me and pulled me between his legs and wrapped my legs around his waist. I could feel him moving under his jeans. He pulled my shirt over my head then I pulled his off him. We wrapped our arms around each other; I was trying to get inside him. I felt him unhook my bra, as he pulled the straps down over my shoulders my breasts fell into his hands. He was kissing my breasts as I leaned over and was kissing his chest and nipples. He sighed as he kissed my breasts. He released my breasts and unwrapped my legs from around him, then pulled me down on the blanket so he could unzip my jeans and pull them off.

He was on his knees and started to unzipped his pants when I told him, "Let me do that." He pulled me to a setting position as I unzip his jeans and pulled them down to his knees then I pulled his briefs down and there was his wonderful manhood right in my face. I couldn't resist I wrapped my fingers around his penis and I heard him moan as he was growing in my hand.

He pulled himself back and said, "Stop, baby stop. I need to make love to you to be inside you. I released him and fell back to the ground. He had grown rigid with the feel of my fingers around him and I was wet with passion. He slid himself slowly inside me, he pushed his penis inside me as far as he would go, and I could feel myself explode with that wonderful throbbing inside.

I wrapped my legs around him and pulled him tight against me. "Just hold me baby don't move, just stay inside me don't come yet. I couldn't stop that one you felt so good."

"Just let me be here inside you. I will try to hold it, but you feel so good to me too."

It didn't take me long Jonathan was holding my butt up tight against him. I let my mind go where he was lying inside me waiting for me and I could feel his slight movement and I started moving my hips as that wonderful feeling was deep inside me. He pushed himself hard against me and I wrapped my legs tighter around him as he started moving in and out of me.

I could feel him grow inside me, "Hold him inside me, don't move hold me tight come with me." As he pushed himself inside me I could feel our rivers mixing together making that ocean and we were going to that place again we never wanted to come back from. We were both in such ecstasy, the sounds we were making scared the birds out of the trees.

We lay there for a few more minutes still connected. "Jonathan, you feel so good inside me I never want it to stop."

"We will never stop unless you want us to stop."

He rolled off me still holding me in his arms.

"This was the most beautiful place I have ever been, and I never want to leave here. I don't know what we have found in each other, but it is like nothing I have ever experienced before."

"You are the only person, male or female I have brought to this place with me. You will always be the only one and I would also love to stay here forever with you, but we may get a little hungry. I am starving and mom's house is not far from here. We can go there and I will make us a sandwich then take off again."

"We are going to your mom's house? Do you think that is a good idea, I don't think your mom likes me. I guess if I was your mom our age difference would make me a little edgy, but I would let you do what makes you happy."

"I want my mom to see us together to let her know how much I love you and that we are going to be together as long as we want."

"Jonathan, do you realize how much younger you are than me?"

"Yes I do, but I don't care I never want to be without you. Age means nothing if you are really in love and I am so in love with you. Do you feel the same?"

All I could do was say, "Yes," and wrapped my arms around his neck as he pulled me close to him and I never wanted him to let go.

We were back on his bike riding to his mom's and I had so many butterflies in my stomach I was scared to death to meet his mom.

We walked in the back door hand and hand and he squeezed my hand and said, "It is okay, she won't bite, I don't think." Oh, how reassuring, I was still scared to death.

He introduced us again as we had met the night before. She was polite, but cool as Jonathan made us a sandwich. I'm sure she thought I was just someone her son was infatuated with and it would pass as soon as I was gone. Little did she realize how much we loved each other and we were not going anywhere, if it wasn't together.

We ate our sandwich then were off on his bike again with his mom on the porch watching us leave I could feel her eyes piercing through my back. I pulled myself as close to him as I could get and wrapped my arms around his wonderful body. If she could only realize how much I loved John. But, I was to learn a lot more about his mother and her obsession with her adopted son.

We flew down the back roads of Checotah, OK, stopping every once in a while so we could hold each other. Jonathan would pull my face to his and tell me how beautiful I was and how he loved my green eyes and every other thing about me and he would kiss me and my whole body would respond to him. I was fifty-three, he was twenty-eight and I had finally fallen in-love.

As the sun was going down I told him we should find a motel to stay in for the night. I remembered a motel that was about two miles down the highway from where Roy and I had lived. We pulled up the drive to the motel and parked where the sign said, "Office."

This is when we realized something was dreadfully wrong as people started walking toward us that looked like zombies. I had started to get off the bike and Jonathan grabbed me before I could get off.

He said, "I think we have arrived at the Hotel California."

This at one time had been a motel, but the man that came out of the office told us it was now a part of the mental hospital in Eufaula, OK.

While we were talking to him we saw a man dancing in the window of one of the rooms, in another room we saw people's faces pressed against the windows. Jonathan pulled my arms around him and started backing the bike away from the bodies that had surrounded us. When we were clear of the bodies we were flying down the drive to the highway.

We stopped about a mile up the road; Jonathan swung around to face me and asked, "Did that really happen? Did you see what I saw? Was that the real Hotel California?"

"I think it was." Then we were laughing and kissing again. We could not let go of each other for a minute.

"There is another motel on this side of Checotah we can stay at." I told him and we were on our way again.

Once we were in our motel room we stood for a few seconds just looking at each other, then he said, "I love you Jewelya and I want to make love to you all night. We only have tonight then you will be gone then what will I do without you."

"You will have to follow me I don't want to be without you either." Then we were undressing each other.

Jonathon was not the experienced lover I had had in the past, but when you love someone the way I loved him all you need is that touch and his touch will be with me forever.

After we made love for the how many times I don't know we showered together and washed each other's bodies then I curled up in his arms and I had never felt safer before in my life, I was in my Jonathan's arms.

When I woke up I turned toward him and waited till he felt me staring at him. When he opened his eyes we were almost nose to nose. His beautiful brown eyes were staring back at me then we were making love again.

"We need to shower; we have a picnic to go to remember?" He asked.

"I want to stay here with you; I don't want to go to a picnic."

"Stay here in Oklahoma with me Jewelya. Please, don't leave me here alone without you."

"I have to go back where my kids are; you come to me and stay with me."

That day at the picnic all I can remember is my Jonathan. There were others there, but they meant nothing to us all we could see was each other. We walked around the park and sat on a large fallen tree just holding each other not saying much. There wasn't much left to say that we hadn't already said.

As the sun was going down Lena said, "Jewelya we have to go to get back to Checotah. We will stay at my son's tonight then go back to my house in the morning so you can catch your bus."

I walked with Jonathan to his bike and held him one more time then I watched him drive off until he was out of sight, just as I had watched him disappear into the woods the night we spent in Lena's car. I walked to Lena's car and got in, tears streaming down my face.

Llena asked, "What in the world happened to the two of you. I have never seen Jonathan like this. The two of you really do love each other, I can see that. I hope you know what you are getting into as Jonathan's mother is not going to let go of him easily."

I lay on the couch that night, but don't think I slept a wink; all I could think of was Jonathan. My heart was already breaking and I was still in Oklahoma.

(I should never have left him. If we could only see into the future just once in a while I would still have my Jonathan. The last time I saw him was in 1994 and I still love him and remember everything about him.)

Lena and Edger took me to the bus station the next day to go home to my children and all I could think of was Jonathan. I had a book in my suitcase, but there was no reading.

My daughter picked me up at the bus station as I was going to stay with her. As I had been gone for my birthday August 11, they were having a party for me; I think that was the last one they had for me. Since Roy was no longer a threat to Manny, Manny's manipulation of my children was about to begin.

I finally got a job at a nursing home as head of cleaning and a part time job cleaning offices at night. I didn't have anything else to do and I needed to get an apartment as I was staying in my daughter's basement. I loved being there with my grandson and he loved having me there. He would come down to my room and lay on my bed with me watching the football games. I still went to Alderman's bar where Roy and I went to shoot pool and all our friends went. I came home one morning at about 9:30 am after an all night poker party at someone's house after the bar closed and my grandson was setting on the couch waiting for me and told me I was grounded for a month. I decided it was time to get my own place.

Jonathon and I had been writing to each other everyday. Sometimes while I was at my evening job I would write him two letters. I was the first at the mailbox at my daughter's looking for a letter from Jonathon and I received one almost everyday. He wanted to follow me and come to see me and wanted to see him so bad. I have never missed a man the way I missed Jonahon, he was all I thought of. Our letters were filled with passion and longing and how we missed each other so much.

I found a small one bedroom apartment not far from my daughter's. I had asked Jonathon for a phone number so I could call him once in a while and he could call me. I called him to tell him about the apartment and that I was coming after him the following weekend. He was so excited about finally being able to follow me.

Again the best laid plans of mice and men, my oldest son was put in the hospital with his heart and the doctor needed to talk to me. I called Jonathon to tell him the bad new about my son and not being able to come after him. He said not to worry to go to my son and he would get there one way or another. When I got home from the hospital there was a message on my answering machine from Jonathan. He was on his way on a Greyhound bus and would be there the next night and would I pick him up.

I had only been about two months since we had been together, but that seemed like an eternity to us. When the bus pulled into the terminal

I was standing there waiting for my knight without his motorcycle. When Jonathan stepped down out of that bus I was in tears. He wrapped his arms around me and was kissing me and I was kissing him back.

He asked me as he wiped my tears away, "Why are you crying, I am here now?"

"These are tears of joy, I am so happy to see you. All I know is I can't wait to get you home and in my bed." I took his hand and ran to the truck and home.

My bedroom was at the front of my apartment so when you came in the front door you were in my bedroom. My son was not too happy about that when he moved me in, but it was the only room that was big enough for my waterbed to fit in, and I wasn't giving up my waterbed.

When Jonathan saw my waterbed he said, "I am going to make so much love to you in this bed you will be sick of me."

"You can try but it ain't gone-a happen, I will never be sick of you."

We stood there for a few seconds just looking at each other then I was in his arms sobbing and holding him as tight as I could. We fell down into my bed and we were almost tearing our clothes off each other. It had been so long since we had made love it didn't take us long for us to go to that place we both never wanted to come back from. We lay wrapped in each other's arms our hearts pounding. The rest of the day we were in bed making love, getting up long enough to fix something to eat and shower. At that point we were the happiest people in the world, just being together.

As I said before, Jonathan was not the most experienced lover I had had, but the best. I so wanted to make love to him and decided to see what happened when I tried. We were making love and I was kissing his eyes, nose, lips then I started making my way down his body and he stopped me and said, "I have never let a woman do that to me before."

"Let me know if you don't like it and I will stop, but I so want to make love to you." I continued going down from his chest to his now erect penis waiting for me. I wrapped my lips around him and was running my tongue around his now very hard penis. Jonathan took hold of my head running his finger through my hair just saying my name over and over as I made love to him.

"Jewelya, you need to stop I can't hold it any longer."

"That is okay, I want to taste every part of you, and I love you so much."

He was still holding my hair in his hands and was holding my body with his knees pressed against me as I felt his penis start to throb filling my mouth with his wonderful juices.

When his throbbing stopped he pulled me up into his arms and said. "Now I know why I have never wanted a woman to do that, I was waiting for you. I have never loved the way I love you and that was wonderful."

From then on Jonathan never tried to stop me when I wanted to love him. He never did get into oral sex as I did. He did love my body and would kiss me everywhere, but his tongue never did venture inside and his kisses all over my body were enough to set me on fire. We devoured each other's bodies every chance we got. If we didn't have too much time then a quickie would work.

We loved being together, the only time we were apart was when I had to go to work and Jonathan had gotten a job at a local steakhouse so I didn't have to work the two jobs. Jonathan loved to cook for me, he said I was getting too thin and he wanted me to eat, my daughter agreed with him so he kept cooking. I didn't mind at all as he was a good cook and cooked different things than I did, but I really didn't want to gain any weight.

Christmas was just around the corner so we went shopping at the local mall. In the middle of the mall was a kiosk filled with trolls.

I remarked to Jonathan, "Let's go look at the trolls, I love trolls."

At the counter Jonathan picked up a troll with blonde hair and dangled it in front of me and asked. "Do you like this one?"

"Of course I do, it is blonde just like me." I answered

"But there is much more to this troll than it being blonde like you. A blonde troll is good luck and if you always carry it in your vehicle you will always make it to where you are going safely."

"Are you messing with me?" I asked him.

"No I am not messing with you."

Jonathan bought the blonde troll for me and when we got back to the truck he hung it on my rearview mirror and said, "Promise me she will always be with you no matter what or where you drive."

"I promise you my love; I promise my blonde troll will always be with me."

Jonathan bought that blonde troll for me Christmas of 1993, it has been in every vehicle I have had, going from one vehicle to the next. I named her Blondie and Blondie is now glued to the dash of my Dodge pickup. When I am no longer able to drive, I will attach it to my walker, wheelchair or whatever it is that gets me from here to there, it has worked all these years and I'm thinking it will keep on working, because my Jonathan is still with me.

Jonathan would call home for time to time to talk to his mom. One day when he got off the phone he told me his aunt was getting married and we should pick up a card to send them.

We went to the mall to pick up a card and when I went to put the address on the card he told me not to put a return address on the envelope. When I asked him why he said he didn't want his mother to know where he was.

"She is your mother." I told him. "She should know where you are."

"No, no, she doesn't need to know where we are, you don't know her, she will do anything to get me back there. Please, do what I ask don't put a return address on the envelope."

I didn't really understand at the time, but I did as he said. I would soon learn how far his mother's arm reached.

When Jonathan decided he was going to follow me he asked me, "Are you a partier, do you drink very much?"

"Goodness no, I am an amateur drinker. Why would you ask me something like that?"

"You and your husband were good friends of Uncle Bill and Aunt Lulu and they like to drink, I just assumed so did you and your husband."

"I really didn't drink at all until I was almost forty after my divorce and my kids were older. I don't like to drink much as then you are not in control the alcohol is and I like to be in control of what I am doing. Why?" I asked.

"Remember when we went to my mom's house and I made us the sandwich and you told me how great the house was and how you liked the big dishwasher? Well my mom doesn't use the dishwasher for dishes, that is where she keeps her drugs and pot and bottles of booze and pills, I want to be away from all of that."

Now I understood more about what Lena had said about Jonathan's mom and how she controlled him.

I started seeing a change in him when I came home from work. We didn't talk as much or make love as often. He seemed moody and fell silent a lot. I came home one day and he was drinking. When I questioned him about it he got very defensive, so I left him alone. One day I came home to him being packed and telling me he was going home, he already had his bus ticked bought. I was devastated, but not surprised I saw it coming. I could always tell when he had talked to his mother as that was when he was moody. I knew instantly that if he left, I would never see him again something terrible was going to happen.

I begged, "Please Jonathan don't go. If you go, I will never see you again something terrible will happen. You can stop the hold your mother has on you if you just stay here with me."

He was so angry at me he yelled, "You don't know anything about it. If I don't go then she will call my cousin Robert to take care of her. She does this all the time to keep me there, I thought this time it would be different she knows how much I love you I thought she would leave us alone."

"Please, please don't go, I am begging you I see things other people don't see. Don't ask me how because I don't know. I do know if you go back there, there is a tragedy waiting for you. Please Jonathan stay here with me. Let her know you are not under her control any more."

He yelled at me from across the room, "You know, I did have a life before you!"

He must have seen the look of pure pain on my face as he rushed across the room. "Jewelya I am so sorry, I don't think I have ever had any kind of life until I met you. I have never had so much love in my life as you have given me."

He gathered me into his arms and said, "I love you so much, but this is something I have to do for us."

There was nothing I could do but take him to the bus terminal. I told him I would not stay to see him off I would drop him off at the door as I don't think I could bare to see him get on that bus and leave me, and that was what I did. It was like reliving leaving Bob in the park and the parking lot of the motel, I cried all the way home.

In the blink of an eye, life changes. The only thing in life that we can depend on is change. The change is not the dilemma, but how we deal with that change, and I was not dealing with this change very well.

The following evening my phone rang, it was Jonathan. When I heard his voice it was hard for me to breath.

"Jewelya, this is Jonathan."

"I know, do you think I could ever forget your voice? Where are you? Are you coming home? Please Jonathan if you don't come back something terrible is going to happen."

"I am in Muskogee; I got a locker to put my bag in so I don't have to carry it. Mom is coming after me, I am going to tell her I love you and I am going back to you so we can go to California to make a new life, will you go to California with me? I can get my old job back you won't even have to work if you don't want to."

"Yes, of course I will go with you, but don't go to your mom's please just get on the bus and come back to me, please Jonathan."

"I have to do this; I will call you when I leave Checotah so you can pick me up. I love you Jewelya and want to spend the rest of my life with you, but I have to set things straight here first."

He said goodbye and was gone and I knew goodbye was right, I would never have Jonathan in my arms again he was lost to me. His mother had won.

I didn't hear from Jonathan first, I heard from Lena. When I answered the phone the first thing she asked me was if I was okay. I told her of course I was okay, why.

Lena asked, "Have you heard from Jonathan? Have you seen the news?"

"No Lena, what is going on?"

She proceeded to tell me that Jonathan had gone to his mother's and his cousin, Robert, was there. There was always bad blood between Jonathan and Robert as Jonathan was adopted and Robert never let him forget it. Robert was twice John's size and was always beating him up and Jonathan's mother used this to her advantage, but tonight something happened I doubt if even she expected. The dishwasher was opened; the drinking, the drugs, the pot smoking and the arguments began. Jonathan went into his room got his gun came out and shot Robert.

When Robert fell Jonathan shot him again saying, "Die you son-of-a-bitch die." Jonathan's mother's boyfriend tried to take the gun from him and the boyfriend got shot in the process, killing the boyfriend. Then Jonathan took off in his mother's car. Lena was concerned Jonathan would come to me. I assured her Jonathan would never hurt me or involve me in this, he loved me too much, but I knew eventually I would hear from him. I didn't tell her, but I knew that when Jonathan called me I would do anything to protect him. I knew he had done wrong, but he also was a victim, his adopted mother made him a victim and she would get away with it.

Every time the phone would ring I would jump out of my skin thinking it might be Jonathan. A day later when I answered the phone it was my Jonathan. When I heard his voice I was in tears.

"Jewelya I have done something terrible, do you still love me, have you heard what I have done?'

"Yes, Lena called me. Where are you Jonathan let me come and get you. We can go to Mexico. I can get away from the police, I don't care what happens without you life is horrible I miss you so much. Please Jonathan tell me where you are."

"I knew you would say that so I am at a pay phone in California down the street from a police station. I am going to turn myself in I have done a terrible thing, not so much to me, but to you. I should have listened to you and stayed, but I didn't and I have to pay for what I have done, I can't take you down with me I love you to much to do that to you. We talked for a few more minutes with me begging him to tell me where he was so I could come to him, but he would not.

Then he said, "I am so sorry for what I have done to us, if I would have only listened to you we would be together, but I listened to her not you. I will always love you." He said goodbye, then he was gone.

I was yelling Jonathan, Jonathan into the phone, but he was gone. The only other people that can cause this indescribable pain in my heart are my children. I still feel this pain when I think of Jonathan.

I cried myself to sleep only to be awakened at 3 a.m. with a pounding on my door and yelling, telling me it was the police department and to open the door. When I unlocked the door, three very large policemen came bounding into my apartment wanting to search my home, I told them to go ahead.

There was a police car somewhere around my apartment all the time. One stopped me when I left telling me he wanted to check my brake lights as he though one was out when I stopped at the stop sign. I knew what he was doing, but I went along with him. I would take them on wild goose chases, they would follow me when I left and I would take them all over.

About a week later Jonathan called to tell me he was in the Eufaula jail. I was so happy to hear his voice, but so unhappy as I knew I would never be with him again, but I would always love him.

He sent me some papers to fill out so I could go visit him. I needed a vacation and Laura was wanting me to come down to Dallas to see her, why not what else did I have to do.

I made the appointment I needed to see Jonathan so when I got my confirmation I headed to Dallas via Eufaula, Oklahoma.

I didn't have a problem finding the jail in Eufaula, as Eufaula is a very small town and most court houses in small towns are in the center of town, Eufaula was no different.

The keeper of the keys led me down some half circle stairs to the basement where I could see bars, lots of bars. I heard a familiar voice call my name and there was my Jonathan standing behind bars looking out at me. I longed for the feel of his body next to mine, but I knew that was not going to happen. I quickly walked over to where Jonathan was and took his hand that he had extended through the bars. As soon as I took his hand the tears started to fall. I pressed my face to the bars so I could feel his lips on mine. How can this be happening? Any minute I will wake up and find this is just a bad dream; bad dream this is a nightmare.

"Jewelya I am so sorry for hurting you so much, I should have listened to you."

"We can't do anything about what is already done let's not waste what time we have talking about what should have been."

What was there for us to talk about except what could have been because the future holds nothing for us. There will be letters, but no more kissing, touching, holding hands all the other things that people in love do.

Jonathan asked, "Will you write to me let me know how you are doing. I can't ask you to wait for me, I will probably never be a free man again, but we have all the memories we made those will always be with me."

"I will write to you Jonathon, that is all we will have. I will always love you and remember the wonderful times we had. When you put yourself in this cell you put me in here also. Someday I may be able to pull me out of here, but a part of me will be in here as long as you are, maybe longer as I will always love you. I have never loved anyone as I love you."

"I know," He said, "I put us both in this cell, but that can't be changed. Drugs, alcohol and pills can turn a man into an idiot, and I was the biggest to have done this to someone I love as much as I love you. I bought you something for Christmas before all hell broke lose, I was going to bring it back with me, but you can see how that worked out. I told mom to send it to you, I made her promise she would send it. It is a Santa troll; it was hanging on the tree that night. Only me, my mom and the Santa troll know what happened that night, maybe someday I will tell you. There is a lot more to me and my mom than anyone knows."

He never did tell me what happened that night, but his mom did send me my Santa troll and he is setting by my blonde troll, that and my memories are all I have left of Jonathan.

The tears were running down both of our cheeks when the guard came to tell me my time was up and I had to leave.

I held onto Jonathan's hand as long as I could then I slowly pulled my fingers through his and told him, "I will always love you, always love me."

I could hear the tears in his voice as he said, "Always, I will always love you."

I could hear him calling to me, "Jewelya, I will always love you, I will always love you."

I could barely see the steps through the tears as I found my way out of the court house and to my car, his words ringing in my ears.

I will always wonder if this would not have happened, would Jonathan and I have made it. Would we still be in love?

When I left the jail in Eufaula, OK where they were holding Jonathan, I called Laura, my friend in Dallas. I was crying so hard she couldn't understand what I was saying. I had just left the man I would love forever in a jail cell probably never to see him or feel his touch again.

I could hear Laura's voice, but had no idea what she was saying, then she yelled into the phone, "Jewelya! Get hold of yourself, this is not going to help you or Jonathan. Get yourself together, get in your car and get here to Dallas. Don't break any speed limits, but get here as fast as you can, then the healing can start."

Laura was waiting for me when I got to her apartment. She already had a twelve pack of Coors Light waiting for me. We drank that and walked down to the liquor store about a block from her apartment to get another. Now I understand why people turn to alcohol, it dulls the pain for awhile, but when the dull wears off the pain is still there.

(After I returned from seeing Jonathan, I didn't care if school kept or not. This is the only time in my life I look back at and think, "What the hell were you thinking? I wasn't thinking of anything except how to stop the aching in my heart. I don't know how I survived, or how so many tears could come out of two eyes.)

Chapter Two

Living Without Jonathan

When Jonathan left to go back to Oklahoma I decided to go back to my second job, I didn't have anything else to do with my evenings. I hadn't taken Jonathan to Alderman's with me as I didn't want to share him with anyone, but I now needed my family. The family that would feel my sadness and help me laugh again.

When I walked threw the door at Alderman's I was welcomed back as though I had never been gone.

Nickie came from behind the bar with a big hug and, "Where the hell have you been."

"It's a long story," I told her "Some day when you have a year or two, I'll tell you, right now, I'll take a Coors Light."

It didn't take me long to get settled in and meet the new people that had joined the family and reacquaint myself with the long timers.

Nickie was behind the bar most nights, but Dee was there on Thursday and any other night Nickie needed him, I think he had become a fixture around there.

I found a new job in Omaha that paid me enough that I didn't have to work my second job. I moved from C.B. to Omaha as it was closer to my new job and Alderman's.

I found my self looking at every man I saw for traits of Jonathan, I missed him so much. I still wrote him almost everyday and he could call me once a month. But hearing his voice left me a mess for days.

I couldn't eat, mostly I drank, therefore; I had lost a lot of weight. My oldest daughter would call to tell me to eat as I was getting too thin, that was when she still cared.

I was shooting pool one night when this young man came up to me and asked if I wanted to shoot darts as he wasn't very good at pool. I told him I wasn't very good at darts, but I didn't want to embarrass him at pool.

He laughed and said, "This could be very interesting, as I'm not very good at darts either."

"This will make us even then, the blind leading the blind."

He was right he wasn't very good at darts and that made two of us, neither of us was any good at darts, but we had fun.

He asked, "Are you married or with someone? This is the first time I have been in here. I quit drinking because my wife wanted me to, but she left anyway so this is how I am drowning my pain."

"I am not married or with anyone right now, I was, but he is gone now, long and boring story."

"Would you come home with me?" he asked. "You can follow me in your car and leave when ever you want. Trust me, I won't hurt you and anyway you will know where I live. What do you say Jewelya?" (Of course, I don't remember his name.)

He was young and slim built, not skinny, but slim like Jonathan. Not too tall, but like most people I had to look up to him. He was clean shaven, not like my Jonathan.

"Why not." I said. "There is no one at home waiting for me."

We finished our beers and waved at Nickie as we left. He didn't live too far from the bar so it only took a few minutes to get there. Nice little house, very clean. We walked through a small front porch and into the front room.

He just stood there looking at me not saying anything so I asked, "Well what now, are you going to stare at me all night?"

We were standing behind the couch in the front room and he slowly walked toward me and kissed me. A short sweet kiss at first then he became more ardent.

He stepped back from me and said, "Not what I expected."

"What did you expect?" I asked.

"There is a big difference in our ages I guess I didn't expect that kind of kiss."

"You mean because I am older than you, you didn't think I could kiss? That is one of those things like riding a bicycle once you know how you never forget."

"Are you as good at everything else as you are at kissing?"

"There is only one way to find out." I answered.

He took my hand and led me into the bedroom then started undressing me as I was him. All the while I was thinking of Jonathan, I wondered who he was thinking of. He was more experienced than Jonathan, but I didn't love him so I was just making do.

After making love for some time he asked. "Will you stay for a while? It has been a long time since some one has slept in my arms and you feel so good beside me."

"I can stay for a while, it has been a long time for me also, it feels good to be held again."

"My wife is bringing my boys in the morning so you will have to be gone by then, but I really want you to stay for a while."

I woke up to him propped up on his elbow watching me sleep, in that instance I thought of Roy. He used to watch me sleep.

"I really enjoyed being with you, much more than I expected. Will I see you again?" He asked.

"No, I really don't think so; do you love your wife? Does she love you?" I asked.

"I love her very much and I think she still loves me just really angry at me. There were no other women, just too much drinking and spending too much time with my drinking buddies and not enough with my family."

"If you want to save your family, then you stop drinking again and get down on your knees when your wife gets here and beg her to forgive you and promise her that your family is more important to you than anything else, but most important, if she forgives you keep that promise. Trust me, I have been in her place all mothers want that faithful, attentive husband and father that comes home to them everyday, sober. If you keep that promise I will never see you again, if you don't keep that promise, see you at Alderman's someday."

I never did see him again so maybe he kept his promise, I hope so. I like to think I did a good thing with this young man and helped him find his way back to his family.

When I got to my truck and backed out of the drive I realized I didn't know where the hell I was at. I couldn't go back as his wife would be arriving at any time and I didn't want that to happen. It took me over an hour driving around trying to find a landmark I recognized. Last night it seemed so simple, it is a damn good thing I don't have to work today.

After Jonathan, I don't think I even know who I was. There were many men, Larry; the thing I remember most about him was he had a very large penis and very small balls. I also met him at Alderman's, one of my stepping stones to get me from one place I didn't want to be to another place I didn't want to be either. Larry was a very nice man and wanted more than I wanted. He was divorced with two daughters. His apartment was just down the hill from the bar so it was very convenient if we couldn't drive. He loved having sex with me and there wasn't anything he wouldn't do for me. He would run his tongue all around my pussy until I would fill his mouth with my juices then he would put that big penis into my wet pussy and we would have sex all night long. When our bodies got wet and sticky we would get up to shower and make love in the shower. One night when we left the bar we drove down the hill to his apartment. When I got out of the car he picked me up and carried me running to his apartment. Once inside the apartment we fell down on the floor tearing our clothes off each other and had sex right there on the floor.

Lying on the floor naked he said, "You are amazing, I have never known a woman like you every minute with you is exciting."

We made our way to the bedroom and he fell asleep almost immediately. When I was sure he was asleep I dressed and went home. I saw him a few times after that, but always found excuses to not go with him; he wanted more than I was ready to give. He would have been a good catch, but there I go again that nice guy thing and stupid on my forehead.

There are so many men around, an abundance of men. There were many that asked, but I ignored them especially if there was no traits of Jonathan, too tall, too muscular, no beard no mustache. There were some I went with and just don't remember what we did, just know we did. Some got mad expecting it to happen again, and it wasn't going to happen again.

One night setting at the bar at Alderman's someone sat down on the stool beside me and said, "Hi Jewelya, how are you doing?"

I looked over and said, "Fine, how are you?" I had no clue who he was.

"Where is your husband?" He asked

"And you are, you know me sorry I don't know you."

"My name is Alan, I used to shoot pool with you and your husband, Roy was his name right?"

"Oh, now I remember you, you shoot pretty good if I remember right."

"Yes I do, but not as good as Roy, he is great, where is he?" He asked.

"Evidently you haven't heard, Roy died almost a year ago. I just started coming back in here not to long ago I went to Oklahoma for a while. Found someone there and lost them too. How about you?"

"I was in a relationship, but that is no more either, so want to shoot some pool?"

He did remind me of Jonathan, dark, medium long hair, dark brown eyes a thick mustache and was built like Jonathan, small build and not too tall. We shot a few games of pool, don't remember who won.

Alan said he had to go he had an appointment, but would see me another time. I told him if he was lucky. He laughed and left.

Another I went out with a couple of times, again don't remember his name, he lived in a really nice house with a sunken front room where we of course made love or had sex is probably a better word. These men at this time, I had sex with not made love, they were just stepping stones.

One night setting at Alderman's having a drink and conversation with Nickie and some other regulars, this man came bursting in and was yelling at me as to why was I in the bar without him. He stood in the door way motioning for me to come with him.

"You are my girlfriend and I want you to come with me, now. If I had your phone number I could call you and not come looking for you."

"What? I am not your girlfriend and I am not coming with you now or any other time so just go away and leave me alone."

When he started coming toward me Nickie and a couple of others stood up between me and him and Nickie said, "Jewelya said she was not coming; now you leave or we will help you leave." Thank God for my bar family, at any other bar they probably would have let him drag me out the bar by the hair, like that proverbial caveman he thought he was.

His face was red with rage as he stormed out of the door, but he was never seen again in the bar.

I did everything I could not to stay at home, I missed Jonathan so much. When I lay in bed at night I would feel the pillow where he slept and run my hand over my body and pretend it was him.

I decided one night I was going somewhere else tonight; I wanted to be alone, but not alone at home. If I went to Alderman's there was always someone I knew and I didn't want to see anyone I knew. There was a bar not to far from Alderman's; I guess I didn't like to get too far out of my comfort zone. I walked up to the bar and set on a bar stool. As I do at every bar I go into the first thing I look at is the pool table and who is playing, and there he stood. This could have been Jonathan's double, brown medium length hair pulled back, brown eyes and a beautiful mustache and full beard. His height and weight had to be the same as Jonathan's.

I was brought to the present when the bartender asked, "What can I get you?"

"A Coors Light and give me some quarters for the pool table."

When I put my quarters on the table Jonathan's double said, "We have a challenger, a blonde, good looking challenger."

I knew when I left there he was going with me if I had to drag him, but I knew when he looked at me I would not have to drag him.

I stuck my hand out and said my name is, "Jewelya, and you are?"

"My name is Steven, Jewelya what a beautiful name. Do you shoot pool often and are you any good?"

"Yes, I shoot pool often and I am good. This is the first time I have been in here, I usually go to Alderman's, but I wanted a change so I came here."

"I'm glad you did. I'm from out of town staying at my brother's for the night and heading home in the morning cattle need to be tended to."

We shot a few games of pool; he won some I won some. He put some money in the jukebox and we danced. He pulled me close so my breasts were pressed against his chest and his beard against my forehead.

He said, "You smell so good, not like perfume, like woman. Do you look as good underneath those clothes as you smell?"

"I certainly do." I answered.

My heart was pounding so hard I thought he would feel it against his chest. He took my chin and pulled my face up to his and was kissing me ever so gently, as my Jonathan had done. I wanted to tear his clothes off right there on the dance floor, but I contained myself. When the music was done, we sat down at a table in the corner.

He asked, "Are you married or in a relationship?"

"No, I was married, but my husband died several years ago and the relationship I was in went down the drain so to speak, a long story and not to interesting, how about you?"

"I am married, but separated. She doesn't think she wants to be married anymore. Things have been so rocky for so long I really don't know what I want anymore. As you said, long story and not to interesting."

"Then let's just think about tonight and having a good time and not think of what was or what might be just what is now. What do you say?"

"Sounds good to me Jewelya. What do you want to do?"

"I want to take you home with me." I answered.

"And I want to go with you, make love to you and spend the night in your arms. It has been a while for me how about you?"

"Yes, it has been some time so I am ready to go when ever you are I don't live to far."

He grabbed a six pack at the bar and we left.

By the time we got to my apartment we had forgotten all about the six pack. We were undressing each other as we went in the door. We fell into my waterbed and into each others arms with only one thing on our minds, each other's bodies.

He started exploring my body with his eyes going up and down my body then said, "You really are a blonde and curly on both ends and you do smell like woman all over do you taste as good as you smell?'

"There is only one way to find out." I answered.

I already had my hand wrapped around his penis and I slid down to where my hand was holding him and replaced my hand with my mouth. I engulfed his penis with my lips while my tongue was going around the head of his penis. He was built so much like my Jonathan I could close my eyes and pretend Jonathan was here.

He interrupted my thoughts with; "Jewelya, you need to stop, I can't hold it any longer, but I kept going, stopping was not going to happen and I could taste him filling my mouth.

I kept swallowing until there was nothing left. He pulled me up beside him and said, "My God woman that felt good, it has been so long. Now it is my turn to make love to you."

He started his kisses on my lips and what great kisses with his soft beard caressing my face. He went from my lips to my breasts spending the same amount of time on each making each nipple as hard as his penis. Then his tongue was trailing down that line of fine hair that extends from my bellybutton down to my reddish-blonde fur ball. With his head between my thighs his tongue was finding every part of my pussy. I ran my fingers through his hair; with my eyes closed it was as though

Jonathan was with me. Even though Jonathan was not as aggressive as Steven, Jonathan was who I was thinking of. I could feel my whole body beginning to throb as Steven was devouring my juices running into his mouth. It is a good thing my neighbors are not close or they would be enjoying the sounds we were making.

Steven lay down beside me and began kissing me, then said, "Can you taste you on my beard? Do you taste as good to you as you did to me?"

"Yes, I can taste me and yes I do taste as good to me as to you and you taste pretty good to me also."

He started kissing me again then rolled over so he was above me and said, "I want to make love to you slowly, I want to feel everything about you."

He was between my thighs and pulled my butt up to him as he slowly entered me. I could feel a slow moan come from both of us as he slowly pushed himself all the way inside me. He rolled over onto his back with me on top of him then sat up and wrapped my legs around him. He was so deep inside me I could feel that familiar throbbing start again.

"Hold on baby," He said. "Wait for me; I want us to come together."

He rolled me onto my back and pulled me so close he had his face buried in my hair as we felt each other come; it felt as though our hearts were beating inside me. We lay there for a moment; when he raised his head a drip of his sweat fell on my forehead, just as Jonathan had done that night in Lena's car.

"Sorry about that." He said

"That is okay, we are both sweating, the hair on your chest is stuck to my boobs and my hair is soaked, both ends. I think we should shower, it has been a long time since I have showered with a man and that is one of my favorite things to do."

We were lathering each other and kissing and laughing and enjoying each other.

I took his penis to wash it and it moved and that was that.

He said, "I don't think he is up to much more tonight, but we will make love before I have to leave you. I need to be back at the bar early, my brother is going to take me home to tend to the cattle."

I knew this was probably something that was not going to last, but I had tonight and will have the morning. I knew Steven was younger than me, not as young as Jonathan probably about ten to twelve years younger, but he didn't know that as I looked and acted much younger than I was.

After we dried each other off we fell into bed and Steven pulled me into his arms and I curled up in the curve of his body and went to sleep feeling content and safe again.

I woke up with Steven kissing my back. I rolled over to face him and he said, "Good morning, beautiful how did you sleep?"

"Wonderful." I was thinking to myself this was the best I had slept since Jonathan left.

He was then kissing me all over and we made passionate love. We showered again, and then left to get him to where he was to meet his brother.

"When I get home my wife and I are going to get together to talk. I don't know how much it will help, but I have two boys that need two parents and I am willing to try if she is. I would like to see you again if this doesn't' work. That sounded terrible, I didn't mean it the way it sounded I really enjoyed being with you. You are the first woman I have wanted to be with since my wife left with my boys."

"I understand what you are saying. I gave up many things in my life for my children, you are a good man and I respect you for this. Our children always have to come first."

"Would you come to the bar Saturday night? I know this is asking a lot and I would understand if you didn't as if she wants to try again so will I and I will give it my best."

"I will come over, if you are there you are there if not then I understand and I wish the best for you and your family."

This was Thursday morning and after I dropped Steven off at the bar, I went on to work. The next few days were like weeks and all I could think of was seeing Steven again, only to me he was Jonathan and I knew in my heart he would not be there, but I would be.

Saturday finally came and I made my way to the bar my heart pounding so hard I could hear it in my ears. I sat at the bar on the same stool hoping Steven was already there, but he was not. I drank my beer and ordered another one, but still no Steven. When I finished my beer I slid off the stool and left the bar with the bartender telling me to make sure to come back. I did go back to that bar the following Saturday, but no Steven and I never returned there again.

Chapter Three

Alderman's & Allan

When I left the bar I got in my truck and drove around and around the block then I went to the only place left to go, Alderman's bar.

I sat at the end of the bar where I usually sat and ordered a Coors Light from Nickie. The bar was pretty full, but I wasn't paying much attention to anyone.

Someone sat down on the stool next to me, when I didn't look to see who it was a familiar voice said, "Hi Jewelya how are you this evening? Are you ready to get beat at some pool?"

"Oh, you are so in trouble Mr. Alan, beat me? Not a chance."

While we were shooting pool Alan said, "I keep asking you to go out and you keep refusing, why?"

"Well, I think you are too young, but what the hell maybe we should do that some time, what can it hurt."

Who knew what would have been with Steven and me, maybe nothing as sooner or later I would have to separate him from Jonathan and realize Jonathan was gone, but I sure would have liked to have tried.

So for now I was back where I had been so many times, my heart was breaking and I needed a man to glue it back together.

Alan and I decided to go to a pool hall in C.B. at that time. We shot pool for a few hours then decided go back to Alderman's. Somehow we ended up at my apartment; I bet that is a big surprise to all of you.

After we made love I got up to clean myself.

Allan asked, "How old did you say you were?"

"I didn't say." I answered.

"Well, are you going to tell me?"

"If you really need to know, I'm fifty-ish." I answered as I walked around the foot of my waterbed, yes the same waterbed.

"You can't be fifty-ish with a body like that, and where are you going I'm not done with you yet."

"I'm going to clean up, then we will see who lasts the longest as I'm not done with you yet either."

I knew I would see Allen again, probably more than I should, but what the hell why not. He knew where all my buttons were and knew what to do, when to do it and how to do it. If it wasn't him it would be someone else, and there were more someone else's, after a while it was only Allan.

I would spend the next almost sixteen years on and off with Allan, more on than off.

Allan was a juvenile diabetic and because he thought he was invincible he didn't take as good care of himself as he should have. November, 2008 he turned fifty and January, 2009 he died from complications of diabetes. I was alone again, except for my bubble baths and beer.

Maybe someday I will write about Allan and our turbulent relationship, but not right now. Right now it is time to find another man with some glue.

EPILOG

O ne of the things we women forget is that by nature we are nurturing people, men are not. Women are born with this bred into us, the mother instinct. Whether we become mothers or not, it is still there, and we have the need to nurture, to fix, to comfort, and men are well aware of this, and know when to move in and take over.

Once a woman is in a controlling relationship it is very easy to fall back into one and very hard to get out, not because we can't, but because we think we can change these controlling men. Men have a way of knowing which of us can be controlled.

The only way we can break that cycle of controlling relationships is to realize we cannot change them, we can only change us. So the next time a man says no you can't do that, RUN!!!!!!

MY REGRETS

I REGRET:

That Loren and I didn't make love the only night we had together. I know he would have been a great lover. I wish he could have been my first lover, not just my first love.

That I didn't get away from Carl and his buddies sooner than I did. Then I wouldn't be carrying all this baggage around, it sure gets heavy sometimes.

That I didn't commit Carl to the mental institute as the psychiatrists wanted me to, maybe they could have saved him from himself.

That I didn't leave with Bob when he wanted the kids and me to go to Florida with him and his daughter. Almost fifty years later and I still love him and remember everything about him. I wouldn't have had my last three children, but you can't miss what you never had. Bob and I would have had our own.

That I didn't make Manny wait a year to get married, just to see if he was still around; of course he would have still been around.

That I wasn't able to tell my birth person no to marring Manny and watch her cringe, what a rush that would have been.

That I wasn't able to tell my birth-person, no to anything long before I did.

That I married Manny the second time around. I already had my children what did I need him for? I thought my children needed a father at home, even if he was an absent father most of the time. I used to think I did the right thing for them, now I'm not so sure; it was definitely not the right thing for me. If I wouldn't have married Manny the second time, then I could have kept having my secret love affairs that I enjoyed so much. I wasn't hurting anyone and I was contributing to the joys of those men.

That I didn't finish my education to be an English teacher as I wanted to do when I went back to school in 1978. But, Manny said no and I did what he said. What a crock of shit. Like I said, when a man says no you can't, "RUN"

That I didn't appreciate Roy more when I had him, and realized he loved me more than any man in my life, before him or after him. Other men wanted to love me as Roy did, but none could. They loved themselves more that they loved me.

That I didn't stay in Oklahoma with Jonathan and live in a tent with him in the middle of a cow field, as he had wanted; he was the love of my life. I still think of that night in the back of Lena's car and the afternoon in the middle of that clover field and I feel those familiar shivers go through me. I still think of riding on the back of his motorcycle with the wind blowing through my hair and my arms wrapped around his slender beautiful body, and the night we found our own Hotel California.

That I wasn't able to keep Jonathan from going back to Oklahoma to visit his mom at Christmas, as I knew tragedy was waiting and he wouldn't be back.

That I didn't stand up for myself more often than I did. I spent so many years not standing up for myself and saying nothing that when I finally did say something, I am a bitch.

And, if I were able to even overcome the first regret, it would change all the other regrets to other regrets, etc., etc. Our lives are based on the domino effect, which ever way the first domino falls, all in its path falls. To every action there is a reaction, think before you react. Oh what a vicious circle we ride around in. Only the strong survive.

There is only one certain-tee in life, and that is change. The change is not the real dilemma; the real dilemma is how we deal with the change.